BEN

THE ALIEN BIRD

BEN

THE ALIEN BIRD

PAUL ARON

JERUSALEM ◆ NEW YORK

Typesetting: Marzel A.S. – Jerusalem
Cover Design: Studio Paz, Jerusalem
Translation: Paul Aron and Alex Auswaks

Edition 9 8 7 6 5 4 3 2 1

Gefen Publishing House
POB 36004
Jerusalem 91360, Israel
972-2-538-0247
isragefen@netmedia.net.il

Gefen Books
12 New Street
Hewlett, NY 11557, USA
516-295-2805
gefenbooks@compuserve.com

Printed in Israel

Send for our free catalogue

Library of Congress Cataloging-in-Publication Data
Aron, Paul, 1930-
[Ben. English]
Ben: The Alien Bird / Paul Aron.
    p.   cm.
ISBN: 965 229 183 8

1. Jews—Denmark—Fiction.   I. Title.
PT8176.1.R52B6413   1999
963.8'1374—dc21

96-35366
CIP

*To my children Michael and Susanne
and to my wife Karen*

Part 1

The engine of the truck makes a terrible noise. It is dark inside. The cold wind whistles under the flapping and snapping tarpaulin. As they drive on, they are shoved one against the other. They cannot even glance outside. They have no idea where they are going, nor any idea of what is going to happen to them.

Now the truck comes to a halt. The strings of the tarpaulin are untied. Ben is first to jump out into the light after the two soldiers.

They are shepherded into a red-brick building. Ben is immediately aware that it is a school. Then they are dispersed in different classrooms.

Ben doesn't know any of the people with whom he finds himself. They look very dispirited and sad. Most of them have placed themselves upon the small desks. Only an elderly gentleman with goldrimmed glasses, a fur coat and black hat is pacing to and fro continuously.

On the blackboard it says: 3A: *TOMORROW DICTATION*. The letters are so beautiful. Their teacher certainly had a nice handwriting! Outside the door a German soldier stands guard.

After a long wait the Danish Nazi in the black coat enters. He sits down at the teacher's desk on which he places a big book like a school register. Then he calls the gentleman with the glasses.

The elderly man approaches the teacher's desk slowly. Just then the young Nazi officer stands up and swings his arm, striking the man violently in the face with the back of his hand! The man's hat and glasses slide to the floor while the Nazi bellows angrily:

– Off with that hat, damned Jew! Haven't you got any manners at all!

White as a sheet, the old man touches his cheek before, confused, he bends down to pick up his hat. His hands are shaking as he gropes his way across the floor until he finds his glasses and puts them on again. His hat he keeps in his hand. One spectacle lens is broken. Isn't that odd... one eye looks much bigger than the other!

The Nazi starts writing in the register, while the gentleman answers his questions.

Ben is sitting in the farthest end of the room. In turn, everybody is to have their name, date of birth and address listed. The Danish Gestapo agent, enthroned behind the teacher's desk, only has to say: "Next!" and frightened, they spring up to him as fast as they can, taking off their hats.

Ben casts a glance out of the window. There they are in the schoolyard, the German soldiers with steel helmets and hand machine-guns mounting guard. Ben knows that he cannot avoid questioning by the Nazi officer too. Should he try to give a false name, say that he was called Poul Jensen? Then they would probably ask why he was going to Sweden, and they would find out that he was telling a lie, and then he would surely be punished.

Now it is Ben's turn. The Nazi knits his brows:

– Well, you were born in 1930, in Hamburg, in Germany!

Ben is compelled to explain:

– We came to Denmark when I was five years old.

– Are they Jews, both of them, your father and mother?

Full of shame, Ben has to admit that it is so. The Dane observes Ben coldly:

– Jews are not German citizens any more... Well, so you thought that you could get away with it so easily? Where are your parents now?

Ben doesn't know. The Nazi is nodding slowly:

– You are not even a Danish Jew, you are stateless!

While the man is writing *STATELESS* in the big book, Ben feels that he is worse off than the other people... he has been convicted!

* * *

The Nazi has gone. They cannot leave the classroom. Ben is thirsty. He could ask to go to the toilet. The soldier outside the door, nodding his head, allows him to slip out. In the corridor leading to the toilet, Ben squints into the other classrooms, but he cannot see anyone he knows.

How nice to get something to drink! Ben has his mouth under the running tap of the wash-basin and keeps drinking.

When he gets out into the corridor, there is a general departure. The Germans are yelling and giving orders:

– Come on! Los! Los! Hurry up! Up! Up, faster, faster!

The people are running down the stairs. They had been waiting all that time!

In the schoolyard the trucks are ready, and the people have to leap onto the trucks as fast as they can, while the tarpaulins are pulled over them. Ben has placed himself nearest the German guard. There he can glance into the street.

It is late in the afternoon. Ben feels how tired he is. On the pavement, people are walking by without paying any attention to him or the others crowded in the German army truck.

A young man and a girl are kissing each other. Of course they haven't an eye for Ben. They are smiling happily and then walk on hand in hand.

Now a lady stops, looking Ben straight in the face with her long amazed look. Then she quickly turns her head away and goes on, but at this very moment Ben's view is obscured by the tarpaulin, which is tied so tightly that he can only look out through a very tiny chink.

The truck is carrying them far away. Once in a while it stops for a few moments, probably because of traffic lights... Ben leans forward and can see a coloured poster with a drawing of a girl, and he manages to read the text, MISS ELSINORE 1943, before the truck starts off again.

* * *

– Mein Gott! It's my Bennyboy! And I thought that... Oh my God, how could this happen? Look, Moritzl, little Ben is here too...my own Benny!

Mommy spotted Ben, who was waiting together with the other newcomers by the camp's red office hut. She runs up to him, embracing and kissing him, laughing and crying at the same time. Ben is just as surprised as Mommy. He can hardly believe it's true!

Mommy and Uncle Moritz had been caught by the Germans at Dragør harbour. They had been waiting for a ship together with many other people, but then suddenly the Germans had emerged, catching most of them. First they succeeded in hiding in a wash-house, and when the Germans had gone, Uncle Moritz thought that the danger had blown over and he went into the street to look around. At that moment a German soldier and a Danish Nazi and his girlfriend had passed by. They arrested Ben's stepfather, then went inside the wash-house where they found Mommy! The German went off to fetch a car, while the others were to guard them. They waited for a long time. Mommy had asked the Danish girl if they would let them go if Mommy gave her her gold watch, and the girl agreed to that. But when Mommy had given her the expensive watch, they were not allowed to run away anyhow. The man had a revolver and was going to shoot them if they were to try to escape, and the woman kept Mommy's watch all the same.

When the soldier returned in an army car with four more soldiers with hand-held machine-guns to watch them, they were taken to this place, the Horserød camp. They had already been here for a week and they were living in one of the wooden huts with a window to the forest with its beautiful trees in ochre autumn colours, and Mommy would see to it that Ben was allowed to stay with them.

* * *

When Ben was just a little boy he was playing in the sand-box in the yard, in Hamburg, where he was born. He was sitting all by himself, very nicely making cookies out of sand and carefully placing them in line on the edge of the sand-box. And Mommy was up there!

Now she was waving from the balcony. Mommy was as high up as the angels in the sky. She couldn't hear him when he was shouting. Ben couldn't reach her, even though he stretched his arms up as high as he could. Suddenly Mommy was gone. Ben couldn't understand it. Where was Mommy? Over and over again he cried for her to come, but she stayed away.

At long last Mommy appeared. By that time he had been crying for a long time. Mommy took him in her arms. Oh, it was indeed wonderful! Then she sang the song about Little Hans, who went out into the wide, wide world, all alone with his stick and hat, cheerful and happy and full of zest for life. But when Little Hans had gone, his mother became very, very unhappy... she cried so much, that Little Hans hurried back home to his mother as fast as he could!

Ben and Mommy sang that song often, and he laughed and hugged her with all his might when Little Hans came home again.

Mommy also sang the song about the poor soldier who died in the field, while the sun rose and the sky turned flaming red:

> – OH DAWN, SO BEAUTIFUL AND RED,
> GIVE YOUR LIGHT TO THE YOUNG DEAD
> YESTERDAY HIS CHEEKS STILL BLUSHING
> IN HIS VEINS LIFE STILL WAS FLUSHING
> TOMORROW IN THE COLD, DARK GRAVE,
> TOMORROW IN THE COLD, DARK GRAVE.

Then he completely forgot that he had just been crying and he was so glad that he had his Mommy, that he held her tight, never to let her go!

Ben loved it when she let him hop a hundred times on her lap:

> *– LITTLE HORSEMAN HOP HOP HOP*
> *FALLING HE GETS UP UP UP*
> *FALLING IN THE GRAVE*
> *EATEN BY THE RAVEN*
> *FALLING IN THE SWAMP*
> *HE SHOUTS WAMP WAMP WAMP*

At the end, mother bobbed him down on his back, down to the floor so that his stomach tickled, whereupon she took him up in her arms to kiss him. And he laughed and shouted:

– Once more!

Mother also knew the song of the dead comrade. It was so beautiful when she sang the sad melody:

> *– I HAD A COMRADE DEAR*
> *NEVER LIVED A BETTER MAN*
> *NEVER LET ME DOWN*
> *WE WENT TO THE BATTLE*
> *THE TWO OF US TOGETHER*
> *THE TWO OF US TOGETHER*
>
> *THROUGH THE AIR A BULLET FLIES*
> *IS IT AIMED FOR YOU OR ME?*
> *IT HIT YOU IN YOUR CHEST*
> *NOW ON THE GROUND YOU REST*
> *AS IF YOU WERE A PIECE OF ME*
> *AS IF YOU WERE A PIECE OF ME*

Daddy always used to lift Little Ben high up in the air with his strong arms, looking him right into the eyes, pressing his nose against the tiny tip of Ben's nose and saying: "BOOOO!"

Later on his mother told him:

– Then I took my pillow and put your little pillow under your arm, and then we left your Daddy and went to Grandma's...

One day, Ben and Mommy were going to visit his father in his shop in the Reeperbahn. But when they got there, his mother wouldn't allow him to go inside. And he had been looking forward so much to seeing him again, as Daddy had so many toys in his shop.

– Now stay here until Mommy returns!

Mother went in, shutting the door in front of Ben.

But, just like Little Hans, he wanted to see the world. So he ran away. He ran into the narrow streets, where he met so many funny and peculiar people. The Chinese lived here! Though full of go, when he had been running for some time, he became afraid of the strange people who were looking at him. He wanted to be with Mommy again, and he looked for her but couldn't find her anywhere. He began to cry again, because he couldn't find Mommy, so he looked again and again...

There she is! How happy Ben was when he saw Mommy! Finally he had found her and he spread out his arms for Mommy to pick him up and kiss him, just like they had done so often before in play.

But things didn't turn out as in the song about Little Hans. Mommy was so terribly angry. She picked him up firmly, pulled down his trousers, gave him a spanking and scolded him! It wasn't a game. This was serious! Ben whined out of pain and disappointment, because he had just wanted to see the world...

They stayed with Grandma and Mommy had to clean all the rooms, which were let to people, so that she had some money to buy food.

Daddy never came to play with Ben any more.

But now Grandma wasn't at home either. She had gone to Copenhagen, and Ben was now such a big boy, that he could stay home all day by himself, while his Mommy was in the office.

When she came home in the evening, Mommy played the piano. Ben stopped playing, sitting quietly, listening to the sound of the music. Mommy would say: – This is Beethoven! – or: – This is Mozart! Her fingers flew easily and magically over the white and black keys, dancing like little dolls, trilling like little bells in a quick tempo... or else Mommy's fingers would tap along slowly and heavily, in deep strong tones, just like the Seven Dwarfs when they were walking through the woods to Snow White after a long working day. Mother could also make the piano sing with long soft notes, when she would smile at her boy, humming the melody, so that the music forced its way through his skin, through his whole body, so that it chuckled and tickled him inside his tummy.

When Ben was walking with Mommy in the streets, they sometimes met the big soldiers marching with a forceful tramp, tramp, tramp of their boots, and then Ben tramped too, just like the soldiers, stretching his legs as far as he could. Mother was greatly amused: Benny was her own Little Soldier!

It happened that they passed by the *ORPHANAGE*. There lived the children who had neither Mommy nor Daddy... they were orphans. He thought of that every time he passed by the orphanage. Once Mommy took him with her and they went inside. Here he watched them play, while his mother talked with a man with a long, black beard.

Sundays, Mommy would take him with her to the Alster Lake to feed the swans, and afterwards Ben had a nice cream puff at the Alster Pavilion, while Mother drank her coffee.

Once one of the big birds assaulted him, hissing with its long, menacing beak stretched towards him. Ben was really frightened... he hid behind Mommy and afterwards refused to feed the swans. Nevertheless, he wanted another cream puff. But when they arrived at the Alster Pavilion, they couldn't get in... There was a sign at the entrance with the words: *ADMISSION OF JEWS PROHIBITED!*

Another day, Mother brought him with her to a big building, where she talked for a long while with a man in uniform. As they were leaving, Mother said HEIL HITLER by way of good-bye; then Ben said in a loud voice so that the man could hear him:

– Mommy, we mustn't say Heil Hitler. We are Jews!

✶ ✶ ✶

When Ben was five years old, they were going to go by aeroplane to Copenhagen, the place where Grandma lived.

How very funny it would be to be flying, how small all the houses would become when you see them from the sky. Ben would get a souvenir pin, to wear on his jacket, so that he could tell everyone he had flown in a real aeroplane!

But as they were leaving, a strange man was there too. Ben had to bow politely saying: "How do you do Uncle Moritz." Uncle Moritz was so nice... they were going to live with him in the new country!

The flight wasn't fun at all. And the uncle wasn't nice either. He didn't say anything when Ben shook his hand, and then he became angry because Ben wanted to sit on Mommy's knee all the time. Ben was to sit properly in his own seat! This meant he couldn't look out of the window! When Ben had to get past Uncle Moritz to look down at the small houses, he suddenly became ill and threw up so that the uncle's trousers became dirty:

– Pooh, ugh, how disgusting, ugh, ugh!

Mommy had to wipe the uncle's trousers with her fine silk handkerchief. Ben should have taken more care! Look, his nice jacket was soiled!

Mommy had to wash his face and clean his shirt. Then Mommy forgot all about the souvenir pin. But he didn't deserve it anyway, the way he had behaved.

* * *

In Copenhagen Ben was to stay with Grandma... not with Mommy! She was to live with Uncle Moritz in a *pension*. Anyhow, Grandma's flat was comfortable, with plenty of room... Ben, then, could visit Mommy on Sundays!

Ben was not at all comfortable with Grandma. And he didn't have his teddy bear any longer. Mommy had forgotten his bear in Hamburg. He had to scrub the floor, even under the cupboards, with the wet cloth which was so disgusting and dirty, and so heavy, that he could hardly pull it out of the bucket of cold water in order to wring it. Every day he had to wind tight bandages round Grandma's thick legs, up to her enormous thighs, fat and white with swollen blue veins... it was disgusting!

Grandma also made soup for a whole week at a time, and Ben had to eat it, whether he liked it or not.

Grandma wasn't at home during the day. She was out selling clothes from door to door. The neighbours were to look after Ben from time to time, or he went to their place, playing in a corner with some copper pots.

After some time, Ben went to the kindergarten in Saxogade. There were a lot of children, both smaller and bigger than him. They glanced in surprise at him, because he talked German. However, playing with them, it didn't take long before he could speak Danish like the other children.

In the morning, Grandma sent him to buy milk. For that, Ben went all the way through the Saxogade, down to Istedgade, because at the creamery there the milk cost one penny less than at the baker's in their own house.

When he visited Mommy, she always put him in the bath-tub at once: – Ugh, how terribly dirty you are, how disgusting! – The water turned black in the bath-tub. But it wasn't strange, because Grandma never washed him. Then Mommy always had to leave with Uncle Moritz, but Ben was such a sensible boy, he could keep himself occupied... so he used to sit on the sofa, rocking on his knees for hours, singing the songs he used to sing with Mommy.

When summer came, Ben was sent on vacation to Jutland with his kindergarten. Every morning they had to eat porridge. It was so thick and lumpy that he was just about ready to throw up.

Mommy had told him of El Dorado, the land where children could eat all the sweets they liked. But first they had to eat a huge mountain of oatmeal porridge! Even with the best will in the world, Ben could not get the porridge down, so finally Mommy had let him off.

Now he tried to eat the porridge with his eyes closed, swallowing it quickly, so that he wouldn't taste it. But it stuck in his throat, and he was forced to throw it up again into the plate. Luckily, one of the servant girls took pity on him and gave him a few slices of bread with margarine instead.

Was he ever going to see Mommy and Grandma again? So he was, indeed, happy when, after the summer vacation, he came back and Mommy was there to fetch him. She had such a tan, that he couldn't recognize her for a moment. She kissed him, saying that now he had grown to be a big boy! He was not five years old any more, but six!

* * *

Throughout the entire winter Ben went to the kindergarten. When spring came and Ben was to start going to school, he was finally allowed to move in with his mother and Uncle Moritz. They had got married, so Ben could call the uncle "father." But Ben didn't like that, so he didn't do it.

Living with Mommy, he had to sleep in a room, which they were not supposed to use, because the man from whom they had rented the apartment had his things in there. Ben had to be very careful and by no means scratch the sofa he was lying on, so that the man wouldn't discover his presence.

What fun to go to school with all the other children in the first grade, to learn to spell and to count, and listen to the stories! Ben was sitting next to Kristian. The teacher, Mrs. Arnold-Hansen, taught them to write and Ben drew the letters as nicely as he could. So did Kristian, but when they went up to the teacher with their copybooks, she always praised Kristian and all the other children, but she never said anything to Ben, even though he spared no pains to do the best he could.

One day Kristian's mother invited Ben to come home and play with Kristian after school. Of course Mommy gave her permission, and so, every day, Kristian's mother, in her car, brought both boys over to her place. What a lot of toys Kristian had! Later Mommy came to fetch Ben, but it wasn't long before he could walk home by himself. On the way he would kick stones if there were any on the pavement.

Mommy was always in a hurry to give Ben his supper and put him to bed before Uncle Moritz came home, so that Ben shouldn't trouble uncle.

Very often Ben thought of the children in Hamburg. The day when he was watching the orphans play, one of the boys asked Ben if he was going to stay there too, and then he had told Ben that the man with the beard was very strict and used to beat them. They all hated him. One of the little boys, Eugen, was teased by the others. They shouted at him all the time: – Prince Eugen in summers and winters has his arsehole full of splinters! Eugen had wept. He had been all alone facing the others, as nobody helped him, not even his big brother.

Fortunately, Mommy would much rather keep Ben. She would never let Ben go, never ever, and in the evening, when Ben was going to sleep on the sofa, which he had to be so careful about, Mommy came to him in the forbidden room to say his prayers with him.

Mother had taken her piano with her to Denmark as well. Ben wanted to learn to play it, so Mommy showed him how. The very first piece Mommy taught him was the tune of LITTLE HANS. Ben was to practise exercises and scales every day. But then he asked if he could play some of the pieces Mother played herself, and Mommy was certainly surprised that he learnt them by heart immediately.

* * *

Miss Tiedelund liked her pupils, and her pupils liked her, because during her lessons they were allowed to talk among themselves without her getting angry. They are going to watch slides. Ben and Kristian help the teacher draw the black curtains. The classroom darkens and then the richly-coloured pictures light up the room, while their teacher tells the story of Aunt Green, Aunt Brown and Aunt Lilac:

– Now you can see the two children standing here, the boy and his little sister, alone in the street, and they are crying, because they were sent to town to do some shopping, and they lost the purse with all the money. They are afraid of being spanked when they come back. And here you see Aunt Brown. She wants to comfort them and asks if their mother and father are really so strict that they need to be afraid of being punished. While the slides are being changed the teacher continues: the children say that they have neither father nor mother – they are ORPHANS – and live with a woman who doesn't like them and doesn't give them much to eat either... Poor children, come with me, Aunt Brown says, and hand in hand she takes the children home to Aunt Green and Aunt Lilac. Look, here they all are at the aunts'! And the children get all the cookies they can stuff themselves with. You have no idea how happy they are, and they become even happier, as the aunts agree to keep the children for ever, but the one who is happiest is the little dog named Spot. Now Spot can play with the children... Just look how they all smile as they walk down the street, the little dog with a bow round its neck, the little boy, the little girl and the aunts!

All the children in the class laugh. Except Ben. He is very quiet, because he too is afraid of being spanked by his stepfather at home... the other night, when they had guests, mother put some cookies on the table. Mommy had baked them herself. After having watched the grown-ups help themselves for some time, Ben thought that he too was allowed to take one – but then the stepfather gave him such a slap in the face, that Ben fell off his chair! Everybody had seen it and he felt so ashamed, that he ran out to cry in his room. Kristian whispers:

– Do you want to play at my place today?

Having drawn the curtains apart, Miss Tiedelund has placed herself by the harmonium. They are going to sing a song. She is trying to be strict without really succeeding:

– Please be quiet children... we will sing *In Denmark I Was Born*. I know you like that song!

And she starts pumping the organ, working both her legs, while she plays on the keyboard with her fingers, and her brittle voice mixes with the young and cheerful children's voices:

> *– IN DENMARK I WAS BORN, HERE I BELONG*
> *HERE ARE MY ROOTS FROM WHERE MY WORLD BEGINS*
> *THE DANISH LANGUAGE, VOICE OF MY BELOVED MOTHER*

Ben liked that song very much, but he wasn't born in Denmark, no! And Mommy couldn't speak proper Danish either... Actually she and Uncle Moritz sometimes spoke German, when they were walking down the street, so that others could hear that they were foreigners. Then Ben would feel so ashamed.

Now Kristian is singing:

> *– AND YOU I LOVE, AND YOU I LOVE*
> *DENMARK MY NATIVE LAND!*

Ben wished he were him, that he had a native land too.

All of a sudden Miss Tiedelund stops playing:

– Why don't you join in the singing Ben?

Ben can't explain. It would, indeed, be too embarrassing to say that it wasn't true, it wasn't his FRESH DANISH BEACH, and that THE APPLE ORCHARD AND THE HOP GARDEN only belonged to the others... When the teacher asks once more if he doesn't feel like singing, Ben just nods, because he has a lump in his throat.

They are just about to start singing again but the teacher lowers her arms. She sighs:

– Oh my legs are tired from pedalling!

And then she looks at Ben and Kristian:

– Who wants to come up here to pedal while I am playing? Ben and Kristian, you would like to, wouldn't you? Come up here!

The boys leap towards the teacher, place themselves by the teacher's feet on either side of her, stamping on the pedals with all their might, while they laugh at each other. They are completely out of breath, competing who will be the fastest, so that Miss Tiedelund has to ask them not to stamp so violently that the whole instrument shakes.

∗ ∗ ∗

It is Kristian's birthday. The entire first grade has been invited. In the large hall of the villa twenty-five boys and girls are playing up and down the broad staircase, which rises in a bend to the first floor with Kristian's room and the bedroom of the parents.

Mother Birgit supervises. Mrs. Vestergaard is busy laying the birthday table in the dining-room. It is decorated with flags and by every place setting there is a small present for each of the young guests: coloured pencils, children's books and nice paper.

At the top of the stairs, Ben and Kristian are fencing with their swords against the other children, attacking them and screaming loudly. But the two of them hold the fort, they always stand up to superior forces. In the middle of the formidable battle, Birgit calls. Ben's mother has arrived. She is standing in the hall. She's brought a present for Kristian and wants to leave right away. By no means does she mean to disturb the children's party... though she would just like to say hello to her little son.

Kristian and Ben have to give up the fight, so that the others, triumphantly, can conquer the landing on the first floor.

– Happy birthday, little Kristian!

Mother smiles heartily as she hands Kristian the present. He opens the package. It's a big smart racing car in blue and red with silver stripes! While Kristian gives her his hand, bowing politely as he says thank you, Ben stares in wonder: How did Mommy ever get the money to buy such a nice racing car? But now Mommy kisses her own little Bennyboy, hugging him really tight.

In the meantime, Kristian runs into the dining-room and puts the car together with all the other presents. He comes back impatient:

– Come on, we have to win our castle back!

And Ben and Kristian again fight their way up the stairs.

Mommy intended, naturally, to leave at once, but she just had to thank Mrs. Birgit for being so kind to her little Benny, that he was allowed to come and play here so often and that they wanted to have him with them on vacation next summer:

– It is so nice of you, you have no idea how happy my Bennyboy is to be here, aren't you little Benny? Well, he is already off... anyway we are so grateful to you!

Birgit doesn't think Mommy has any reason to thank her:

– It really is we who are so happy about having Ben here. Kristian and Ben always stick together. My son says that the two of them are stronger than the rest of the class put together!

Both mothers laugh. Mommy's heart warms to her:

– He is such a good boy, my little Benny, don't you think so too?

Sure, Birgit thought so, certainly!

Mommy hesitates for a moment. She wanted so much to tell Mrs. Birgit even more, but she thinks better of it. She couldn't just tell Kristian's mother all her worries... She contents herself with sighing as she takes her leave:

– I do care so much about my little boy. He is my only comfort.

* * *

In the dining-room Ben is standing by the sideboard. It groans under Kristian's presents. He picks up the smart-looking car which Mommy brought, running his fingers along its smooth surface and along the grooves on the radiator. The bonnet can be opened so that you can see the engine inside. It has real rubber tyres, which you can remove. The front wheels can be turned by the steering-wheel! There is a battery in the car, so that the headlamps emit a white light and the rear lights are red. Ben just has to try that. Then he puts the car back carefully.

Now all the children enter, making a great noise. Birgit spots Ben:

– Ben, you sit here, next to Kristian.

Finally they are all seated! Two ladies arrive, in black dresses, with their caps on, each with two huge pots full of hot chocolate. They begin to pour, and all the children may help themselves to whipped cream, just as much as they want... It tastes wonderful, ah!

Now Mrs. Vestergaard arrives with a fantastically huge birthday cake with seven burning candles on it! Everyone is quiet while she walks carefully all the way alongside the table up to Kristian and then places the cake in front of him. He gets up, taking in all the air that his lungs can hold, then blows as hard as he can. He succeeds in blowing out all the candles except one, so he has to take in air again, giving the last candle an extra puff... like this!

Everybody is shouting with joy, laughing and clapping hands! Now is the time to sing the birthday song! They all sing, all of them except Kristian, because he is the one to be celebrated:

> – TODAY IT'S KRISTIAN'S BIRTHDAY
> HURRAY HURRAY HURRAY
> WE'RE CELEBRATING KRISTIAN
> HAVING LOVELY CAKE AND CHOCOLATE
> HAPPY BIRTHDAY, KRISTIAN, HURRAY!

When they end, mother Birgit shouts:

– Long live Kristian!

Now everybody screams, waving their little flags, screaming with all their might, for nothing is so wonderful as yelling as loudly as you can! Even Ben shouts so loudly that he becomes red in the face:

– Long live Kristian! Hurray! Hurray! – And the long shout: Hurraaay!

* * *

During the night Ben dreams that he is playing with a beautiful music-box. It is playing melodies and has a hundred lampions shining and sparkling red, green, yellow, blue – all the colours of the rainbow. All of a sudden it breaks. It won't play any more, it won't light up any more, however much he tries to make it. Ben cries and cries...

* * *

Ben and Kristian are now nine years old and in the third grade. In the schoolyard all the children run about, playing noisily. The weather is lovely, but Mrs. Arnold-Hansen, who supervises the yard, gets into a foul mood anyway, when she discovers Ben and Kristian. Are they really using the hymn book for playing hopscotch? Of course it was Ben's idea! She hadn't liked it either when she got this little black-haired lad in her first grade three years ago. What were those strangers doing here, anyway? Couldn't they go somewhere else? And his mother, always smiling to excess, trying to ingratiate herself... Upon my word! Ben is kicking the hymn book again! That is the limit. Those strangers don't have any respect at all for Denmark's cultural values!

Mrs. Arnold-Hansen resolutely approaches Ben. Seized by long accumulated anger, she takes the boy's arm and shakes him violently, so that he can't stand up straight. She pulls him up by his hair, shouting at him, her face so close to his that it gets wet from her saliva:

– How dare you kick the hymn book! Well I never! A boy like you shouldn't be allowed to go to the same school as decent people's children! Damned little devil!

The teacher picks up the hymn book and hits him hard over the head before she turns around to leave with the ill-fated book. Now the brat can go and get it himself from the headmaster.

Ben has fallen to the ground confused and scared to death.

Kristian is pale with fear. He helps Ben to his feet, and hand in hand they run to hide in the farthest corner of the schoolyard.

∗ ∗ ∗

One morning, very early, Ben wakes up because the whole sky is rumbling. He jumps out of bed, runs into the kitchen and climbs the table by the window, from where he can see beyond the roofs of Copenhagen. An aeroplane sweeps quite low. It steers right at him, and with a roar that almost makes him lose consciousness, sweeps over the roof just above him, so that he ducks his head.

He looks up again: There are more, a lot more. The whole sky is full of them! Everything buzzes hollowly. A large flock of planes like tiny black birds, swarms above the white clouds in the bright sky, and when they come closer they grow in size and become big, black ravens. He tries to count them, but they keep coming, more and more of them, so he gives up.

Once again, one is separating from the swarm, sweeping towards him faster and faster, growing bigger and bigger, until it snarls over his head with a bang, so that the window sill shivers and a couple of frightened pigeons fly up from the gutter, flapping their wings.

– Mommy, Mommy, look at the aeroplanes!

His mother comes running up. She has been wakened too, standing there in her night-gown with her hair mussed up. She isn't wearing lipstick either. At first Ben hardly recognize her.

Now his stepfather arrives – unshaven and in his pajamas – and mother clings to him. He puts his arm firmly around her, while both keep staring up at the sky.

Ben had never seen his stepfather hold Mommy before. In fact, he couldn't remember having seen his stepfather so much as touch her.

Mother is on the point of weeping:

– The Germans, the Germans are here... Mein Gott, what are we going to do, Moritzl? What is going to happen to us now?

Stepfather is looking at the aeroplanes, and suddenly Ben realizes that his stepfather is afraid! But he is so big and strong! How odd that he too could be scared. Ben gets a strange sensation in his stomach.

His stepfather's voice sounds unsteady:

– Unglaublich! Don't worry, Tanya... we won't get hurt, even though it never occurred to me that Hitler...

– But Moritzl, are you sure that we won't get hurt?

Mother's eyes have a haunted look. His stepfather hesitates:

– Yes, I'm sure. They all say that, don't they! We won't get hurt!

– But then they all said that it was absolutely UNTHINKABLE that the Germans would invade Denmark. They did say that, didn't they, Moritzl?

His stepfather looks at the aeroplanes for a while, then resolutely shakes his head:

– They won't do anything to us, not here in Denmark, you can be sure of that, Tanya. King Christian will protect us!

But Mommy's eyes still look worried:

– Are you sure of that Moritzl, that our king...?

– Yes, mein Schatz, I am. The Danes would never allow it to happen and the King of Denmark will see to it, that they don't harm us. Anything else is UNTHINKABLE!

It was just as if the parents didn't see Ben at all. Why all the aeroplanes? He stretches towards Mommy. She turns to him to take him in her arms.

Mommy wants so much to spare her little boy's feelings. Ben is, in fact, far too young to understand what's going on. He is so sensitive and he can't bear all the agitation. Smiling sweetly, she pretends that nothing unusual has happened:

– There is nothing to be afraid of, my little Benny. Just go to your room and play!

But you cannot fool Ben. He can feel that something is wrong. He won't leave Mommy. Reluctantly, he jumps off the kitchen table but remains standing in the doorway.

Now his mother begins to lose her patience: – Why don't you ever do what I tell you? Come on, go now, Benny. Can't you hear?

But then mother is, indeed, sorry for her little boy. She gives him a little kiss on the cheek, before she gently pushes him away:

– Couldn't you go to your room and make a nice drawing for your Mommy? You are so good at drawing horses! Benny, draw a nice horse for Mommy. Make Mommy very proud of her little boy and happy. Come on, go now!

But Ben doesn't feel like drawing a horse at all. Because the last time he had drawn a horse and proudly shown it to Mommy, she had laughed so strangely. For Ben had drawn the horse with a big penis. He himself had seen that they had one. Mommy had shown the drawing to all the grown-ups in the living-room, and they had all laughed at him, and he couldn't understand at all what was so funny about it and he got so embarrassed. After that he had always drawn horses without a penis.

Now he is drawing a big aeroplane instead.

* * *

You had grown accustomed to the presence of the Germans in the country. The President and the King had called on the population to take a dignified attitude toward the Wehrmacht. Mommy and the stepfather took it easy now. Apparently, the Germans weren't going to hurt them. It was true, then, that King Christian protected the Jews, and every morning the king rode on his white horse through the streets of Copenhagen as usual. And when they happened to meet the King on Saturday morning, Uncle Moritz took off his hat and bowed deeply and Mommy told Ben to take his hat off too. Everything seemed normal, as if Denmark wasn't occupied by the Germans at all.

One day Ben came home from school early, so he and Mommy went into town to do some shopping. It wasn't very often that Mommy took Ben with her by herself, so they really enjoyed being together. They went into several shops to try on dresses, as Mommy loved looking at dresses. Ben would sit on a chair, watching when Mommy came out through the curtain of the dressing-room, as if she were performing at a theatre. Then she walked back and forth, while still looking at Ben, but smiling and looking at herself in the mirror with coquettish glances, and she pirouetted in front of Ben, asking if he liked the dress.

Mommy was so beautiful! Ben, actually, had never seen a woman as beautiful as his mother! Not even in the pictures of beautiful ladies on horseback in the big album his Grandpa had collected. Grandpa, Mommy's father, had been the most handsome man in the world, Mommy always said so, and because Ben was born on the very day his Grandpa died, Ben was named after him.

They also went into a milliner's and Mommy tried on all sorts of hats. Some of them were tiny and meant to sit a little askew on one side of the head. Others were huge, with broad brims, so that you could hardly see Mommy's face. Then Mommy made some very funny faces. She pursed her lips, which she always painted red, but only in the middle, so that her mouth was to look as small as possible, and then with her forefingers she pulled out her temples to the side, so that she looked like a Chinese woman with slanted eyes... For every new hat she figured out some other display, and this made her so happy as she tilted her head to one side in a seductive way, eyes twinkling merrily to herself in the mirror, and Ben laughed with her.

Now Ben was to decide which hat Mommy should buy. He thought that they all suited her. Finally, Mommy chose one with a small veil reaching halfway down her little nose, which she always powdered white to make it look even smaller. Mommy's brown eyes were just like two stars, glinting behind the veil.

They also went to a shoeshop named Hector. At the entrance to the shop there was a big dog, made out of painted wood, with shining eyes. Mommy chose a pair of shoes for Ben, which he could grow into. When he tried them on, he was made to put his feet with his shoes on into an instrument. You could look down through a pane in the instrument to see your own feet inside the shoes to check if the shoes weren't too tight.

At the Town Hall Square there is music. A lot of people are standing by the corner just opposite the German headquarters. Following the music, Ben pulls Mommy over and manages quickly to push his way to the front row: It is German soldiers who are playing. People stop to listen. You might as well do that. It can't harm anyone...

The orchestra is playing a march and Ben nods his head to the music. How exciting to listen to it! There they are blowing into the long black clarinets, piping in such a funny manner. The flutes play, and in the back row, the great tubas honk with their deep tones that sound like cows lowing in beat to the march: – Moo, moo, moo, moo!

But the most beautiful of all the instruments are the trumpets. They sound truly fantastic as the fanfares are blown! Eight soldiers are playing the trumpets. Ben counts them several times.

The conductor wears white gloves, beating time to the strict rhythm, raising and lowering his arms in short abrupt movements: – up – down – up – down... the baton flicks in the air.

Right behind the German military band, on the high plinth, stands the famous statue. Ben knows it very well. It is THE LITTLE BUGLER, dating back to the war against the Germans in 1864! Ben is looking at the soldier who carries the little boy with the bugle on his shoulders. The boy wears a uniform. Even though he was so young, he participated in a real battle. Mortally wounded and having to be carried by the grown-up soldier, the boy is blowing his bugle bravely to encourage the Danes to go on fighting. Until he is thoroughly exhausted. Ben would have done the same thing too.

Now Mommy is pulling his hand:

– Come on, Bennyboy, you're dreaming again, aren't you!

✴ ✴ ✴

One evening Ben is playing the andante of Mozart's C major sonata. Mommy is listening: How wonderful! He formed the phrases of the music all by himself! He was as musical as... a child prodigy! But of course, one mustn't by any means let him know it.

Ben is fully absorbed in playing the piano. All his soul is but melody and sound, the flight of the music carrying him away... he is roused from his reverie by his stepfather's rough voice coming like a gunshot from an ambush:

– Isn't that boy supposed to go to bed? It is after half past eight!

Mother starts. Ben was playing so beautifully and there is only the last half page left. She looks pleadingly at her husband:

– Ach, Moritzl, couldn't you allow little Benny to finish the piece?

But his stepfather wants peace now. At once! As a former non-commissioned officer in the German army, he was used to being obeyed, Ruckzuck, now!

– You can't read your paper with that strumming all the time!

Mommy wants to avoid irritating her husband on any account. Moritzl had, indeed, so many worries, in making ends meet, and then he had been to the Chilean consulate today... little children must have their sleep, that is best for them, so that they can grow up to be strong. Mommy kisses Ben good night:

– Well, it is right, honey, you have to get up early tomorrow to go to school. Hurry to your bed quickly, little Benny!

Ben had been so frightened that he couldn't have continued playing anyway. Mostly he used to play only when his stepfather wasn't at home, but this time his mother herself had asked him to play. He gets up to disappear in a hurry or he might easily get a slap in the face. But before he manages to escape, Mommy stops him:

– Aren't you saying good night to Uncle Moritz, little Benny? Come now, like this: "Good night, dear Uncle Moritz"... that's good! Isn't he a dear boy, Moritzl? And don't forget to brush your teeth, little Benny!

Ben has to overcome his fright and disgust, pretending to kiss his stepfather's rough cheek.

Moritz grunts something, which is supposed to be "good night." He also feels embarrassed, but Tanya insists and what don't you do to please her! It was only reasonable for the boy to show respect! Later, when Moritz was lying in Tanya's embrace at night, he forgot how much the boy annoyed him, forgot all the things enveloping him. Therefore it was even more irritating when the boy was ill at night, so that Tanya had to get up... and it happened often that something was wrong with that boy! She mollycoddled and spoiled him too much!

Now Moritz wants to listen to the news. It was good that they had managed to come to Denmark before the borders had been totally closed. He switches on the radio and after a little while a snarling, hysterical voice rises above the general noise. At first it sounds like an incomprehensible yapping, a dog's barking, getting louder and louder in pitch and strength and falling back to become a growling, hoarse spiteful whisper... only, suddenly, to bawl again, threatening and frightening. Single words are repeated all the time:

– Juden... Schweine, dirty pigs... damned Jews... rats... wipe out all of them... ausgerottet, exterminated! Jews are our disaster... Juden sind unser Unglück... Jewish devils!

And then the enormous roar of applause from the huge crowd, jubilant and screaming with hatred.

Moritz gives Mommy a darkened glance and she looks inquiringly at him. He is silent, he feels helpless. He has learned that things are very bad for the Jews in Poland and participates in organizing the collection of clothes and food to send to Warsaw. Yes, it was indeed a good thing, that they got themselves out of Germany in time and had been lucky enough to get into Denmark. If only the residence permit... Last week three families had been sent back to Germany by the Danish authorities. You couldn't get a work permit either. What luck for him that he had his Danish business friend.

Then Moritz discovers Ben standing in the doorway, listening to Hitler's curses on the Jews. Moritz gets furious:

– Isn't that boy in bed yet?

Mother claps her hands: Why is Ben standing there without his pajamas? He will catch a cold! And he is putting Moritz in an even worse mood! Why doesn't Ben recognize that there are certain things he is far too young to understand? It certainly didn't do him any good to listen to the radio! Even Mommy is upset:

– Now you go to bed immediately, Ben! And your teeth, did you brush your teeth?

But then Mother becomes kindly again:

– My little Bennyboy, go now! Mommy will come and help you say your prayers in a while.

Ben goes into the forbidden room, puts on his pajamas, and very carefully climbs on the sofa, which he wasn't really allowed to sleep on. He has left the door slightly ajar, so that he can see the streak of light from the living-room. He has also felt the sinister tone of the voice on the radio: Juden... Jews... But they were Jews themselves! What was going on?

Ben listens to his parents' conversation, until he finally falls asleep.

Mother, who would rather not talk about war and persecution, wants with all her heart for Moritz and Ben to become real friends. Therefore, she always tells her husband what a good boy Ben is, and every time she expects Moritz to share her enthusiasm. If she keeps on that way, it is bound to happen some time:

– I say, Moritzl, our Bennyboy and Kristian play together so well, and Kristian's mother is so kind to our little boy... don't you think it's wonderful, Moritzl? And Kristian's mother has even invited Bennyboy...

This annoys his stepfather still more:

– Bennyboy! I have other things to think of! Waldburg has been caught by the police, and he had foreign currency on him.

Mother gets worried again:

– Foreign currency? But we have that too, haven't we Moritzl?

Moritz has explained this to Mommy several times:

– Tanya, you know, that it is strictly forbidden to take money out of Germany. They have blocked all Jewish bank accounts. Therefore it's illegal, even in Denmark, to try to exchange our money. They call it currency fraud, and the immigration authorities will send us right back into Hitler's arms if they discover it. It is extremely dangerous, and Waldburg had a large amount.

– I wish we could get away, some place where we could live in peace!

Mommy sighs. Now they had settled down, got a proper home and were happy to be here. To break up once more is hardly bearable... and there is Kristian's mother who is so fond of Ben...

Moritz had written to Tanya's brother-in-law in South America. He would, of course, like to help them to a fresh start if they managed to get over there:

– It's very difficult to get a visa to Chile. At the consulate they said that we had to be patient, but our residence permit soon expires... I have to renew it next week, and the immigration authorities are urging us all the time to leave!

Tanya would like to cheer up her husband. She talks about Ben again, for Moritzl can't help caring for him, he is such a sweet boy:

– You know what, Moritzl? Kristian's parents have again invited Ben to vacation at their summer residence! Isn't it wonderful?

But Moritz is not at all enthusiastic:

– Why does he have to go to a Christian school together with all these *goyim*? And they teach him about Jesus! Why don't we send him to our own Jewish community school?

Tanya never stops struggling to make everything go smoothly, to make sure that Ben isn't a nuisance to his stepfather. It is just that Ben gets on very well at that school, even though the form-mistress wasn't very kind, but you had to accept things as they are. Ben had told her that the children had been at Mrs. Arnold-Hansen's place, and he had seen that the teacher had a portrait of Hitler hanging on the wall! But it was probably better not to tell Moritz about it, because Tanya wanted so much for Ben to stay at the school where he and Kristian had such a good time... Right now, she just had to comfort her own Moritzl:

– You are quite right, my dearest. Then our Benny wouldn't have such a long way to go to school and we could save the tram fares! But it will be wonderful for our little Benny in the summer, won't it Moritzl?

And to make the stepfather realize the advantage to him in this, Mommy adds:

– Then he is OUT OF THE WAY, you see Moritzl?

* * *

Ben is now eighteen years old. The war is over long ago. Nobody thinks of it anymore. Nobody talks about it.

The two friends had become three: Ben, Kristian and Grete are sauntering across the schoolyard through the hullabaloo, like swans quietly sailing through flocks of chattering ducks. They are in the top grade at school, and the young pupils give way respectfully to them, just as they once had had to do themselves for "the big ones."

They always stick together, fond of one another as they are. They are looking – with a little pang in their hearts – at their old school... soon they will be leaving. Indulgently they watch the poor little wretches who still have to stay at the institution. With pride of ownership they approach "their" bench... Good heavens, some creatures are sitting on it!

– Beat it, toddlers! You know that this is ours!

Ben sits down beside Grete, who laughs with her dark eyes on both of them. Suddenly Kristian pinches Ben's thigh hard and runs off. Ben goes after him with a yell! Kristian takes advantage of it, returning to Grete, capturing the seat beside her. But then Ben runs back and sits down on Kristian with a bump, so that the three of them fall over, laughing loudly. Now Ben walks to the other side of Grete, so that she is in the middle. She likes sitting so close, puts her arms around both of them and feels the comfortable warmth of their bodies. She sighs happily:

– Take it easy, you two. Control yourselves! One might believe that you are crazy... This is very, very serious! By the way, what's our next lesson?

Kristian jumps up and starts dancing, hobbling about as he waves his arms with spastic movements:

– We are going to have Danish, Danish with Børge, we are going to have Danish with dancing, Danish Børge!

Obviously Kristian was trying to imitate the teacher. Børge had once had polio. Therefore he moved awkwardly and was only able to write clumsily with his left hand.

Now Ben also gets up and takes Kristian by the hand, both hobbling giddily around, shouting in chorus to their leaping waltz:

– We are going to have Danish with dancing Børge, with the dancing Danish Dane, Børge of Denmark!

Grete thinks they are much too rude:

– Stop it, you ought to be ashamed of yourselves!

The two young men stop, embracing each other, acting with extravagant gestures:

– But we really care about our Børge. Actually, he is our favourite teacher!

And as they sit down with Grete again, Kristian adds:
– And actually, Ben is his favourite pupil!

* * *

Outside is the most wonderful spring weather. The air is singing, the sun glittering through the open windows into the classroom, where the atmosphere is still heavy from the diligence of winter studies.

Master Børge also takes a long look at the blue sky with its floating, fleecy cotton clouds:
– You may open the other window, too!

But duty calls. They would have to complete their set task painstakingly. Now for it! And the poem "The Birds" by Christian Winther was so appropriate for the season and the mood: These youngsters would soon fly away! Børge watches the class from his raised desk. There are Kristian and Ben, always together... and all the others. He had followed them all, seen them grow up from being children, seen them develop through the years until they were now adults. It would soon be over. He would probably never see most of them again...

Dreamingly, Ben looks out of the window, where the white birds fly with loud cries. What strength they have in their wings! How easily they rise up, up on high and then dive again through the air: Freely, without worries, they let the light breeze carry them far away. Suppose you could...

Ben starts as Kristian pushes him. Kristian is ironic:
– Our highly esteemed senior master Børge most kindly asks the young gentleman if he would graciously condescend to recite the last stanza of Christian Winther's poem... if you'll wake up!

Ben just has to let go of his dream. He starts to read, first with some hesitation... but soon he lets himself be carried away by the words of the poet, experiencing the joy as if he were flying through the air, feeling the trembling fear and the sweet pain, which intoxicate him and makes him so happy at the same time, so that the words come alive, becoming his own, expressing what he was concealing in the most secret corner of his heart.

> – FLY, BIRD, FLY ACROSS THE WAVES SOUNDING ON THE LAKE
> DEEPLY, THE NIGHT BREATHES A SIGH
> THE TREES WHISPER IN AN UNEASY HUSH
> BOWING THEIR HEADS IN GOOD NIGHT.
> DIDN'T YOU LISTEN TO MANIFOLD PAIN

EVEN WITH THE FEATHERED FLOCK,

SAY GOOD NIGHT TO MY TREMBLING HEART

SAY... YOU KNOW WHAT IT IS.

It is as if one could hear the stillness like a distant echo follow for long seconds when Ben's voice falls silent. Everybody is looking at him. Grete feels as if he had spoken inside her chest. Until now it had been natural for her to care equally for both boys, but could it go on in this way?... The blonde-haired Lily, who is sitting next to Grete, is also looking thoughtfully at Ben.

Master Børge clears his throat:

– Thank you, Ben, I have never heard it recited like that before. It was beautiful. It doesn't need further comment... And now we can tackle *EARL HAKOON*, the great romantic drama of Oehlenschläger. It is the last piece we are to get through before your days off for examination preparation. Please read the introduction for next time.

* * *

On their way home from school, the two boys are in high spirits, clowning and trying to push each other for fun off their bicycles, to show off to Grete, pedalling peacefully behind them. The bicycle track goes along the railway line and as a train is passing with a roar at the very moment, they stop to look at it.

Where was that train going? They all have the same indeterminate yearning to travel, experience something, get away from the accustomed... They have this expectant itch in their midriff. Kristian takes a deep breath:

– Only three weeks left, then we'll be at it for exam work. We have only Earl Haakon left! Well, Børge is funny, isn't he? "His" Earl Haakon, "his" Adam Oehlenschläger... Adam Oehlen-Beerswiller!

All three laugh and Ben gives Kristian a slap on the shoulder:

– Beerswiller, that's funny! Cheers old man... but Børge is O.K. and the piece is really exciting. I have read it already.

Grete's mind has wandered off to mathematics – not her favorite subject.

– By the way, what result did you get in the second problem?

Kristian remounts his bicycle:

– You can have it when we get home, but you have to change it a little...

They drive on, chatting in confidence. Kristian wanted to see the whole of America, hire a car over there and drive through all the states. Ben was enthused by the thought of Paris, Vienna, and especially of Rome – the Eternal City. Grete dreamt about Venice, with its wonderful palaces, rocking on the waves, while she floated slowly past them in a gondola on the Grand Canal, waving her white lace scarf in the warm Venetian night. Torchlight would be reflected in the water and the moon would light the sky mysteriously, while the gondolier pulled at the oar, so that the boat was weaving smoothly as he sang amorous canzones in his light tenor... Grete closes her eyes dreamily:

– And afterwards we will all dance to the music on the Piazza di San Marco, with the wonderful church with the gilted onion-shaped cupolas, together with a thousand other people in the whirling carnival in flowing, many-coloured draperies and white and black masks.

∗　∗　∗

And then Ben was out of the way.

Kristian had every kind of toy you could think of in this world. They used the floor in Kristian's room to fight great battles between the Indians in colourful plumages with their bows and arrows, and the Royal Canadian Mounted Police in their uniforms, armed with rifles. Kristian also had German and British soldiers with cannon and tanks, which the boys placed in companies on the wooded battlefield with its river banks. The cannon could shoot for real, with matches as projectiles, and the tanks on their caterpillar tracks could drive up and down over all the obstacles.

They also had planes and cars, some of which the boys had pasted together themselves, realistic models like those seen in the streets, big battleships, aircraft carriers on which aeroplanes could land, frigates and corvettes, and they named the ships, pasting red, blue and white colours on the British ones and the black swastika on the German ones. Of course the Allies always shot down the nasty and cowardly Germans.

But they must remember to do their homework, too! Kristian looks at his mother:

– Yes, Birgit, we will!

It was strange that Kristian said "Birgit" to his own mother, as Ben always said "Mommy" to his mother, never "Tanya." It was only his stepfather who did that.

The boys place all the soldiers in neat rows on the shelves of the book case and don their Musketeer suits with the smart plumed hats. With their swords drawn, they run into the garden, fencing on the sizeable lawn. Ben is d'Artagnan and Kristian is Athos. They fight side by side, defend the King and defeat the cardinal's cowardly guard, while the big brown dog jumps around in excitement, barking martially.

Mother Birgit calls from the terrace but the boys run between the bushes, hiding in their cave. They are busy. Now the big moment has come. Quietly – only the sound of their breathing can be heard – they sit huddled, looking solemnly into each others' eyes. Ben takes out his fine sharp sheath knife, holding it against his left forefinger, while they both say, slowly and ceremoniously: – To eternal friendship and fidelity in our secret league, we swear that to each other, by God and mankind!

Ben makes the decision and with a rapid gesture he passes the point of the knife over the outermost joint of the finger: Ouch! – The dark blood runs out of the cut over his white finger, dripping down on the brown earth.

He hands the knife to Kristian, whose blue eyes light up amidst the leaves of the branches in the dusk. Kristian sucks on his finger, takes the knife and cuts himself unhesitatingly, so that his blood gushes out. He holds out his finger towards Ben, who squeezes his finger against Kristian's finger, mingling their blood. Now they are brothers for life!

They can hear Kristian's mother call again from the house, but don't some of their enemies walk in the pathways behind the hedge? Yes, indeed!

And so now they are patriots. Quietly, huddled up, with their machine-guns ready, they sneak up between the bushes behind the detested Germans:

– Bang, bang, brrrrr! Death to the traitors, brrrrr! Damned Nazis! Bang, bang! Hitlerschwein!

Now Birgit is calling for the third time. The boys run to the villa. They are delighted:

– We got them! How scared they got!

* * *

Birgit puts the cocoa cups on the floor next to the boys. She strokes Ben's hair, while the boys are busy building a big crane out of Meccano. As Ben looks up at her, she feels the sadness in his eyes, even when he enjoys himself most. He didn't feel comfortable about his stepfather. His mother had also confided that to her... Birgit feels so powerless, if only she could do something.

The boys hardly have time to drink the cocoa, it's so exciting to finish the crane. They swallow their drink in a hurry and Kristian's mother takes away the empty cups. Since Ben had begun to visit them, she felt that she had two sons.

In the afternoon Kristian's father comes home. What a splendid crane! It's almost finished! Kristian looks at his father:

– We lack only two angles to make it work. Do you have ten crowns, Knud, then we can go get them?

Of course the chief physician has ten crowns, and off the boys go from the villa to the toyshop on Strandvej.

Ben borrows Kristian's old bicycle, even though it is a bit too small for him. He could have taken Mrs. Vestergaard's bicycle, but then he would have had to ride standing up, because it was a high lady's bicycle, and that was rather difficult, especially when he had to put his hand out to signal a turn.

Now they are waiting in the shop. What a lot of things! Imagine if Ben, too, had a father who gave him ten crowns if he just asked for it! Mommy had, indeed, promised that she would give him ten pence a week. However, she forgot about it every time. Mommy didn't have any money anyway, she always quarrelled with Uncle Moritz about money. That's why Ben never said anything to her when she forgot to give him the ten pence... But if he'd get ten pence a week, how much time, then, would it take to save up ten crowns... Kristian's father must be incredibly rich!

The boys know exactly which two pieces of Meccano they want. Now that they are there anyway, Kristian also buys two pulleys, twenty screws and twenty nuts. It comes to a total of six crowns.

Next, they ride to the news-stand, because Kristian would also like to buy the new Tarzan magazine. As they are about to enter the kiosk, they narrowly avoid bumping into a couple of German soldiers, who can hardly get out through the door, because two girls, who are hanging on their arms, won't let go of them. The two girls and the soldiers are laughing loudly, they think it is ever so funny. The girls say something in Danish, and the Germans, in their green uniforms, don't understand a single word of it! The girls are dying with laughter.

Ben glances at the soldiers. Were they really that dangerous? They were amusing themselves, laughing... How could they? Ben was glad that he didn't touch them by accident.

The Tarzan magazine costs fifteen pence and Kristian puts a crown on the counter. As he gets the change, the woman puts the money on a newspaper. It says *FIGHTING SIGN*, and there is a drawing of a disgustingly ugly man with a huge nose, black hair and a black hat. As Kristian slides his hand over the paper to take the coins, Ben reads the big letters over the drawing: *THE JEWS ARE YOUR DISASTER!*

Ben gets such a strange feeling in his stomach. The drawing portrays the abominable man, the Jew, about to strangle a little blonde girl screaming for help! What was the purpose of that?

Kristian takes Ben by the arm:

– Come on, Ben, we are going to finish that crane!

The boys hurry away on their bicycles, working the pedals hell for leather.

∗ ∗ ∗

On Sundays Mommy often sent Ben to Tivoli. Then he got fifteen pence for the entrance fee. It cost that much to get into the amusement park before 11 a.m. He had to run all the way to make it, because after that time it cost twice as much.

At the children's playground there were seesaws, swings and a slide you could go down on your behind. It was all free. There was a big sign with drawings telling you how to cross the street. The black figures crossed straight from corner to corner. The red figures crossed the street diagonally. You mustn't do that! Therefore the red figures were crossed out. Ben knew exactly how to do it correctly.

Best of all was a swing called "The Fish," where the playground nannies pushed you, so that your stomach leapt into your mouth. Once in a while, the nannies played singing games, the children holding each other's hands while dancing in a circle. Playing "Sleeping Beauty" Ben was once allowed to be the prince who awakened Sleeping Beauty with a kiss, and he jumped around inside the circle while the other children were singing, as if he were riding a real horse. He kept jumping on and on till his face was red from exerting himself so much to do it right.

When Ben got thirsty he could always drink water from the pump. It didn't cost anything either. If he put his head too far under the water jet or if one of the others pushed him while he was drinking, the water would squirt inside his shirt as far down as his stomach. But then Ben would shove the boy who had pushed him, so he got wet too.

At 5 p.m. the playground was closed and the nannies went home. Ben would run around in the Tivoli Garden, looking at people trying the amusements. It must be fun, indeed, to row boats on the lake or try one of the big merry-go-rounds... or the roller-coaster!

The most exciting thing was the dodgems. Ben could stand there for hours looking at the people driving, bumping into each other. The most experienced among them were those who could avoid getting hit and just drive all the time, escaping the others. Ben found out the secret technique of the most experienced and figured out some smart tricks himself. Now if he were driving, then he would surely be the most superior, the most diligent of them all!

Often, Ben also watched the lemonade sellers' stands. They had red lemonade, orangeade and lemon-flavoured lemonade. A glass cost fifteen pence. You could also get lemonade mixed with soda pop and ice, so that it fizzed over the rim of the glass. It was called "ice-cream soda" and cost twenty-five pence... He even imagined that perhaps the ladies would give him a lemonade one day, but that never happened.

Ben always ran to listen to the musicians playing at the promenade concerts. It was free, too, if you didn't sit. Each time, among the audience, there was a strange little man conducting with a baton, even though he didn't belong to the orchestra. People laughed at him, saying he was crack-brained and something of a character. But the man didn't worry about the bystanders. He just swung the baton in the air, totally in a trance, with a mournful expression in his eyes.

Pierrot was the funniest of all. Ben loved to watch the pantomime, and it was free too. Because Ben was so small, he was allowed to stand inside the line of rope, where the Tivoli attendant saw to it that he could watch without problems. How he laughed when Pierrot fell on his behind! How he would like to play with them too, up there on the stage! Then he would be Harlequin and fool all of them and get sweet Columbine in the end.

After the performance – when Pierrot had made all the children scream HURRAH as loudly as they could – Ben ran home. After spending the whole day in the Tivoli Garden the poor little thing was so tired that Mommy just gave him something to eat in a hurry before he was sent to bed, not to disturb Uncle Moritz.

✳ ✳ ✳

For the last ten minutes of the gymnastics class the boys were allowed to play ball. Børge blows his whistle, making it trill:

– Time for your showers. Off you go!

The boys charge into the changing room, take off their gym suits, put them in their bags, hang them in the cupboard. They jump under the showers, stark naked.

Børge has turned on the hot water so that the the entire room is filled with white steam. Ben and Kristian are fooling about with the others, having fun, shouting with joy, snorting and laughing, enjoying the water pouring in thick hot jets down their bodies, filling their mouths with water and squirting it out again.

Børge is standing by the cupboard calling:

– Ben, where is your bag? You've forgotten to hang up your bag!

Ben runs out of the shower, dripping wet, to the bench where he had left the bag, takes it and brings it to the teacher. Børge hangs it in the cupboard and gives the boy a friendly smack on his behind sending him back to the shower:

– Now get back under the shower, you little puppy!

Once more the teacher checks that the bags are hanging on their pegs, before locking the cupboard carefully. Then he approaches the tap... And now the boys scream and shiver, squirting each other, because Børge has turned on the ice-cold water. He does it every time, and every time it is just as horrible and just as funny.

Soon most of them have had enough, running out to dry themselves and dress. Only Kristian and Ben are still jumping about, having fun under the cold water. Suddenly Kristian stands still, glancing with surprise:

– How come your wee-wee looks like that? Look at mine!

And Kristian throws out his stomach, shaking his little limb. Ben looks at himself:

– It's because I am circumcised.

Kristian knits his brows:

– Circumcised? Did they really cut it? It sure looks funny, your piddle!

Kristian turns around and runs to dry himself.

Ben remains alone and doesn't feel how cold the water is now. Most of all, he wants to disappear in a hole under the ground, so embarrassed is he. He had, indeed, noticed that around the head of their penises the others had a small piece of white tapering skin, while his own was more bare. He had asked Mommy how this could be, and she had answered that he had been circumcised when only eight days old. All little newborn Jewish boys were circumcised! Then Ben wanted to know why, but Mommy wouldn't talk about it any more. And he hadn't thought of it any more either, even though he always changed quickly, so that the others wouldn't notice anything. Finally he had forgotten all about it and had also forgotten to take care that they didn't see him.

He really never thought what the word circumcised meant either. But now he suddenly understood that they must have cut off that little piece of skin, which he was missing. Could he recollect the great pain at that time, could he feel his helplessness, his loneliness? Could he still see the gigantic, bearded faces looking at him from above? Could he remember how he had been totally in their power? Could he hear their deep voices sing, so that he became terrified? Could he remember when the knife cut into him, so that he screamed, screamed, screamed... – until he lost consciousness from sheer exhaustion?

Børge has come to turn off the water. He finds that the boy is still standing there:

– Ben! You'll get a cold! Come on, hop it. Go and get dressed!

Ben starts. Short, thin, blue with cold, he runs holding his hand in front of his penis, hurrying to put on his underpants, drenched as he is, doubling up, turning against the wall. Only then does he take his towel to dry himself.

Actually the teacher has to wait for Ben to finish dressing. Børge cannot help sounding a little impatient:

– Hurry up Ben, you are always last!

* * *

In the warm weather, the three musketeers are sitting on the terrace of the big, venerable three-storeyed brick house, a suitable residence for the chief physician's family.

The big brown dog is leaping, barking happily on the lawn. Now it approaches Kristian with a ball in its mouth, but there is no time to play. They have to do their homework, even though it's difficult to concentrate when you feel more like running into the green wood and just keep on running and running...

Luckily, Kristian's mother brings them something refreshing. It is a wonderful opportunity to have a short break.

Birgit wants to know if Ben has decided what he would like to do after the summer vacation. Ben gets a distant look in his eyes. He doesn't know for sure if he is going to let on, reveal his innermost desires, so he just breathes:

– Dreams... dreams... dreams...

Kristian can't help teasing him:

– Dreams... ice-cream and candy-floss! No, bitter medicine, that is what people must have. Bitter things for the stomach are healthy for the soul!

The two of them love to be funny, but sometimes there is seriousness even behind their jokes. You can often allow yourself to be sincere, pretending it's all for fun:

– The fact that you are going to become a physician has been decided ever since you were slobbering in your cradle... but I!

And Ben spreads out his arms in a wide gesture:

– Le Théâtre, mon ami... Le Théâtre Royal, le Théâtre du Roi!

To his surprise Kristian feels a little stung. What kind of a sore spot was it that Ben had touched? But he brushes the thought aside:

– *TO BE OR... NOT TO BE!*

Ben laughs, then he becomes thoughtful and softens inside himself. Again he is itching with expectation:

– You just *WAIT AND SEE!*

They are all hit by the quiet passion in Ben's voice. Birgit wants to know what it is:

– What are you dreaming of, Ben?

But Ben locks his secret away again and looks inquiringly at Kristian, at Birgit and at last at Grete:

– What is wrong with dreaming?

* * *

The air is so hot that you get dizzy when breathing it in deeply... the sun is shining, glimmering over the waters of the Sound, while the waves quietly lap up on the beach, and if you let your eyes run over the beautiful green beeches on the big lawn and across the water, you see hundreds of white sails, moving out there against the background of the blue sky!

It's almost unbearable to live within such a moment! You do not walk on the ground but you fly across it. Time is before you... an eternity of time, full of promise and secrets, waiting for you to discover them!

Ben and Grete are walking on the ramparts by the fort of Charlottenlund, past the big old cannon, pointing with their thick long round barrels over the Sound. They do not notice how heavy their schoolbags are. As if by themselves, their hands have found each other and neither Grete nor Ben wonder at it. Who would feel like studying in such weather? At least Grete wouldn't! Ben doesn't sound particularily convinced either of the need for it:

– Wasn't this what we came for?

Grete laughs happily:

– What a lot of ships out there!

And she points at the cannon:

– How quaint they are, those old cannon!

Ben cannot help laughing either. How often he and Kristian had played on them, crawling up them until they straddled their high barrels:

– When I was a little boy, I sat on the cannon shouting: "Why the hell mustn't I say damned?" Because Kristian had said that you mustn't say that! I couldn't understand it, as I had learnt it from the big boys in the yard where I lived with my Grandma, when I came to Denmark. The boys had taught me all the worst swear words and, of course, I didn't have the slightest notion of what they meant... What a language I spoke when I started school in the fashionable suburb where you speak properly! They must have stared at me! And Mother, who was so proud that I learned to speak Danish so quickly, long before she herself could... She couldn't comprehend why people were smiling and shaking their heads at the dreadful language of the guttersnipes from the gloomy quarter of Vesterbro they overheard as I chattered along!

Bubbling over with joy, Ben runs along with Grete, pulling her across to the lawn that smells of fresh grass. They throw their bags to the ground, and he puts his arm round her waist, swinging her about, completely indifferent to the wondering glances of an elderly couple sitting on a bench by the high hedge... and dancing round and round they shout and sing at the top of their voices:

– Why the hell mustn't I say damned? Why the hell mustn't I say damned? The hell, you mustn't say damned! Damned you mustn't!

Finally they swing round so quickly that they lose their balance, tumbling over and rolling, embracing each other, till they are finally lying quietly in the grass... They are looking right through into each other's souls. The whole world around them has ceased to exist. Their feelings have snapped into life, so powerfully that they gasp for breath... only gradually, after a long time, they calm down completely.

They hear each other's heartbeat, feel the divine spark in themselves. They are celestial beings, like gods. They abandon themselves to each other, discover each other in themselves, becoming one living creature. Irresistibly their mouths meet, and as Ben feels Grete's soft lips against his own lips and breathes her warm breath in a kiss, his body is lifted weightlessly... and he is soaring, free as a bird, up in the air... and now he is holding Mommy in his arms, flying with her above the clouds in the heavens so high! And Mommy draws him close to herself, seductively, smiling she is offering him her open mouth, and Ben closes his eyes and allows himself to be absorbed by her...

– Ben, Ben...

Ben wakes up slowly and finds Grete looking at him with her shining eyes in which his own face is reflected. She shakes him gently, bends over him, kissing him, so that warmth courses through his body:

– Ben, where have you been?

Ben lets his hand run over Grete's slender back. He feels the warmth of her downy girlish body. Her face is completely open. He has never met such beauty before. This must be the meaning of it all. It made life worth living:

– I've been flying!

Grete puts her head on his chest, breathes in his scent and sighs lightly, as she looks at the sky where the seagulls are flying high up:

– *FLY, BIRD, FLY!*

– Yes, to be a bird, flying up to the moon...

And Grete holds him tight:

– I will fly with you up in the sky, up to the stars...

– Yes, to the end of the world, together... The two of us, you and I!

– Yes, Ben, up to the sun, the two of us... You and I!

✱ ✱ ✱

In the 6th form they are about to finish studying Earl Haakon. After that they have fulfilled the examination requirements. Børge understands very well that his pupils are tired of school, they are so many other things engrossing their young minds to a far greater extent than what they can read in books written centuries ago... And it's spring outside!

Master Børge has to pull himself together. He would also like to fly somewhere far away, where he had never been before. But he has to stay here in his cage. He has chosen to do that... to stay here on his perch and look after himself and his family... to take care of the young people, to whom he would like to give some proficiency, not knowledge – they must acquire that for themselves – but proficiency for ballast when they fly away. Sometimes, true enough, he too stretched out his wings, but then he had to admit that his wings were clipped. They weren't able to carry him in winged flight.

Now he hadn't been sitting here, dozing, had he, being sentimental, devoting himself to worn-out cliches? It was, indeed, Oehlenschläger's Earl Haakon that mattered! Only that the youngsters don't notice anything! The teacher throws a secret glance at the class... Maybe they, on the contrary, would even be content, if he took a quiet little nap... Then they could snore over the books too. He must pep them up a little! He raises his voice with annoyingly great zest:

– Now the dramatic meeting between the two heroes, the proud heathen Haakon and the Christian Olaf, takes place!

The teacher looks at Ben and Kristian. Those two, yes exactly, those two:

– Ben, would you recite Haakon's lines... and Kristian, please, would you read Olaf's lines!

Ben starts reading:

– You call me a heathen?

And as he says the word HEATHEN, all at once he feels Earl Haakon's pride and in addition the humiliation, the slight of being outside the community of the other Christians, a feeling that penetrates him like a knife, so that he, all of a sudden, shouts loudly:

– Honorific name!

He shouts with such might that all his classmates, and Børge too, give a start while Ben, doggedly, goes on reciting:

– By Odin and Thor, Olaf, thou shalt not put out Norway's giant fire!

Kristian reacts with lightning speed. In reality the two brothers always stuck together, defended each other, had the same opinions, formed a united front against the rest of the world. But now something moves inside Kristian, so that he too declaims with a strength surprising himself:

– Well now, that depends, we part...

And his voice shakes threateningly:

– Woe unto you when next we meet!

Ben is deadly serious:

– Woe is me if I do not crush you!

Kristian feels the deadly blow as if it hit him bodily. But he also feels, with a peculiar sort of pleasure, his own rage growing and making him stronger. He clenches his fist:

– Heaven will strike you with its flames!

As if Ben had actually been struck by lightning from heaven, he is now screaming Oehlenschläger's words as if he would smash everything and everybody into smithereens:

– No, Thor shall splinter the Cross with his hammer!

Børge is completely overwhelmed by this clash between two such strong temperaments.

All of a sudden the drama had acquired a new dimension. At this very moment it had come alive, in a way Børge never thought possible. He must calm down the two young men, and himself too:

– Thank you to both! As you see, Ohlenschläger doesn't reveal who of them, the heathen Haakon or the Christian Olaf, will emerge the winner! And that maintains the excitement, the suspense.

Grete didn't look into her book at all. Fascinated, she has been watching Ben and Kristian. She is shocked by the violent passion her two friends revealed. It was literally as if spurts of flame were fired from one to the other. That sort of thing she had never known with them before. They seemed so beautiful to her, both of them, as they sit there, silently engrossed in their own thoughts...

The other pupils are sitting in strained attention as well. Wasn't there something new, something dangerous about the situation? Lily is contemplating Ben steadily. Her light blue eyes are shining with an extraordinary radiance.

The classroom has been totally silent for some time. Grete now looks at the teacher:

– For me, Earl Haakon has a fantastically strong effect...

Børge agrees. One must imagine that so far one doesn't know how it will end:

– There is also an undertone of something ominous about this meeting, like a presentiment...

✳ ✳ ✳

It's almost 8 p.m. Mommy and Ben are waiting for Uncle Moritz to come home for dinner. Mother has been to the kitchen several times to light and turn the gas off again under the soup. She is used to it, because Moritz is always late. Surely he must be busy everywhere, getting around, doing business, and then he has a weakness for chattering, can never break loose, and so he forgets the time.

Mommy tastes the soup to see whether it has enough salt... Mommy's nice chicken soup. Without soup it isn't a proper meal! Benny sets the table for dinner. Such a good boy! Tonight is Friday night. Sabbath Eve is a special time: Then Mommy serves a particularly good *kosher* dinner, chopped chicken liver, soup, stuffed fish, and roast veal with gravy and potatoes. On Sabbath Eve the table is set especially nicely with an embroidered table cloth, the beautiful soup tureen, the china with the gilt edges and the precious silver cutlery for 24 places, which Grandpa had given to Mother when she married Aron. Mommy is dressed up and looks so very pretty, while Ben's hair is plastered down with water. Mommy has made his parting herself to make sure it is straight, and he wears a clean ironed shirt. Friday night is sacred to all good Jewish housewives and mothers, and for Mommy the old family traditions are the most important things she knows.

Finally Moritz arrives!

– Good Shabbos!

Mother speaks loudly and a little ostentatiously, looking at Ben to see if he says *GOOD SHABBOS* to his stepfather too! She approaches the dining table with the Sabbath candles in the polished silver candlesticks.

Ben is looking at Mommy. She says a prayer in Hebrew and lights the candles, after which she covers her face with her hands, saying a prayer to God quietly, so that Ben cannot hear the words. He can only see Mommy move her lips. She is not allowed to say it aloud. But Ben knows that she is praying for God to let all be well and everyone happy.

Then his stepfather rises in his seat. He wears a skullcap. Ben, being a male, puts on his small black embroidered skullcap too, while Moritz takes out the Hebrew book, murmuring the Sabbath prayer, "Baruch Ato Adonaj," while he holds the silver cup with the sweet Carmel wine in his hands. At a certain point in the blessing over the wine he stops, as if he cannot read the Hebrew text, after which he clears his throat and then continues. He does the same thing every Friday and Ben has often wondered why he does not learn the single word he cannot cope with, as he stumbles over it every time. Uncle Moritz drinks first, then Ben and Mother last, because she is a woman.

Ben likes the wine. It tastes wonderful, but it disgusts him to drink out of the same cup as his stepfather. He takes good care to place his lips at the opposite edge to the one his stepfather drank from. Mother drinks only a drop. The remainder she gives to her husband.

Now the master of the house takes out the white braided loaf, which Mommy herself had baked. It is hidden under a dark red cloth with Hebrew letters sewn with gold thread. He breaks off three pieces with his hand, sprinkling salt on the bread, saying the blessing this time loudly and clearly chanting the last words: "Ha Moutzi Lechem Min Ha'aretz!" Then Moritz eats his bread, handing Ben and Mommy their pieces, each pronouncing the same blessing.

Ben now fetches the soup tureen Mommy has prepared in the kitchen and then she starts dishing up. Mother is doing everything with beautiful, graceful movements, as she lowers and lifts the big silver ladle, seeing to it that as many of her delicious meatballs as the Balabos, the master of the house, would like to have are in his serving of the clear soup. Mother smiles, full of goodness:

– The first plate is for the father of the family. Here you are, my dear Moritzl!

And Mommy hands it to Ben who takes it, placing it very carefully in front of his stepfather. Ben is so good at helping, Mommy doesn't need to say anything to him... He does it all by himself! Then Mommy dishes up the soup for Ben, with the same beautiful and loving gesture, and finally for herself.

Mommy is satisfied. She takes such trouble to cook, in order to make it a really cozy, and kosher, Jewish Sabbath every Friday night. It is the climax of the week, when the family is gathered in joy and happiness around the table, on which the candles are reflected in everybody's eyes. She is doing her very best, to make them feel good with each other. Look now how Ben dips the Sabbath bread in the soup! Isn't it marvellous that her little Bennyboy loves her soup and dips the bread in it, just like her own daddy used to do... Benny is, indeed, wonderful!

Moritz is eating silently. He is in a bad mood. Tanya would like to cheer him up, and little Ben has been so sweet today, she just has to tell Moritz about it:

– Imagine, Moritzl, when I came home from the butcher, Bennyboy had baked a cake for us! He remembered the recipe all by himself and he mixed the dough with cocoa to make a Madeira Cake, all by himself, just as he had seen me do! It was to be a surprise, a surprise for the two of us for tonight. Isn't it marvellous, what little Benny has done, Moritzl?

Mommy is smiling, beaming at her husband and Ben is looking stealthily at his stepfather. But as the latter answers only with a short grunt, continuing to eat his soup without so much as glancing up, Ben casts his eyes down in embarrassment. Mother can't help laughing:

– But then Benny showed me which bag of flour he had used, he had taken the rye instead of the wheat... isn't it a scream? We can't eat that, of course, Ben must eat it himself, because he doesn't want us to throw the cake away... but the fact that he wanted to make us happy is so sweet of him, don't you think so too, Moritzl?

Mommy has to laugh again, it is too funny! Ben has crumpled. He looks down at his plate and doesn't feel like eating any more. Most of all, he would have liked to crawl under the table.

Moritz continues to eat without saying a word. Then Mommy notices Ben. Well, I must say! Didn't she teach him to sit properly at table?

– What manners! Just look at the way you are sitting, Benny! Straighten yourself up and sit properly, with your elbows at your body, you know, so that you can hold a book tight under each arm... and why aren't you eating?

Now eat your soup, you do like it so much! You also know what happened to Choosy Charles, don't you? He became so thin that he died! And Mommy baked a nice apple pie for tonight. You would like to taste it, wouldn't you, Benny?

Moritz has finished his soup. He is waiting. Always that boy! Can't Tanya think of anything else? But then Mother sees that the master of the house has finished his soup:

– Would you like a little more soup, Moritzl?

And as he nods, she smiles, happy and flattered. It is true. Her soup is something special. She chooses the chicken herself very carefully, just like her mother taught her to do... But is Ben dreaming again?

– Benny! Didn't you hear Uncle Moritz ask for more soup?

Ben has been looking at the painting hanging on the wall opposite him. It is a representation of two Spanish boys in brown and other colours, eating grapes. If they hadn't worn those funny old-fashioned clothes, it might well have been Kristian and himself... At the sound of Mommy's voice, Ben jumps to his feet, takes his stepfather's plate and holds it, while Mommy ladles another portion of soup into it. This time, just a little less than before, because the delicious roast veal is waiting for them too, and she knows her own Moritzl well enough, so this time he gets only three meatballs in his soup!

Moritz is really anxious. Waldburg had been caught and the police had confiscated all his money. He himself was, indeed, lucky that he hadn't... Well, it had been close! You had to be very careful nowadays! Fortunately, he could prove that his Danish business connections were still trading with his old firm, which the Nazis had taken over:

– Waldburg has been questioned today. The immigration authorities have found out that his residence permit isn't in order either...

At this moment Ben drops the plate with the hot soup right into his stepfather's lap, so that it squirts all over and the fine china plate crashes down on the floor, breaking into a thousand pieces! Uncle Moritz's nice trousers are ruined! His legs are scalded. For a moment, Ben is paralysed.

Then, with lightning speed, the hard smarting blows hit him, so that he tumbles over on the floor. He doubles up like a little animal and covers his head with his hands and arms to protect himself.

His stepfather is white-hot with rage. Tanya is always covering up for this audacious, impudent and sly little fox, who is whining all the time, pretending to be innocent... and you can't tear him away from his mother's apron strings. Moritz's anger gushes from him, the anger he has to swallow when he feels so powerless outside his home. He bends over the boy and hits him again and again, trying to strike him on his side, to slap him in the face:

– Damned snotty brat, little devil... You did it on purpose, Rotzjunge! I will show you, you shameless rotter!

Mommy wants to intervene. However, when Moritz gets angry you can't stop him! He does have such a violent temper... But he shouldn't beat her boy like that! She had tried to defend Ben so many times, but it only made things even worse... They argued for nights on end and then Moritz would be cross for weeks afterwards:

– But Moritzl, Ben couldn't help it, it was an accident!

Now Moritz gets angry with Mommy too and turns against her. His eyes are swollen under the bushy grey eyebrows and the veins in his face and on his bald top stand out blue in agitation. He screams away, totally out of control, so that mother shrinks:

– Like hell it was an accident! It was on purpose!

Terrified, Ben takes the opportunity of saving himself by running out of the room, while Moritz continues to thunder as if he would never stop:

– Los! Raus! Get out! In the street, auf die Strasse! He can sleep in the street! Out! Raus, out of my home! I won't set eyes on him again! He ought to live in a reformatory! Out, in the street! Auf die Strasse...!

Mommy is in despair. It was her Friday night! Silently she sweeps up the broken pieces of china, serving a new plate of soup to her husband. She doesn't speak a word until they are eating the wonderful roast veal with the delicious sauce, which her Moritzl is so fond of, pretending as if nothing had ever happened.

∗ ∗ ∗

Ben has been crying, all alone, while the words ring in his head: "Auf die Strasse, in the street! He can sleep in the street!"

No one in the whole world to help him! But then he clenches his fists and sets his teeth:

– I'll kill him when I grow up! When I grow up I'll kill him!

And he feels a hatred that almost chokes him.

– I'll kill him, kill him...

But it would take a long time, it would take many years before he became as strong, and even stronger than his stepfather.

Ben goes to look out of the window. Raindrops are drumming against the window, gliding down in streams. He leans his head against the cold pane of glass, so that his forehead and eyes are cooled and numbed...

– Or I will run away from home! And then I might be run over by a train or a car... and when I am dead, then you might regret it, then you might weep and mourn for me!

He feels Mommy's soft hand stroke his head. After having served her husband apple pie and a nice cup of tea, and after he had switched on the radio that played a lovely classical concert, Mommy had slipped out to look after her little boy, bringing him a piece of cake without Moritz noticing it!

Ben throws himself into Mommy's arms, hides himself clinging to her, closes his eyes and feels her warmth, her intimate fragance, and Mommy keeps caressing him while he sobs. But only for a short time, then he stops. Because it is so wonderful to be with Mommy that he forgets all about his loneliness and despair just now.

Mommy hugs her boy in her arms, passionately and softly at the same time. She feels both happy and unhappy. She kisses Ben and presses her cheek against his:

– Don't be sad, little Bennyboy! Mommy is so fond of her own boy... It is because I love you so much that Uncle Moritz gets jealous of you! Because when I love you so much, then he gets angry... Well, that's how it is, you cannot change him...

And while she is comforting Ben, an old distant feeling wells up alive in her, a feeling from a long time ago, when she was a little lonely girl herself, who experienced an emptiness, a pent-up longing for something which she was still missing.

– It is because I love you so much, and he won't accept it, that he gets jealous of you, you must understand that, my own sweet boy.

Ben enjoys Mommy's caress, while listening to her sad melodious voice. Even though he doesn't really understand what Mommy is saying, there is a feeling of happiness inside him, of satisfaction. He no longer cares about what happened just now. If only his Mommy stays with him.

* * *

Ben dreamt that he was a little elephant standing in a house, together with two big elephants. The two big elephants were standing in one box, while he was standing in a small box by himself, separated from the others by a partition. But then the bigger of the elephants reached out his trunk for the little elephant, laying its trunk on his back, holding on to him. The little elephant was standing quietly and did not dare to move to shake off the trunk, even though it lay heavy on his back, because the little elephant was afraid that the big elephant might hurt him. He was just standing there, totally motionless, pretending he was not there at all.

* * *

– But you were always so happy as a child. Why are you blaming me? You had such a happy childhood!

Mother is sitting on the bed in Ben's room or "Locum" as the students call it. She MUST visit her son, as he has not been home to see her since he graduated two years ago.

Mother doesn't understand it. Ben had been so lucky... and he had done so well, of course, to get a scholarship, gain admission to this fine residential hall, and then he was not one bit happy.

Ben is standing by the window, looking down into the yard with the bumpy paving stones and the lime tree in the center. Now he was living within The Red Walls, the old buildings of reddish brown brick, standing in the heart of Copenhagen, where the students lived. He was in *REGENSEN*, Collegium Domus Regiæ, which King Christian IV himself had built for his students more than 300 years ago.

– Yes, I had SUCH a happy childhood!

Mommy looks into her handbag and finds a picture... she always carries a photo of her wonderful little boy:

– Look for yourself, Benny dear, how you smile and how happy you are. You are only eight years old, and see how happy you look! You used always to be at Kristian's place, he had so many toys...

In a flash Ben visualizes Kristian's table abounding with presents:

– Kristian's toys, Mother! It was Kristian's cars, Kristian's soldiers and Meccano set, Kristian's Tarzan books... not mine!

But Mommy doesn't listen at all:

– And what an imagination, you had! When you were little, you could be playing by yourself for hours. With an empty matchbox, you could turn it into anything. Often I would sit all quiet, admiring you, you were amazing! I dressed you in the little red pinafore with the yellow ship embroidered on the front pocket, do you remember that, Bennyboy? And then you would think out some little songs with your own melodies, and you invented short plays and talked to monsters, fairies and pixies, as if they were present. And then you yourself were a terrible monster, or a fairy godmother, and all of it was just your imagination! You didn't need toys!!

Ben takes hold of Mommy's arm to make her listen:

– But you, mother, you hadn't imagination enough to guess that I would have liked to have toys of my own like the other children, who had so many things!

Mommy doesn't want to know:

– You were always so happy to visit the others. You began to play, immediately, you didn't notice if I were there or not. Sometimes I did wonder if you were sorry when I left, but you were already engrossed, and at Kristian's you could play with everything... You really were so happy!

– Happy! Because I didn't have anything myself! Don't you think that I asked myself why the other children got so much from their mothers?

Ben looks into the yard, where some of Ben's friends are sitting in their dressing-gowns, having discussions, while puffing at their long pipes. On this hot day the open windows, painted white against the red brick background, look like the cross on the Danish flag, Dannebrog. He runs his eyes over the assembly hall building with the small clock tower in the ridge of the roof and at the Round Tower which rises proudly behind the hall. *CHRISTIAN IV* 1642 is written on the tower in large gilt letters, and in Hebrew: *JEHOVAH* and in Latin: God shall guide justice into the heart of the crowned king!

– Happy... I had to be happy... because I soon learned to adapt myself to be the way you wanted me to be. Then I smiled and was happy!

– Bennyboy, believe me, I didn't have any money to buy you toys! Uncle Moritz gave me only five crowns a week for myself, we were so poor...

Ben bangs his fist on the keys of the piano... his own piano! Which he is paying off with money he is earning himself! The sounds burst into the room in a shrill dissonance:

– Like hell! We weren't poor! I've heard you lament that you had no money a thousand times! But it wasn't true! You could afford to have a woman clean the house for you. And of the five crowns you had for yourself... you didn't have tenpence for me!

– You are not fair now, Benny dear! I did spend the money on you. I went to the finest photographer and had your photo taken. I dressed you neatly in clothes sewn by a real tailor, and that was expensive, believe me! And you got a nice tie, so that you looked like a real little gentleman in a white shirt and suit! You were so sweet, you could tie your necktie all by yourself, and you were only eight years old!

– Yes, I was your little cutout doll, which you could show off, so that your fine friends could praise you!

– I paid for your piano lessons, with a real concert pianist!

– What was I to do with tailored clothes when only five pence could have made me happy? Your cleaner, Mrs. Jensen, she told me about all the things she bought for her children and spent in Tivoli, with the money she earned from you! And I had to listen to that! Kristian only once came to play with me at my place... and never again! I was simply ashamed that I didn't have one single thing we could play with! And Moritz was sitting at the dinner table like a thundercloud, we didn't even dare to look at each other. You never gave me anything, mother... not even for my birthday!

Mommy is totally taken aback:

– Didn't I give you anything for your birthday?

Ben flares up again:

– Can't you ever stop telling lies? A thousand times you said: "The 12th of July is my sweet Benny's birthday!" But when July 12th came, then year after year you forgot your own sweet Bennyboy, while you were staying at a holiday hotel with dear Uncle Moritzl!

Mommy had been in such a tight spot at that time:

– What do you want from me? Why do you keep on pestering me? I couldn't have done it differently. I was a divorced woman without a fortune, indeed with a child! Your father had escaped to Paris, and he never sent me a penny. Grandma didn't help me either, she just left. And there I was all alone. I had to clean the flat and let out the rooms, I worked in an office during the day, do you think that was easy? Moritz only agreed to marry me if I had no children, but I had you! His mother, the whole family were against me! They literally hated me. He could have easily made a much better match, his mother told me so, and then Moritz took you as well anyway... otherwise we would have stayed in Hitler's Germany!

– Was he, perhaps supposed not to take me with you to Denmark? Would you, perhaps, have left me at the orphanage?

– I really had no other way out, Benny dear! Moritz saved you and me, can't you understand that?

– But we aren't his slaves because of that! You might still have celebrated my birthday!

– You know that Uncle Moritz is the most avaricious man in the whole world. He walks two miles to save twenty cents tram fare. He never gives me enough money for housekeeping. I still have to argue with him when the bill comes from the butcher. So I didn't dare to ask him for money for you too...

– You bought expensive birthday presents for Kristian!

– But it was for your sake, Benny! Mrs. Birgit and Doctor Knud were so nice to you. I wanted to make a good impression for your sake!

– You didn't celebrate my birthday, because my birthday wasn't worth celebrating... you yourself told me so a hundred times: You didn't want me!

Mommy gets sad:

– On your birthday you were always on summer vacation with Kristian. I couldn't celebrate with you when you were not at home... and you were so sweet, you understood me, young as you were! You never asked me for anything, you never pestered me as other children did.

– But when it was "nice Uncle Moritz's" birthday, then you suddenly had money and you sent me out to buy HIM a present! I remember once buying a fine hanger for him on which he could hang his clothes. It cost eight crowns, eight crowns! A luxury hanger. How sweet, little Benny gives his dear stepfather a birthday present, to him who never gave me a friendly word!

– You see, I wanted Moritz to care for you, Bennyboy, just a little.

Mommy has just received some money from her rich sister in America. She takes out the banknotes:

– Here you are, 50, no 100 crowns, Bennyboy, take it and buy whatever you want!

– Now it doesn't matter, I earn my own money. Then, when I was a little boy, that is when I needed it...

Dejected, Mother puts her money back in her purse:

– You should have asked me for it. Then I would have given you... you never asked me for it!

Ben's whole body is heavy with grief:

– I thought over and over again how I was to make you understand! When I was in the summer house on my birthday, Kristian's parents made a day of it with chocolate and a flag on the table, but I wasn't really happy. I was ashamed, because I had such miserable parents, that there wasn't even a card from you. That's why once, before the vacation, I asked you if you would give me twenty-five pence... I don't think I had ever asked you for money before, and I hadn't really expected you to give it to me, so I was rather surprised that you gave it without any objection at all! And do you remember, there was a bookstore down at the corner which had second-hand books in boxes outside in the street? Boys' books at tenpence and some, a little better, at fifteen pence... I stood choosing for a long time till I found the two best books, one from each box, two books about Indians, looking as little used as possible, so that one might believe that they were in fact new. Then I wrapped them up in brown paper, tied a bow around them and drew red flags on the paper. I showed the packet to you Mother, and told you what I was going to do with it, yes I did! In the summer house, the first thing I did was to give the present to mother Birgit. She was not to give it to me until my birthday. I said to her that I didn't know what was in it, but it was a present for me from you and Uncle Moritz... and on my birthday I pretended to be very surprised! I hoped that they didn't notice that the books weren't new... Kristian gave me a big sheath knife with a fine handle of real horn and a broad sharp blade. And then you say I never asked you for a present.

Mommy is silent for a long time:

– I didn't understand it, I didn't, believe me, Ben! Moritz's mother, she was so hard on me, completely merciless... everything I did was wrong! And she even put up Moritz against me! I had to make it appear that you were the least inconvenience possible, Benny dear, I had so many worries for your sake...

– Worries! For my sake!

And now Ben recalls what happened in Hamburg. He was at home all by himself. The day before, Mommy had bought a delicious ice-cream for him in the café in the street. It certainly tasted wonderful! And he had often seen Mommy take money from the drawer in the kitchen... But he couldn't reach the drawer, he was far too short. Then he had dragged a heavy chair to the dresser, climbed up, opened the drawer and taken the money:

– Do you remember, Mother, when I went to the café to buy an ice-cream? The woman asked me how big I wanted it, I could have an ice-cream as big as I wanted... and I wondered why it could be so big, and I kept eating the gigantic ice-cream till I was totally stuffed... I had left the front door open so that I could get in again, and I didn't tell you anything about it when you came home. I must have had a feeling that something was wrong about what I had done, especially because I could get an ice-cream as big as I wanted, and not just a small one... And then you discovered that the money was missing! You got so awfully angry, so extremely furious, you beat me!

Mommy had been in court that day. Aron didn't turn up. The shop in the Reeperbahn was totally in debt. As he wouldn't make an appearance at all, the court had agreed with her and the divorce had been granted. But when she came home, she had been so terribly disappointed that her own little boy could do such a dreadful thing as steal, that her son was a thief! Would Ben become just as unreliable as his father?

Mommy is far away in her thoughts as she hears Ben's voice shouting:

– Witch, witch!

– But you can't say that to your own mother.

– Yes, I do mean witch! You became a cruel witch! You hit me, screaming that I was a thief, that I had stolen your money! A three-year-old thief! You shouted that I wanted to kill you – and worst of all: You'd take your own life, because I was so naughty! You'd call the police, so that they'd come and take me and put me in prison! I was so terrified of you... And then you took me into the living-room, to the corner cupboard, which I always avoided by taking a long detour round it, because in there was the whip, Grandpa's horsewhip, which you had shown me one single time...

– But I didn't hit you, I never hit you with the whip!

– You showed me the whip...

Mommy is almost crying.

– But I never hit you with it! I didn't mean it like that, dearest Benny, I just wanted you to become a really good boy, and then I said to you that there were OTHER children who were so naughty that they got whipped, but not you! I swear it, because you were not as naughty as the others! I always told you that you were my sweet well-behaved boy and then I had to teach you once and for all, really thoroughly, that you must not steal! I was so desperate about what you had done, and that you should never ever take Mommy's money again!

– Well, you taught me really well, Mother, that I wasn't allowed to take your money... it was YOUR money, I had no right to it! It was theft...

Ben is calm again. He remembers how sorry he had been, for the terrible thing was that he was exactly as naughty as his mother said he wasn't! He did take Mommy's money and therefore he had deserved that the police would put him in prison. The truth was that he was a bad boy!

– You should have whipped me then, Mother!

– How can you say such a thing, Benny?

– You may think that you did a good thing to me not to punish me, but it was not! Because now I became frightened of you, you could turn into a witch again at any time! Because now I had punishment coming to me! You never mentioned it ever since. It was just hanging there on the horizon like a black cloud. That's why I never dared to ask you for anything. Then I thought that one day, when you gave me a present without me asking you for it – and you were going to figure it out yourself, all by yourself – that then you had finally forgiven me! I kept hoping and waiting, year after year, from birthday to birthday. I thought about it every single day throughout the year. I thought that on my next birthday you might, perhaps, give me a present, if I was really nice... But it is not easy to be nice 365 days in a row, something easily happens during a whole year... Once, I wetted my bed by accident: – Ugh, ugh, how disgusting – you said, and then I even did it once more the following night... However, you promised not to tell Uncle Moritz, so that he wouldn't punish me. Then we had this secret, this guilt together. But then there was one more reason for me not to expect any present that year. And I hoped anyway... But you never forgave me my guilt!

After a long while Mommy whispers:

– If I had only known... I never thought... I never thought of it like that, dear Bennyboy...

Ben is sitting immobile. It is as if a knife were cutting its way through his body, from down in his stomach, through his chest and up through his throat:

– I hate you, Mother!

✳   ✳   ✳

In the middle of the night Ben wakes up in a sweat. He had been dreaming that he saw a little baby lying quietly without moving. The baby was completely naked and white, but it had long red stripes over its whole body. The baby was lying in a crooked fashion looking into the air.

✳   ✳   ✳

Ben continues to go to school in Hellerup, even though they have moved to the City. Mommy only needed to accompany him once, then he was able to manage by himself. First he went by tram No. 3 to the Triangle, then tram No. 14 to Strandvej, right to the end of the fare stage. He had to walk the last part of the journey, or rather to run...run, because Ben was so often late for school, as there was always something Mommy didn't have time enough to get done.

– Los! Aufstehen, up you go! Hurry up, Ruckzuck! Los, Up!

Every morning Uncle Moritz wakens Ben, knocking at the door with a clenched fist, bellowing:

– Get up, husch, husch! Come on, now! Los!

Ben jumps out of bed at top speed! He hurries, like a frightened hare, to get dressed, being careful not to get in the way, as Uncle Moritz might fetch him a blow with the back of the hand.

Mother is busy packing his lunch. There is only time for Ben to have a glass of warm milk. Ben hastens to put on his coat. Such a dark winter morning is cold and he would like to catch the early tram.

Mother asks if Ben remembered to brush his teeth, and as he hesitates a little, he has to do that as well. When he finally gets his mouth rinsed out and is about to leave, Mother comes to think of the most important thing:

– Your cod-liver oil, Ben! You must take it, otherwise you will not be big and strong! It is for your own good, Bennyboy. The other children take it too!

Mother gets hold of the cod-liver oil bottle and pours a tablespoonful, filling it to the brim. She thrusts it into Ben's mouth, who has to swallow the thick, sticky trash. There mustn't be the least bit left on the spoon. It has to be completely clean! He is just about to throw up. But it is healthy for him! For a long time afterwards he has the loathsome taste in his mouth.

There isn't a minute to waste! Ben is frightened by the thought of what Mrs. Arnold-Hansen will say, as Mommy holds him back again:

– Your scarf, Ben! You must not forget it or you will catch cold! Come here, Mommy will tie it for you, sweetheart!

Ben shuffles his feet, while Mother is tying his scarf around his neck, giving him a little hug on his way out, before he can finally rush down the stairs.

In the tram Ben gets a seat, a window seat. Mommy had taught him, that he always had to get up for grown-ups, but when Mommy wasn't there, he kept sitting anyway if he got a seat.

Now a lady places herself right beside Ben and keeps on looking at him to make him get up. Ben just ignores her and remains sitting, staring out of the window, taking care not to turn his head lest he see her. He can actually feel her gimlet eyes at his back, so that he gets a bad conscience, but he remains sitting anyhow, looking out at the snowflakes shining brightly when they get into the glare of the car headlights.

When Ben changes to No. 14, he stands on the front platform, just beside the driver. He can lean against the crossbar and watch how the conductor turns his stick when he was to start forward. And when they pick up speed, the tram driver turns his stick backwards with a cracking sound, so that they drive in neutral and the tram sings on the rails for a long distance before he turns the stick again to reduce speed, so that the song of the tram becomes a deep whine, and finally he uses the hand-brake until the carriage, with a weak buzz, glides to a complete stop.

At the fare stage Ben has to get off. His tram card is not valid any further. He shakes himself and bends down to rub his knees, blue with cold, while the tram drives on along the Strandvej.

As a matter of fact, he is wearing short trousers. But when he passes the newsstand on Strandvej he forgets all about the cold. There it is, the Popeye magazine with the pictures of Prince Valiant. Then he remembers that he is already late for school and darts off, while supporting his schoolbag so that it won't swing to hit his legs while he is running.

All of a sudden a voice calls. It's mother Birgit. She has just driven Kristian to school and stops by the pavement:

– Ben, come on, jump into the car. It's after 8 o'clock!

Ben sits on the front seat next to Birgit, while she drives the last part of the way to school. She casts a glance down at his trousers:

– Aren't you cold with those bare knees?

Ben shakes his head energetically.

The bell has rung a long time ago. The schoolyard is empty, as Ben slips out of the car and dashes towards the school building.

∗ ∗ ∗

The classroom has been nicely decorated with fir branches, coloured hearts and Christmas stars. Mrs. Arnold-Hansen has drawn pixies and Santa Claus in red chalk on the blackboard, and Miss Tiedelund has put an Advent wreath with four candles on the teacher's desk. One candle has already burnt down a little, and today they are going to light one more, so that two candles will burn at the same time. The teacher did promise that.

Next to the blackboard hangs the Advent calendar. Every day, during the first lesson, the children will open a new calendar window in turn. It is so exciting to see every day what will be the new picture!

The children have been allowed to enter the classroom, while Mrs. Arnold-Hansen has just gone to talk to the headmaster for a moment. Happily and noisily they jump about between the desks and don't notice that the teacher is already back, standing silently in the doorway with drawn eyebrows. Didn't she tell them to sit nice and still? Now Mrs. Arnold-Hansen raises her voice:

– What an awful noise! For heavens sake, this isn't a Jewish school!

How the children hurry! In no time they are by their seats, standing straight, stretched to attention like stiff little dolls beside their desks.

The teacher relents. After all, it soon will Christmas, it's only natural that they are happy and a little frisky.

At this very moment she gets a shove from behind. It is Ben who, out of breath, crashed right into her as he tried to slip around the teacher to get into the classroom, and once more Mrs. Arnold-Hansen feels a distinct dislike for the boy:

– You are late again... Blockhead! Now hurry to your seat!

Ben tumbles into the classroom. On the way to his desk he happens to stumble over a schoolbag on the floor, and on top of that he gets a grumpy "Bungler!" from behind, before he stands stiffly beside Kristian, fingers outstretched along his sides, blushing while trying to hold his breath to stand as quietly as he can, like a little mouse.

But as it is Christmas soon, teacher suppresses her anger:

– Now then, you may sit down, children. I want you to sit really properly, yes, that's right, really properly...

And the children are sitting as properly as they can, hands folded on the fine polished desks. Kristian and Ben don't even dare look at each other.

Satisfied, Mrs. Arnold-Hansen looks down the straight rows of the childrens' little raised heads with their expectant shining eyes. That's fine, that's the way they are to behave, properly and decently. Then she looks out of the window. It has stopped snowing and the day is dawning. Now it's time for the calendar to be opened:

– Whose turn is it, anyway, to open the calendar? Who did it yesterday?

Eagerly, the children shout all at once:

– It was Kristian, it was Kristian!

The teacher has to shush them again:

– Will you PLEASE stop talking all at the same time! Let me see, yesterday was the 9th, so it must be the 10th calendar window which is to opened today. How exciting it is to see...

Ben knows very well that it is his turn today. He is sitting next to Kristian, isn't he? He figured it out already the day the calendar started. He is looking forward to it so much that he has butterflies in his stomach. He gets up and slowly approaches the blackboard.

Then he meets Mrs. Arnold-Hansen's cold glare. Ben's heart stops beating and he stands still when he hears her unfriendly voice:

– So it's you!

Ben nods insecurely. After a while her voice sounds even sharper:

– Have I said you might come up here?

Ben's throat contracts. He cannot say a word. It was true enough that he didn't wait to get up before he was given permission to do so. Again he had done something wrong. And now the inevitable happens... the voice of the teacher sounds as if it comes from very far away:

– You must wait till somebody calls you! Coming up here without permission! I must say! One can't behave like that!

And searchingly she runs her eyes over the class and calls up in her sweetest voice the little girl at the desk behind Ben:

– Come up here, Lotty. You may open the window... it was No. 10, wasn't it?

Mrs. Arnold-Hansen doesn't see Ben any more... as if she had totally forgotten him... as if he weren't even there! Luckily the other children in the class didn't look at Ben either, otherwise he would certainly not have been able to keep the tears back...

Slowly he returns to his seat, sitting down beside Kristian. He swallows hard to make the lump in his throat disappear. Then Kristian slips Ben's hand into his and Ben squeezes it, pressing so hard that it hurts, and Kristian cannot help giving a little moan.

– Look at that beautiful picture! It's an angel! And what does the good angel do? She descends from heaven and she has someting in her hand... a present! In a daze Ben hears the teacher's enthusiasm:

– How the calendar picture fits in with the carol Silent Night in which the angel descends from heaven... Wouldn't you like to sing that song now? Come on, children, let's sing Silent Night!

The teacher and the children start singing:

> – SILENT NIGHT, HOLY NIGHT
> ALL IS CALM, ALL IS BRIGHT

And all of a sudden the calendar picture comes alive: The angel gets bigger and bigger and turns into a real living angel, descending from the picture, approaching Ben, smiling at him...

> – ROUND YOU VIRGIN, MOTHER AND CHILD
> HOLY INFANT SO TENDER AND MILD

And look: The angel is mother Birgit. She is smiling, holding out her hand towards him, and he takes her hand. How soft and warm her hand! And now she is singing the song too...

> – SILENT NIGHT, HOLY NIGHT
> SHEPHERDS QUAKE AT THE SIGHT...

And she gives him the present with the red bow, and Ben can hardly believe it... is it really for him? And Birgit nods! It is... yes!

> – GLORIES STREAM FROM HEAVEN AFAR
> HEAVENLY HOSTS SING ALLELUIA

Ben abandons his doubts. He decides to believe that it truly, really is a present for him, that even he is getting a present, just like the others!

> – *SLEEP IN HEAVENLY PEACE*
> *SLEEP IN HEAVENLY PEACE*

And now Santa Claus, and all the pixies on the blackboard, come alive too. They also have presents for Ben, lots of presents, mountains of beautiful presents, containing all sorts of toys which he has seen in the shop windows!

> – *SILENT NIGHT, HOLY NIGHT*
> *SON OF GOD, LOVE IS PURE LIGHT*

A couple of days ago, Christmas catalogues had been put through the letter slot, with pictures of all the things he could ever wish for, and Ben had written them down, all of them! He had filled in a whole page from that list! But he had never thought that he would really get any of it. He had hidden the list under his bed...

> – *RADIANT BEAMS FROM THY HOLY FACE*
> *WITH THE DAWN, REDEEMING GRACE...*

– Mommy! If we believed in Jesus too, then we would have Christmas too, wouldn't we, Mommy? Then we would also get some presents, wouldn't we, Mommy? Just like the others!

> – *CHRIST THE SAVIOUR IS BORN...*
> *CHRIST THE SAVIOUR IS BORN...*

Now Mommy's voice sounds sad and comforting at the same time:
    – But we don't celebrate Christmas, you know that all right, my own little Bennyboy. We have our own celebration, HANUKKAH, and we don't get any presents, then, but we celebrate lighting the Hanukkah candles, first one candle, and then one more every night until all eight candles are lit together on the last evening... It is so beautiful! We have our own religion, little Ben, and you should be very pleased with that. We are Jews, we are not like the others. You ought to be proud of it, my own boy, proud and happy! Aren't you happy, my own little sweetheart?
    But... Ben isn't really happy anyway. And while dreaming, he draws Santa Claus with his sharp pen on the newly-painted desk.
    Mrs. Arnold-Hansen's mind has become calm and generous:
    – You would like a Christmas fairy tale, wouldn't you?

Of course the children would like that! And while they are shouting with joy the teacher gets the fine-looking book with the Christmas tales and all the lovely drawings. She used always to walk with the open book down the aisles in the class, so that those at the back also had an opportunity to see the pictures:

– Well then, I'll read the tale about Søren's music box. You know, little Søren wouldn't stop making a noise with his music box during the lesson, so that the teacher had taken his music box and locked it in the cupboard. But then he forgot to give the music box back to the little boy before Christmas, and it was the only present Søren had ever received. But as good luck would have it, it did occur to the teacher on Christmas Eve itself, and then he hurried back to school for it, so that little Søren had his music box after all...

– Are you kidding? You're off your head Ben! You can't do that!

Kristian whispers, pushing Ben so that he wakes up with a start:

– What can't I do?

– You've been drawing on the desk!

Ben gets into a fright, discovering the Santa Claus he himself had scratched on the shining surface of the desk. Only yesterday Mrs. Arnold-Hansen had admonished them, now that the desks have just been done up so nicely for Christmas, the children must not on any account ruin them!

Ben tries to cover it over by pushing his swan reader over it, but Lotty had already seen it and put up her hand to sneak on Ben.

The class is as silent as death. Oh, gosh!

Mrs. Arnold-Hansen gets up. Now she is stalking slowly towards Ben to inspect the calamity... and as she comes closer she gets bigger and bigger, growing, becoming overwhelming, and Ben becomes so very very small, he doesn't even dare to look up at the colossal figure looming over him, huge and threatening. Oddly enough, the teacher's voice is soft and kind, as she stretches her hand towards the boy:

– Now, come with me, my little friend.

Ben puts his hand in the teacher's big hand, and she walks out of the classroom with him. The boy is surprised. Could it be that it wasn't so bad after all, what he'd done? The teacher holds his hand quite lightly and Ben joins her willingly. Where are they going?

They walk out into the schoolyard. It is empty. The cold wind is whistling around the corner of the buildings. The teacher stops looking around. Ben is waiting. What will happen now? She bends as if she were going to say something to him... and then, like a bolt out of the blue, she strikes his open face, hits him again and again, first one cheek, then the other... and she keeps on beating! Ben doesn't even try to protect himself, as the teacher hisses:

– Take this! And this! And this! And another one! And one more, and more... Little sheeny... ruining our fine desk... Jewish scum...

Then Mrs. Arnold-Hansen grasps his arm and drags him across the yard into the gymnastics building.

Ben doesn't resist. He doesn't cry, he only feels his cheeks smart. He doesn't understand what is happening to him until the teacher is pushing him into the cupboard where the gym suits hang. The cupboard door slams and the key is turned from outside.

Everything is black around him. From outside comes Mrs. Arnold-Hansen's voice, merciless:

– Now you stay in there as punishment!

The teacher's firm steps are gradually lost in the distance.

✳ ✳ ✳

Ben cannot see anything. The cupboard is so narrow that he can hardly move. He tries to turn and hits his head against something. He takes it in his hands... it's a bag with a gym suit. No matter where he turns, he is hit on the head by a bag. He can't stand erect, but must duck in order not to hurt himself.

As time goes by, Ben begins to see a tiny light dimly coming from a chink at the top of the cupboard door. There is not a sound around him, but the acrid animal odour of sweat from the gym suits and rubber shoes, reeks in his nose, while inside his head the teacher's voice rings incessantly: *as a punishment... punishment...*

Ben presses against the cupboard door, but he cannot get out. Panic seizes him: He beats the door with clenched fists, again and again, so that his hands hurt. He stops panting heavily and listens. All he hears is his own heart beating, so that it is drumming in his ears. He would scream, but it is as if his voice will choke him. Then he hits the door again: Ouch!

The air is heavy and sickening. Ben is feeling giddy... he is near collapse.... He doesn't try to call, as nobody can hear him, nobody knows that he is there, except Mrs. Arnold-Hansen.

He doesn't cry. He just stands there. The seconds pass like black eternities. Is it like that when you are dead? But then you go to heaven, if you have been good enough. But he hadn't been...

Suddenly it gets lighter inside the cupboard. Ben looks up: It is the angel! She is smiling at him, moving her lips, speaking to him... But he cannot understand her. In her two hands she is holding towards him the big present, tied with a bow...

Ben is just about to take the present, when he is dazzled by a glare of light. The cupboard door has been opened and Ben blinks at seeing Mrs. Arnold-Hansen's angry face. Before he manages to understand what's going on, he is pulled by his arm, so that he stumbles out on the floor.

* * *

The teacher pushes Ben into the headmaster's office:

– Here is the sinner!

The headmaster is grey-haired. His big cold eyes are looking disapprovingly at him. He gets up, growing terribly tall, as he walks around the desk towards Ben, stating dryly:

– So it is you who scratched the desk... I see!

The man stares severely into Ben's eyes, bending down, squeezing and twisting Ben's cheek with his right hand's strong thumb and forefinger:

– Then it's you who ruined the desk in the geography room as well, isn't it?

Ben is taken aback... he has never been in the geography room, he doesn't even know where it is.

Then he gets a hard blow on his back from Mrs. Arnold-Hansen. He falls forward, so that the headmaster's firm hold tears his cheek and mouth:

– Can't you answer?

And the headmaster tears at Ben's cheek even harder. Ben's mouth bleeds, he tastes his own blood.

– You scratched the other desk too, didn't you?

The big man lets go of Ben's cheek, waiting. Ben's head tingles. Next his arms are grasped from behind. The teacher turns him around and shakes him violently, screaming into his face:

– Come on, admit it, you little liar!

Ben's face is wet from her saliva. He is afraid of the tall people. But he will certainly not lie, saying that he has done something he hadn't!

With a jerk, the headmaster turns Ben towards him again:

– Now you have to admit it, you will!

As Ben shakes his head, the headmaster decides that they should go to the geography room, the three of them. Here the tabletop is scratched all over with lots of lines. Ben looks at it. It was evident that it was done by someone who could not draw, so when the headmaster asks him again Ben answers, and this time loudly and clearly, that he had certainly not done it. The teachers cannot get anything further out of him.

Mrs. Arnold-Hansen gives him an evil look:

– What a stubborn lad! He wants to lie his way out of it! Take your clothes and go home!

∗ ∗ ∗

It's the middle of the morning. Ben is plodding along the Strandvej. Actually, he was still supposed to be at school, but now that he has time to look at the toyshop, he doesn't feel like doing it at all. What is he going to do? Go home? Then Mommy would ask him why he was back so early, and what could he answer to that?

At a loss, he walks on to the newsstand, while letting his schoolbag swing, smacking against his bare thighs at every step. Having looked at Prince Valiant in the Popeye magazine for a while, it doesn't interest him any more.

Then, in the show window, he notices a lottery ticket poster from Children's Welfare Day, with the drawing of the little boy in the cap. There were no more tickets, but if you could get hold of one, you might win anything you could think of... The boy with the big cap down his forehead looks with his brown eyes right at Ben.

Ben turns down the side roads until he is standing in the square with the trees in front of the villa with the high hedge around it. Could he ring the bell? But what would they think of him coming alone, while Kristian was still at school?

Now the gate of the back entrance opens. It is mother Birgit, wearing a thick fur coat, coming out together with Mrs. Vestergaard. Ben hides behind a tree, watching the two ladies. After some time Birgit walks along one of the roads, luckily without noticing him, and the cook returns to the house. It was no use, anyhow, going up there, now that Kristian's mother wasn't there...

Ben trudges back to the fare stage where the tram is waiting for him. There are lots of empty seats in it.

Instead of changing at the Triangle, he remains sitting, continuing to King's New Square. Here he gets off and walks down a street where he had once seen a sign. Yes, it is still there, saying: HELP CHILDREN'S WELFARE in capital letters.

Ben reads the sign once more, then he walks up the three steps, opens the door and remains standing there, a little despondent. A woman appears, looking inquiringly at him.

Ben doesn't know how to explain himself. The little boy in the cap is looking at him from the posters on every wall. Finally, the woman asks kindly:

– Is there anything I can do to help you?

But it is too complicated. The words stick in his throat. Ben turns around and walks down the stairs again, into the street.

The lady shuts the door after Ben with a shake of her head. It is so awfully cold outside.

* * *

– You never told me that Mrs. Arnold-Hansen locked you up in the cupboard!

Mommy is dumbfounded. She remembers all right that she had been called to a meeting at the school to be told that Ben had ruined the expensive desks. Mommy couldn't comprehend it. Ben had always been such a good boy. But they said that it was Ben who had done it and that he had admitted it himself. "He is not to show up at this school any more!" the headmaster had said, and she didn't dare object. As a Jew, she had to be careful not to create *Rishes*, animosity... Nor did she ever talk to Ben about it, because she had been so sorry that her own boy could do anything as bad as this, and to Moritz she'd only said that it was time for Ben to enrol at the Jewish community school. But she had never had the least suspicion of...

– Locked up in that cupboard! Oh my God, why didn't you ever tell me about that?

– I knew it was useless. How often it happened that you never defended me.

– Did I ever not defend you? I have done nothing but try to protect you all my life!

Mommy had been looking forward to the two of them having a really nice afternoon together... Last time, leaving, she had put the 100 crowns on the piano all the same, and she had been so happy, when Ben had called her to thank her for the money. Then he had accepted it after all. Mommy couldn't comprehend that her own Bennyboy should hate her, hate his own Mommy! It was impossible, it was unnatural! Most of all, she would have liked to visit Ben immediately, but then she had other things to do. Today, being in town to buy silk for the sofa cushions... In fact, she had the passbook which Moritz didn't know about, and as she happened to be near Regensen anyway, she bought some delicious cakes and came up here. Nevertheless, they started quarrelling again!

– Bennyboy, haven't I always been your little hen mother, trying to protect you, keep you under my wings! When Uncle Moritz was really furious I hid you from him...

– In the kitchen cabinet! You hid me in a cupboard! There I stood with the brooms in the dark!

– But it was to protect you, so that he wouldn't find you and beat you!

As a child, Ben had, in fact, often wondered what might be wrong with him, since his mother always sent him aware to other people.

– When I needed you... either you weren't there, or you were late!

– Dear me, is it that bad? I can't help it, Benny. Dear, I also had to have time to visit the old people at the rest home, you do understand that, don't you? Well, I am a little late once.

– You always had time to visit the old people at the rest home, you had time for them, just not for me... either you weren't there when I needed you or you were late!

– Dear me, is it that bad? I can't help it, Benny. I am a little late once in a while. Can't you forgive your own Mommy for having such a little defect?

– A little late! Once when I was playing in the yard and had forgotten the time, you gave me such a slap in my face! I was astounded when you hit me... and I was sent to bed without dinner! All of a sudden you wanted to educate me, teach me to be on time, while you yourself... and Moritz who was late for dinner every day!

That day Moritz had, for once, come home early for dinner and they had been waiting for Ben with the hot meal:

– I really was so sorry afterwards, dearest Benny. Uncle Moritz was in such a bad mood...

– And you always cheated me, "Mommy will be here in a minute, just stay here with the nice aunt, then Mommy will be with you again soon!" And you just stayed away for hours, days, weeks... I remember once you had gone on vacation without telling me anything.

By that time Mommy had known Moritz for a year and had the opportunity of going on vacation with him, and she wanted so very much for him to feel attached to her. But what was she going to do with Ben? First Mommy had thought of the orphanage, but fortunately Aron's sister offered to have him with her. And sweet Benny didn't cry when she left him, and when she came back, he had been smiling so happily:

– Aunt Alice played the piano for you, yes she did, and you were so pleased to stay with her.

– But mother could have told him that she was leaving! He had thought that she had left him for ever! What else could he have believed?

– But all mothers do that! I didn't think that you'd notice the difference between a few days or weeks. I did it in order to spare you. It was to avoid you getting depressed!

– Do you think that I didn't get depressed when I discovered that you stayed away? And one thing more: Children's Welfare Day!

Mother gets insecure again. Why is Ben so angry with her all the time?

– What Children's Welfare Day?

– Of course, you have forgotten everything about it...! I was living with Grandma and you had come for me. People were celebrating in the streets. That particular day was the day of the year you were to help children. You promised me that I would be allowed to have a big candybar and try all the rides on the merry-go-rounds and the swings, just as many as I wanted, and I might even buy a lottery ticket and maybe win a big prize in the tombola! I could hardly believe it! You promised me all the things I had always only seen other children being allowed to have, and the price didn't matter! But you had promised me something so many times, which you just forgot afterwards... Anyhow I thought: This time it is true! I kept asking all the time: "Is it true, is it really, really true?" And you answered: "Yes, put on your best clothes, and we'll go!" And then I decided to believe you. I began to look forward to it, first very cautiously, and then more and more. At last I was looking so much forward to it that I couldn't contain my excitement. I was nearly bursting and could hardly breathe with expectation: Me! I was going to try all the amusements that had been so unattainable... I was floating on clouds when we went outside into the street. Now finally, we were, indeed, going to have fun! And then... Do you remember we were going by tram to King's New Square, where all the candy shops and the merry-go-rounds were? And then we entered the tram, and when the conductor came for the fare, he asked how old I was. You said that I was only five years old! But I said proudly: "No! I'm six years old!" You yourself had told me that I had had my birthday when I had been with the kindergarten in Jutland. But then you said again: "No, he is only five!" Then I shouted, "You are lying Mommy, I am six!" – I didn't know you said it only to save a lousy tenpence, as children of five were allowed to ride free of charge... and then you gave me a slap in the face! Because mothers never lie! And then we had to get off, and we walked back to Grandma's, and there I was left alone for the rest of the day as a punishment... No amusements, no rides on the merry-go-round! Because I had been naughty!

Mother had never thought of it in this way:

– Bennyboy, I really... I always meant it honestly when I promised you something, really, my sweet boy! Now after so many years... Can't you just forget about it?

– It is easy to say...

* * *

In the schoolyard the three musketeers are sitting, as they usually do, on "their" bench. Their schoolmates are chatting all around. Grete is sitting between Ben and Kristian, everything is as usual, but nevertheless Kristian has a notion that there is something between Grete and Ben, without really being able to explain to himself what it is... this something between the two of them that he doesn't share...

Of course he couldn't help thinking of what had happened during the Danish lesson, reading Earl Haakon aloud. But it wasn't that which made him uneasy, it was their mutual silence, the way Grete was turning her back to him ever so slightly. And why did Grete only talk of the strength of Earl Haakon, without mentioning King Olaf, whose part he himself had been reciting?

Nearby Lily is standing with some of the others. Sometimes she laughs out loud, stealing a stealthy glance at the three friends on the bench.

Finally she comes to a decision, walks up to Kristian and sits down next to him. There is just enough space for her beside him. She takes his arm, leaning against him:

– Didn't you say that you have the latest Duke Ellington records?

Kristian is torn away from his thoughts. He pulls himself together, trying to be cheerful:

– Yes that's right. And they've got that swing, you can bet your hat on that!

Lily shows eagerness. She always wanted so much to join their gang, but she never really dared to approach the trio before. She ingratiates herself as much as she can:

– I would so much like to hear them. Can't we go to your place and listen to them?

Kristian finds that an excellent idea. He gives Grete a little shove:

– How would you like to slip away after the geography lesson and go home to listen to a couple of records?

Lily is enthusiastic, pressing herself even tighter to Kristian:

– That's great! I'm crazy about the Duke!

Kristian is flattered, even though it doesn't entirely suit him. They are used to being only a threesome, and now Lily, unexpectedly, crashes in on them. He casts a glance at Ben, but Ben is just sitting there without participating. It annoys Kristian. It strikes him that, in fact, it was Ben who started things in the Danish lesson...

In order to think of something else, perhaps also to impress Grete, who apparently didn't seem to care that Lily was actually clinging to him, Kristian begins to fool about. Couldn't he say something funny? There was that joke! He had passed the headmaster's office this morning. There, the English teacher, The Tail, as he was called, because he swung his behind in a funny way when he walked, was standing. The teacher had told the story to the headmaster and Kristian had heard how they had both been laughing, finding the story awfully funny!

Kristian raises his voice to attract attention:

– Now, listen to the latest joke fresh as a fish from Newhaven! A little Jew is sitting in a basement pub having his beer. Some sailors enter the bar. They have had plenty of drinks inside their bellies, pretty well plastered, you see, and suddenly one of the sailors goes up to the Jew and socks him in the snout, like this!

Ben gave a start when Kristian said *JEW*. He does so every time he hears the word. If, for instance the word JEW appeared in a newspaper, it was this one word which caught his eye instantly. He could spot it amongst the thousands of words, as if it had lights flashing over it. He feels his midriff burning. All of a sudden Kristian becomes a complete stranger to him.

Kristian gets into stride, spreading out his arm in a gigantic sweep: SLAM! And he keeps on making fun, rubbing his cheek, doubling up, holding his arm above his head to protect himself and whimpers pitifully, pretending to be the poor JEW:

– Ouuuuch! Why are you beating me? I haven't done anything to you!

Their classmates have stopped talking and approach to listen. Kristian is now playing the strong sailor, showing off, reeling his broad shoulders, lurching around, shaking his head, distending his eyes wide open as if he were drunk, and with a hoarse comic bass he stammers:

– Beca..ca..cause you cru..crucified Jesus!

And then Kristian doubles up again, making a pitiful face as the Jew, snuffling through his nose in a falsetto pitch and in bad Danish to make it a scream:

– But me cannot help it! It is doch happened soo much years ago!

Whereupon Kristian growls as the drunk sailor with a foolish expression:

– But I only got to know it today!!

Kristian slaps his thigh with laughter and all the young people laugh loudly. He is feeling an odd sort of satisfaction, but at the same time he has the sensation that he'd rather not have told this joke.

Grete and Ben have been torn out of their twosomeness. Grete feels how much it hurts Ben, and Lily, who was at first laughing with the others, stops immediately when she looks at Ben.

Ben turns more and more despondent. Every time he heard these Jewish jokes, whether they were anti-Semitic like this one, because the accusation that the Jews were guilty of the murder of Jesus had, indeed, been the cause of pogroms and massacres of Jews through centuries, or if it was the jokes, which amused many Jews themselves and which they themselves, and his stepfather too, loved to tell with great enthusiasm, it got him depressed. He asked himself if the Jews couldn't see the degradation in these stories. Most of the jokes were both embarrassing and discriminating. They were mostly about Jews who were cowardly, avaricious and sly, knew how to cheat the stupid Christians, and in this way they actually confirmed the filthy prejudices, which anti-Semites used as an excuse for oppressing and persecuting the Jews. And now this particular one: What about it, if the little Jew had his neck broken? What about it, if he had left a wife and children? Ben knows well enough that Kristian does not mean any harm by it. The point of it should be, anyway, that it's the sailor who is stupid! That's probably why the others are laughing... nevertheless Ben has a bad taste in his mouth.

The bell rings, break is over. Ben tries to push his thoughts away. But he remains sitting, when Kristian reaches out for him to join him. Grete stays with Ben too.

Kristian bites his lip on his way to the classroom. In a lightning flash he realizes how foolish he has been. He is angry with himself! That he could put his foot in it! But he had told it, that idiotic joke...

A voice is calling from the staircase of the main building. Lily has come back for them:

– Come on, Grete and Ben... The geography teacher is here!

* * *

Of course Ben had seen the Tivoli Boys' Guard. He had admired the big boys in the orchestra, as they marched, music blaring, through the Tivoli Garden in their beautiful scarlet uniforms and those splendid bearskin hats. There were also smaller boys playing fife and drum, and there was the Old Guard in the blue uniforms of the previous century.

You could become a Tivoli Guard at age nine! In the yard at home there was a boy... his older brother was a colonel in the Boys' Guard! It was he, with his shining sabre, who was riding the white horse. But he was already sixteen years old! He said to Ben that he would tell him all right, when there was the next entrance examination for the orchestra. Then Ben just had to turn up.

As Mommy hadn't come home yet that day, Ben went all by himself to the barracks of the Tivoli Guard and played the piece of Mozart which Mommy also used to play. The conductor asked Ben if he would like to learn to play the flute. But Ben would rather play the trumpet, and he was allowed to do so.

In the contract which Ben and Mommy signed it said: IT'S AN HONOR TO BE IN THE TIVOLI BOYS' GUARD!

* * *

The following summer, Ben and the colonel's little brother were the two youngest boys in the Tivoli Boys' Guard. Ben had to learn to play the trumpet before he joined the orchestra. In the meantime, the two little boys marched in front of The Old Guard. Ben carried a bugle and actually had the same uniform and the same kind of bugle as the statue of the Little Bugler!

Ben was proud! He also had his picture taken by a street photographer in Tivoli. The photographer sent the photo to Mommy, and Mommy was so elated! Even though she had to pay for the picture...

However, when Ben joined the orchestra the year after, he never had his picture taken any more, even though he now wore the scarlet uniform, as Mommy had so many expenses for his sake, the white gloves, the black socks and the black shoes, all of which he absolutely had to have.

In the Boys' Guard Ben earned money! 15 cents every time they marched through the Tivoli Garden and 25 cents when they played a concert on the tribune on Sundays. The boys received all their pay once a year at the end of the season. Mommy then made a deposit for Ben in a closed bank account. This meant he'd get his money when he was 18. It was the most rational thing to do.

Mommy naturally thought that Kristian's mother also ought to see how sweet Ben looked in the Tivoli Boys' Guard uniform, so she arranged for mother Birgit and Kristian to meet her on a Sunday by the marble bust of Pierrot with the white face and the thick red lips.

The Guard is marching through the Tivoli Garden playing THE COPENHAGEN MARCH. Ben is perspiring. It is not so easy to keep time while marching and playing and to ensure that the music notes don't fall down, and in addition to keep straight rows. Ben catches sight of them. They are standing just over there... His face is red, because the bearskin is heavy and hot, and then it is a little too big for him, so that it continuously drops down on one side, awry, and when he gives a shake of his head, it moves to the other side. Furthermore, the high starched collar rubs hard, so that his neck is sore. But he has his eyes stiffly directed at the music, and he is blowing his cornet with all his might, pretending not to see Mommy, Kristian and mother Birgit, when marching at a stiff pace just past them, while Mommy, pointing at Ben, is bending to say something to Kristian.

Mommy is touched! It is indeed her own dear Bennyboy in that beautiful scarlet full dress uniform. Mommy's own brave little soldier, who protected her as a little boy in the street in Hamburg, just like a big soldier.

Mommy walks with Kristian and his mother, following the Boys' Guard past the Pantomime Theatre with the gilt Chinese pagoda and the fantastic, gigantic peacock, opening out its tail feathers in all the colors of the rainbow like an enormous fan covering the entire stage.

Mommy is so proud that Ben, all by himself, had managed to be admitted into the Tivoli Boys' Guard.

– Ben had asked me to accompany him to the entrance examination, but I had forgotten about it... I hurried to the Tivoli as fast as I could and when running up the stairs, filled with other parents and children, I heard the last tones of the sonata by Mozart: "It's my son who is playing! Yes, my own Bennyboy!" I shouted and ran into the room where the music came from... And there he was, sitting by the piano, and around him the captain and the conductor of the Tivoli Boys' Guard listening! They were very satisfied and wanted to have Ben in the band!

Mommy is smiling proudly at Birgit while they proceed through the garden under the trees with the fairy lights:

– He managed it all by himself, playing for all the strangers without me being there! Just fancy: When Ben was only three years old, he already knew the book Slovenly Peter, Der Struwelpeter, by heart! I had taught him all the stories, and he told them with the correct intonation, exactly as I did! Once when I was at the dentist's, Ben had brought the book with him, while he was waiting for me. When I came out again, a lady in the waiting-room asked me, if it was really true that such a little boy could read already! She had, indeed, believed that Ben could read!

Mommy takes Kristian by the hand so that he can listen better:

– Because Benny had turned the pages exactly when he was supposed to, while he was reciting the stanzas about "Choosy Charles," who got so thin, so very, very thin because he wouldn't eat his soup... and finally he died of starvation! Because it is indeed true that children have to learn to eat up the food on their plates, isn't it?

Mommy looks at Birgit, waiting for her to confirm what was so evident to her, so she gets a bit confused when mother Birgit doesn't agree with her:

– I think that children should eat until they have had enough. And when they don't want to eat any more, they don't need any more, either.

It takes a moment for Mommy to recover from her surprise. But then she agrees with Birgit immediately:

– Well, certainly, it is quite right, what you are saying!

And Mommy bends down to Kristian, confidentially:

– It is such a good book, indeed! Of course you know it too, don't you Kristian? The mighty Nicholas who dips the boys into his deep ink-stand when they are naughty, so that they become totally pitch-black!

As Kristian never read it, Mommy wants so much to tell him all the happy tales, while they are walking around the Tivoli Lake, observing the ducks grubbing under the water, and the lovely flowers and all the cheerful people sailing in the small boats:

– Now listen to the story of the little girl Paulinchen! Even though her mother told her not to play with matches, she does it all the same, when her mother goes to town! And then the fire takes hold of her dress and her hair, and it doesn't help the least that she is screaming for help: She is burnt by huge flames! Finally there is only a small heap of ashes left of her. And the two pussycats are the only ones to cry over her...

The boy is listening with his eyes wide open, but the tale certainly doesn't seem to please him. In fact, Birgit doesn't like the stories very much either, but as Mommy means well, Birgit would rather not stop her. Mommy is completely affected by her own narrative:

– And then there is the story of Ugly Frederick. He is so awfully naughty! He hits his own nanny with a whip, his own dear Anna. But then the dog takes the whip away and eats his food, so Fred goes to bed hungry... And Fussy-Philip won't sit properly at the table, but rocks in his chair, so that he overturns the entire dinner, which falls on the floor, even though his father told him to sit properly... What a mess! So naughty Philip got a regular spanking! But the best of all the stories is the one about Konrad, the Thumb-Sucker. He wouldn't stop sucking his finger! As soon as his mother left him, POP! His finger went into his mouth! But then the tailor came with his big scissors and cut off his thumbs: CLIP CUT, CLIP CUT, both of them! And Konrad didn't get the delicious figs his mother had gone out to buy for him either...

And Mommy sings the stanzas from the book:

> – *WHEN THE CHILDREN GENTLE BE*
> *THEN THE CHRIST CHILD THEY SHALL SEE*
> *HANDLE SILENTLY THEIR TOYS*
> *TAKING PAINS TO MAKE NO NOISE*
> *AND WHEN A PLEASURE WALK IS PLANNED*
> *LET MOTHER LEAD THEM BY THE HAND*
> *FOR EVERY BLESSING THEY MAY LOOK*
> *AND GET, BESIDES, A PICTURE BOOK.*

They have passed by the multi-coloured Chinese pagoda with the dragons' heads putting out their tongues from every corner of it, and they get to the square in front of the barracks of the Boys' Guard.

Here a lot of people are standing looking at the guard boys, who have turned out for parade in ruler-straight rows. The colonel is sitting on his high horse, with his long shining sabre sticking up along his right shoulder. They are going to play the regimental march.

Kristian runs ahead and pushes himself between the onlookers, so that he can get a good view, just opposite Ben who is standing straight in his row, staring right ahead. Kristian whispers: – Pssst! And Ben winks at Kristian with one eye, without turning his head, because now he has to be attentive.

In the meantime, Mommy and Birgit have reached Kristian. They are smiling at Ben. Now there is complete silence.

The colonel gives the command:

– Attention! Present... arms!

The drum major signals with his drumstick and the orchestra plays the regimental march, slowly and ceremoniously, while the lieutenant and the standard-bearer carry the Danish flag, Dannebrog, past the ranks, marching with short rhythmical steps and outstretched knees and insteps, keeping time to the music. The colonel salutes the colours by slowly lowering the point of his sword in a curve from his fine black bearskin down to the heel of his boot.

* * *

The three of them, Mommy, Birgit and Kristian, are waiting for Ben when he streams out of the barracks together with the other boys, after having changed into plain clothes. Mommy embraces her boy, she is so proud!

So is Ben, certainly! He is still hot and his cheeks are quite red. Now they are going for a walk in the lovely garden on this wonderful summer evening, crowded with people smiling happily, and what great fun they are having!

When they pass the merry-go-round, Kristian's mother asks if the boys would like to try it. Of course they would, but when Birgit is about to buy the tickets, Mommy insists that she wants to pay for them.

The boys each jump on a horse, just beside each other, and now they go round and round, and up and down. They are shouting and laughing, holding hands. Together they are going to conquer the whole world. They have such fun, that they must have another ride, and Mommy absolutely insists on paying for it again.

* * *

When the Tivoli Guard had their summer holidays, Ben would take the train, all by himself, to Kristian's parents' summer cottage, called The Cabin. It was, in fact, a real cabin, taken from a real ship, once stranded on the coast. The Cabin had round portholes with thick double-glazed windows. The benches were built into the walls, complete with lids, like chests you could open up to put things into. The tables and chairs had iron legs fastened to the floor with screws, in order to resist the sea.

The Cabin stood on top of the cliff with a view of the sea, on which it had once sailed, Kristian's father always said. There was also an old water tower on the plot of land. Plants and bushes grew wildly, as Doctor Knud didn't want the grass to be cut. It was the boys' prairie, where they could hide in their secret hiding-places in the thicket.

The water tower was their fortress, impregnable to all enemies, and they had a rope ladder to climb up and down the tower.

In the morning the boys went down to the station to get the newspaper, and they bought tasty warm and fresh bread at the baker's. Ben rode on Kristian's old bicycle, which the family always brought with them into the country. And what a delicious breakfast, with milk fresh from the cow from the neighbouring farm, scrambled eggs, bread and butter... Porridge... thank you, not for me!

And then: Let us be off! Down the steep slope with the 113 steps to the beach, where Kristian and Ben got swimming lessons from Tarzan himself! That was the nickname of the big bronzed muscular lifeguard! On the beach the boys would play all day long, and when Kristian's father gave them 25 cents each, they darted off to the ice-cream shop in town, where the greengrocer's daughters with the swelling bosoms were selling delicious cornets with lots of whipped cream and strawberry jam!

Sometimes Knud and Birgit, Kristian and Ben bicycled to picnic in the Trolls' Forest. They carried luncheon packets and the schnapps liqueur bottle. Birgit mustn't ever forget the schnapps. This was very important, Knud always said. At first Ben had been a little uneasy about going there, but the Troll Forest was thus named because the trunks and branches of the trees were so crooked and twisted that they resembled real monsters.

The boys also made their own newspaper, "Cabin News," in which they drew cartoons and wrote stories of their own creation, and then they sold the paper to mother Birgit and Knud, and to all relatives and friends who might be around.

The last week of the vacation they sailed around Zealand in their big sailing boat. Certainly they got somewhat seasick the first day crossing Køge Bay in a heavy sea, but already by the same evening both boys were so accustomed to the sea that they could hardly walk on land without rolling their hips like hardened tars.

Knud sat by the tiller, wearing his captain's cap, smoking his pipe, while the two brothers were sitting in the bow, enjoying the boat lifting them up and bringing them down again with a long rocking rhythm into the troughs of the sea, making their stomachs jump. The cool seawater spurted on their faces, so they could lick the salt taste off their lips. The boys got tanned bodies like Norn guest's sons in the book by Joh. V. Jensen, which father Knud loved to read aloud.

* * *

Ben now went to the Mosaic Boys' School. It was named after Moses. It did sound better, anyway, than if the school were called something like *JEW*... But strangely enough Ben had to repeat the third class.... He already knew all the stories in the reader!

Of course Kristian was still at school in Hellerup, and Ben continued to go to Kristian in the afternoon, even though he was busy practicing the piano and playing the trumpet in Tivoli too, where the Boys' Guard Orchestra had rehearsals twice a week.

The two boys often went down to the harbour where Doctor Knud had his big sailing boat. There was even fishing-tackle on board. Then the two of them would sit with their legs dangling over the rail, catching gigantic whales and dangerous sharks with teeth sharp as a sword, or they were explorers, fighting with pirates or with enormous octopuses, which had shining green eyes and deadly tentacles, long and thick as boas, and when Kristian was stuck in their suckers, Ben came to rescue him... Or they were flying in their spaceship, right up to the moon, just as in the novels of Jules Verne.

One day when Ben came to visit Kristian, he was in bed. Kristian was battered all over. He had bruises on his arms and legs and an enormous black eye. His lips were swollen and bleeding. He had come to blows in the schoolyard with a big boy two years older. The boy had called out during recess that it was a blessing that they had been released from Ben dirtying the school, and had mocked Kristian, because he was a friend of such a sheeny... Kristian became furious and attacked him, even though the other boy was much bigger, and in the end Kristian succeeded in striking him down, giving him a real beating, until Mrs. Arnold-Hansen had separated them and sent Kristian home from school!

Mother Birgit had to dab his eye with moist cotton wool and cleanse his wounds with iodine, and that was painful! But after a few days Kristian was again top dog, immensely satisfied that he had given that ignorant ignoramus such a thrashing that he had something to think about.

* * *

At the Jewish school you were only supposed to study the Old Testament, but Ben knew, nevertheless, all the stories about Jesus, as he had read them at the school in Hellerup. Even Miss Rasmussen, who was a Christian, talked a lot about the sweet little infant Jesus, though they were supposed to learn mathematics. She was so lovable and nice, but Ben didn't like her all the same, because she was unjust to Kalle and John, giving them poor marks, only because their parents were exempt from paying the two crowns monthly school fees.

They had a teacher with a small goatee. He was called "The Goat." The boys often teased him so much during lessons, that he ran exasperated after the wags between the desks without being able to catch them, thus making a big fool of himself.

Ben never participated in teasing him. He felt sorry for the teacher, who was so desperate sometimes that he was nearly sick. He had such kind eyes, and Ben always learned scripture so well that The Goat took a special liking to him and gave him full marks both in Bible and Hebrew, though Ben wasn't able to find out what the Hebrew words meant.

Their music teacher was nicknamed "Rabbit." He too was fond of Ben, and he was the one who taught Ben to sing a very long piece in Hebrew for his Bar Mitzvah, his confirmation at the synagogue. Ben knew it by heart and the synagogue had been completely silent while he was singing.

In the nature study room there was a cupboard with a stuffed squirrel with a beautiful bushy tail. Ben made a drawing of it, so that it seemed almost alive, and he also drew some fine Alsatian dogs. These pictures were on view and shown to the entire school.

In gymnastics they had a former warrant officer, who drilled the boys as if they were little soldiers. When they took their showers, Ben noticed that the other naked boys looked just like himself, so he didn't have any reason to be shy.

In Danish, they had the headmaster himself – Mr. Painer – a big grey-haired gentleman. He was a Christian and very strict. He always biffed the boys on their heads with his knuckles. First he pulled them up by the hair on their temple till they were standing on tiptoe... and then he biffed them! That hurt! The boys were fearful of him. If it was one of the pious boys who always wore a skullcap, the boy first had to take it off, and then: SLAM! He got a knock on his nut!

One day during the break Ben had walloped the boy sitting next to him in class, one of the orthodox boys, and he peached to the headmaster, so Ben was to have a knock. Mr. Painer biffed him, beating so hard with his sharp knuckles that Ben nearly fainted. Ben would remember him for that... and also the pious one!

There was another teacher who wasn't a Jew either. He was a young man called Mr. Ermin. Sometimes he came to school in a civil defence uniform. He was a breath of fresh air from the world outside the stuffy atmosphere of the school and was extremely popular. Mr. Ermin taught woodwork too and he allowed Ben to make a fine bookcase with curved corners for himself.

Once when Ben was far away, his thoughts soaring, dreaming, plaiting his curly hair with his fingers, paying no attention, he got a sudden brutal box on his ear from the teacher, who bullied him to wake him up. It was Mr.

Ermin. Ben got deathly scared and after that he never ever said a word to Mr Ermin.

In the schoolyard there was a pear tree with a bench around it. During the intervals, Ben would often sit there with one of the small boys from the first grade on his lap, tickling him so that the little boy gurgled with laughter.

In the autumn it was a matter of getting hold of the pears! The boys dashed down, when the bell rang, to be the first ones to pinch the pears which had fallen off the tree. One could also be sly enough to ask for permission to be excused in the middle of the lesson, then you had a great chance, eventually, to get hold of a deliciously juicy pear or two. Unfortunately, Ben wasn't the only boy who had figured that trick out: There was a constant running of boys to the toilet during lesson when the pear season had come. The boy who got the most pears was Kalle, because he had been lucky enough to be chosen to ring the bell when the time was up. This gave him permission to leave the class a few minutes before lessons had finished.

* * *

The school day is over. The boys rush out of their classes and down the stairs. Ben too is hurrying down to see if he can wangle a pear, but they have already been taken by those who got there first.

Kalle, however, has a slightly battered pear in his pocket, which he slips into Ben's hand. As they are going out of the school gate, some big lads are riding by on their bicycles. They are waving arms, shouting contemptuously:

– Jewish brats! Soon the Germans will come and take you away!

* * *

Ben is pacing nervously up and down his room:

– When you placed me in the Jewish boys' school you put me back to the 3rd grade, even though I had been promoted to the 4th grade together with Kristian.

Ben recalls that he had been so ashamed when people asked him what grade he was in; he couldn't understand at all why he wasn't promoted.

Mommy sighs:

– I never suspected that it was so important for you! Everything was so confused at that time, Benny dear. You had to change from one school to another in terrible haste. And then in the 4th grade there were some boys who had been ploughed, twice moreover, so that they were two years older than you were, and they would certainly be sorry if you did better at school than they did. And the headmaster thought it was the best for you. Mr. Painer advised me to do it. You were to learn Hebrew, too!

– Hebrew! I never learned Hebrew. I read it without understanding a word, I learned the grace by heart, so that I could say it on Sabbath night to your great delight! That's all...

– After all, Bennyboy, what does a year mean at that age?

– You just say: What does a year mean!

Ben had thought of it every single day at school. His thoughts continue to revolve in his head:

– The stupid lies of grown-ups! It's simply unbelievable: I was more than ten years old when I found out that it wasn't the stork that brought the babies...

Now Mommy can't help smiling:

– Bennyboy, you can't be serious! Everybody told their children that. Grandma told me when I was a little girl... And I even told you that after the stork had laid all the little babies, each on the leaf of a water lily, I chose just you! Of all the sweet little babies! Because you were the dearest, sweetest of them all...

Ben remebers what a shock it had been for him! Not the fact that children grow inside their mother's womb, but by the fact that his mother could bring herself to lie to him!

– You had made a fool of me, treated me as if I were stupid. I was ridiculous to the others who knew better! One night when Moritz wasn't at home I was allowed to lie in bed together with you. You were reading a book called The Good Hearth, and I was reading it too. The book was about a Chinese woman who worked in the field, and then she suddenly got pains and lay down in the ditch to give birth to her child... and then you hastened to close the book. From the look you gave me, I could deduce that it was something I wasn't allowed to know:

– I was so concerned that you shouldn't learn to find out about it in a nasty way!

– Why didn't you tell me yourself then? And... You always promised me so many things: "When you start school you will get a big bag of candy, just like your cousins!"

He visualizes the pictures his mother had shown him with his cousins standing with their enormous candy bags... and his playmates getting Easter eggs and decorated birch-rods...

– But when I had my thirteenth birthday, I came from the countryside to

Copenhagen because I was going to my Bar Mitzvah at the synagogue. Now I am home for my birthday, I thought, now Mommy will celebrate it...

– Bennyboy, we couldn't celebrate twice, both your confirmation and your birthday...

– Why not? Other parents do it anyway!

– But we made a fine Bar Mitzvah celebration for you, didn't we? You sang solo in the synagogue... and all the others said that you had sung so beautifully! I gave you a creamed egg yolk with sugar before you sang, in order to soothe your throat, and you did get fine presents – a fountain pen, a book and a wristwatch! We celebrated for sure – we had thirty guests for dinner...

– But you, Mother, did YOU say to me that I sang beautifully? And you sent me to bed at a quarter to nine! At the only party ever made for me... before dinner was over! I was just allowed to eat my dessert while you were still eating the main dish. I knew that a father usually makes a speech for his confirmed son, but Moritz wasn't my father, so I couldn't possibly expect that of him... and, of course, he didn't. You didn't say a single word either! I wasn't mentioned at all. I was totally ignored, while you grown-ups were drinking and feeding like animals. When I was told I had to go to bed, I pretended not to hear anything. It was my party after all! I could stay up late, couldn't I! Then you came up to me, whispering in my ear that if I didn't go to bed immediately Uncle Moritz would get angry. A glance at him was enough! I slunk into bed...

Mommy had done everything to arrange a really fine party for Ben and she had been so happy on his behalf!

– But that was for the sake of your health, Bennyboy! It was, indeed, such a fatiguing day for you! You surely were so very very tired, my poor sweet little thing...

– And your poor sweet little thing who was so very tired, was crying into his pillow, while you were having a good time... until the last guests left...

– But you were happily sleeping tight. I was in your room to see you!

– I was pretending to sleep...

Mother refuses to comprehend. The only thing she wants right now is that they would be comfortable when together:

– Shouldn't we stop thinking of all the sad things, Bennyboy? Please, let's be friends... I get so unhappy when you talk like that! What is the good of saying that I should have done things differently? I did all I could do... And we have had so many happy hours together! Do you remember when you were a little boy and I sang the song for you about Little Hans? I was so happy because I had you! You were so mild, so compliant, so dear! We were to be together forever and ever.

Mommy closes her eyes, starting to hum, rocking backwards and forwards as if hugging her little boy:

> – *LITTLE HANS, LITTLE HANS*
> *WANTS TO SEE THE WHOLE WIDE WORLD!*
> *HIS HAT, HIS STICK SUITS HIM WELL*
> *LITTLE HANS IS BRAVE AND SWELL!*

Ben has never forgotten that song. It has been inside him from his very first sensual perceptions:

–Yes, brave and swell! I wanted to see the whole wide world!

Mommy keeps on singing:

> – *BUT THEN HIS POOR MOMMY CRIED*
> *HER SORROW IS TOO GREAT TO BEAR*
> *SO LITTLE HANS HURRIED BACK*
> *HOME AGAIN TO MOMMY DEAR*

– And then, Mother: You punished me!

Now Mommy's heart beats faster in sheer agitation:

– It was so dangerous when you ran into the nasty streets of the Chinese quarter, and you were only two years old! Didn't I tell you to remain standing there properly! But you just ran away without obeying!

– You left me in the middle of the street.

Mommy, who used to relate the episode as if it were a humorous anecdote, now relives her fear:

– When I came out of the shop, you were gone! So I ran like a maniac through the streets. I was looking for you everywhere, in shady pubs and sinister staircases. In my mind's eye I already saw how you had been kidnapped by the Chinese and that they had cut you in bits. I was so terribly frightened, I cried and shouted to everybody: "Have you seen my little boy?" And when I finally found you, I gave you such a hard spanking! I pitched into your sweet little bottom, I smacked again and again, until it was bright red, your sweet little bottom.

Ben tries to explain:

– I was so happy when I finally found you again... I had been so scared and now you came to protect me at last, and what did you do? You beat me!

Mommy had just wanted to talk about something pleasant, something funny, something that the two of them had in common... and now it went wrong again.

– Anyway, it was good luck that I found you, wasn't it? Afterwards you promised that you never ever would run away any more and always keep to your Mommy. Something could have happened to you! Thank God it all ended well, so that we can sit here today and be amused by it!

But Ben doesn't think that it's so funny. This was his mother's favourite story, which she just loved to tell to anybody, and they had, of course, laughed when she gave a vivid description of how red his bottom became.

Mommy tries to find a subject which is not dangerous:

– Bennyboy, do you remember that you instantly wanted to play the same pieces that I did? And you played Chopin waltzes after only a year! I was so proud of you! Now I'll make a nice cup of tea to have with the delicious cakes I brought with me...

* * *

Even though Ben had completed his thirteenth year and had been Bar Mitzvah and consequently had "entered the company of grown-ups," he was still short and thin, so that he still looked much like a boy of nine.

His hands are moving easily and adroitly up and down the white and black keys of the piano. Sometimes he plays sensitively and expressively, sometimes sonorously, powerfully. Beethoven's Sonata in C minor – the Pathétique! Mommy admires how easily he plays the quick passages and the technically difficult parts. As a young girl, Mommy had kept practising the same piece over and over and now Ben was playing it as a matter of course, so she can hardly help being a little envious of her own boy...

At that moment Uncle Moritz pitches forward into the room. Mommy and Ben stare at him with amazement. He never shows up so early in the afternoon. Out of breath, he is standing there in his hat and coat, in the living room. He is trembling all over:

– It is terrible, schrecklich...

Mommy is suddenly overcome with fear:

– Moritz dear, what has happened? What is it?

– The Gestapo has broken into the community's office and got hold of the list of names. Nobody thought of removing the card index of all our names and addresses, and now the Germans are going to arrest all adult males! I have to go underground immediately! Hurry up, Tanya, pack some clothes for me!

The parents run into the bedroom and Mommy starts packing Moritz's things into a bag.

– Go underground... Oh my God! But they said it was UNTHINKABLE!

Ben has followed them. He is thinking of Hitler's voice on the radio and feels his stomach tightening.

Moritz is nervous:

– Just the most important things, Tanya. I can't attract attention in the street. It's so frightful! And worst of all I must tell you: Waldburg has taken his own life!

Mommy lets go of the bag and has to sit down. She cannot choke back her tears:

– That distinguished cultured gentleman! How awful... My God, and his poor wife who is expecting! But... didn't the King promise to protect us?

Moritz helps her to her feet gain:

– Come on, Tanya, I must get away in a hurry! We have no time to lose, the Gestapo may be here any minute!

Ben is dumbfounded. Mr. Waldburg had always been so kind, smiling in such a friendly way at him, saying "Hullo, my little friend, how are you?" How often hadn't he wished that Mr. Waldburg were his stepfather, instead of Uncle Moritz.

Mommy pulls herself together and manages to put the last things into the bag:

– Where are you going, Moritzl?

Moritz runs quickly to the entrance, Mommy and Ben hurry after him.

– I am going to the grocer's, then I'll let you know.

Mommy is confused:

– What about us, then? The Germans could be here any moment, as you say. What about Ben and me?

Moritz starts down the stairs without even looking at Ben:

– They say that they are only after the adult males. No need to worry! They won't hurt women and children! Bye-bye, Tanya. As soon as I can, I'll let you know...

After Moritz has left, Mommy remains in the doorway for a moment. Then she closes the door, turns the key from the inside, takes Ben in her arms, hugging him tightly.

Ben is looking into his mother's eyes. The Germans, obviously, were doing exactly the things they said they wouldn't do. Uncle Moritz must have realized that too. What a coward he was to run away and hide like that and

leave Mommy and himself alone! And if it was adult males the Germans were after, then he himself had already had his Bar Mitzvah...
– But... if the Germans will come anyway?

* * *

The following night Ben dreamt that he was out sailing on the wild sea in a fishing-boat. And King Christian the Xth was with him! The boat rocked in the storm, and water from the heavy, salty sea washed over the deck. The king who was, of course, a lot taller than little Ben, would leave the cabin for the cab of the boat, but he couldn't maintain his balance. He was just about to fall and get washed overboard. But Ben came running to help the king, supporting him to save him from drowning.

* * *

The Germans didn't come that night. But the following day Ben and the other boys were sent home from school.

On the way, Ben, as usual, went past the Forum. Ben opened his eyes wide: The whole immense building was in ruins! The Forum had been blown up by the resistance movement, because the Germans had been using the building for their troops.

Now, suddenly, they all, women and children included, had to run away. Apparently Hitler didn't care about King Christian and wanted to catch all the Jews. Apparently, Hitler didn't care about God either.

It had to be done in an awful hurry. Ben is wearing three sets of underwear, two shirts and two pullovers, and even two pairs of trousers... and a jacket. It would be too conspicuous, if he were carrying a suitcase, wouldn't it! In addition, Mommy dresses him in his new coat, but even though it was bought two sizes too big for him to grow into, Mommy can hardly button it up. Ben looks like a big stuffed doll and has difficulty moving. He also wears the new watch which he got as a Bar Mitzvah present.

Mommy also wears one dress over the other. She puts on her Persian lamb coat, the hat with the veil, her expensive gold watch and all her jewels. She ties Ben's scarf around his neck, kisses him fiercely and gives him 35 pence:
– Here is the money for the tram, for the stop after the fare stage as well. And always remember your scarf! It's very important or you will catch a cold! And you will walk very composedly and naturally in the street, so that people won't notice you! Be sure not to attract attention! You will give my regards

to Doctor Knud and Mrs. Birgit. May God stand by us, so that we will meet again in Sweden! You are such a big and brave boy! You'll manage it, Mommy will think of you all the time! Now you go down the backstairs and go straight to them...

And she kisses him goodbye for the second time:

– Take care, my dear boy! Hurry up, we have no more time. Mommy is going to meet Uncle Moritz in ten minutes.

Mommy's eyes are wet as she closes the back door behind Ben. Crossing the yard, he waves his hand at her, seeing her standing by the window, before he turns out of the gate.

∗ ∗ ∗

Ben walks quickly along the hedges towards the villa, kicking the withered leaves on the road. The ride on the tram, everything considered, was all right. All during the ride, he stood next to the tram conductor behaving as if nothing had happened. And yet he had a feeling that people were glancing at him, wondering why he was wearing all those clothes, even the conductor... but he just watched how the tram rode on the shining rails.

In the villa they are expecting him. Ben has hardly rung the bell before the door opens so that he can slip in. Doctor Knud, mother Birgit, Kristian and Mrs. Vestergaard are there to receive him. Birgit helps him to take off all the superfluous clothes, and Knud tells the boys that they can play all over the house:

– But you can't play in the garden!

What a pity, because out there they had their cave, but Kristian is glad:

– You are going to sleep in my bed. We can easily lie in my bed together.

Daddy Knud suggests that they step upstairs to the attic, all of them. On top, under the pitched roof, there is a big cupboard. The father pushes the heavy cupboard aside, and behind it a small room appears with a mattress, a pillow, a thick woollen blanket, a big flashlight, some Popeye magazines, two bottles of fizzy water and a box of cookies. Knud explains:

– As you see, it's a real little cave! We have arranged it in case the Germans should come looking for you. Then you will run up here and hide. They can't find you here, and then you will wait silently, until we let you out again.

Daddy shows how he pushes the cupboard in front of the opening and then pushes it aside once more. Birgit smiles, patting Ben on his head:

– We have left cookies for you to cheer you up in there. Try to crawl in there, then you'll know how it is, and you know, it is just for fun! The

Germans probably won't come at all, so it won't be necessary... it's just that you know how it is.

The boys look at each other. They are aware that it isn't altogether just a game. Ben crawls inside, placing himself on the mattress, and Knud pushes the cupboard into place in front of him.

Ben is now in the pitch-dark black hole, everything around him is silent. His heart is throbbing. Then, Mrs. Arnold-Hansen's sharp threatening voice rings out: *You stay there as a punishment... punishment... punishment...*

Ben can hardly breathe, it is as if he is about choke... He starts hitting at the back wall of the cupboard, beats with all his might without noticing how much his fists are hurting. He hammers away, again and again, until the cupboard is pushed aside and the light reaches him and he sees the doctor's smiling face:

– Hello little man! Come out here!

And Daddy Knud helps Ben out:

– Was it dark in there? Why didn't you turn on the flashlight? That is why we left it there! You didn't get scared now, did you? We were out here, all of us, all the time!

Ben is pale and short of breath, and he doesn't calm down until Birgit takes him in her arms, stroking his hair:

– Nothing happened really, Ben... and, most likely, the Germans won't come at all...

Ben holds Birgit tight and only after a while lets her go.

Even Kristian has gone pale. Daddy Knud suggests that the two boys should try to go into the cave together, this time with the flashlight switched on, but they are not in the mood to play games any more. Birgit, too, thinks that they had better go downstairs, all of them.

In the dining-room they have coffee, chocolate and cakes. Ben is really being spoiled and may eat as many cakes as he wishes... and Mrs. Vestergaard asks him what he would like for supper. Ben would like to have rice pudding with cinnamon and sugar and a big lump of butter on top. He really likes that a lot. Sometimes his Mommy made it for him!

– But that is a Christmas treat!

Well, Mrs. Vestergaard will make it anyway.

* * *

During the day Kristian went to school as usual. Of course he did not say a word about Ben being at his place, and Ben, meanwhile, read Kristian's schoolbooks, in which there were so many exciting stories which Ben hadn't read yet, because Kristian was a grade higher. He read each one of his Tarzan books, Kristian had all nineteen of them, and those you couldn't borrow from the library!

In the evening mother Birgit came to tuck both boys up in their eiderdowns. They slept with their heads opposite each other in Kristian's bed. Knud then read Norn Guest to them, which he had commenced in the summer vacation. Ben could imagine vividly how Norn Guest's sons were swimming about in the sea until they literally got webbing between their fingers and toes. Kristian always fell asleep, but Doctor Knud continued to read aloud for Ben till the chapter was finished.

Although Kristian's father was the one who made decisions in their home, Ben knew that he was, nonetheless, kind and gentle. Ben couldn't grasp it at all, that one could have a father you didn't have to be afraid of.

If the Germans should suddenly turn up, they had agreed that Kristian would hide Ben's eiderdown in a box under his bed, Knud and Ben were to go up into the attic, while Birgit went down to open the door.

* * *

A couple of days later Kristian comes home from school. During the Danish lesson Mrs. Arnold-Hansen had said that it was a blessing Denmark finally had been purified of Jews and of all kinds of rabble who were poisoning the whole society.

Kristian had got up and walked out of class. The headmaster was supposed to punish him with detention, but Kristian would not submit to that and had gone home. Doctor Knud, consequently, called the school and had a talk with the headmaster. Nothing more happened regarding that matter.

One night they went to the Royal Theatre. Ben was brought there by car by one of the actors. They saw Shakespeare's Twelfth Night and Ben and Kristian were sitting in the second row. What fun! They were amused and entertained, and Ben was laughing so loudly that the actors on stage noticed and wanted to meet him. During the interval Ben and Kristian were to go backstage, and the actors and the beautiful actresses shook their hands, asking Ben if he was the one who had laughed so much, if he really thought it was so amusing? He certainly did!

* * *

It didn't prove to be necessary for Ben to hide in the attic, and one morning, a week later, a young dark-haired lady arrived. She didn't take her coat off but just waited in the hall. Ben was to put on his coat. It was time for him to leave.

Knud hands the woman an envelope:

– It's for the fisherman... it's four thousand.

Ben could hardly believe his ears.. That was a lot of money! And they were paying so much, just for him! The doctor turned towards Ben:

– This is Tove. She is a nurse in my hospital. She is going to Sweden, too, and she will see that you get on a boat from Gilleleje. Now listen: If anybody asks your name, it is Poul Jensen, Tove is your mother and you live at 84, The Boulevard. And do remember that you are going to stick with Tove all the time, you must do that!

Ben nods and looks at Birgit, who is holding Kristian's hand. Her voice is almost inaudible as she addresses Tove:

– Take good care of him...

Knud opens the front door. Outside the wind is blowing so hard that the withered leaves are stirred up among the trees. The sun is shining, but it is chilly.

The doctor makes the decision:

– You'd better go now.

Mother Birgit lets go of Kristian and holds Ben tight in her arms before at long last she lets him go:

– God bless you, my boy.

Ben shakes hand with the father, then with Kristian, and goes with Tove out in the bracing weather.

After having crossed the square, Ben turns and looks back: They are still standing in the doorway, all three of them, waving to him, and Ben stops to wave back before he turns the corner.

He can hardly believe that it was real, what happened to him at this moment. It was as if he didn't participate in it himself, but rather as if it were something he was dreaming... or as if he were an actor in a film or as if he were reading about it in a book...

Birgit is still standing there, looking at the empty road. She raises her hand to wave once more, although Ben has already disappeared. Then Knud gently takes her arm to lead her back into the house, closing the door to the autumn.

* * *

Ben has a window seat and is watching the landscape gliding past, while the train rolls slowly through North Sealand.

A young doctor is there too. He is Doctor Knud's assistant, and he is to see to it that everything is done right. Ben is wearing his warm coat. All his extra clothes have been left with Birgit. She would send them to him afterwards, when he was safely in Sweden.

While they are talking, an elderly gentleman and a lady enter the compartment. It had been agreed that if any other people came into the compartment, the youngsters would stop talking. Tove is smiling encouragingly, and Ben responds with a hint of a smile, but he looks solemn once again as he watches the elderly couple.

Neither of the others says anything. All you hear is the rhythmical sound of the wheels against the rails, as if they were chugging the melody: *The Time When I Set Out, Boom Boom...*

The door of the compartment is pushed open. The train conductor, wearing his cap, wants to punch their tickets. The doctor and Tove show theirs. Ben has his own and he hands it to the conductor, who looks inquiringly at it for a long time – and then at Ben – and then at the ticket again. It was all right, wasn't it? At last he hands it back to Ben and hardly checks the tickets of the elderly couple before he leaves.

Just then some German soldiers pass by and look into the compartment, but the train conductor swiftly slams the door so that the Germans walk on, even though there actually are some vacant seats.

* * *

In Gilleleje they get off the train, and the doctor accompanies Ben and Tove to one of the low houses in the narrow alleys of the small fishing town. There he takes leave of them and they are shown into the house by the fisherman himself, as Tove hands him the envelope.

In the narrow room a few other people are waiting with their coats on. Ben discovers that it is Kalle and his mother and his little brother Jacob. Ben nods at him and Kalle winks back without daring to say anything. Ben and Tove sit down on the red plush-covered chairs along the wall. They will just have to wait.

The fisherman has gone off. The door to the living-room opens and a couple of small girls enter, looking at Ben and the others with wide open eyes. They are the fisherman's own children. Only a few moments pass before their mother pulls them out again by their arms, very determinedly, indeed: They are NOT to go in here, but keep away... whereupon she closes the door firmly, from the outside, and that's it!

On the wall of the room there is a painting of a fishing boat in stormy weather and on the sideboard there stands a bottle with a small ship inside. Ben would like to have a closer look at it, but Tove indicates that he'd better stay beside her.

It gets hot sitting for such a long time with your overcoat on. After a while, little Jacob starts crying so that his mother has to unbutton his coat and take him on her knees to comfort him until he has calmed down again.

* * *

The fisherman didn't come back till the afternoon. Now the time had come. They have to go down to the port. The man shows the way:

– Do remember to walk composedly! Down at the pier a boat will be waiting for you! And don't walk too many together, or you will be noticed!

Ben goes with Tove, as he had been told to do, while more and more people pop out from narrow alleys and houses, all of them wearing overcoats, some of them carrying bags and suitcases, all walking in the same direction towards the harbour. Gradually the people have gathered into quite a big crowd, although they had been told to move in small sparse groups.

All of a sudden somebody screams:

– The Germans! The Germans are coming! Run! Run!

More people take up the cry, desperate and frightened:

– The Gemans are here! The Germans! The Germans!

Everybody starts to run, faster and faster. Even Ben is fidgeting with impatience, drawing at Tove's arm. But she cannot run so quickly... so Ben lets go of her and, agile as he is, he is running along and is soon at the head of them all, and can see the boat, its steam up, lying at the farthest point of the pier. He turns to look for Tove. He waits and waits, while the others catch up with him again and hasten past him. Then he runs all the way back to her and takes her arm to help her. If only she would hurry up!

Now all the people are crying out desperately, without heeding the warning to be quiet. What was he to do? He could easily manage to get on the boat, he was the fastest runner in his class... if it hadn't been for Tove, but Doctor Knud had told him to stick to her...

At this very moment Tove stumbles and falls heavily to the ground. She gives a cry. Ben tries to help her to her feet, but she cannot stand up. He looks around in perplexity and sees the fisherman who has been following them.

He shouts to Ben to wait, rushes into the nearest house and returns shortly after with a barrow. With great effort they manage to place Tove in the barrow and the fisherman starts to push her, while she groans and moans unceasingly.

Once more Ben runs ahead and gets all the way down to the ship. Its motor is chugging with powerful strokes, while black smoke intermittently puffs out of the funnel. Many of the people are already on board and the rest of them are completely hysterical, crowding and pressing their way forward to get on the ship. An old man is so agitated that he loses his suitcase, which falls with a splash between the boat and the quay.

The fisherman has now gone a fair distance along the pier with Tove in the barrow. Her whimpers are pitiful. Suddenly she waves her arms, so that she tips out of the barrow, screaming desperately:

– My scarf! My scarf! I lost it on the road! Ben, will you get it for me! Hurry up, now, run!

Roughly the man reloads Tove and gesticulates to the cutter to wait.

Ben is in doubt. He could easily get on board if he ignored her request, but he was so used to doing what he was told, and a scarf was so very important! And he was also supposed to stick with Tove! If he dashed off as quickly as he could... then he might manage it!

Ben rushes all the way back up to the road and fortunately he finds the scarf at once. Then he sprints out onto the pier again and, gasping for breath, hands it to Tove. She has to put it on at once and ties it round her neck, so that she nearly falls off again, while Ben helps the fisherman push the barrow the last part of the way.

But there are already a few metres of water between the cutter and the quay, while they are pulling the last refugee on board over the gunwale.

There they are. The boat sails farther and farther away, and the chug-chug of the engine is getting weaker and weaker, while the stretch of water separating them from freedom is getting broader and broader.

They are the only ones left behind.

Ben looks up the road to see if the Germans really were coming now to take them. But there was nobody... There weren't any Germans!

– You'd better hide in the boathouse!

The fisherman wheels Tove over the stony, rugged ground till they get to the small boathouse in the middle of the wharf. Here he helps Tove to get out of the barrow. He supports her up a small ladder to the flat loft inside the house, where she and Ben can crouch behind some planks. The man has to leave immediately:

– Stay here. I'll be back later!

✳ ✳ ✳

Wake up Ben! Come on, wake up! What's wrong with you? Are you having a nightmare?

Grete tugs at Ben lying in the fragrant green grass on the big lawn under the warm spring sun. Ben is confused. A moment ago he had been dreaming such a wonderful dream with Grete in his arms, and then those awful memories, which he thought he had thrust aside into black oblivion, had still emerged...

– Grete, but...?

She places her hand gently on his chest. It beats like a captured bird. She nestles against him, whispering very close in his ear:

– Ben, you are here, here... with me! Look at the sun! Our sun! It is shining on us! I get so scared when you moan like this in your sleep!

Ben can feel her soft body against his own. He is looking into her eyes, and at this moment he gives in, opening out his inner senses, streaming out of him in a broad river, breaking through a dam which held back its long accumulated force, the foaming waters splintering all resistance and, liberated precipitously, flow over the thirsting dried-up landscape as he sobs, he cries, dissolving the tortured knot in his chest, letting it flow down the river as he holds on to Grete, clings to her, weeps as long waves flush through his whole body, over and over and over again... What a relief to let go of all that he has suppressed for so long, to let it out, all of it, in the presence of Grete's confident warmth, the mild air, the touch of the shining sun, and soft melodies resounding from the floating clouds spreading all over the sky in an azure haze, from all the way beyond that extreme, where every pain disappears.

For a long time they remain in companionable silence, listening to each other's breathing. Then Grete laughs softly:

– Actually, we were supposed to study the French Revolution and revise the last act of Earl Haakon.

Now Ben is laughing too, after so many tears:

– Earl Haakon! No, I couldn't bear it now...

Grete caresses his forehead and cheeks with her palm, wiping him below the eyes. She touches his lips:

– You really recited like an actor, really...

Ben again feels the slight itch inside himself:

– Being an actor! Well, that's life! Sometimes I think that my dreams are more real than everyday life itself!

Grete is more down-to-earth:

– Life is everyday life, too. And you must have something to live by in your everyday life...

Ben, however, won't think of such things right now:

– Let's enjoy this moment! Enjoy each other, be happy that we are together, that we are alive!

He kisses her lips, and she abandons herself to him. But as he leans back again and looks at the sky, and his thoughts set out on a long voyage, Grete feels a little pang. It is as if she cannot reach him! Sometimes Ben could even frighten her a little with the strength of his feelings. She must call him back:

– A penny for your thoughts!

Ben feels sadness. Isn't it possible to be happy, cheerful without being sad at the same time?

– Every time I want to enjoy life, really enjoy it, it is as if something prevents me... the bitterness...

Grete feelss insecure. That's exactly what she wants to fight against. She will defeat the black monster, the past! She takes Ben's head in her hands, leaning her forehead against his, pressing her breast hard against him, prevailing upon him with her entire will:

– Ben, you are here, here! With me now! Forget about the past, throw it away! Away, off! We belong together, the two of us! We can manage it together! I can feel you now... and you can feel me!

✳ ✳ ✳

Børge heaves a sigh of satisfaction, but he cannot help being a little sad too. They have finished Earl Haakon and with that the last Danish lesson is over. They had coped with all the examination requirements and the pupils must surely be relieved to have done with it...

The teacher tidies up his books while the pupils are leaving the class. Only Ben remains sitting, deep in thought. For some years, there has been a special relationship between them: Børge has treated him as his equal.

Børge notices that Ben is still here. He approaches him with his awkward steps, swinging one of his legs in a curve every time he moves it forward. What might ever become of Ben... It's not easy to express one's feelings.

– It won't be long before our ways will part Ben, and you'll fly away from

your nest. I wonder if you will come and see your old teacher once in a while...?
– I probably will. Why shouldn't I?
– Youth does forget easily! Once you get whirled into the carnival of life...
Finally Børge gets it off his chest:
– You meant a lot to me, Ben. It was indeed an event that I got you back in my class after the storms of war!
Ben smiles lightly, but then knits his brows. The storms of war! It was already four years ago... When he observed his classmates, it seemed to him that most of them hadn't grasped anything at all. Of course they had not experienced anything on their own bodies, but still... they were incredibly immature, and... a certain thing had been annoying Ben during the entire lesson:
– Even now, after the war from which people ought to have learned something, you can hear them use the word *JEW* in the sense of *THIEF*. Just now, before the lesson, someone said: – Who *JEWED* my Earl Haakon?
Børge has heard it before and it strikes him hard every time. Moreover, this is happening in Ben's class! You cannot ignore it, but you could try to explain:
– It is pure thoughtlessness, Ben, they don't reflect upon it, they don't mean anything by it...
– Don't they? I start every time I hear it!
– I do feel with you. They ought to consider it more... But aren't you a little too sensitive?
Ben gets indignant... Børge as well! But can't he comprehend that Ben feels the contempt they are showing for the Jews! And then he was not supposed to be offended?
– Too sensitive... Is that possible? Is there a law laying down a limit to how much you are allowed to feel? Shall anyone else decide my feelings, restrict them according to what they find reasonable? I feel what I feel! I have a right to that, haven't I? Are they, perhaps, not my feelings? Every time I notice people who look typically "Jewish," I can't help wondering what the others, the non-Jews, think of them. And it fills me with distaste if they, the Jews, by any chance behave noisily or strangely, so that it could give occasion for someone to criticize them. Then I get ashamed! Other people may behave badly, why not Jews? If I read in the paper that a Jew has cheated someone, or appears to be a slum landlord, then I feel guilty... me! And that's absurd! And then I get furious with myself!
Børge would like to reassure Ben:

– At least you don't look typically Jewish yourself.

Ben laughs sarcastically:

– And so what if I did? Some people have even told me so: You can't be more than half! Half Jewish they mean! Are they flattering me? Is it supposed to be a compliment? Or do they mean to comfort me?

– It is not easy, indeed, but you are too touchy, Ben, too sensitive. Like I said, can't you stop being annoyed?

– It's easy enough for you to say when you aren't in such a situation yourself!

Børge must admit the justice of Ben's view. Many people don't consider such matters when pronouncing their own cocksure opinion.

There is something else which is rankling inside Ben, too:

– I really shouldn't talk about it, but why did I never ever get any prize for diligence on prize day? Kristian and the others, who don't get such good marks as I did, they get one!

Even Børge has wondered why he had met that sort of opposition amongst the teaching staff. It was also a defeat for him personally:

– Honestly, Ben, I have proposed you every single year, and every time some of the teachers are against it.

He won't tell Ben about the condescending remarks with which these colleagues used to turn him down, but it was painful indeed!

Ben is aggressive:

– And WHY are they against it?

Børge is confused. He has been reflecting over it, but then one is led to think thoughts that are UNTHINKABLE!

– I don't know Ben, I really can't comprehend it!

Ben has no doubts. There is no need to explain it to such an intelligent man as Børge. He calmly looks his teacher straight in the face, holding his gaze:

– I know why!

* * *

Now they were there. Tove didn't say anything, she just whimpered because her foot hurt so much. Ben didn't say anything, either.

In the gable of the loft there was a small window. Ben crawls over to it so that he can look out over the wharf, the fishermen's low houses, the pier and the ships. For a long time there is no living soul anywhere. It is getting dark.

Then he thinks he can see some soldiers running on the road, but they soon disappear again.

He can hardly distinguish Tove in the dark. She is breathing heavily, having probably fallen asleep. Well, he does not care, he doesn't feel like talking to her.

At long last he hears footsteps outside the house and the door is opened. It is the fisherman, together with another person. Tove is totally confused when she wakes up, but the man calms her down:

– We'll hide you in the church just nearby. It's a good place, and then you will get to Sweden tomorrow.

They help Tove down the ladder, and when they support her under her arms she is able to stand a little on her leg again. She is, in fact, not doing too badly over the short distance to the church. Ben is walking beside her, listening into the dark night, lest someone is pursuing them. But everything is silent and empty around them.

* * *

In the church they are welcomed by the vicar, who shakes hands even with Ben. It's so dark that they can't see his face.

The fisherman and the vicar help Tove grope her way up the narrow stairs, and they enter the loft which runs the full length of the church. In the dark, a crowd of shapes are discernible all over the floor. Everybody has to be silent. Only a few people whisper.

Ben and Tove sit down like the others. It is beastly cold, even though Ben has his warm coat. They had been sitting motionless for hours in the boathouse.

As Ben gets used to the dark, he can distinguish, in the gloomy light of a small opening, the posts which support the pitched tile roof. Ben approaches the skylight and tries to open it. He pulls and pushes the bar. Oh yes, he can manage to open it. But the small roof window is too narrow for him to crawl through.

Outside the sky is clear, even if it is a dark night. The stars are shining from high above. But there is a man-made gleam too. It comes from the other side of the water. It is freedom, shining from the coast of Sweden, where they have no need for a blackout.

Now he notices the clockwork sounding through the silence: tick – tock – tick – tock – tick... like a heart beating, and he discovers a narrow staircase in the middle of the loft leading to the small bell tower. Ben slips around the many human bundles and takes a few steps upstairs, but the tower seems to him too small a hiding-place even for a little fellow like himself.

He crawls down again and accidentally stumbles over someone lying in the dark:

– Kalle! I thought you managed to get across on the boat! Have you been here long?

So they didn't get to Sweden either. Kalle's mother had become so scared when they called out that the Germans were coming, that she ran into the nearest house, and there they had been concealed in the cellar. Shortly after they got a message from the vicar that they should come over here, up into the loft. They had been the very first people here, but then all through the day a lot more had come.

A little later a flashlight glimmers by the stairs. A woman has arrived from the Red Cross with food and blankets.

Tove is calling Ben, so he had better go to her. She hands him a cheese sandwich and covers him with a blanket:

– Where have you been? You can't leave me this way. You have to stay with me, you know that!

Ben chews his food without answering her. The woman from the Red Cross hands him a mug of milk, which he downs in one gulp.

For some time there is a muttering and a rummaging in the loft, until all have had their food. Then there is silence again. Only once in a while is there some noise and light when newcomers arrive, until such time as they have been accommodated.

Ben keeps thinking: Why do things have to be like this? Why did so many things happen? Why hadn't Mommy taken him with her, when she was going to Sweden, too, together with Uncle Moritz? Around him people are snoring, and soon Ben also falls asleep.

* * *

Ben wakes up with a start. Glaring cones of light cut through the black of the night. Harsh roars and commands resound, the tramping of boots with metal heels, hollow thuds, screams, and children crying:

– Los! Los! Aufstehen, get up! Hurry up! Hurry! Get moving! Up, up! Sheenies, Jewish pigs! Judenschweine! Filthy beasts!

Quickly he extricates himself from the blanket, on the lookout now to see if he can slip away somewhere.

German soldiers flicker their lights in the loft. An elderly woman nearby, who does not get up fast enough, wails loudly as a soldier kicks her.

Ben doesn't care about Tove. Like a hunted animal, he creeps forward, hiding behind people and behind the posts. He reaches the staircase of the bell tower, but after climbing just a few steps, he is caught by the leg and dragged down again as a rasping voice howls in Danish:

– That's what you think, you little sheeny!

A Danish Nazi in a black coat flings Ben across the floor.

Ouch! Dazzled by the glare of the man's torch, Ben stands up. His new coat is dirty and the belt torn. Ben gets a blow on the back and has to go to the stairs, where people cluster to get down, while the Gestapo soldiers bay like vicious hounds, driving and pushing the people forward:

– Los! Get moving! Schnell! Hop! Hop! Get going, Jews!

✳ ✳ ✳

Day is about to dawn when Ben gets out of the church. German soldiers stand in two dense ranks from the door all the way to the road, where a number of grey-green military trucks are lined up. The enormous soldiers point their rifles with fixed bayonets at the captured people, who have to walk between the two lines up to the trucks. Ben feels how his stomach hurts as he passes the many long sharp bayonets turned on him so closely that they nearly touch him.

Just in front of him are Kalle and his mother, with her younger son in her arms. Little Jacob is crying. He is afraid that the soldiers are going to shoot him.

As they reach the trucks on the road, the prisoners are commanded to get up on the vehicles. All the time the sound of that hoarse bellowing is heard in the grey morning. As soon as one vehicle is full it sets off, and then a new truck drives forward for the next lot of prisoners.

Kalle's mother gets a blow with a fist in her back:

– Make that damned kid stop howling!

It was the man in the long coat who had caught Ben just before. He was the one who ordered all the others about.

Kalle's mother almost falls as she mounts the truck, having to press her hand against Jacob's mouth to make him quiet.

Ben can't see Tove anywhere. She has probably gone with one of the first trucks. On the truck in front of him hardly anyone can get in any more. It is crammed. Ben is the last person to get up there. He hesitates for a moment, but a yell from the Danish Nazi officer makes him jump inside, so that he accidentally treads on Jacob's toes and the little boy starts crying again. Finally they all have to press even closer, because now two more soldiers get inside the truck. They are supposed to sit on the edge, their rifles to ensure that nobody tries to escape.

Ben happens to stand close to one of the soldiers. He tries to look the soldier straight in the face. But the soldier's face and eyes are completely blank...

The overhead tarpaulin is secured from outside and the truck starts with a jolt that makes them all fall against each other.

✷ ✷ ✷

Ben dreams that he is walking all alone inside a long dark tunnel under the ground. The tunnel gets narrower and narrower, threatening to bury him. Far, far away he can see above, the light marking the entrance to the tunnel. Over there is freedom and fresh air, but he cannot get his feet out of the mud. They are stuck, and the more he exerts himself and struggles to get free, the further he sinks. When he tries to cry for help, his mouth fills with earth. The ground under him gives way, and he falls deeper and deeper, until he wakes up with a bump as he hits the floor on the side of his bed.

✷ ✷ ✷

It recurs every single year: The most magnificent weather when you have to prepare for an examination. The beeches stand with their light-green leaves so succulent that you could eat them. Plants and bushes are in flower, filling the air with their overwhelming fragance.

The sky of the summer night, which could never persuade itself to darken completely, gives out light from a milky-white haze from up there, where you only dimly distinguish the dots of stars. The swelling fairy-tale shapes of the clouds continuously assume new forms, like a rose-violet army of faces, drawn over the vault of heaven, illuminated by the gleam of the sun resting just below the horizon ready to ascend and radiate over the new morning.

The two blood-brothers are sitting in the library. They have been studying the whole day long and even most of the night. They had passed mathematics well enough the other day, and now on to biology!

Kristian is sitting with his feet on his father's writing-table and Ben is lying sprawled on the leather sofa, while they go over their notes and alternately test each other.

Birds are chirping, chattering and singing so loudly that it all rings in your ears with sound and music that drowns out every thought.

It isn't strange at all that Kristian can't concentrate any more:

– Aren't we to have a little drink? There should be some whisky left...

He walks up to the corner cupboard and takes the bottle with the liquid. Ben jumps up from the depth of the sofa:

– I'll get water and ice. We have only a few more pages to read!

While Kristian is pouring out the drink, a little swishing of dog's paws is heard along the parquet flooring. The dog has been wakened and now comes to sit with Kristian to be patted on the head.

– Is it worth going to bed at all? It's almost 4 o'clock...

Ben has returned from the kitchen:

– We might as well have a break and go down into the garden.

The two brethren sit down on the garden bench listening to the enchantment of the summer night. Glow-worms gleam in the dusk and the elf maiden and other wizards are muttering and rummaging in the shadow of the leaves.

Kristian laughs a little:

– After biology we have three days to prepare for Danish, and after that we shall never again see Børge arriving on his bicycle every morning at PRECISELY three minutes before eight, no matter how bad the weather.

The figure of the chief physician looms from the shadow of the terrace. The consultant is now being a senior staff member at a big hospital in Copenhagen and recognized even abroad:

– Birgit is still asleep, but I'm damned if I could sleep for all that noise the birds are making. It sounds like a symphony, whose every single instrument plays its own melody, fortissimo!

Kristian smiles at his father:

– We will have done with the subject soon, but if we go to bed now, we'll be sleepy tomorrow.

Doctor Knud sits beside them:

– When I was a student, even I read all night through. Well, it will be nice when you have it over and done with! I certainly hope you'll go sailing with us for a fortnight in July. Later on Birgit and I are going up to the Cabin, and you can come too, whenever you like...

Ben leaves for a moment and returns with a glass:

– Can I serve you a whisky, Knud?

– Yes please, thank you Ben. By the way, have you decided what you want
to do?

– I don't know yet for certain... Literature maybe...

Knud hasn't the least idea how close he's getting to the truth right now:

– I do recall the school comedy last year. You were certainly outstanding
in the part of *I WANT TO BE SOMEBODY ELSE*. Maybe that is what you wish,
is it? Do you want to go on the stage?

Ben won't make a statement, but Kristian can't help thinking of the
Danish lesson:

– You surely did show promise, when we were reciting Haakon and Olaf
the other day, didn't you Ben?

Ben looks right into Kristian's face:

– And so did you!

And the tension between the two of them now is let out in a releasing
laughter.

Knud, pensively, is observing his son:

– It's biology, isn't it, Kristian? A very important subject for a future
medical student!

– The deadline for the application to the medical faculty is in July.

Ben drinks his whisky thoughtfully:

– You don't have such a difficult choice to make...

After a moment of silence the doctor clears his throat:

– There is something I want to tell you now, as we are three grown-up
men, and Ben, you know that you are like a son to me, so there is really no
reason to conceal anything... I want to tell you without beating about the
bush: My dissertation was rejected at that time! And naturally this has given
me pain all these years...

Kristian is about to drop his glass in surprise:

– But Daddy! I've always thought that...

– I couldn't avoid some competition, even rivalry from some of the
professors. I must confess it was a bad blow for me. Amongst my colleagues
there are those who are rather embarrassed because of that. That's why
nobody ever mentions it.

Kristian is quite exasperated:

– But your method has been quoted in International Medicine and is
practiced in hospitals all over...

Knud has regained his peace of mind:

– That's the main point, and a consolation too. But my honourable
colleagues and professors at the university did not want to have me by their

side... Well, now you know about it! I'm glad I finally had the opportunity to tell it to you, my sons...

Ben is also shocked:

– Then it's up to you, Kristian, to write that thesis and rehabilitate your father in this way!

Kristian nods resolutely:

– It will be a real pleasure for me.

Knud is pleased:

– I couldn't help wishing that one day you would do this for me... Competition exists always, even inside the medical profession.

Kristian raises his glass:

– I promise you to do it, Knud, you can rely on me!

The chief physician wants to go up to his bed again:

– Listen, boys, I advise you to go to sleep for a couple of hours nevertheless. I'll wake you at 7 o'clock, before I'm off to the clinic... It's good that we talked it over.

∗ ∗ ∗

In the spacious basement room of the villa, they had put a new top on the billiard table to use it for table tennis.

Some relaxation is necessary even while you are cramming for examinations. Lily has joined the clan and is playing ping-pong with Grete. They are cheerful, parodying the heroes in Oehlenschläger's romantic drama. Everything is a lark, everything is a playful prank. At every stroke they applaud, yelling with joy, or else making all sorts of gestures to show desperation.

Right now it looks as if Grete is going to win. She hits the ball so hard that it smacks with a clank on Lily's side of the table, and from there down to the floor.

Ben is waving his arms:

– Grete, my fair maid, what a smash! Magnificent! Divine!

Lily takes the ball with a tragic air:

– Help me in my agony, good Sir Kristian!

Kristian cheers her up:

– The battle is not lost yet, by Odin and by Thor. Strike with your formidable backhand!

Grete is already triumphant:

– Only another point, and you are a defeated woman!

But Lily hits the ball heroically:

– I'm still fighting like a she-wolf defending her cubs closely pursued by a pack of hounds!

In spite of her big words, the ball races into the net.

Ben embraces a strutting Grete!

– Victory! Victory! The brave Lily falls in action... in the gloomy night.

But Lily keeps up her part as tragedienne:

– I've lost a battle but not my honour... Oh, my dear Kristian, here I am, to seek comfort from you!

He wipes mournful tears off her cheek, then lies down on the floor, grotesquely flinging his arms and legs about, howling at the top of his voice:

– Tu-whoo tu-whoo! Here I am, grinning like a troll!

And Ben recites:

– This is our glorious heroine!

Grete states:

– The glorious heroine, though, is thirsty!

Kristian quickly stands up and goes to the cellar:

– Okey-dokey! What do you wanna drink?

Grete wants an orange lemonade. So does Lily:

– S'il vous plait!

Ben stammers:

– Gi-gi-give m-me a be-be-beer plea-plea-please!

Kristian is the cupbearer, serving with solemnity:

> *– ALL MERRY NOW, CHILDREN,*
>
> *MAKE THE HORN GO ROUND*
>
> *SO THE FINE MEAD*
>
> *MAY FRESHEN OUR THROATS!*

Lily looks directly into Kristian's eyes as she receives the glass and whispers meaningfully:

– Thanks, Kristian, thank you so much!

Now Ben raises his glass in an expansive gesture:

– Let me with unchained hands seize the strong golden beer! What did old Adam Oehlen-Beer-swiller and his faithful disciple Børge say?

Upon which all four recite in chorus:

> *– ONE FOR ALL AND ALL FOR ONE*
>
> *A BEER FOR ALL AND A BEER FOR EACH – CHEERS!*

Impulsively, Kristian grasps the ping-pong bat:

– Come on, you lazy Haakon! I challenge you to a duel, cowardly wretch! Let's see who first scores eleven!

Ben isn't slow, and soon the ball flies with smashes to and fro between them on the table-top: Dok-dok, dok-dok, dok-dok...

The two of them have been playing each other for years and have achieved an enormous virtuosity... They are equally good, and are familair with each other's smallest tricks and movements. Like two chivalrous heroes, they are combatting with the strengh and agility of youth in front of an elegant female audience... And each of them wants to prove that he is able to win!

The first points are won by Kristian, who sings proudly:

– *WAKE UP! WAKE UP! DANISH HEROES!*

And Ben:

– *SPRING UP AND BUCKLE ON YOUR SWORD!*

Kristian gloats:

– Two/love to me!

Ben pulls himself together, hitting the ball:

– *IN ALL REALMS AND COUNTRIES...* Two – one! *I FOUGHT WITH OPEN HELMET!...* And another point: Now we are even!

And Ben keeps scoring the next points:

– *BY ALL VALHALLAS I STRIKE YOU ON YOUR HEAD!...* Hurray! Three – two, I'm leading!

Grete applauds enthusiastically:

– Well done, brave Haakon! Give Olaf the Christian his mortal wound!

Lily throws her fine silk scarf into the arena to Kristian:

– Olaf, my noble knight, I lay my trust in your strength!

However, Ben wins scores again, leading four – two and Kristian swears revenge:

– *BY SATAN AND ALL HEATHENS! HEAVEN WILL STRIKE YOU WITH ITS FLAMES!*

And Ben answers so that it resounds in the basement:

– *NO, THOR WILL SPLINTER THE CROSS WITH HIS HAMMER!*

and succeeds in smashing, so that the ball ends up at the other end of the room. He raises his arms as the winner:

– Ha, did you see that hammer-stroke? Five – two my favour!

Kristian shakes his head despairingly as he fetches the ball. Lily runs up to him, suggesting a little kiss on his cheek, gently whispering:

– Take courage, my hero!

Kristian nods with clenched teeth:

– I'm gonna get him!

In defiance of all his will-power, Kristian's ball ends up in the net. He must submit to Ben laughing right in his face:

– Poor Olaf! Six – two! What do you think of this service? Bang, smash: seven – two! And another one! Eight points for me and two for you! *YOU TURN PALE AND YOUR EYES ARE DULL...* Please serve, sad Olaf!

Kristian serves – across the table! Immediately Ben attacks him howling:

– I'm winning! I'm winning! Two – nine, my advantage! Now you are at the bottom! *LOOK WHAT NASTY AIR APPEARS ON OLAF'S COUNTENANCE...*

Kristian gets more and more savage. Without uttering a word, he plays as determinedly as he can, while the girls watch the exciting match with bated breath. Kristian is on the defensive, Ben keeps smashing harder and harder, and no matter how many times Kristian returns the ball, it does not help him. Ben seems to be totally invincible... at last Ben hits the ball with such power that Kristian cannot reach it. Ben dances wildly, jubilant with joy:

– Ten points to me! I only lack one point before you bite the dust, dear Olaf! Your serve... the match ball!

While Kristian serves the decisive ball, Ben recites as elegantly as Cyrano de Bergerac during his fencing matches:

> – *WITH THIS SMASH I THEE TO VALHALLA SEND*
> *THEN WE SHALL SEE THAT THY DAYS WILL... END!*

And Ben executes that fatal blow, a gigantic smash, precisely timed for the last word of the verse.

The duel is over. Annoyed, Kristian throws the bat away. At this very moment he hates Ben, and on top of that, Grete embraces him:

– Magnificent Haakon, what a stupendous fight!

While Ben joyfully holds her tight.

Kristian throws himself into an armchair, totally exhausted, while Lily, affectedly playing the comforting angel, puts the beer bottle into his mouth, letting him drink as if he were a bottle-fed baby. She dabs his face with her fine scarf:

– Let me wipe the sweat off your forehead, Knight Olaf... Soon a better fortune will smile upon you.

Reluctantly Kristian has to stick to the game. But it doesn't please him at all. He is more ill-tempered than he would ever admit, and now Ben is taunting him even more:

– Wherefore art thou so blue on thy lips? Poor, poor Olaf!

Lily glances at him with her azure eyes:

– Why so silent, noble lord?

Kristian has to swallow his anger. If he'd betray to them how furious he is, seriously, they'd surely tease him even more... he forces himself to smile:
– Shall we go up and listen to the Ellington records again?

∗ ∗ ∗

At Camp Horserød the meals, the best that the Danish Red Cross could provide, were served by smiling Red Cross nurses.

Ben was so happy to be with Mommy again. He didn't worry about the German soldiers with the machine-guns standing by the entrance to check everybody coming and going, so that it was quite impossible to escape. He wasn't even seriuosly concerned about the SS men in their black uniforms with the skulls on the collar. As long as he was with Mommy.

His stepfather didn't shout as he used to do, neither did he object when Mommy sat down on Ben's bed in the evening, stroking his forehead until he fell asleep.

Tove did not appear at all. She had been set free immediately, as she was only half Jewish.

Those who were married to Christians could get out too, even if they were full Jews. Ben went with Mommy to the gate of the camp to watch those lucky ones. Some of them were weeping in a frenzied manner. Mommy was told that one of the ladies was desperate, even though she was going to be freed, because she had to take leave of her old mother and sister, both of whom had to stay in the camp.

For October, the weather was exceptionally fine. The sun shone every day out of a cloudless sky, and by noon it was so hot that you could strip to the waist and sunbathe. The food was excellent, and they had it served! If the soldiers and the barbed wire around the camp had not been there, you could almost believe you were in a summer camp.

Moreover, the Germans weren't so strict any more, either, and they had made you understand that you could count on staying here in Horserød, which wasn't the worst thing that could happen. You might be told to do some light work and at the end, you might even be set free, because it was rumoured that King Christian Xth himself would intervene on behalf of the Jews and maybe talk to Hitler himself... and everybody knew that Hitler certainly had the highest respect for King Christian!

The King had even averted their having to wear the Jewish star. Then he would also wear the Jewish star on his own chest and wear it with pride, the King was reported to have said. Maybe things weren't that bad, after all. If only you could stay here in Denmark! The Danish Gestapo agent himself, Henning Juhl, had even allayed Uncle Moritz's fears in that regard when asked.

The Danish Red Cross had also procured schoolbooks for the children, and Ben and Kalle were doing their lessons every morning, together with some little girls who were there too. Thus a week went by, and some cautious smiles began to turn up among the prisoners.

But then with a blow the optimistic atmosphere vanished: The Gestapo officer announced that they all were going on a transport to Germany! It came as a shock! Now, just as they had thought that...

– Ready for departure at 5 o'clock tomorrow morning!

Perplexed and confused, they are running about in order to get everything ready. Mommy and Uncle Moritz are busy packing.

The fine weather is gone too, the wind has risen, autumnal and cold. Ben walks to the entrance of the camp. They are still standing there, the German soldiers with their guns. Ben watches them for a long time. Even the military cars have to stop, and the drivers have to show their papers before they are permitted to pass.

He strolls along to the square in front of the office hut. Just then Mommy comes out of the door together with the tall Danish Nazi, Henning Juhl. Mommy is talking and smiling at the Gestapo agent while pointing at Ben.

Then she starts running and, short of breath, reaches Ben. She embraces him and begins to explain so fast that the words stumble over one another while the Nazi slowly comes closer...

– Now listen Bennyboy, I have just told the Gestapo officer that you aren't at all the son of your father but that I bore you by another man, that is, by a man who isn't a Jew, do you understand? So you are, as you see, not a full Jew but only half Jewish! Because your father, who is a Jew, is not your real father; your real father is an Aryan who... and you know that those who are only half Jewish can get out of here. So you aren't going to Germany with us! You are going to be free! It is to save you...

Ben is thunderstruck! Uncle Moritz wasn't his father, obviously... but now his own father wasn't his father either, but a person he has never heard of before! And who was it anyway? And then Mommy says that she said it to save him... but was it only something she made up... or was it true? Then why didn't Mommy tell him about it in advance...?

Meanwhile Henning Juhl has come up to them, offering Ben his hand:

– Come here, my friend, the two of us are just going for a little walk. We have something to talk about.

Mommy wrings her hands watching Ben walking with the tall man towards the barbed wire fence at the far end of the camp.

It's an odd feeling to hold the hand of a person whom everybody is so afraid of. Most of all, Ben would like to withdraw his hand. But he doesn't dare to do that, so he lets his hand remain in that of the Nazi. It is even stranger that the man is friendly towards him, being, at the same time, so dangerous! What was going to happen now?

Only at the barbed wire fence, where they are all by themselves, does the officer start talking in confidence, almost inspiring trust:

– We have agreed, your mother and I, that because you have an Aryan father you may decide for yourself! Because you know well enough that you are all going to be sent to a labour camp in Germany... so it is for you to decide, whether you want to travel with your mother or you want to get out of here, because you are, as I said, only half Jewish! You have to think it over thoroughly before you answer... But you must make the choice now. If you get out from here you might get to Sweden afterwards. But then you are separated from your mother, aren't you?

Ben's brain goes blank with surprise at what he has just been told. His thoughts are whirring in his head: Be set free? Get to Sweden? And then what about Mommy?

After waiting a little, Henning Juhl gets somewhat impatient:

– We do not have much time, my little friend. You have to answer me now: Do you prefer to be free? Or do you want to travel together with your mother? You must make your decision. Come on, decide now!

The Nazi officer becomes friendly again and smiles persuasively:

– You wouldn't think of leaving your own mother! You do prefer to stay with your Mommy, don't you?

Ben comprehends with the speed of lightning. There is not a shadow of doubt in his mind. He nods slowly.

∗ ∗ ∗

The sun is still high in the sky, shining down at the ramparts around the Citadel of Copenhagen. The beautiful old buildings surrounded by paving-stones stand reflecting the sunlight from their red walls and tiled roofs. The air is warm and has a scent of greenery.

The two brothers are walking deep in thought on the high earthworks. The sunbeams penetrating the blanks in the foliage fall sideways in shining spots on the black-brown ground. But if you want to grasp the white ropes of light seeming so tangible, your fingers will slip through them, closing on air. You cannot catch sunbeams.

Birds sing in the crowns of the trees, but if you look high up, you are totally dazzled by the intense light glinting among the leaves of the branches.

Without talking, they walk past the mill with the big angular arms on the green lawn, and further around the iron cannon, past the Citadel church situated on the square about twenty metres under them between the wings of the barracks. The airy white clouds in the sky are coloured slightly pink. The sun can hardly make up its mind whether to set today.

Kristian is reserved, in a gloomy temper. Once in a while he slaps at the bushes along the path.

Then he takes off, sliding down the grassy slope, so that pebbles and clods of earth roll between his feet down to the middle level of the rampart.

And Ben after him! Why use the stairs when you can tumble down through the bushes as if you were flying on wings? And yet again, they go down the last slope until they are standing on the bank of the moat.

In the still water a big white swan sails calmly between the green rushes, its wake spreading out behind it like a rippled fan. From the top of its long neck it casts sidelong glances down upon the short brown quacking ducks, which have to draw aside for it like small boats giving way to an ocean liner.

For a long time the two young men stand by the life buoy. Now at last the sun begins to sink behind the hills. Kristian cannot rid himself of his discontent. It keeps preying upon his mind. What was going on between Ben and Grete? It annoys him, too, that Ben is in such a damned good mood.

Ben interrupts the silence:

– I want to travel... see the world! As a guide you can even earn money when travelling! Italy! Rome! The Forum with the triumphal arches of the emperors... You don't say anything! Are you totally tongue-tied?

Only now Ben notices Kristian's unsympathetic air, and he comes to think of their combat and his victory. Ben enjoys his triumph once more, just like the ancient Romans! He can't help feeling genuine malice... True enough, he also has an account to settle with Kristian. That joke! And the sweet pleasure, when Grete kissed him in congratulation. He claps Kristian hard on the back:

–Are you sulking because you lost?

And Ben guffawing, roaring with laughter, thumps him again on the shoulder with such a resounding smack that Kristian nearly falls into the water. Ben gestures with his arms, declaiming, as if he were standing on the Royal Stage:

– NOW I AM GROSSLY REVENGED!
NOW HIS GHOST IS ONLY HAUNTING...

Kristian can't stand any more... The humiliation! And then Grete! He must throw him off his high horse! He wants to hurt him, so that he'll feel it thoroughly! Blind with rage, he hisses:

– You Jew!

Ben stops his laughter abruptly. He must have misheard it. Both of them stand completely motionless for long seconds. Then Ben breathes and almost without moving his lips:

– What did you say?

And Kristian repeats, very clearly:

– I said: You Jew!

Ben cannot believe it. It cannot be true! All goes black, his chest is squeezed tight, he is gasping for air:

– You can't be serious...?

Kristian turns his back on him and goes.

Now it cuts through Ben like a knife, going through his chest down to his stomach, and then up again through his throat and his head, through his eyes and his brain, up to the roots of his hair. His legs stagger under him, everything around him is swimming, so that he must grasp at the life buoy not to fall. And now it comes: All that he has in his stomach is pressing its way up through his throat, so that he is choking. He bends forward, opens his mouth and vomits, spits out, again and again, big lumps. His stomach turns inside out until, at long last, he has spat out every last drop of phlegm. Groaning with exhaustion, he reels to the slope and falls to the ground.

✳ ✳ ✳

It is still pitch-dark when they are wakened by loud shouts. People are running to all the huts, knocking at the windows. Frightened, Mommy gets up in her bed:

– What time is it Moritzl?

The light is switched on, hurting their eyes. Ben is awake too, looking at his beautiful new watch: Is it true that it's only 4 o'clock? Nervously Uncle Moritz puts on his glasses:

– We have to be ready in an hour!

Now they get busy. Everybody is going to the washroom at the same time. They press and push to get in. Mommy is deathly tired. She didn't fall asleep till after 3 o'clock. They must pack their last things, and remember the nightgown... And Ben must remember to brush his teeth!

They must also get breakfast in time. In the dining-hut coffee, milk and oatmeal is ready. The nurses from the Red Cross are serving, and there is one big lunch packet for each person to take along on the journey.

They all sit with their overcoats on, eating. Nobody talks. The nurses don't say a word either... and they don't smile encouragingly as they used to.

The sky is still dark when in the light of the searchlights from the watch-tower they line up in two rows in front of the office hut. Once again commands crack through the air. The lines are to be exactly straight! That takes time.

Then they are counted, and they are counted again and again, until it is correct. Henning Juhl is in control of the whole operation, and when he passes, he nods his head at Ben as if saying: "It's a good thing, that you are going too!"

They have to remain standing there, while the officers go into the hut again.

After that, five German army trucks drive into the square... The drivers have to wait, too, and sit there, looking at Ben and the others, who just have to remain standing.

Gradually the dawn came.

The SS officers comes out of the office again. The prisoners are counted one more time, and yet again. And then once more. Was anybody missing? After that the Germans enter the hut.

Ben wears his good coat and Mommy her Persian lamb coat; nonetheless they are cold as they stand there... Nor are they permitted to move out from their line. Ben tries to take just one step away, and immediately a soldier glares threateningly at him, so that Ben hastily steps back into his place between Mommy and Uncle Moritz.

Some of the old people, who can't bear to stand for so long have to be supported by those standing next to them.

Time passes. It is light. It's almost 9 o'clock when, at last, Henning Juhl orders them to climb into the trucks. Now it has to be at breakneck speed: – Los! Los! Get moving, fast, fast! – Once again there is total confusion until they are all inside the trucks.

They set out. They would be going by train from Elsinore...

* * *

At Elsinore they are to line up in straight rows once more on the platform of the railway station. SPECIAL TRAIN is written with big letters on the railway carriages. But they must not get on the train yet.

They just have to wait, and they are to stand still all the time. Something in particular must be going on, because Henning Juhl runs backwards and forwards along the lines several times, looking very agitated, staring angrily at the prisoners:

– A packet of 200 cigarettes has been stolen! It's deadly serious! If the thief doesn't own up voluntarily, you are all going to be sent to Poland instead of Germany, and it will go hard with you! From there nobody has ever returned safely!

The stepfather becomes deathly pale:

– Poland! This is awful...

They all look at each other in fear. Even Ben is glancing about, and all of a sudden he looks right into a pair of big brown eyes: It is Lea, a little girl of eight with long curls. She had been doing school lessons in the morning too. She is looking just as frightened at Ben.

At long last a man in a cap breaks away from the row and walks slowly towards Henning Juhl. Apparently he was the one who had taken the cigarettes. The Danish Nazi tears off the man's cap, pitching into him so that the man falls to the ground and must be dragged away by two soldiers.

Now they are allowed to get on the train. There is plenty of room in the large common compartment. Ben has a seat to himself opposite Mommy and Uncle Moritz as the train rolls towards Copenhagen. The trees have lost their leaves. He has a sudden impulse. Mommy gives him an inquiring glance as he rises, but he is just going to the toilet.

To get into the toilet he has to pass the Wehrmacht soldier who is keeping guard by the door of the corridor. He locks the door behind him and shakes the window with all his might, but he cannot open it. There is nothing to be done about it. It is spiked.

When he gets back, he sees that the soldier has placed himself with his big rifle just beside Mommy! Mommy is talking to him in German, smiling charmingly, and the soldier is answering her gently. He is smiling too, talking about his family at home and showing Mommy a photo of his wife and children... and as Mommy is so tired he suggests she rest her head on his shoulder.

How could Mommy behave like that! Why is Uncle Moritz submitting to it! He really ought to say that Mommy had better rest her head on him...

Ben is tired out. He doubles up, lying down on his bench, listening to the rhythmic chug-chug of the wheels against the rails. Now it sounds just like the song he used to sing with Mrs. Tiedelund and Mr. Rabbit:

– FIGHT FOR ALL THINGS DEAR TO YOU
IF IT MATTERS, EVEN DIE,
THEN LIFE NEVER WILL BE HARD FOR YOU,
NOR WILL IT BE TO DIE

* * *

Only a dim light penetrates the narrow chinks in the shutters high up inside the roof into the overcrowded dark box of the carriage. It is like being locked up in the gym closet... Ben presses close against Mommy, as they sit there huddled up on the floor. Around them people stand or sit in dense clusters. Shivers run through one's body as the wheels of the carriage bump and click on the rails, sometimes fast, sometimes slow, going like a shudder through your spinal cord.

The locomotive groans, it howls slowly and piercingly. Where is it going?

The stepfather is sitting on the other side of Mommy. He keeps saying:

– If only we aren't going to Poland! Not to Poland...

Yesterday, when they arrived in Copenhagen they had been taken to the harbour. There they had to stand with their faces against a wall, hands over their heads. They had to stand like this for a long time, while they were counted again and again.

After that they had been ordered to get on a ship and go down steep steps far down into the bottom of the ship's hold, where they huddled together in the narrow space with their coats and luggage... and their lunch packets which they certainly must take care of!

The ship was at sea all night long. It rolled, and what foul air down there! Many had fallen ill and were groaning and wailing... Little Jacob had been crying all the time, and then he had puked over his clothes. It smelled disgusting, but at long last he fell asleep... and Ben too.

The next morning they arrived in Germany, at Warnemünde, exactly as Uncle Moritz had predicted.

They were to climb up the steep steps again, and in a hurry, so that they nearly fell over one another, and then with vociferous yells from the SS soldiers, they were hustled ashore. Those who weren't across the landing-stage quickly enough got a clout on the head, no matter whether they were old or young. But all the same, it was nice to get up into the fresh air.

They had had to line up again and were counted once more, and the SS men were lashing with horsewhips those who didn't stand properly. Ben had to beware not to get lashed himself.

Ordinary Germans had passed by men and women who had brought their children with them. They were shouting a stream of coarse invectives, spitting at the prisoners standing there; some of the German children even threw stones at them.

After some time had passed, they were hustled into three box wagons – more than fifty people to each – and it wasn't easy at all, especially not for the old people, to climb inside the high wagons, which stank and were so filthy, because they were normally used for sheep and cows. And incessantly the SS were screaming:

– Schneller! Los! Hurry up, Jewish beasts!

Then the sliding doors had been shut by the Germans from the outside and it got dark in the carriage, where everybody was pushing, trying to make themselves as comfortable as possible.

Outside someone gave the order: – ZUSCHLIESSEN! – The door was bolted with a bang, and with a creak a key was turned in the lock.

Now they are here inside the box, rolling along. The wind whistles coldly through the carriage. Ben nestles even closer to Mommy's fur coat. She sighs and fastens Ben's scarf around his neck. Only the monotonous dadunk, dadunk, dadunk from the rails is heard, as if the SS officer's voice repeating: *Jude Jew Jew Jew...* Or Mrs. Arnold-Hansen: *Punishment punishment...*

Hours go by. Mommy asks if Uncle Moritz and Ben are hungry and fumbles for the lunch packet from Horserød. Even though you cannot see anything and you can hardly move, Mommy succeeds in making sandwiches with cheese, sausage and liver paste.

Ben isn't really hungry, but he must eat in order not to get cold and become sick. He has hardly taken the first bite, when he realizes that he actually has an enormous appetite. Mommy carefully packs the rest of the food away. You never know what might happen, so she had better save something for later.

Ben needs to go to the toilet. There is a bucket in the other corner of the carriage. Ben pushes his way over. Several times he nearly falls over the other people as the train sways from side to side from the speed at which it is running!

Beside the bucket some men are smoking cigarettes. But seeing that the bucket is full, its contents splashed out and flowing over the wooden floor, Ben changes his mind. What a disgusting smell. The men are standing so close that they can watch him. How is he to keep his balance without getting filthy? He'd rather contain himself! Ben presses his way back to Mommy.

They had been travelling all day long. Sometimes the train stops for hours and Uncle Moritz gets up and tries to look out through the chinks to read the names of the stations, so he can tell the others where they are and in which direction they were going, if they possibly aren't going to Poland anyway...

Towards evening the train stops again and shouting from outside is heard. After quite a long wait the key is turned in the lock, the door is unbolted and pushed open. The train stands in the middle of nowhere. They are allowed to come out!

There is a hurry to get out! As soon as the people have jumped out, they squat down on the ground to relieve themselves without the least embarrassment, they are in such haste! Ben sits down in the field... as far away from the others as he can. Fortunately, Mommy gave him a napkin to wipe himself with.

Suddenly one of the soldiers calls out! Eight-year-old Lea has run too far away! Her mother must bring her back again, and the little girl is compelled to sit down close to the soldier so that he can watch her.

After the break they are hustled inside the cattle trucks again. What a stench in there, even after the bucket had been emptied. Luckily, Ben, Mommy and Uncle Moritz sit at the opposite end of the car.

Now they are travelling on. Night has fallen. No more light comes in through the shutters. The journey seems never to come to an end. The train rolls, then it stopps, waits for a long time, and then it rolls on, and then it stand still for some time, and then it goes on again, and every time Ben wakes up and falls asleep... The whole night goes on like that.

The whole of the next day passes in exactly the same way. They are not permitted to get out any more, so the bucket in the corner has long been full to overflowing.

Uncle Moritz is still looking out once in a while, but now he doesn't know either where they are. It was is if they have been inside the dark rumbling box for ages and will never ever get out again.

At long last, when the train stopped once more, the lock was opened, the sliding doors were pushed aside, and someone shouted that they were to get out. A second day had almost passed. Ben was numb with cold and exhaustion. It was a relief to stretch one's legs and breathe the fresh air.

They had come to Theresienstadt, not very far from Prague. That was very lucky, as Uncle Moritz had heard that this was the best of all the camps.

✳ ✳ ✳

There is a nervous atmosphere in the hall outside the examination room. Lily bites her usually well-cared for nails as she glances through her notes on Christian Winther.

They are waiting for Ben to come out. What a long time he has been inside! Some classmates are talking and laughing by the door. Lucky chaps, who already have got it over!

Now Ben comes out of the room. Grete rushes up to him:

– How did it go?

Lily looks Ben straight in his brown eyes:

– What do you think you'll get?

Kristian approaches Ben. He has been awake all night, wondering how he could make it up again. Surely it was because he had been so mad, so completely blind with anger, that it was only afterwards that he had realised how deeply he had wounded him:

– What was your subject?

Ben lets go of Lily's lingering look, meets Kristian's searching glance and looks him right in the face:

– Earl Haakon! I don't think I did too badly!

And he turns his back on Kristian. At this very moment Børge, with a broad smile, pushes the door to the classroom wide open with his awkward gesture:

– It went all right, Ben, just as it ought to have...

And after a minute's pause, enjoying everybody's attention, he happily relieves the tension triumphantly:

– Full marks, Ben! There weren't any better!

Cheers of joy from the girls! Lily takes the opportunity to push herself in front of Grete to give Ben a kiss on the cheek before Grete embraces him, kissing him on the mouth:

– Congratulations! What a wonderful thing, indeed!

Now even Kristian goes up to Ben clutching his shoulder. He loves Ben. He wants to tell him how sorry he is... Ben is his brother! He didn't mean to hurt him.

– You are a lucky dog, aren't you Ben!

Now Børge is calling from the room with the green cloth on the table:

– The next living creature is you, Kristian! Come on!

Kristian cannot break away from Ben. He cannot live being on bad terms with Ben. He is feeling sick inside. Ben MUST forgive him!

– Ben, listen...!

But Ben observes Kristian with a cold eye:

– Børge is calling you! Now it is your turn to be slaughtered!

So Kristian has to go in without having made it up after all, while Ben basks in his victory:

– Shall we bet that I get full marks in German, too?

Grete laughs, scolding him happily:

– Stop it, you boaster!

Lily pretends to be offended:

– Never mind all your full marks!

∗ ∗ ∗

Can it be anything but marvellous weather when the students are celebrating their graduation? With Dannebrog, the flag with the white cross on the red cloth, heaven's gift to Denmark, and large bunches of flowers around the platform, the headmaster is making his speech to the graduates. He is full of well-intentioned advice about the world as an open road before them, the course of life which they are about to choose, and when the time comes, the responsibility that is theirs to take over after the old pass away...

The assembly hall is packed with pupils, teachers and parents. The graduates in their red and white caps sit ceremoniously in the front row, boys in freshly-ironed shirts and dark suits, girls in white frocks with their hair done up and with lipstick and powder on. They sing the Danish anthem *Our Beautiful Land* and *In Denmark I Was Born*. The students, one by one, go up to the headmaster who, in honour of the occasion, is wearing white gloves, and they get a handshake together with their certificate.

Afterwards there is a chaos of people in the schoolyard. Outside the gate a horse-drawn carriage, beautifully festooned with coloured balloons, is waiting for the students, to drive them about in the King's own Copenhagen. Master Børge stands by the horses, patting their soft patient muzzles. He smiles contentedly at the young people climbing up on the wagonette.

In the midst of the whirl of people in light summer clothes, Mommy stands there with Mrs. Birgit and Doctor Knud, waiting for Kristian and Ben. All Mommy's thoughts turn towards Ben:

– To think he wrote a letter to me when he was only in the first grade: *MOMMYIRUNNEDFROMYOU!* He wrote that, indeed he did! All because I wasn't home that morning to send him to school. So he left by himself and then I found the letter. This is exactly how he wrote it: *MOMMYI RUNNEDFROMYOUBECAUSEIHAVETOBEATSCHOOLBY12O'CLOCK ANDNOWITISALREADY12..!*

– He had written all the message as one word, but I was able to read it all the same! He is absolutely wonderful, my little boy...

Mommy's eyes seek confirmation from Kristian's parents, as if to dispel any shade of doubt.

Birgit nods and smiles with sympathy, and so does Knud, but he doesn't get to put in a word before Mommy continues:

– In fact, at first I didn't want to have Ben at all, really not! I went to the doctor because I did not want to have you, I did tell him that a hundred times! But then the doctor said: – Dear Madam, the other day I met a lady with a sweet little daughter with long curls and azure eyes, and the mother went up to me saying: "Thank you, doctor! Look what a sweet little girl I have, because you persuaded me to have a child anyway! I'm so grateful to you!" – And then the doctor said to me: "Imagine that you got such a sweet little girl, too, like the mother who thanked me!" – So therefore I decided to have my child all the same! I told Benny that many, many a time, I did!

Mommy has been living through what she has just been telling so forcefully that she feels relieved now:

– Thank God, the doctor persuaded me! It was a blessing that he said "Imagine that you got such a sweet girl too..."

Now Birgit can't help correcting Mommy:

– Ben is, actually, a boy, not a girl... like our Kristian, am I right, Knud?

And she laughs as Knud nods kindly:

– Our boys do stick together like two brothers.

Mommy, who was a little disconcerted for a moment, now abandons herself again:

– Yes, he is such a lovely boy, my Benny, indeed he is! When he was a baby, I always used to call him "my little angel." But then my sister-in-law Alice heard that and she said: "You can't call your child an angel..."

And Mommy regrets what she said, because she realizes how presumptuous it is, indeed, to call one's own child an angel. What would people not think of her...

– And of course, I stopped calling him my angel...

But in the same instance, Mommy smiles in sheer defiance:

– But he is, anyway, my little angel!

Doctor Knud puffs at his pipe:

– We certainly have some magnificent boys... but they aren't so little any more, after all! They are grown-up men now! I'll soon have to say MR. to Ben...

All three of them laugh. Mommy is bending her head coquettishly:

– It's unbelievable that they have grown so big... how time flies! It's like it was yesterday Ben was a little boy of three! And now he is a tall and strong man!

Now one more thing comes to Mommy. She must simply tell them about it:

– Already when he was two years old, when I walked with him in the street, he was watching the girls! When he caught sight of a nice little girl he might say: "Oh my! How sweet she is!" – Can you imagine that? And one day he said to me... he was four years old then: "When I grow up I want to marry you!" – Of course I said: "You can't do that, you have to find a girl of your own age to marry, Benny dear!" And can you guess what he answered?

Mommy anxiously watches Knud's and Birgit's inquiring faces. Then she smiles in ecstasy:

– He answered so sweetly, so modestly: "If there will be anyone left for me!"

And Mommy is jubilant with delight:

– "If there will be anyone left!" Isn't that fantastic?

Birgit doesn't really know...

– Ben, in fact, deserves better than just the one who is left!

But there is no more time for talk. Both youngsters are coming now, waving their red and white caps, and Børge is coming from the gate calling the two "Highwaymen"! They all salute one another, and Mommy is effusive, congratulating Kristian...

Kristian walks with his parents to the carriage, where all the families and friends have gathered.

Børge approaches closer. He has something on his mind. Ben had given his teacher a poem NACHSCHUB, The Extra Meal, in which he described how once he was standing in line hoping to get a little more to eat. Børge had shown it to some of his colleagues, who had shaken their heads dismissively, but the poem had impressed him deeply. Surely it was a work of art, in its content as well as its form, written by a young soul in a completely new and original way, in free rhythmical verse! And every evening, at supper, when Børge picked up the breadcrumbs on the tablecloth, and he didn't leave one single crumb, he thought of Ben, that he had been starving... He glances solemnly at Mommy:

– May I congratulate you sincerely on your son's... please accept my heartfelt congratulations!

Mommy is radiant with pride:

– Thank you so much! I'm so happy that my little boy did pass his examination...

Ben gets embarrassed. Did Mother perhaps not expect him to pass? He cannot hold back:

– Mommy!

Børge comprehends. But isn't there something true, something eternal in it too...? Today is the day of joy:

– To our mothers we will always remain little boys, Ben, no matter how old we get. And that's just fine! You ought to be happy for that, Ben! And you, madam, have surely reason to be proud: the highest average in the school!

Ben, though, can't conceal his disappointment:

– But I didn't get any book prize this time either!

Mommy immediately swoops down on him like a hawk: Can't he stop drawing attention to himself! People would think that he is a braggart! Didn't she try to teach him to be modest?

– You don't say things like that Ben. Don't you know how to behave?

Mommy must apologise to his own teacher:

– He isn't ever satisfied with anything! Be pleased, Ben, with what you did get!

Børge is a little puzzled. He had had to suffer a defeat again. He had been arguing in the teacher's staff assembly that Ben, this last time, finally should get a prize for diligence. But the opposition wouldn't give in. They had simply smothered his arguments by voting against him. Børge has a sensation that he is betraying what he in his heart feels is right and true. He chooses his words carefully:

– My dear Ben, your mother is right. You can be pleased with an exceptional achievement, with your impressive exam result. Be pleased, really, with your effort, which I appreciate fully!

And master Børge walks with his characteristic hobbling steps towards the gate:

– Come now, Ben, come to the carriage, they are all waiting for you...

Ben remains standing there. His blood is racing with pent-up emotions. They are so damned right! He only has to obey orders and be glad, be pleased with being passed over! When he ought to have been given a prize! And Mother acts as if it didn't have any importance...

Ben is forced to lower his voice, so that the other people around them won't notice:

– Always and every time you hinder me from speaking my mind, God damn it! Can't you let me say what I'm thinking? I am old enough to know my own mind!

– No, apparently you are not! You are behaving like a child, ruining everything for yourself in that way! Defiance and disobedience only lead to disaster! It's merely to prevent you from making a bad impression, can't you see that?

Mommy looks up at the clear sky, at the red and white Dannebrog waving in the warm breeze, at all the cheerful people around them and at Ben wearing that beautiful cap. Isn't he handsome, her son! She takes his arm, stands on tip-toe and gives him a kiss on the cheek:

– Now be just a little sensible sweet Bennyboy! To spoil such a glorious day both for you and for me! Do your own little Mommy the great pleasure of being happy together with her! I am so proud of my big son, I really am!

Ben lets his mother kiss him and escorts her to the carriage. But why, why did Mother never agree with him...?

Grete has reserved a seat for Ben between her and Lily, who is clinging to Kristian. Ben swings his cap, shouts HURRAY and leaps up on the waggonette, where Grete puts her arm around him.

They are sitting so close, the classmates, that they almost squeeze one another, but that's exactly the wonderful thing about it! What high spirits! The coachman cracks his whip and the horses start, the carriage rolls along while the students sing:

– *GAUDEAMUS IGITUR...* Let us rejoice!

And Ben is cheering with them, louder and louder, to overwhelm his inner self. Now that he is sitting here with Grete, everything else is a matter of indifference...

* * *

From the train they had to carry their things to a place called "The Sluice." Besides the Gestapo soldiers and the Czech gendarmes there were also some men who helped to carry their luggage. They were wearing a yellow star saying *JUDE* sewn on their coats in letters which looked like Hebrew but they were ordinary letters after all, which you could read.

Inside the Sluice, an ugly barracks, the Jewish mayor, also called "Jew-elder," Paul Eppstein, bids them welcome, as if they were dear guests:

If only you comply with the rules of this place, you can be all right in Theresienstadt. But you should absolutely not try to escape! Recently six young men attempted to flee. They were caught, hanged, and their corpses left hanging on the gallows for a whole week. This was meant as a warning. They have to give up all their luggage, all their valuables, such as money, jewels and watches. It was of extreme importance to give up all of it! The Jew-elder stresses that if somebody was found trying to conceal anything on himself, he would be shot.

The yellow Jew-Star was handed to all of them. From now on they always had to wear it, indoors as well. They might be checked and if you didn't wear the star, you were sent to The Small Fortress. That was the camp penitentiary. It was certainly not to be desired!

Mommy fixes the Jew-Star on her lamb coat and on Uncle Moritz's and Ben's coats, provisionally with safety pins. Later they would be given more stars to be sewn on all their clothes.

It takes a long time to give up all their things. They also get a number, each one of them. Ben is standing in line, watching how everything goes on. Quite a few people have brought considerable amounts of money. Uncle Moritz also has to give up his expensive gold watch and all the money he has, more than twenty thousand crowns! That was meant to be the payment for the voyage to Sweden and for their living costs over there.

Mommy gives up all her jewels, the necklace of real pearls and the brooch with the large diamonds, which she inherited from Grandpa. The German official who receives the things puts them all in an envelope, writing everything down carefully. Wedding rings had to be surrendered, only Mommy may keep only her fur coat because she is wearing it.

Now it is Ben's turn. He gives the German his fountain-pen, which he got for his Bar Mitzvah, and gets the prisoner number XXV-3-21. XXV indicated that he came from Denmark, the 3 meant that he was on the third transport, and 21 was his personal number. They did not have to have their number tattooed on their arms as Uncle Moritz had been told was done in the other camps. This was proof, indeed, of how well they were being treated here!

The German has already written Ben's name and now looks up inquiringly. Ben looks into the man's eyes and then down at his watch, which is half peeping out from under his coat sleeve. Hesitatingly he raises his arm in order to take it off. He had always wanted to own a watch, ever since he was a little boy, and now he had finally got it... All of a sudden the German man leans forward whispering very low, almost without moving his lips:

– Keep your watch! Hide it under your sleeve!

Ben cannot believe that he got it right and looks at him inquiringly, but the man winks at him a few times. Then, in a flash, Ben understands and withdraws his arm with a quick gesture, so that now the watch is not visible under the sleeve.

When all had surrendered their valuables and received their Jew-Star, they were supplied with a saucepan and a spoon.

It has become night long ago. Now they bring the soup from the kitchen. There is also a small piece of dark bread, a scrap of margarine, and a bag containing two teaspoonfuls of sugar. The bread was to last for three days, while you were to make do with the margarine and sugar for a week.

The soup looks disgusting, with dirty potato peels in it. Most of them don't want to eat it and prefer to eat the rest of their lunch packet from Horserød. Mommy gave Ben a cheese sandwich instead. But the Jews from the kitchen fatigue said that the Danes certainly would learn to eat the food in Theresienstadt. It would definitely not be long!

Part 2

In Theresienstadt all the streets were straight, going either lengthwise or crosswise. It was a fortress town with deep moats around it, and it had a beautiful coat-of-arms, but that was about the only beautiful thing in the town. Well, there were also the banknotes, the Ghetto-crowns, with a fine drawing of Moses holding the commandments on them. Only you couldn't buy anything with them.

The town was a collection of miserable low houses and big, dirty military barracks with streets of clayey earth. In the middle of the town there was a large square with a church, which was always shut.

The part of the camp where the Germans had their quarters, the Aryan area, was blocked off with wooden boards. It was forbidden, on penalty of death, to cross over there, and who would ever like to try do that?

When the Gestapo officers, Obersturmbannführer Karl Rahm and the feared Rudolf Haindl, walked the streets in their shining black boots with a whip in their hands, it was a matter of life and death not to tear off your hat and stand stiff as a candle, if you couldn't manage to run away and hide in time.

Theresienstadt, in Czech Terezin, was situated about sixty kilometres from Prague. Two to three thousand people used to live there. But the former inhabitants had been driven away by the Germans. Now it was crammed with Jews, in cellars, houses, lofts, in the barracks, also in the shops, store rooms and stables: More than 55,000 prisoners from various countries: Czechs of course, you were in their country, Germans, Austrians, Hungarians, French, Dutch... and Danes!

Two transports from Denmark had already arrived earlier, so now there were 468 inmates from that country all in all. Chief Rabbi Friediger from

Copenhagen was there too. He was one of the prominent people, Mommy said, with great respect in her voice.

They learned that Grandma had arrived with the first Danish transport. She had gone back to her flat to get some of her things, and someone in the house had peached on her to the Gestapo. The Germans came immediately to arrest her.

Moritz and the other men were quartered in the loft of one of the large barracks, which were all named after German cities, like Hanover and Hamburg Barracks... Under the roof, their "beds" were straw mattresses on the floor pushed as close together as possible.

One began work at 7 o'clock in the morning, then there was a break for lunch from 12 to 1 p.m. and the work continued until 7 in the evening. They even had Sundays off! Uncle Moritz was quite optimistic. Here they could live almost in freedom... they were allowed to walk about all over the ghetto and to be together in the breaks and in the evening until 9 o'clock. In other camps, men and women weren't permitted to see each other at all!

The women and children were lodged in some wooden huts just outside the entrance to the town.

At first Ben slept with Mommy in the women's huts. There were bunks in all the rooms and Mommy and Ben got a bed in the middle with straw mattresses and a thick black blanket each. There were about thirty women and children in the room: Lea and her mother, Kalle's mother with little Jacob, a girl named Rebecca, and there was a woman with a protruding stomach... she had a little girl named Sara and was expecting a baby.

As there was very little room, everybody kept all their things, even the bread and the saucepan too, in their beds.

In the middle of the room there was a table and some wooden benches. Of course they couldn't sit there, all of them, at the same time. They had to take turns. There was also a small stove in one corner. They had to take turns sitting there, watching their potato slices if anyone had any... It was necessary to take turns to clean the place. Such things weren't easy to agree on. Mommy ended up arguing with the other women about the smallest things, and it seemed as if they all banded together against her.

At one end of the corridor there was a wash-house. The water was ice-cold, and even there the mothers fought about the space and whose turn it was. Ben didn't mind, however, since he could therefore often escape washing. There were also two toilets, the walls of which were smeared all over with streaks of brown and black shit. That was because they didn't have any paper. Some people wiped themselves with their fingers and afterwards wiped their fingers on the wall. Ben always took care to collect fallen leaves from the road with which to wipe himself.

In the yards of the houses and barracks latrines had been built. These were sheds or shelters where an oblong hole had been dug into the ground with a long board over it. Here, squatting beside one another, they relieved themselves into the evil-smelling grave. Even though they tried to keep it clean, there was often shit on the board, so Ben had a technique to avoid squatting, doing it standing on his feet. One had to be very careful not to get typhoid fever, too.

Every room had to have a chief, a room elder, who was supposed to maintain discipline and see to it that the beds were properly made. Above them, there was a house or hut elder; the next rank – a block elder, who was under the board of elders led by the Jew-elder, the mayor. The Jew-elder then bore the entire responsibility before SS-Führer Rahm.

When the hut elder inspected the room and it wasn't properly tidy, if only a blanket was a little out of place or wrinkled, he had a fit of rage. Suppose the Germans would come and see it! It meant being sent off to the Little Fortress! The bed was to be redone properly and you were watched redoing it.

Mommy wanted to be elected room elder, but so did Lea's mother, and so everybody started quarrelling again. Then Kalle's mother spoke her mind, saying that she couldn't stand Mommy altogether, shouting a lot of ugly things about Mommy, so the end of it was that Lea's mother was elected. Mommy got furious about it and told Ben never to speak so much as a word to Kalle any more.

In the morning you queued up in the yard for hot black coffee, of which you could have as much as you wanted, because it wasn't real coffee. In the lunch break you were to line up again with your saucepan. They cut off a coupon from your food card and then you got today's meal. That might be soup from potato peelings, or millet soup, or a dumpling, or 2-3 potatoes with a sauce containing bits of tendons or meat, or a portion of soup cooked from swedes. In the evening you got the thin millet soup or coffee again.

It wasn't many days before everybody had eaten the leftovers of the Danish lunch packets. The men from the kitchen fatigue proved to be right about what they had said regarding the potato soup.

The bread you were to ration out to yourself. Most people ate it up on the first day. But, of course, it was better if you could make it last all three days. Then, naturally, you had to beware that it didn't get stolen.

Kalle was to live with the men in the loft of the Hamburg Barracks, because he was over thirteen, and after a short time Ben couldn't live in the women's hut either. He had to move to a boys' home in a big yellow house beside the church.

John, who had lived on the Isle of Amager and was always late for school because the bridge was up – at least that was what he said – had arrived with the first Danish transport a week earlier. He was the tallest and strongest boy in Ben's class and was also living with the men in the loft.

One day John had noticed that one of the older men, a gentleman with gold-rimmed glasses, had hidden his bread in his straw mattress, leaving for a moment. John then took the bread and ate it. But he was exposed. The old gentleman howled and bawled, and then Uncle Moritz and some other men thrashed John really hard, so that he was black all over his face. He ought to have been glad that they didn't report him to the barracks elder, who would have punished him far worse!

Ben and Mommy went to see Grandma. She was living with thousands of other old women in the stables which had been dug inside the earthworks. In the boxes where the cavalry horses used to stand, there were bunk-beds on which the old women, with their rumpled grey hair, hollow cheeks and receding mouths, lay staring into space. Only a few small lamps lit their long, dark cells. The floor, consisting of cobblestones and earth, was wet, because it was raining outside. Grandma was sitting with a rug hung around her bed to try and keep warm, as there was no stove. In the middle of the stable there was the latrine and buckets for those of the old who couldn't go out.

Ben preferred to wait for Mommy outside because of the stench.

It was almost impossible to ration the small bag of sugar and the margarine you were given once a week. If Ben just dipped the tip of his tongue in the bag of sugar, just to taste a tiny, tiny bit... the bag was empty before he knew what he was doing.

When Mommy asked him where his sugar ration was, Ben had to admit that he had eaten it. Mommy got angry. Ben had better not open the bag at all when it was handed to him at the boys' home but bring it and the margarine to Mommy immediately. She'd take care of it for him.

* * *

In Terezin everybody talked about food. They imagined all sorts of delicious dishes. They dreamed about all the favourite courses they longed for, or told what they got at this banquet and Bar Mitzvah or that wedding, New Year's Eve or birthday... or even the weekly Sabbath evening! Everybody imagined how wonderful it would be to eat one's fill when they'd come home again, so that their mouths watered.

Ben could imagine well enough how good it would be to taste a freshly fried hot egg on a piece of bread with melted butter. But ordinarily he didn't suffer hunger. Rather, he had a constant pressure, like a sucking in his stomach, a sickening feeling in his midriff, as if he were constantly carrying a balloon inside.

When he then did get something to eat, he swallowed it with the greed of a hungry wolf. Mommy admonished him to chew slowly, making the food last longer in this way. So he kept a bit of bread or potato in his mouth until it more or less disintegrated by itself.

In the morning he would drink two or three cups of the so-called coffee. It warmed the stomach for a while, but afterwards his stomach was full of air again.

Some time after their arrival, all the Danes are called to the Sluice Barracks. There all of them are handed a postcard, pen and ink. They are supposed to write home.

The Jew-mayor impresses on them that they HAVE TO write that they were contented here. It was severely forbidden to write anything unfavourable about the conditions, especially not a word that you lacked food. They had to write precisely 25 words. The letters would be censored, and the worst things could happen to anyone who didn't write as they had been told to do.

Of course Ben writtes to Kristian. He wrote that they should give his regards to Uncle Houlberg and Aunt Irma, as Houlberg was a sausage factory and Irma was a shop selling butter and eggs. Then Birgit and Knud could figure out that he was hungry. The day after, both John and Kalle told him that they had written exactly the same things.

∗ ∗ ∗

Amidst the rhythmical clack-clack cluck-cluck of horses' hooves, so like the sounds of a xylophone, the students' waggonette arrives at beautiful King's New Square.

Now they are going to dance around the equestrian statue towering above the beds of flowers in the middle of the square. Since time immemorial, students have been doing this. Moreover, their spirits have not flagged after having been to various parents' homes for a drop, or even a drop too much, at each place. Actually they don't care two hoots whether it's a Christian or a Frederick who is sitting up there on horseback and what number he has after his name. They will not be examined on that any more!

Mommy too would have liked, so awfully much, to invite the entire class... Moritzl certainly did not mind in the slightest! But Ben would not hear of such a thing!

And the good Philistine citizens of the town, grown-ups as well as little ones, and tourists from foreign continents, and sailors coming out of basement barrooms in the colourful houses of Newhaven with their accordion music, jug of beer and the reek of stale tobacco, and the errand boys on their bicycles, Copenhagen's famous "Swayers," everybody stops short, looking, smiling or gaping, admiring or envious, at the young students, ready to laugh and not too steady on their feet, letting themselves go and, singing and treading a measure in a circle... even the trees rallied round the square nod approvingly with their fine light green leaves.

You are in the heart of Copenhagen, the centre of events! Ben's eyes run from the white columned facade of the hotel... that some people can afford to live there!... past the solid building of the bank's head office to the majestic Royal Theatre with the statue of Denmark's great poet Oehlenschlager, its classical dome and the Pegasus horse above the portal. He has a sinking feeling: Imagine belonging there, to be on the stage and to be cheered, to have the audience in the hollow of your hand, to fascinate them all, to be loved and adored! It had been like talking to creatures from fairyland, as fantastic as talking to the angels in heaven, that evening before he was taken prisoner, when he had been talking to the actors. There the desire had emerged in him that he wanted to be one of them.

– Come on, Ben, you are dreaming!

Lily is pulling his arm. He jumps out of the carriage and courteously, with Kristian and the other young men, helps the girls over the wrought iron lattice which fences the park with the royal statue.

Then Ben has to get over himself. The fence is in front of him, rocking back and forth, and see: Suddenly it is swinging behind him and he is on the lawn... without being aware of it, really, he had simply shot over the fence like a rocket!

They are drawing him into the whirling ring of dancers, going round and round:

– LET US SING OF THE STUDENT'S CHEERFUL DAYS..

Until all of it, the trees, the people, and the king whose name you can't recall, swim before your eyes if you just try to stop short.

Suddenly Mommy is there! She has dragged Moritz along into the bargain. Ben would rather pretend he did not notice them, but it was not possible. Mommy is beckoning him enthusiastically:

– Bennyboy, come here, Moritzl wants to congratulate you!

Ben lets go of Grete's hand and walks reluctantly towards the fence. Moritz holds out his hand.

Actually, it is the first time Moritz shakes hands with Ben, since Ben shook hands with his UNCLE when he was five years old.

Even Moritz has to overcome a resistance in himself, to show kindness and appreciation, as he never took the General Certificate himself. Well, he did it for Tanya! The other day his friends in the synagogue had also congratulated him on "his son" having passed the examination. Moritz mumbles as if it were a lesson he had learned:

– Congratulations...

With a slight shiver Ben shakes off Moritz's limp handshake, releasing himself from the disagreeable sensation of the physical contact with his stepfather.

Mommy looks expectantly at her husband:

– Uncle Moritz is so proud of you, Benny!

Then, discovering Grete who stands near by, she bursts into exuberant kindness:

– But that sweet young lady over there is Miss Grete, isn't she? Won't you come up to us, please? Congratulations, dear Miss Grete! May I introduce you to my husband? Moritz, you know that this is the young lady who is in the same class as our Benny! Well, Ben has told us so much about you, Miss Grete, he certainly has!

Ben loathes watching Grete touch Moritz by the hand. What might Grete think?

Resolutely he takes Grete by the arm:

– Let's get on with the celebrations!

And runs away with her to dance around the equestrian statue, singing of the cheerful days of a student. But now his joy is flawed, and he avoids looking at Grete...

✱　✱　✱

All four of them are walking, breathing the summer air in the soft dawn of the Deer Park. It's the shortest night of the year. The black silhouettes of the trees stand out sharply against the milky way of the sky, and the branches high above them form enormous vaults of rustling foliage, like a Gothic cathedral supported by the slender columns of the trunks.

Grete, Ben and Kristian with Lily on his arm, are walking towards the multi-coloured flood of light emanating from the entertainment area: the circus tent, restaurants, merry-go-rounds and all the other amusements:

> – THE MOST BEAUTIFUL BOUQUET
> IS TO YOU, MIDSUMMER DAY...

Ben is in a good mood, even though he has this sensation of somebody else being inside him all the time, someone who is watching how he is having fun. So many things had happened which they hadn't talked about and yet, you couldn't ignore them either...

Even the others keep certain thoughts to themselves, covered up by their cheerfulness. Grete thinks of the last couple of days, when she had been talking so much and so seriously with Kristian.

> – TIED BY THE HEARTS OF SUMMER
> SO WARM AND SO HAPPY...

Kristian MUST put an end to the matter now! Ben hasn't shown him any resentment but has just given him the cold shoulder. He lets go of Lily and walks towards Ben, grasps his shoulders and hugs him, and while they walk on singing, he looks inquiringly into Ben's eyes: Ben's eyes are glistening with tears in the dusk, and Kristian feels as if he is relieved of an enormous burden. He could kiss Ben! He shouts with joy and Ben joins him at the top of his voice, yelling just as loudly:

> – MIDSUMMER DAY, MIDSUMMER DAY
> WE SEAL YOUR GLORY
> WITH THE BOUQUET OF OUR FRIENDSHIP
> BEAUTIFUL MIDSUMMER DAY!

Both drown confused voices inside themselves, finally silencing them. How wonderful to be really happy again, how it makes you feel good not to have to be obstinate, what a relief to give in! And Ben holds Kristian's arm in the same heartfelt grip...

Lily is bewildered... and hurt. She has taken Grete's arm. What is going on between the three of them? Kristian just walked up to Ben and left her behind where she was... Lily feels shut out. It was as if Kristian merely put up with her. Every time she thought that she had succeeded in getting on intimate terms with him, he slipped away... and honestly, really: Was it Kristian whom she most of all desired to be with?

The girls have stopped singing, walking thoughtfully in silence. But the two boys continue a little longer. Then they fall silent too, as they enter the entertainment area with the noisy crowd of people on Dodgems, past the Danseuse Pavilion, walking towards the roller coaster.

All of a sudden Kristian takes Grete by the hand and makes off with her. Ben doesn't really comprehend what is happening, but they are already gone and he is looking straight into Lily's dark blue eyes. Then he laughs, taking Lily by the hand:

– Hey, where did they go? Off we go, to get them!

Ben tugs Lily along. She is squealing, because he is pulling her so vigorously, and now she stumbles, so he has to catch her round the waist to stop her from falling. They start running again and Lily holds on to Ben's hand with a strength that surprises herself. Breathless and laughing, they reach the roller coaster.

Kristian has bought tickets for them. He is sitting in the front seat with Grete, reserving the seats just behind them for Ben and Lily.

The roller coaster gets under way. At first it moves slowly, as if it can hardly drag itself along, till they get up above the booths and the treetops, from where they can see the swings and the Ferris wheel turning round and round, swinging up and down, gleaming red, yellow, blue and green.... And then all at once the roller coaster darts headlong down: HUUU! Like a deep dive into a bottomless hole, it is sucked down at a furious speed and it races even faster up the next steep grade, at the top of which it pauses for a brief moment, to plunge down again so that your stomach ends up in your mouth.

The girls shriek and the boys yell at the top of their voices as they gasp for breath between the tops and bottoms, and the velocity is so mad that Lily must cling to Ben and so must he to her. What delight and fear at the same time, the contact between the young bodies, while they hold on tight to each other, not to lose their balance! Kristian and Grete cling laughing to each other too, holding on to their student caps so that they won't be lost in the abyss. Finally the long, pitch-dark tunnel. Ben feels Lily's breath burn close and hot against his cheek. The tunnel turns sharply in the dark, making them sway from side to side, until they finally come through, and the cars glide along slowly to a stop.

Their legs tremble slightly when they get solid ground under their feet again. Now they are hungry. Kristian knows what to do:

– Let's go to Peter Liep's to get something to stuff ourselves with. This is on Daddy!

In the restaurant, Ben again sits next to Grete.

* * *

Teaching school in the ghetto was forbidden. It would carry the death sentence if the Germans found out about it. Nevertheless, the Danish children went daily for a walk on the rampart around the camp with two teachers who were giving lessons. But soon it became far too cold and a classroom was set up in which the children were taught secretly. They were about 12-13 pupils, and even Lea and Rebecca attended. The small children and the big ones were in the same class, but of course kindly Miss Sulamith was trying to instruct them according to their ages. They didn't have any school-books, but they did have paper and pencils, and little Lea made a diary with fine drawings in an exercise book about her being captured by the Germans and about Theresienstadt.

Kalle and John didn't go to school. They were fourteen years old and had to work, so they got one more slice of bread every third day.

John worked in the stable, while Kalle was a carter. Ben sometimes met him in the streets pulling a cart with dead bodies, arms and legs sticking out from under the black cloth.

The cart was the same as the one used for bringing bread every third day. Every morning Kalle was told from which houses to fetch the dead people. Those were either very skinny, hardly weighing anything, or they were blue, swollen with bloated stomachs.

Kalle and his mate Alex had to carry the corpses down to the cart. Ben would have liked to know why the black cloth was not larger so as to cover the dead bodies, but Kalle could not tell why. This way everybody could see what they were carrying as they pulled the cart along the streets to a small mortuary established inside the earthworks. There the bodies were laid in coffins, whereupon the rabbi held a little ceremony for the deceased.

John drove the camp's team of oxen. He drove all the dead people farther away to the crematorium. His carriage could hold twenty-eight coffins. Usually he had to drive out there two or three times. That's why John knew exactly how many people had died, and every day the number was all over Theresienstadt: One day it was only 47, another day 52 or 56, and when there was typhoid fever, it was as much as 85 or 92, or even more than 150 daily.

At the crematorium, the Jewish workers took the corpses out of the coffins and put them on a bier. They examined their mouths and pulled out any gold teeth. There was a strict check to ensure that the gold was turned over to headquarters. They cut off women's hair, to be used for mattresses for the German population, and even the dead people's glass eyes were removed... everything could be of use. Then the bodies were shoved into the ovens, four at a time.

The ashes of the deceased were kept in cardboard boxes with their names on them. John drove back to the mortuary with the coffins. Of course they were to be used again.

Ben wished to earn that extra piece of bread, so he ceased going to school and reported for work. But he was not to drive the hearse with Kalle. Instead he was set to shovelling earth on the outer rampart, where they were cultivating potatoes and vegetables for the Germans.

* * *

One day, when Ben was working on the rampart laying out vegetable gardens, SS-Haindl arrived to watch their work.

They were a hundred men, ten in each row, and they were shovelling in rhythm. The earth was heavy, wet and sticky, so that it stuck to the shovel, but at the very moment they see the German they tear off their caps, and then go sharp about it, *EINS-ZWEI, ONE-TWO, ONE-TWO...*

John is standing by his team of oxen fixing the harness, without noticing the German. The Gestapo officer goes up to John and, striking him with his clenched fist, yells:

– Off with the cap, swine!

John rolls over on the ground where he remains lying. Ben's heart throbs while he continues digging. Thank God, it isn't me, flashes through his mind.

Not until the German is far away, does John stand up from the cold ground where he was lying, pretending that he had fainted.

Queueing for soup that night, John has much pain in his ear. Never ever in his life, no matter if it be rain or snow, will he wear a hat, so that he will not have to take it off for anyone.

* * *

Ben is dreaming that he is shovelling earth on the rampart, while the SS officer is beating John lying on the groud. Then Ben, with all his strength, strikes the German's neck with his spade so that his head is almost cut off and he drops dead, his blood spurting all over. All the others are yelling and crying, scolding Ben because it is his fault that now they will be punished. Ben wants to hide the corpse and digs a hole, but none of the others will help him. Suddenly Kristian appears and helps him dig in the heavy sticky soil until the hole is big enough. With great effort they manage to throw SS Haindl's corpse into the hole and cover it. But before doing that, Kristian had taken the German's pistol and cartridge belt. With the gun they will shoot the camp commandant, Rahm, if they should be found out.

* * *

Three Czech teachers are in charge of the youth centre where about 800 boys and girls are living. One of the teachers plays the piano. His name is Mr Klein, even though he was a tall, grown man and "klein" means small...

In Ben's room there are boys from many different countries, so he soon learns to count in Czech, and to understand all German dialects from Berlin to Low German.

Mr. Klein talks daily to the boys about how they would be living in freedom again after the war, and they sing about how they will assume responsibility for their own lives and learn a profession so as to be able to shift for themselves. The boys never speak of their parents or about going home again. They all want to go with their beloved teacher to Palestine, to build a secure home for the Jews, and they fasten small banners to their beds with drawings and catchwords such as FELLOWSHIP and BROTHERHOOD, and signs with the professions they wanted to acquire: FARMER, TEACHER, SHOEMAKER, DENTIST, MECHANIC, CARPENTER, EXPLORER... when one day they will get out of Terezin.

Every Friday the boys and girls assemble in the yard for parade. The cleanest and most orderly room of the week is awarded a streamer. Ben and his comrades are really proud of their own room and get the award. They sing:

WE ARE FORTY IN A ROOM
ALL OF US ARE DIFFERENT
WISE, GOOD, HONEST AND DILIGENT
NAUGHTY, FOOLISH, LAZY AND CRAZY
BUT ALL THE SAME WE LIVE WELL TOGETHER
WE NEVER GIVE UP HOPE
WE WANT TO WORK AND TO LEARN

THE SUN RISES FAR AWAY
IT WILL SHINE AND LIGHT FOR US ONE DAY
AND THE PAST WILL ONLY BE A DREAM

In the home the children make drawings. The teacher teaches them to draw, and she encourages Ben, too, to draw. It isn't prohibited to draw. It is not considered to be knowledge.

The boys and girls make a Czech/German newspaper, and that is secret. Every week when the paper is produced, it is read aloud in their room by the oldest boy, Pavel Friedmann. He has just completed his fifteenth year, has handsome dark wavy hair and warm brown eyes. Ben likes him very much!

One night, just before they are going to sleep, Pavel reads a poem to them that he has written:

LITTLE BUTTERFLY
WITH YOUR COLOURED WINGS
HOVERING YOU REST
LIKE A FLOWER UPON A FLOWER
THEN AGAIN SO EASILY
YOU ARE FLAPPING
UP IN THE AIR,
AND DOWN TO ANOTHER FLOWER
AND AGAIN FROM FLOWER
TO ANOTHER FLOWER!

– LITTLE BUTTERFLY
SO LUMINOUS YELLOW
SHINING BRIGHTLY
LIKE THE RAYS OF THE SUN,
RADIANT TEARS FALLING
ON THE WHITE GLARING ROCK.

– IT WAS THAT SUMMER WHEN I WAS STILL AT HOME
NOW I AM IN TEREZIN
AND HERE IN THIS PLACE
FOR BUTTERFLIES THERE IS NO SPACE

One of the boys, Teddy was his name, has to lie on the floor because he pees in his sleep. Every morning his straw mattress is heavy and wet with pee, so that he has to place it in the window to dry. Boy, is he teased and called Teddy the Bed-Pisser. However, he doesn't care and laughs loudly. But in his heart he is probably sad.

Before the boys fell asleep, the bunks often shake. Ben is lying in a middle berth. The boy above Ben especially is given to making the entire bunk rock vehemently. He isn't ashamed of it at all. On the contrary, he boasts how often he does it.

There he is, standing stark naked on his upper berth, shaking his penis for everybody to see, roaring like a ferocious ape from the Tarzan books. The boy has begun to get hair around his piddler and can push his skin up and down the head of his organ. He is not circumcised. Also he has swollen nipples. He is called Fritz and is named after his grandfather, who had been a General in the German Army!

One night Fritz climbs down to Ben, creeping under his blanket and whispering, asking if Ben has ever seen a naked woman. In fact, Ben never has, but he doesn't like to admit it. Once in the kindergarten a little girl had shown him her tummy, but Ben hadn't really been able to see anything. When he was five years old, he had once entered the room at Grandma's while Mommy was about to try on a bra. Mommy had squealed and turned around covering up her breasts from him, and scolded him because he didn't knock on the door, so Ben had to go out to wait in the kitchen.

Reluctantly, Ben tries to say something about Mommy having round breasts, and then Fritz begins to shake the bed:

– Tell me more! How is your Mommy lower down on her stomach! Tell me!

Fritz is very excited. Actually Ben doesn't feel like answering, but then at last he says anyway that Mommy's tummy is white and round. And when Fritz pants and asks Ben to tell what Mommy looks like between her legs, Ben finally admits that she is white and smooth between her legs too. Fritz shakes even more violently all over his body and then calms down. A moment later he crawls up into his bed again.

None of the boys in the entire room, except Ben and Fritz, has a mother. All the others have neither a father nor a mother any more, just like the boys in the orphanage.

The smallest of the boys, ten-year-old Klausi, has a mouth organ on which he plays little ballads, *SAW A BOY A ROSE SO RED...* Sometimes, in his sleep, he crouches under his blanket in his bed high up in the corner, cries and calls his Mommy. Then in the morning he sits on the teacher's lap. What luck, Ben has his Mommy...

The teachers wake them every morning at six o'clock with a *DOBBRI*

DENN which means "Good day" in Czech, and they see to it that the boys make their beds properly. Every day the teachers bring the bread for the boys. They don't have to keep bread for three days, but get a slice of bread every day.

Shaking out the blankets and straw mattresses, they see the fleas fall on the floor in large numbers. There are fleas everywhere, as well as in the hut where Mommy is living.

You can't avoid having them on yourself. They are in your clothes, in your stockings, biting your ankles. When you catch a flea you can squeeze it between your fingers, but if you open your hand it leaps away until you have learned to put the flea between two nails and press hard, and when it cracks, the flea is dead.

However, the bedbugs are the worst. They live in the chinks of the wooden beds, in the floors, in the benches, wherever they can find the tiniest crack. They were able to hang on to and wander across the walls, ceilings and posts. There are a lot of them, hundreds of thousands crawling in unbroken living streams up to the sleeping person, or they fall down from above upon him in never-ending lines. They can be as small as dots, like red pinheads and they can be as big as ladybirds, bulging like blisters with the blood they sucked in. When Ben pinches them, the blood splashes out, making large red blots. Ugh, ugh! And then it is his own blood!

And the itching! You can't help scratching yourself, so that the wound festers. The bite of the fleas always leaves white blisters filled with liquid on your skin, while the bedbugs leave wounds with black crusts.

Some of the boys also have itch mites between their fingers... and head lice! They have their hair shaved off so that their heads look like white eggshells.

Sometimes at night Ben can't stand the itching... He scratches himself again and again. At some point beyond endurance, he gets up, shakes his blanket and goes out into the corridor, where the floor is made of concrete, and there he bounces up and down, up and down, to shake off the bedbugs, stamping his feet on the ground to smash and crush them with his heels, and kill them, kill them! When he is cold all over, he climbs into his bunk again. Then he is so tired that he doesn't care about anything and allows the bedbugs to guzzle him, and fell asleep.

* * *

At Bellevue Beach the last weary flames are licking up the scraps of the charred smoking branches of the Midsummer Night's bonfire on the white sand.

Most people have already gone home, now that the sky begins to brighten from the coast of Sweden on the other side of the black-blue Sound. You can dimly see the lights glimmering over there, fading away while the outline of the land stands out more distinctly.

It is only an hour's sailing from Denmark to Sweden over the Sound, lying there so calm, grooved by tiny ripples, while the cool air breathes faintly over the water.

Ben is sitting on the stony slope. He picks up a branch which escaped being devoured by the fire and draws in the sand with it. Kristian is sitting next to him and Lily has placed herself besides Kristian, although he has been avoiding her more openly than she'd like to admit.

Grete is standing a little apart, glancing over the water. In her light summer dress, her slender figure is silhouetted against the slowly blushing horizon. She breathes deeply:

– Summer holiday... at last!

Lily agrees. She gets up, raising her arms:

– Yes, school is over, no more school! Now we are free... free!

Kristian raises his forefinger in didactic irony, like a wise old man:

– My young friends, the school of life is only starting now!

Ben assumes Børge's well-known tone of voice and schoolmasterish look:

– Most correct my dear colleague, then Kristian will turn into the great medicine doctor, Big, big bwana!

They try to laugh a little even though it isn't very funny. After a while Lily professes, but not very convincingly:

– I'd like to become a nurse...

Grete is meditating. She cannot push it aside any longer. She looks at Ben with a little pang and then at Kristian. There is something they must by all means settle. But as long as Lily is present...

– First a really long, long holiday...

Kristian has figured out a quick repartee:

– And you'll become the famous Maestro Toscanini, 'the great musical doctor!'

Again Ben gets the familiar prickle in his stomach, because it's true, it is, what Kristian is saying. It's exactly what he desires:

– Yes, so much is ahead of us...

Ben looks at Grete and all of sudden it seems as if she is totally different, as if she has changed...! Where has their sweet secret gone?

He feels a pang, gets up and walks to the water. He stands on the wet sand, so close to the water that the ripples touch his toes, draw back and come up again and again. Sometimes they swirl over his toes, but he does not move, he just lets it happen.

He feels a light pat on his shoulder and turns round. It's Grete:

– Ben...

Grete's eyes are glancing at him with a fervour which burns into his soul. He looks towards Sweden again, the land of rescue and freedom! In the silence between them they can hear each other's breathing above the quiet gurgle of the ripples.

– Look at the lights over there, Grete. It's like that time when...

– But Ben, it is NOT that time any more, it isn't!

It makes Grete suffer so much. That is why it is so heartbreaking, so that she cannot bear the thought that she would have to live with it. She could cry...

– Can't you understand it, Ben? It is not that time any more, no, it isn't...

They don't speak for some long minutes. Now she must say it, even if she would die:

– I'm going to study medicine after all...

Ben cannot understand anything:

– Aren't you going to study literature any more?

– No! Kristian and I... we want to study together.

Ben is seized with the fear he has known since he was a baby, the fear of being rejected, the fear of being thrown out into loneliness:

– Well?

Grete has to go on:

– Kristian and I are going on holiday together too...

Ben feels as if he had a knife at his throat:

– What are you doing?

At this point Grete is quite relieved at saying frankly:

– Kristian and I are getting engaged.

Ben's legs give way. He must sit down in the wet sand. Grete bends down, giving him a long firm kiss on his mouth. Then she breaks away from him and walks quickly up to Kristian, who is standing with Lily on the Strandvej.

Ben wants to weep, but he doesn't weep. He wants to howl, but he doesn't howl. He wants to die, but he doesn't... Deep inside himself he recognizes that age-old disappointment, which exhausts all his strength. At long last he stands up, following the others.

* * *

Ben dreamt that he was going to sing the solo part at an important concert at the Tivoli concert hall. Just before he is to ascend the platform, he is informed that they had chosen another singer whom they considered better. Ben is standing there, all alone, while tears stream down his thin cheeks. "How beautiful you are when you are weeping," Mommy says.

∗ ∗ ∗

The entire class of students is invited to a party at Kristian's place. The dining-room has been cleared for dancing. Daddy Knud saw to it that there was plenty to drink. It's over there, right on the side table, the young guests may help themselves!

They had been welcomed with champagne, and the buffet at the Ritz couldn't be better.

The young girls are looking lovely, dressed to the nines with their hair taken up for fun. Kristian is wearing tails and Ben is wearing a beautiful suit, which Mommy insisted on paying for, so that her own boy could look good now that he had become a student.

They have been celebrating for many hours already, and Birgit and Knud discreetly retired upstairs long ago. The couples are dancing, clinging to each other, and Ellington's soft rhythms are weaving through the half-light of the suggestive summer night. Some of the students are enjoying the gentle air on the terrace and a few couples have disappeared to walk among the fragrant bushes in the garden...

Ben is dancing with Lily, feeling her body against his own. But he cannot abandon himself to dancing. In his heart he has a big gaping hole, just in his front, in the middle below the ribs!

Lily has noticed that Kristian has been avoiding her all night and that he has danced only with Grete. Now she is enjoying dancing with Ben, although he appears so far away, so unattainable to her. Are only the others around her really happy?

She casts a glance at Grete and Kristian and starts: They are kissing each other while they are dancing, a really long and intense kiss! She looks inquiringly at Ben. He has seen it too, she has no doubt of that... Lily can read Ben's eyes, and gets so furious that she could cry. She lets go of Ben and runs out, away from the party, away from them all!

Ben remains on the dance floor, while the shadows of the dancers swing and rock around him.

Grete noticed it. She drags Ben towards the table with the many bottles:

– Come on Ben, let's touch glasses, cheers!

Ben is not angry, and now he feels warmth and his heart grows soft. Grete made her choice. He wishes them every happiness. Kristian joins them, filling the glasses. Ben raises his glass ungrudgingly:

– Well, cheers, you two... and congratulations!

They glance long and silently at each other.

Grete is both happy and sorry. Maybe Ben will understand her too... when time will have gone by. Her eyes are wet.

– We'll always stick together the three of us, won't we?

Ben doesn't struggle any more, he nods:

– Sure, we will!

Kristian feels that Ben has forgiven him. A little embarrassed, he lifts his glass:

– One for all and all for one!

Too much of a good thing, they laugh, all three of them.

Kristian puts his arm round Ben and hugs him, and Ben squeezes him with all his might, so that their muscles tighten. They squeeze harder and harder until they both let go with a gasp and have to puff and blow for a while.

Kristian and Grete are going to dance again, while Ben gives them a lingering look. Now he must pull himself together! He walks into the study and sits down at Knud's writing desk, supporting his head with his elbows on the table.

Then Birgit sits down beside him. She had come downstairs and seen him. Why is he there all by himself? During the war, when the Germans had sent him far, far away, he had never been out of her mind. And when he had come back, he had been so silent about what he had experienced. She had never really wanted to question him. The main thing was, of course, that he had come home again, and apparently had got over it without injury. She strokes his hair as she has done so often:

– Aren't you happy, Ben?

Ben lets his eyes circle slowly through the dark library that he knew so well and used to look at with admiration since he was a little boy: The distinguished oak armchairs with light-brown leather, shiny from use, the old paintings of Kristian's grandparents in heavily carved gold frames, and the bookcases filled with leather-bound books up to the high ceiling.

Now he is sitting here at the consultant's broad desk with the marble pen and ink set and the rack of pipes properly arranged according to size, and in the next room they are having fun, dancing!

Ben avoids looking into Birgit's eyes:
– Sure, I'm happy...
Birgit isn't convinced at all:
– What are you going to do after your holiday, then?
Ben has made his decision. He has, indeed, been returning to the same idea for a long time:
I want to be an actor!
Birgit becomes suddenly so pleased on Ben's behalf:
– That is, indeed, an excellent idea, Ben! It is really the right thing for you to do! I do wish that for you, my dear boy, believe me!

Grete and Kristian join them. Kristian gives his mother a hug and pulls Ben up from the chair:
– Come now, Ben, let's find some good records.

Ben feels relief at having confided in Birgit. He won't let himself be knocked out. He walks between the dancing couples up to the gramophone where they rummage in the stack of records to find one with the right swing... Just then Grete takes his hand.
– Come, Ben, let us dance, come on!
And Ben lets her draw him into the dance.

She swings him round, but little by little he takes over the initiative so that he swings her round and round, and they turn faster and faster until everything becomes a flickering flying ring of people, faces and bodies rotating around them in the glimmering lights, and they sway with the jazz music, while the improvisations of the clarinet and the trumpet are mixed with cries, smiles and laughter. They hold tight to each other, hand in hand, letting themselves be turned around by the weight of their bodies, and Ben sees only Grete's eyes, her dark glowing eyes, as his only fixed point, while he whirls at speed through space.

* * *

The following morning, very early, Ben is lying in his bed, dreaming. He is conducting a large symphony orchestra in a crowded concert hall. They are playing Mozart's Linz Symphony, which he knows by heart from Knud's records. The music ends. He bows to the audience. They applaud him furiously.

* * *

One day Ben is queueing for his food in the barracks yard. It is drizzling, and there is a cold wind. Moist white steam rises from the pots in the kitchen. Ben is standing in the wet clayey earth with his food pail...waiting. His feet are wet and cold, as his shoes were completely ruined by the work in the field.

Uncle Moritz might be able to procure him a better pair of shoes, as his stepfather knew somebody who was working in the Clothes Depot, where the newcomers' clothes were seized before being given to the German people. This man could eventually organize a pair of shoes for Ben and smuggle them in. That would cost two slices of bread.

At the food distribution point, some old people are pushing and pressing to get at a big pot in which there had been some porridge. They search in the pot energetically, scraping its inside with their spoons, sticking the spoon quickly into their mouths, digging in immediately again with the spoon to get more, and then licking the spoon clean again: Down with the spoon, up into the mouth, down and up, down and up, as fast as they can. They go on like this, until there is not the least scrap left.

There are still many people ahead of Ben. Nearby is the extra course queue, the *NACHSCHUB* queue. Those people have already got their ration and are hoping that there'll be some food still left. Sometimes you could be lucky enough to get a small extra portion. They are looking a little hostilely at Ben, who still has his meal due to him.

Once in a while, Ben has tried to queue for Nachschub to get an extra portion too, but so far he had never been lucky enough to get anything...

Now the kitchen staff is ladling out the ration of soup and three potatoes into an old woman's bucket. Unfortunately, she drops everything and the potatoes roll across the ground. Hastily some others dash into the mud, managing to pinch two of her potatoes, swallowing them in one gulp before she is able to get hold of the last one. Her spilt soup has turned into a dirty puddle.

How come people put up with this? Why don't we resist? Why did we let them capture us like helpless sheep? Why does nobody revolt? Why don't we defend ourselves? Why don't we conspire and fight? If we stick together we are strong enough against our oppressors, against those who are murdering us! But we stand here, struggling against each other for a crust of bread or a potato...

Recently, while standing in the Nachschub queue, the people around him had gazed in amazement at Ben. Even the guard at the distribution point had turned around, and Ben realized that he had been shouting at the top of his voice, standing there all alone! Frightened, Ben, with his heart beating, and without moving, remained quiet, pretending not even to be there. The guard, who had come nearer, calmed down after a while and returned to his post.

The following night Ben had a dream which afterwards recurred many times:

NACHSCHUB

I AM STANDING IN THE QUEUE
SHIVERING FROM HUNGER
AND FROM THE COLD
WILL THERE BE SOME SOMETHING LEFT?

ICY RAIN
DIM BLACK COATS
GHOSTS WITH YELLOW STARS
SILENT AND SAD
COLD WHITE STEAM FROM THE FOOD POTS SHROUDS US
FEET ARE STAMPING
INANIMATE GLANCES.

I AM STANDING IN THE QUEUE, WAITING
AND WAITING
WAITING

NOW IT BEGINS
THE GREY GHOSTS COMING ALIVE
PRESSING FORWARD
TIN BOWLS FALL RATTLING TO THE GROUND
THE ROW IS MOVING
EYES ARE ASKING
WILL THERE BE SOME SOMETHING LEFT?

WILL THERE BE SOME SOMETHING LEFT?
WILL THERE STILL BE SOME SOMETHING
WHEN I ARRIVE?
OR WON'T THERE BE ANYTHING
TODAY EITHER?
AM I TO RETURN – DISAPPOINTED AND HUNGRY
ONCE AGAIN – TO THE HUT?

I AM STANDING IN THE QUEUE
COUNTING THOSE STANDING AHEAD OF ME
STILL TWENTY-TWO – BUT WE ARE MOVING
IT WON'T LAST SO LONG ANY MORE
NOW EIGHT – NOW SIX!
SOON I'LL GET SOMETHING
TO EAT... SOON

ALL OF A SUDDEN EVERYBODY BECOMES STRUCK DUMB
ANXIETY SNEAKS ALONG THE LINE
WHAT IS GOING ON?
CLOSED
NOTHING MORE LEFT
NOTHING MORE... NOTHING
CLOSED
THE HUMAN SHAPES
RETURN TO BEING... GHOSTS

YET NOW A LOW GRUMBLING STARTS
GETTING LOUDER, BECOMING WORDS
SHOUTS, CRIES, CURSES
COME ON, LET US STORM THE KITCHEN
THERE MUST BE SOME POTATO PEELS LEFT
OR SOME PORRIDGE
SURELY THERE MUST BE
THEY ONLY KEEP IT FOR THEMSELVES
THE SWINE EAT THEIR FILL
LETTING US STARVE
COME ON, LET US STORM THEM
WE ARE HUNGRY

BUT IN THIS VERY MOMENT I BEWARE
FOR I AM HERE – ALL ALONE
HAVING SCREECHED MY LUNGS OUT
NOBODY IS BAWLING
NOBODY IS CURSING
NOBODY SCREAMING
NOBODY IS STORMING
ONLY DISAPPOINTMENT
IN THEIR EYES
DRY EYES – DEAD EYES

MUTE – THEIR HEADS BENT
THEY DISAPPEAR IN THE DARK
SILENT GHOSTS

At last Ben reaches the big pots where they cut off a coupon of his ration card and he gets his meal.

By the soup barrel, as usual, some starved old men and women are wailing: – *NEHMEN SIE DIE SUPPE?* Do you take your soup?

Because it might be that someone didn't want the thin millet soup after all. Then one of the old people could have it.

Ben takes the soup as well. Even though he doesn't eat it himself, Uncle Moritz is sure to do so. He hurries to the women's huts.

* * *

Mommy is pottering about at home. She attaches importance to having a nice home, even though it isn't as big as the home where she grew up... her thoughts dwelling on her father. He was such a fine man, a real gentleman. It is enough to look at his pictures to see how handsome he was. He looks exactly like a Russian baron in his beautiful fur coat... or the picture where he is sitting in his car! There weren't many people at that time, before the First World War, who had an automobile, but her Daddy did have one!

Mommy was born in Odessa, but when she was seven years old, her father and mother moved to Hamburg. Mommy is still able to speak Russian. She speaks Russian with Grandma, who never learned to speak German properly and has even more difficulty speaking Danish. Ben can also say some proverbs in Russian, which Mommy's father used to quote, and he says them with a proper Russian accent! *Bies hlieba nie obied* was one of grandfather's favourites, and it meant, *It's not a proper meal without bread.*

Mommy is proud of her father. He had the sole agency for Singer sewing machines for all Russia and Poland... and Finland! That's why he had travelled so much. When the revolution came, he lost a great part of his fortune.

How she loved her father! But as he wasn't at home most of the year, her mother always decided everything. What a magnificent person, he did not get to be very old either, only sixty, poor Daddy...

It was the inflation, when he lost the rest of his money, which knocked him out. Then he lost all desire for life. Ben was born the very day... the 12th of July...

As a little girl, Mommy had missed her daddy very much, especially when her mother had been severe with her. Then she had wanted so much that her daddy would come and protect her.

Mommy adjusts the lace cloth on the dining-room sideboard by the big carved mirror reaching from floor to ceiling so that you can see yourself full length. What luck she had Mrs. Jensen, who came twice weekly to take care of the hard work, while Mommy dusted and watered the flowers herself. Mommy made it a point of honour to cook delicious Jewish-Russian meals. She had even been interviewed by the newspaper about her recipes. Moritzl grumbled because she spent so much money, but he wasn't dissatisfied at all when she served their guests the good old traditional Jewish dishes on a Friday night.

In the living-room Mommy is smoothing the expensive silk cushions on the fine covered sofa. She had also bought an oriental carpet recently, paying for it in instalments. Bennyboy is going to have that, when she isn't there any more...

Well, Mommy certainly doesn't need to be ashamed of her home. She has reason to be proud of it – especially considering that she had to sell most of the furniture after the divorce from Aron, leaving the rest in Germany. She lost everything once more, when they arrested her and took her to Theresienstadt. But the piano that her father gave her on her twelfth birthday survived all upheavals. She brought it with her to Denmark. It was the very first thing she bought back again after the war. It was her best present from her own Daddy!

Mommy is smiling... How many hours hadn't she and Benny played that piano! She moves the framed photographs on the piano a little: The wedding picture of herself and Moritz, Mommy's sister and her husband in America, and the photo of herself with Benny... Wasn't he cute and sweet! And the large picture of her father! It was the last one of her Daddy, when he was already very ill, and as her father looks at her from the photo with his solemn brown eyes, Mommy feels a pang. How she loved him!

But now she has her own Benny... and her Moritzl too! She had been so proud, when Ben danced around the statue together with the other students!

In the dining-room Mommy stops in front of the mirror, fixing her hair and smiling coquettishly to herself. They all said that she looked ten years younger, and then she hadn't even told them how old she really was! Mommy purses her lips, so that her mouth looks just as lovely as a young girl's. Alas, when she was a young girl... But my God! There's her own boy, in the mirror behind her!

Ben has entered the room and Mommy turns around, embraces and kisses him, adjusting his student cap... it's on lop-sided!

– May I ask my big Mr. Student to dance with me? Come, dance with your proud young mother. I am so proud of you, really!

And Mommy moves her feet in dance steps, trying to make Ben dance with her, closing her eyes, humming:

– *SING OF THE STUDENT'S CHEERFUL DAYS...* Didn't the song go like that?

Ben dances a few steps, then stiffens. He isn't in the mood. But Mommy doesn't notice Ben holding back:

– And Grete, how lovely she looked when you were dancing with her. Well, you both looked so sweet, as if you cared really a lot about each other...?

Mommy looks up with curiosity. Ben has grown so big, that she can't march him about any more as she would like to... he must be tired from yesterday too, she understands that well enough, so Mommy stops in front of the mirror. She nods to their reflection in the mirror, leaning against her son's shoulder, smiling charmingly:

– Don't we look like brother and sister? You are my big brother and I am your little sister!

Ben disengages himself.

– Mommy you aren't sixteen any longer. You are soon fifty... Why are you always putting on an act?

Mommy remains unruffled, patting Ben on his cheek:

– I really cannot grasp that my own son has become so big and so grown-up. I can hardly reach up to you even if I stand on tiptoe when I give my Bennyboy a little kiss... And believe me, I did notice how Grete was watching you all the time!

She wants Ben to confide in her the sweet secret, which she guessed a long time ago:

– You bet I noticed it! What time did you go to bed then, Bennyboy?

Ben shakes his head:

– Not so late...

Mommy recalls quite well what it was like when she was young: To dance all night and walk in the spring morning in the light of the green wood, where only the bees and the birds have risen. Mommy is so pleased, that she has to laugh:

– Not so late! That's how it is when you are young! Not at all late but early, early! I can see from the dark rings under your eyes, that you have been out all night!

And Mommy can't control her curiosity:

– Are you going on holiday, you and Grete, then?

Ben might as well say it plainly:

– Grete is going on holiday with Kristian.

Mommy is taken aback... and disappointed! She had imagined that... what a pity for her own boy! But before she manages to say anything she hears the front door. It is her Moritzl!

Mommy has to be careful! Moritz has been on an errand, and she had had to use all her persuasive powers to make him go about it. She knows only too well that Ben cherishes completely crazy fantasies. In real life, however, you are better off with both feet firmly planted on the ground. It is up to her to make Ben come to his senses. Weren't they wise, the words, that his headmaster had pronounced: Now the young people have to choose the career which is the very right one for each of them.

Mommy is all optimism:

– Uncle Moritz has some good news for you, Benny, don't you Moritzl? You have spoken to the stockbroker, haven't you?

Yes, Moritzl would do anything for Tanya, wouldn't he! The stockbroker had even opened his eyes wide when he had told him Ben's average mark and would very much like to have him in his firm. Moritz couldn't help feeling a little proud. He is literally kindly now:

– It is settled, Ben can start at the broker's next week.

Ben is staggered. Mommy had – and she is doing it time and time again – poked her nose into his affairs, involved his stepfather and, on top of it all, some total stranger!

– At a stockbroker's? Not for anything in the world! Did I, perhaps, ask you to do that? You don't have to make any effort for my sake! I might as well tell you now: I have decided to go on the stage. I want to be an actor.

Mommy pretends to be surprised:

– But my sweet Ben, now that you have passed your General Certificate!

Moritz frowns. He has done Ben a favour and... not even a bit of gratitude:

– One of his crazy ideas again. A good secure job is the only right thing in this world...

When Mommy was in for a cure at the Skodsborg Sanatorium, she had spoken to an actor who happened to be there too, and he, who was one of those who never got anything but small parts, had advised most strongly against her son going on the stage. "If you can possibly live without doing it, you must do so," he had advised. And of course, Mommy was now deeply worried:

– Bennyboy, you can't imagine all the disappointments you'll meet with.

I know you since you were a little baby... you won't be able to bear all the disappointments, you never could bear disappointments, never! A man who is an actor himself told me how it is. Besides, Uncle Moritz has just done everything to get you a job...

– And you expect me to arrange my life in accordance with *Uncle Moritz* taking the trouble to get me a job?

Moritz is annoyed. Who does Ben fancy himself to be? Moritz himself, when he was a boy, had to get up, helping in the shop at five o'clock every morning before going to school, and if he was disobedient, he could spend the night in the coal cellar! Moritz's own father had brought him up with a leather strap, strictly but justly, and that hadn't harmed him in the least! Every penny Moritz owned he had earned himself, working hard... Now Ben with his stupidity! Tanya always spoilt him, so that he always got this and he got that without becoming familiar with life's realities:

– You can't live nor die from going on the stage!

Mommy is seized with fear. She already pictures to herself Ben living in extreme poverty:

– Most actors get nothing but small parts, Bennyboy, and even then they have to be lucky to get them! An actor I spoke to said: "If you can possibly live without going on the stage, you must do so." That's what he said!

– But I might well succeed! Mother, why not? Why couldn't I be successful as well?

Mommy is just about to cry:

– No Ben, it's impossible! You are going to be ill-fated! You will go to the dogs... Bennyboy, why do you want to ruin everything for me? Why are you going to bring disaster upon yourself? At most, only a few of the talented ones who are selected ever make it.

– I have never heard such nonsense!

Moritz is mad. He has made a fool of himself in front of the broker:

– The theatre! That good-for-nothing always thinks he is a genius! Not only is it an insecure career, but it's also utterly improper for people from a well-regulated family!

Mommy seizes at Moritz's words as if they are a life-raft:

– Benny, listen to what Uncle Moritz is saying. He means well! First you must secure a decent job for yourself! Then you can devote yourself to the stage in your spare time, as your hobby! Only very, very few people make it! If only you were talented...

Now Ben is shouting:

– What do you know about it? Who do you think YOU are to decide if I am talented?

Mommy is in doubt:

– Have you asked anybody who knows anything about it?

– Why don't you believe in me? You, my own mother! I'll apply for admission to the Royal Theatre school!

Moritz laughs contemptuously:

– And where is the clever gentleman going to get the money from? What is he going to live on? Of course, he hasn't even given that a thought!

Moritz addresses Ben directly:

– You might as well know it once and for all now: You are not going to get so much as a penny from us!

Ben looks firmly into his stepfather's eyes. He had long ago stopped expecting anything from this man:

– I never expected anything of you either! Did you ever give me anything at all?

Moritz flares up:

– Didn't I give him a roof over his head, food to eat and clothes to wear? Ungrateful too, that's what he is, that snotty brat!

Here Mother realizes the danger of this argument. It could develop into the most terrible quarrel. She must intervene, sweetly and persuasively:

– Please be sensible, my Bennyboy. You could study at the university if you don't want to become a stockbroker. That's both accepted and respected as well! For that kind of study you can get scholarships or bursaries. Then you would become someone. Someone that everybody looks up to. You might study German! You speak it already...

– But mother, can't you understand? It is my life that it is about. My own future I will decide myself! All my friends will do what they want to, Kristian is going to start studying medicine...

And Mommy, who always dreamt of having a doctor for a son:

– Well, medicine, if only you would...

Moritz also has an opinion on such matters:

– The study of medicine isn't just twaddle and fiddlesticks! And, furthermore, he has a father who can afford to pay!

Ben again looks straight into his stepfather's face:

– Yes, Kristian... he has a real father!

Now Mommy must deflect them by every possible means or things will get out of hand. She has such an excellent idea:

– Bennyboy, haven't you always loved to devote your time to literature? I know that from your teacher, Børge. He is so enthusiastic about you!

– But my only desire is to go on the stage! It isn't something I've just thought of today. I've been thinking about it for years...

Moritz is irritated again. Tanya is always thinking of Ben, and Ben alone!

– Bragging! He has always shot his mouth off! A ne'er-do-well! Grosse Schnauze! Braggart!

Ben tries to explain again, very calmly:

– You see, what I need is that you support me in what...

Moritz is triumphant:

– There you are, Tanya! That's what I always said! Lazy fox, he simply doesn't care about taking an honest job!

– But won't you just try to understand me! It isn't money... I want you to have confidence in me, support me by believing in me!

Mommy once appeared in a charity performance when she was a young girl, even playing the leading part in a musical comedy. Her father had been so proud of her! Everybody said that she had such a delightful voice, looked so lovely that she ought to go on the stage... All the same, her Daddy had made her realize that it would be very unwise to do such a thing. Of course, she complied with her father.

– I had my dreams, Bennyboy, you know that, but I had to give them up...

Ben is all eagerness now. Here, finally, is something Mommy can understand:

– That's no reason that I should do the same is it? It really ought to please you, if I achieve what you desired but couldn't do for yourself!

But Mommy is seized by a terrible fear:

– Don't do it, Ben! For my sake! You'll starve to death, you'll become a drunkard! Bennyboy, you will die a dog's death!

– Die a dog's... But why should I? Are you completely insane, Mommy?

Mommy is unable to restrain herself any longer:

– Why do you always rebel against us? Why do you always make me so unhappy?

– Mommy, it's exactly the opposite of what I will do! I want to make you happy, doing what you yourself once dreamt! Just imagine how happy you will be, seeing me on the stage...

But Mommy works herself up more and more, as if some dormant spirit, which had been locked up inside her, has been suddenly released. She whines and wails, moans and weeps like a Jewish mother out of the Old Testament, until at last she breaks down:

– No, no... you make me unhappy, Ben! You, my own son, make your mother unhappy, your own poor Mommy! You never listen to me or to Uncle Moritz... always obstinate and contrary! Night and day I worry about you. I have so many worries on your behalf! You couldn't care less! As far as you are concerned, your own poor Mommy can live or die! Well then, go ahead, do it! Be my death! Oh, oh, oh, what an unfortunate woman I am, to be the mother of such a son! What am I supposed to do with such a son! Whether I die or not, you don't care a damn! Poor, poor me, who must go through so much for your sake...

Ben, who at first felt frightened, now becomes furious:

– What sort of deranged accusation is that? You are totally hysterical! Haven't I myself the right to decide how I want to live my own life...

Mommy turns to her husband for support:

– Isn't it true, Moritzl? We have only his best interests at heart! Sweet Benny, listen to your own Mommy, I beg you, give it up! For my sake! It's for your own good, your own good!

Ben screams at the top of his voice:

– I bloody well know for myself what's for my own good!

This is more than Moritz will endure! Doesn't it say: *HONOUR THY FATHER AND THY MOTHER?* The threatening voice of the former non-commissioned officer now blares out:

– He is not to shout loudly in my home and be rude to his mother!

Desperately, Mommy reaches for the last means at her disposal, one that has never failed:

– My little Bennyboy, you do love your Mommy, don't you? For my sake! For your own sweet Mommy, darling! Be sensible! Your very own little Mommy loves you so much! If you really love me...

Moritz is shaking all over in exasperation. That brat has embittered his marriage!

– He can clear out! Raus! Los! Out! In the gutter, where he belongs! Raus auf die Strasse, into the street! Out of my house, clear out!

And he fetches Ben a blow right on his impertinent nose!

Ben has been humiliated for so many years, enough is enough! With all his strength he shoves his stepfather crashing up against the wall, raising his arm at long last – as he had dreamt of doing innumerable times – to strike his fist into his stepfather's detested face...

Mommy grasps his arm, hanging herself onto him, crying:

– No, no, you can't do that, Ben! No, no!

Ben has to let go of his stepfather, who quickly moves to a safe place on the other side of the dining table. Ben's heart is battering inside his chest. For the first time ever he'd dared to touch his stepfather, to show him his own strength. He would have murdered him! And just then, as Mommy would get in the way...

Moritz, shivering, wipes his glasses. He is really scared... Ben was actually going to hit him back! He had never experienced that before. His voice trembles:

– I forbid him ever again to set foot in my home!

Ben disengages himself from Mommy's hold:

– In his home, exactly! It was certainly never mine!

Ben leaves without closing the door. On his way down the stairs he hears Mommy sobbing:

– Ben, don't go! Stay! You can't leave like that, my son! Come back... Ben...

* * *

Dream: Ben is sitting on a ramshackle scaffolding. On the ground an enormous yellow-black striped tigress is watching him with its menacing, shining green eyes. The tigress begins to climb. She comes nearer, digging her sharp claws into the scaffolding rocking under her weight. Ben tries to get away, scrambling up to the top plank, from where he cannot escape. The woodwork creaks. The tigress reaches Ben, places herself heavily over him. He feels the hot breath of the animal on his face, but she does not claw him. Instead, the tigress opens her jaw, nuzzles his cheek with her fangs, but does not bite. Only her whiskers tickle his nose and his ears. The weight of the animal is so heavy that he is unable to move.

* * *

On November 9th there was to be a census. They said it was because some people had escaped. Ben had also considered running away, but realized that it was impossible. He couldn't rely on hiding with anybody, as the population probably was anti-Semitic... In Denmark it would have been different. There he could have expected protection by knocking on any door... Furthermore, he couldn't speak Czech either. And if they saw him naked, they would know that he was Jewish and then they would surely deliver him up to the Germans...

November 9th was an extraordinarily dangerous day for the Jews. It was the anniversary of Crystal Night, when the Nazis had killed many Jews, smashed up all Jewish shops and torched synagogues all over Germany.

Hitler wanted to avenge himself on the Jews, because the Germans had lost the First World War in 1918, so Uncle Moritz thought.

The order was for all of them, exept the most sick, to line up in the valley of Bauschevitz a few kilometres outside town.

They were to be standing there at 6 o'clock in the morning, so already at about 4 o'clock, in the middle of the cold black night, one had to get up and start walking out there. The room elder, the house elder, the block elder and the council of elders had the responsibility, on pain of death, to ensure that every single inmate, without exception, was present.

Ben is on his way, leaving the youth centre, as Mommy arrives, running with two men carrying a stretcher. She had talked to the Jewish mayor himself, saying that Ben was so ill that it was impossible for him to stand outside for such a long time. Ben was to lie down on the stretcher and lie very still, pretending to be seriously ill. They would carry him to the hospital, and that way he would be saved.

Isn't that odd? Ben isn't ill at all... And he would rather stay together with Mommy. He has his warm coat!

He is carried into a ward. Here he has to share a bed with an old man rattling constantly, whimpering like a baby, a sweet stench emanating from him, and staring at Ben with big bewildered eyes almost falling out of his emaciated face.

The hours pass and it begins to dawn. He is the only boy in the entire ward, all the others being old men. Nobody utters a word, they just moan all day.

Ben's stomach hurts as he lies there, hearing the frightening thunder of the aeroplanes which, from time to time, fly low over the houses. He hardly dares to move, because if he did, he would brush against the old man beside him. And the fleas!

At dinner time they get something to eat. It is only millet soup, not even a potato to go with it.

The old man isn't to have anything. He is rattling once again and then he is quite still. He has stopped breathing.

After endless hours it gets dark again. But it was long, very long before, late at night, footsteps and low mutters were heard. Now they finally got back to Theresienstadt, and at last, after another long while, Mommy arrives and hugs him passionately.

They had been so afraid out there in the valley all day long. There were soldiers with machine-guns pointing at them from the surrounding hills, and when the Germans flew low above their heads, they thought that they were going to be shot, all of them. They had the sensation of being saved again, so happy were they to see their safe, secure Theresienstadt again! Mommy is so glad to see her own Bennyboy!

Shortly after, Ben became seriously ill. He developed a high fever, his mind wandered, and he couldn't keep his food down. He was placed in the sick bay of the boys' home. They had a chair with a hole in it on which you sat to relieve yourself. That's why it was known as "Stuhlgang," to go on the chair.

Mommy came to see him every day during the lunch break. She was afraid that Ben had typhoid fever. After about a week, even Uncle Moritz came to see him. His stepfather had organized an apple, which he had smuggled through the gate. Ben got a third of the apple and Mommy and Uncle Moritz were to share the rest. But Mommy gave him her share as well, so that Ben got two-thirds of the apple.

He ate it very slowly, he hardly chewed it but let it dissolve by itself in his mouth.

After a couple of weeks Ben recovered and was allowed to move back to the boys' room. However, the doctor wrote a note which exempted Ben from working in the field, because he weighed less than 20 kilos. Ben also got one quarter of a litre of skimmed milk once a week as an extra ration for two months. Usually only children under five could get that. He could also go to the secret Danish school again.

In December they had their first *HANUKKAH* in their confinement. Of course, the Germans mustn't get wind of the celebration. It was held in the men's loft. Ben and Mommy and all the other Danes were present. The Chief Rabbi read the Hebrew prayers aloud as in the synagogue. It was the Festival of Lights on the darkest day of the year. Into the bargain, they had "organized" some real candles! On the eighth day they were all lit at the same time!

Little Jacob was allowed to light them. He was so proud standing there with a skullcap on his curly little head. It really looked wonderful with all the candles shining in the dark loft. Then they sang the Hanukkah song. Afterwards they had to sneak home to avoid being detected.

✴ ✴ ✴

Knud is rigging the boat down in the harbour. This year he and Birgit were to set out to Sweden's Skerries and for the first time he had engaged an able seaman. It was a little disappointing, going to sail without the boys. He was surprised and, of course, pleased that Kristian and Grete had become engaged. They were probably in France by now. He had lent them the Chevrolet, as he could easily make do with the Opel for everyday use. Grete was a really sweet girl. Knud had actually known her since she was a little lass with braids. She would certainly help and support Kristian in the writing his thesis. That would be a matter of great satisfaction to Knud... His son would certainly show those fellows at the university... Ben didn't want to go sailing with them either. He might have done it all the same.

* * *

Ben doesn't know what he is going to do with himself all summer, now that Grete and Kristian have gone on vacation. In the evenings he plays for hours at the grand piano in the drawing-room: Chopin's funeral march or the emotional adagio from Beethoven's Pathetique Sonata. Birgit is at her needlework, listening. Ben stops:

– I've rented a room at Frederiksberg. I'll pack my things tomorrow, before you leave.

Birgit stops working. She feels as if something is breaking inside her. What was she supposed to say? She can't interfere... can't hold him back:

– You know that you can stay here as long as you want to...

Ben knows. But it is not possible any more. After the showdown with Mommy and his stepfather he had lost something forever. He must get out, away from any kind of dependence. He must find his own self! Birgit... she understands him. All things would have been so easy with her...

– I am going to study languages after all. I have enrolled for German literature at the university.

Birgit feels a pang of disappointment:

– German? Why German of all..?

– I speak it already, you know...

Birgit had been so pleased, when Ben told her he wanted to be an actor, and now, all of a sudden, he is giving it up:

– But what about the stage?

– I can always have the stage as a hobby in my spare time.

Ben doesn't sound enthusiastic at all. Birgit has a notion of who is behind his choice:

– What does your mother think of it, then?

– Mother? I guess she is supposed to be quite satisfied.

– Supposed to..? What do you mean? Haven't you..?

– I've stopped seeing them!

Birgit looks at Ben:

I so much wanted the stage for you, Ben... well then, I really hope that you'll be happy with your choice...

Ben feels like a surgeon who inserts a sharp scalpel deep into the patient's flesh and nerve fibres without being affected by the fact that he is cutting a human being...

– By going to university I can get scholarships. And then I'll be studying something which is "sensible."

Birgit looks down at the floor. It is as if she is to take leave of a Ben whom she'll never know any more:

– You know that you can stay with us as long as you want to...

– I must look after myself now, I must find out how things are for myself!

* * *

They had to economize on the coal. They got only one bucket of coal for each room every third day, so they could afford a fire only at noon. Not even Lea's mother was able to make them cease their unending quarrelling about who was going to warm up food or sit nearest the stove...

It was so cold that everybody stole – sluiced off, as they called it – whatever they could find to burn in the stove. Even the children found stumps of wood and bits of branches, anything at all that could be used to heat with.

One day Ben came to the hut during his lunch break to find the whole room in commotion. Little Sara, who was only five, was gone.

Sara's mommy had given birth a few weeks before to a baby boy, even though it was forbidden for Jews to have children. She had, in fact, been pregnant when she was captured...

They had searched all morning and were absolutely desperate.

All the women were out, helping to look for the little girl. They were afraid that she might have run outside the barrier and been shot by the Germans, or had fallen into the moat and drowned. While they are in deep despair, Ben's Mommy comes running with Sara in her arms, crying out:

– I've found her! I've found her!

Little Sara had been walking along the road where it was deadly dangerous to pass! There she had found a large piece of wood, bigger and heavier than herself, and then the little girl had been lugging and toiling for several hours to smuggle the stump home, so that they could burn it in the stove... so that her new little brother shouldn't be cold.

Rebecca and her parents were very orthodox. Every day, when her father came to the women's hut, he said his prayers in Hebrew and kept his hat on while they ate together on the lower bunk in the corner.

Once in a while Rebecca's father talked with Ben, too, and he was very nice and kind to him. Then Ben would be both happy and sad at the same time.

The men who brought their meal to eat together with their wives had to stand up between the beds. As there were only a few seats at the table, Mommy always saw to it that Moritz could sit. Then she was the one who had to eat standing up.

Moritz had a job at the post office. With a small group of men, he had to go daily outside the barrier to fetch the mail from Bauschevitz station. Of course, it was under surveillance, but the guards were Czech gendarmes and they could be quite nice.

His stepfather had begun to get on top of things again and was always in an aggressive mood. He told all and sundry what a naughty boy Ben was. No matter how much Ben went out of his way not to upset him, his stepfather raged and scolded him. At such times, out of pure embarrassment, Ben would have liked to conceal himself in a little hole! At times like that Rebecca and the other children looked the other way, but Lea always glanced at him with her big eyes, and little Jacob also got frightened, so that he cried.

Sometimes his stepfather would throw him out. Then Ben had to eat alone outside the hut. He might just as well have stayed at the youth centre to eat with the other boys.

Once he had asked Kalle's mother to tell Mommy to come and see him at the boys' home, but Mommy never did, probably because Uncle Moritz was likely to be mad.

Next Lea got head lice. Her mother was so angry! She had been combing Lea's hair with the fine-toothed anti-lice comb every day till she cried, so much did it hurt, and then Lea anyway...

Lea was very upset when her mother dragged her along for delousing. Ben's mother said loudly enough for all to hear, that now they could see for themselves what kind of a mother Lea had.

Lea had her hair shaved off, her scalp rubbed with alcohol and tar, and she wore a towel round her head. Her scalp smarted and itched and smelled disgusting, but she was told to be glad that it wasn't worse! Her mother scolded her that it was really too awful that this should happen to her own daughter!

It would be long before her hair grew again. Lea had tears in her eyes, but her mother told her not to cry. A big girl didn't cry! Ben knew that feeling very well...

Eventually, Rebecca's father didn't come any more. He wouldn't eat food that wasn't *kosher*. When they had sauce or soup, naturally, it wasn't made according to Jewish precepts, so he didn't eat anything except bread and potatoes. At last he had lost so much weight that he couldn't survive any longer.

The winter never seemed to end. It continued to freeze, sometimes the temperature dropped to twenty degrees below zero.

John had to take more and more Danes to the crematorium.

✳ ✳ ✳

One day Uncle Moritz had been storming and raging yet again, because Ben had been sitting in Mommy's bed, so that the blanket had become crumpled. Only the presence of the other people prevented him from thrashing Ben, who crouched behind the bedpost making himself as inconspicuous as he could. Lea and Jacob hid themselves, just like Ben.

The grown-ups in the room didn't say anything, pretending that nothing was happening. Ben felt so ashamed. Mommy was so unhappy, she did not know what to do to smooth things over...

At long last Moritz stops roaring and sits down to eat the millet soup which Ben had brought. Slowly the others start talking again.

After a while Mommy embraces Ben, comforting him:

– Bennyboy, listen my dear, now you are a good boy again, aren't you? You know you have that fine watch, don't you my love? And you also know that Uncle Moritz had to hand in his gold watch. And he is a grown-up man! So he needs a watch much more than you do, you can understand that, can't you? You are only a child! Now if you give Uncle Moritz your watch... just as a loan, of course! Then I'm sure he will be fond of you. Then he can see what a nice boy you really are, and then Mommy will be so fond of you too, sweet Bennyboy, then you are my sweetest little boy whom I love more than anybody in the whole world!

Ben doesn't know for sure... He looks at his watch, the only present, the only thing he ever owned. Even the German had allowed him to keep it... Nobody else in all Theresienstadt owned a watch! But now Mommy gives him another hug:

– I will go and tell Uncle Moritz that he may borrow your watch, can't I, my own darling boy? You will have it back again, for sure. You will have it back again after the war, I promise you!

And Mommy reaches out her hand for the watch:

– Now, give it to me little Benny! You know that Mommy loves you so much...

Mommy kisses him again and Ben cannot resist, loosens his watch strap, and Mommy takes it and hides it quickly in her hand:

– I'll give it to Uncle Moritz a little later tonight... as a surprise. Then you bet he will be glad!

The next time Moritz did not scold Ben. He was proud to be the only one to have a watch! But he did not utter a word to Ben that he was glad that he could borrow it.

* * *

Ben's left hand moves at a furious pace over the keyboard. His fingers run like waves up and down the keys, each touch of his fingertips like a mild electric shock flashing from one key to the next. The bass roars and thunders, rising and falling like a storm incessantly approaching and withdrawing again. The fingers of his right hand, curved into a bow as strong as steel, hammer the triumphant fanfares in fiery staccato rhythms.

It is revolution! Rebellion against the oppressors, against gross power and tyranny! The murmuring bass has risen to a rumbling mass of sounds, rising in a crescendo to an overwhelming fortissimo. Ben's fingers strike the keys with the strength and passion of youth, the notes increase in dramatic ecstasy, rise higher and higher to a shrill climax... when suddenly he stops so the silence can be heard.

Ben holds his breath. Mommy has entered without his noticing. She is smiling admiringly:

– Oh Chopin, my dear boy, how sweet! Alas, do you remember, Bennyboy, when you were just little... How sweet it sounds!

Mommy unpacks the things she has brought in her bag, bustles about, takes off her coat, even her fine hat with the veil, bending down to Ben at the piano to make him kiss her, and doesn't notice that he barely touches her cheek with his lips.

Mommy is playing the eternal comedy for herself and for the whole world, that all is well and everyone is happy! She will not acknowledge the distance between herself and her son.

Ben feels spied upon. Here comes Mommy poaching on his preserve with all that stuff she is bringing. She should have given her presents to him at that time...

– I'm not playing "sweetly..."!

Mommy opens her eyes wide:

– You aren't? Then how are you playing?

– WELL! I'm playing well! Well! Well!

– Alright then, you are playing well... Are you content now?

Mommy does not really know what she is doing wrong. Sensing, though, that something still remains unsettled, she hastens to talk about other matters:

– Just look what Mommy has brought her own boy: A delicious Madeira cake. You like it so much, don't you! Do you recall, you once wanted to bake one for us? That's when you put rye flour into it instead of wheat flour... and you had to eat it by yourself!

Mommy is laughing.

– Yes, alas, what a sweet boy you were!

As Ben doesn't share the fun Mommy is having, she changes the subject again:

– How are you getting along with your studies? You never tell me anything.

Mommy wants so much to be on intimate terms with her boy, and honestly there is something which makes her suffer much pain:

– Why don't you ever come home to visit us? I know you see Mrs. Birgit often, but I am your mother, am I not?

Ben doesn't answer. After a while she says:

– Uncle Moritz asks after you so often!

– Will you stop that nonsense!

– But I swear to you, Uncle Moritz is really proud of you! He tells everybody how talented you are! He has told everyone at the synagogue, "Our son has been given the big scholarship..." He has always appreciated you, believe me.

– Yes, when I used to carry the dustbin down into the yard, he usually switched the light off in the room where I was doing my homework!

Mommy gives in. And now she discloses what she came for in the first place, as Moritzl has talked about it several times:

– There is something we are very sorry about, especially father...

Ben flares up:

– He has never been my father! What is all that idiotic nonsense? My own father, you took him away from me!

– How can you say such a thing, Benny?

– I found three postcards from him from Paris in which he asked after me. You hid them from me! My Daddy writes that he is longing for me, that he loves me... loves me! And he asks you to get me write to him. You stopped me from writing to him, yes you did!

– But your father ill-treated me! He never gave me a penny! I had the most terrible rows with Aron! Your father always came home drunk, he went to pubs with other women, and then he beat me... You must have felt it while I bore you under my heart: He beat me!

Ben doesn't really know what to think. The fact that his father hit his mother must be true. As a small boy he felt awfully sorry for his Mommy, he couldn't grasp that his own Daddy could do such a thing, and he had sworn that he would never be like his father, ever, ever! He had hated his father for it and had comforted his Mommy. But Daddy must have had some reason to do it. Mother must have infuriated him in some way... or made him unhappy! Maybe Mother had not just been the poor victim who had made his infant soul suffer for her...

All of a sudden he understands his father! Couldn't it be that his Daddy would much rather have stayed at home instead of going to pubs... It must have been horrible for him to lose every penny he owned! But Mother had always made it sound as if it were entirely his father's fault, that he had been so mean towards Mommy, that she didn't want to have his child.

But it was in fact having Daddy's own child that Mother rejected! It was she who didn't want to have him! How would his father have felt about that? Why did Mother go to the doctor to have the child, Ben himself, "removed"?

His own mother actually wanted to kill him before he was even born! Ben feels dizzy and only little by little he hears Mommy's voice coming from far away, feels her hand patting his cheek:

– You have always been my only comfort, my own faithful little soldier...

Ben is sad:

– You even begrudged my father one single greeting from me before the Gestapo took him away!

– But can't you understand, Bennyboy, how distressed I was? In all these years, Aron only once sent you a little money and some clothes... everything depended on me. He surely was a bad father, he was!

Ben becomes indignant:

– And what did you give me instead? When Moritz had been really hard on me, you consoled me by saying that my own father was much worse!

– But it's true, sweet Benny!

– It's a lie! It's in his letters. My Daddy loved me! AND I LOVE HIM! I was only two... when I saw him last, but I can still feel his warm embraces, when he lifted me up in his arms, I remember his eyes. I have missed him so much, need him, and you spoiled that for me! When you said he wasn't my father when we were in Horserød!

– That was only to save you from being taken with us to Theresienstadt!

– What was I to believe? I didn't care where we were going. Even if we were going to die, I didn't want you to send me away!

– But I wanted to rescue you, Bennyboy, even if something should happen to me! The day of the census, when we were to go out into the field at Bauschewitz, I talked to the Jew Elder in person and had you sent to the hospital even though you weren't ill... We were standing on the wet ground in rows from 5 o'clock in the morning while it was still dark, hour after hour, all day long. The Germans ordered us to give each other a clip over the ear, slap each other in the faces, as hard as we could. And if someone didn't strike hard enough, they hit him with their whip until he beat the other person with all his might... Hour after hour passed like this. There we stood, more than 50,000 people, and it had to be the correct number. They were counting us over and over again and we got nothing to eat or drink all day long... And then I was thinking of you, my own Bennyboy, and it consoled me to know that you weren't experiencing this hell too! It hurt so much all over the body, to be standing there so long, it was so cold, and it was raining and windy. The old people who couldn't endure standing up had to be supported by the others. Nobody was allowed to sit down. On the hills around us soldiers pointed machine-guns at us, and in the afternoon military aeroplanes were flying right above our heads. We thought for certain that we were going to be shot or bombed to death.

Mommy puts her arms around Ben:

– If we had been shot, it would have been a comfort to me to know that you were still alive...

– All the same I would rather have stayed with you! I was lying there, lying together with all the dying old men... alone. I was so scared, it was always the sick people who were sent on transport first...

Mommy is sorry. Why did they always talk at cross-purposes? She feels the need, the longing for confidence:

– Ben, it's such a long time ago. Fortunately we are both alive! Let's be happy that we have survived and not always quarrel. We do have one another!

– Do we really?

– Yes, we do have each other, dear Benny! But I'm only so sorry that... and Uncle Moritz too...

Ben gets angry again:
– He isn't my uncle either! Can't you stop it? You married him...
– But I had no alternative! I told you about it a hundred times! Without a husband, a woman is nobody at all!
– And so you got yourself another name. We didn't even have a name in common any longer! I, this little boy, always had to explain: I do have a mother too! It's the lady over there, that's my mother, yes she is! She only has another name!
– Because Moritz wouldn't adopt you, he would not! He didn't want you to inherit from him! If we, him and me, had a child together, he didn't want you to be his heir too!
– There you can see: Even after his death your dear Moritz begrudges me anything at all! I was outlawed. When I got letters, he just opened them and tore off the stamps! Off my letters! Even the stamps on the three postcards from my father he tore off, just stole them! And he opens your letters too and reads them, to this very day...
– Should I argue with him about that as well? I do have enough to struggle for all the same...
– Yes, you were always quarrelling! And it was always my fault. How you screamed, running round the dining-room table, with him after you! And then he bawled, pounding his fists on the table, that he would kick me out into the street, AUF DIE STRASSE!
– But my sweet Bennyboy, your uncle... I mean Moritz, couldn't have been as bad as that. Now you are exaggerating!
– Exaggerating? One night – I was always alone in the house – I had used some matches. I knew very well that it was strictly forbidden. I also knew the story of Paulinchen from the book and how she was burned to a heap of ashes, so I struck the matches over the lavatory bowl so that nothing could happen. But you discovered it when you came home, and you woke me up, and you said that I was going to be punished the next day. I was so frightened that I caught a fever. I was in bed for three days with nightmares, so scared to death was I of Moritz's punishment. Not until three days later did the fever drop. Then, I thought, you might feel pity for me and perhaps show mercy. But for me, little sinner, there was no mercy! In my world, forgiveness for my crime was not possible. I got, after three days of waiting, a thrashing I never forgot...
Mommy presses him to her breast:
– I also regretted so much that I had told Moritz when I found the spent matches! And then you didn't come home after school the next day. I called

the headmaster and was told that you hadn't even been to school. I was in despair and phoned Mrs. Birgit and she, too, became terribly worried. I explained to her that you had to learn how dangerous it is to play with fire. We waited all night with your dinner. You never told me where you were that whole day...

* * *

Ben had been running about in the streets of Copenhagen... If he ran to Kristian's place they would, of course, ask what was wrong. Then he ran down to the harbour and watched the men fishing. They didn't catch anything for a long time.

Finally, one of the men got a bite, pulled a small fish out of the water and put it into a sack. He smiled at Ben several times, asking what was he doing there, if he wasn't supposed to be at school. Ben got afraid that the man would report him to the police. So he took himself off so quickly that he was nearly run over crossing the street. The car driver was forced to brake, tyres squealing, and he shouted that Ben ought to look where he was going, stupid good-for-nothing! Then Ben had run into a yard, where he hid in an empty bicycle shed. There he waited for many hours until he was sure that the police were not after him.

Following that, he had run past the imposing statue of the naval hero Niels Juel, who with outstretched arms directs all the tramcars from his high pedestal.

It had become dark and there were a lot of people in the street. They were so busy going in and out of the shops that, fortunately, they did not notice Ben. He had run past the Nikolaj Church with its high tower, towards High Bridge Square, where the fishermen's wives were shouting with their hoarse voices. Ben could not understand a single word they said, as they scraped off fish scales and wrapped fish up in newspaper with their numb red fingers, scratched and chapped like old carrots.

Ben went on up to the Town Hall Square, where he stopped by the Little Bugler and looked at him for a long time. The infant soldier up there had been hit by an enemy bullet. He was a hero, and the grown-up soldier who carried the dying boy on his shoulders loved him.

It had begun to rain. Ben got wet and cold. The lights from the houses and cars cast their reflections on the black asphalt. Should he run home now? He simply did not dare to. They would have had dinner by then, it was far too late... and what would Uncle Moritz not do to him?

Ben kept on running through the penetrating rain. Each time he saw a policeman he hid or ran the other way. What was he to do? Should he hide in some cellar and sleep there tonight? He was soaked to the skin, shivering with cold. At the end he had just kept running in the same direction the tram took and finally reached the villa.

All the other houses were in darkness, but here there were lights in the windows. He had rung the bell and Doctor Knud had opened the door at once.

– Ben, do you know that it is past midnight?

Father Knud had taken Ben inside, Birgit took off his wet clothes, gave him some of Kristian's, and wrapped him up in a warm woollen blanket.

Kristian was still not in bed. Ben got some hot chocolate and two egg yolks mixed with sugar, after which the boys were allowed to play, even though it was the middle of the night.

While they were playing with Kristian's soldiers, Ben occasionally glanced at Knud and Birgit talking in low voices. He caught Birgit's eyes and could hear her ask:

– Can't we keep him here?

But Knud shook his head:

– We must take him home to his mother. She is worried, of course. You had better phone her and say that I am on my way with him.

Then Knud had lifted Ben up. First Ben tried to shout:

– No, I don't dare go home! I want to stay here forever!

But then he gave in, and father Knud promised to go with him all the way up to Mommy and see to it that he wasn't punished. Birgit would phone Uncle Moritz himself and tell him not to beat him.

Doctor Knud held Ben's hand tight all the way up to the fifth floor. Mommy opened the door and Doctor Knud talked to her and also to Uncle Moritz, before he said goodbye to Ben, who had to let go of his hand to go inside.

Mommy was so happy. She kissed Ben and put him to bed at once. Nothing happened to him. Afterwards his stepfather did not mention Ben's running away.

✳ ✳ ✳

Ben had a new pair of boots. They were watertight, so that he could now work in the fields without getting his feet wet. They were several sizes too big for him, but he just stuffed them with straw.

In breaks from work, as usual he always went to the women's hut to eat with mother.

Months went by. The winter was cold, seemingly it would never end. Sometimes transports arrived with thousands of unhappy people, sometimes transports went off with even more unhappy people. Nobody knew where they were going.

Spring came at last and it started to get warmer.

One night he was sitting outside the hut, talking to Rebecca. They were watching the sky, where the first stars were appearing. Rebecca pointed up:

– My Daddy is up there! I think he is looking down at me right now... Yes, I'm sure he is!

Ben looks up at the stars, too. It was as if some of them were twinkling... could it be that his own father was up there too, looking down at him?

∗ ∗ ∗

Ben was liberated from the hard labour of digging earth on the ramparts. He was placed again in a pottery workshop. The man there had been a professor at the Academy of Fine Arts in Vienna. There were also two ladies making urns out of wet clay. Ben lent a hand in placing the urns in the kiln and putting them on shelves. It was a pleasant job, because nobody scolded him.

With summer, Mommy became very ill. She was in bed as well the day Ben completed his fourteenth year. She could hardly speak when she whispered congratulations to him. She had become thin, weighing a mere thirty kilos. Uncle Moritz was nervous and very solemn. Ben couldn't imagine that Mommy could die...

Fortunately, and quite unexpectedly, Ben received a parcel from the Danish Red Cross. Ben himself went to the post office to sign the receipt. Uncle Moritz was watching how the Czech gendarme checked that the parcel was really for Ben. The coffee and the cigarettes were taken out, they were contraband and were to be given to the Germans, and the gendarme also removed a big sausage, placing it inside his pocket.

In the parcel there was cheese, oatmeal, crispbread, butter, milk powder, and some bacon... INCREDIBLE! Now Mommy got real food! It did her good, and little by little she recovered her strength again.

From now on all prisoners from Denmark received food parcels from the Red Cross once a month. The Danes, who used to be the poorest in Theresienstadt, suddenly became the richest of all the Jews.

The professor at the workshop was modelling a clay horse, which Ben admired very much. Ben also tried to work with clay, and even though he had never done it before, Ben also made a horse, a powerful drayhorse with a round stomach and muscular legs. The professor praised it highly, saying that Ben could certainly go on to become an artist.

The urns they produced at the pottery were to be filled with flowers and placed in a park, because a commission from Denmark was expected to visit the ghetto. The park was supposed to look like a real cemetery, with nameplates on the graves and the ashes in urns.

In actual fact the dead weren't buried at all, but their ashes kept in cardboard boxes in the casements under the rampart. So the ashes had to be removed. Obersturmbannführer Rahm ordered all Danish children to throw the ashes of the dead into the river.

There was a sense of outrage. First the mothers refused to let their children do such a thing. But it was rumoured that if the children didn't obey the order, they would go on the transports. Even Lea's mother, who had protested most of all, had to give in.

It took all day to carry the boxes down to the water and empty them. The boxes were to be collected afterwards. They could, of course, be used again.

Little Lea was so scared. The Nazi had been bellowing all the time:

– Hurry! Schneller! Los! Los! Quicker!

They cracked their whips on their long black boots, and when Lea opened the cardboard boxes to pour the ashes into the water, there were frequently bits of bone amongst them.

Lea cried and Ben put her head, wrapped up in a cloth, against his shoulder.

Rebecca was silent for a long time, just gazing into the air... then she confided to Ben that while she had been throwing the ashes into the river she happened to read the name on one of the boxes, and it had been her father...

* * *

One day, unexpectedly, Obersturmbannführer Rahm enters the ceramic workshop. He wants to see how many urns they had produced. As he discovers the professor's and Ben's horses he is beside himself with rage.

Ben, who luckily happens to stand behind the urn shelves, crouches so that he cannot be seen, while the German is beating and kicking the professor, who has fallen on the floor:

– Judenschwein! Damned! To Auschwitz with you, pig! Jewish swine, dirty sheeny! To the gas chamber, filthy Jew!

In his frenzy, the Gestapo officer pushes the shelves so that the whole pile of urns tumbles crashing down on Ben's back, burying him completely.

Ben is aching all over when he arrives the following day to clean up the place. The professor is gone. He had been taken to the Little Fortress.

✳ ✳ ✳

Ben walks to the window and cannot stop thinking of his childhood:

When we came to Denmark you let me stay with Grandma for a year, you let me live with her for a whole year!

– But I was forced to do it, dearest Benny... And Grandma was nice to you, wasn't she? I know she went to the Tivoli Gardens with you.

Ben shook his head:

– Do you know what Grandma called me, when she thought I was naughty? Murderer! She called me a murderer, and I was five years old!

Mommy is astounded:

– I cannot believe that, Bennyboy... How could Grandma ever say such a thing to you? It can't be true Benny, you are mistaken!

And Mommy makes the oppressed little girl inside her, who would have experienced a thing like that, become silent.

Ben continues:

– And when I was allowed to stay with you later on, I had to sleep in the forbidden room.

– But in this way I got you home with me. After all, it was better than staying with Grandma! And I always did come to put you to bed, to say the night prayers with you, didn't I, Benny dear?

– You prayed to God and the angels that they should protect me, and I didn't dare to turn round in my sleep, lest I scratch the polished mahogany sofa I was sleeping on. It came out anyway! There was a terrible quarrel between the owner and you, we were thrown out of the flat, and you had to pay damages to the man, and again it was my fault!

– But we were refugees, Benny! We were at risk of being sent back to Germany. A lot of people were much worse off. They had to sleep in the street! We must be happy that Moritz was able to get us a roof over our heads... a home!

– A home! Moritz grudged me my food! I lived off his charity! As if I were

stealing something from him when I ate... And then I had to be grateful that I didn't starve like the small Chinese children who were dying in the streets!
– Bennyboy! I was afraid of him too! You must know that! I'm still afraid of him to this very day! He always gets so terribly violent when he gets angry. But... where should I go if I were to leave him?
Mommy recalls her awful fear and loneliness as a little girl:
– My mother tied me to a chair when I was a small child. Daddy was never at home. I was convinced that Grandma couldn't be my real mother, I thought she was my stepmother, since she could be so cruel to me! Once I ran away from home to my aunt. I was only four years old... I couldn't believe that she was really my own mother...
Now Ben shouts:
– I don't give a damn about Grandma tying you to a chair! I couldn't care less! You've told me about it a thousand times! That has nothing to do with me!
For a long time Ben and Mommy do not talk. Then Ben starts to play the piano to get rid of the thoughts which keep on whirling inside his head. He wished that mother would leave him alone. He also had to prepare his homework for tomorrow...

* * *

In the lofts of the barracks, in the basements and wherever else you could imagine, religious services were held, lectures delivered or cabarets and chamber music performed. It wasn't allowed, but the Germans apparently shut their eyes to it.
During the summer, these activities didn't have to be secret any more. They were now – with the exception of school teaching and services – actually ordered by the Gestapo!
A leisure and culture department was established, musical instruments were brought to the ghetto from the opera house in Prague, and the Germans encouraged the Jews to compose satiric songs about the "merry" life in Theresienstadt.
Commandant Rahm himself sent for the actors to entertain him, and praised the artists when the songs were really ironic and politically audacious. Did the Nazis really mean so well by the Jews?
Sometimes Ben went to the revues. One of the songs was sung in Vienna waltz time by a well-known actor with the refrain: *THERESIENSTADT, YOU*

ARE OUR OWN, THE WORLD'S MOST BEAUTIFUL TOWN! It was, of course, on everybody's lips:

> *– THERESIENSTADT, THERESIENSTADT*
> *YOUR SUNNY DAYS MAKE ME SO GLAD*
> *WHAT DELICIOUS MEALS WE ALWAYS GET*
> *WHAT JOLLY AND HAPPY DAYS, YOU BET!*
> *THERESIENSTADT, YOU ARE OUR OWN,*
> *THE WORLD'S MOST BEAUTIFUL TOWN!*
>
> *HERE OUR LIFE IS CHEERFUL AND LIGHT*
> *JUST AS OUR PROPERTY HAS LOST ITS WEIGHT*
> *WHEN AFTER TWELVE HOURS' TOIL AND MOIL*
> *I SING YOUR PRAISE AMIDST THE SOIL:*
> *THERESIENSTADT, YOU ARE OUR OWN,*
> *THE WORLD'S MOST BEAUTIFUL TOWN!*
>
> *WE LIVE HERE IN OUR OWN LITTLE TOWN*
> *PROTECTED, SECURE. QUITE ON OUR OWN*
> *EVEN IF DEEP IN OUR HEARTS WE ARE CONCEALING*
> *A LONGING, A HOPE WE ALL ARE FEELING:*
> *THERESIENSTADT, YOU ARE OUR OWN,*
> *THE WORLD'S MOST BEAUTIFUL TOWN!*

They also sang about the Jewish tourist who had paid a fortune to the German state to undergo treatment at *TEREZIN SPA,* having been told it was a health resort with hotels and modern conveniences. One of the popular songs was about the town *"AS IF"*:

> *– THE PEOPLE HERE ARE LIVING*
> *AS IF IT WAS A LIFE WORTH LIVING*
> *REJOICING OVER EVERY RUMOUR*
> *AS IF IT REALLY WAS WORTH BELIEVING*
> *AND EVERYBODY WALKS IN THE STREETS*
> *AS IF HE WERE JUST PROMENADING*
>
> *THEY DRINK THEIR COFFEE IN THE MORNING*
> *AS IF THE LIQUID WAS WORTH DRINKING*
> *AND EAT THE DIRTY POTATO PEELS*
> *AS IF THEY WERE DELICIOUS MEALS*
> *WRITING LETTERS TO HUSBANDS, TO WIVES*
> *AS IF THEY HAD NEWS ABOUT THEIR LIVES*

YOU BEAR IMPRISONMENT AND SORROW
AS IF FREEDOM AND PEACE IS TOMORROW.

Of course everybody wondered if they'd ever be liberated again, and when the Danish rabbi walked in the streets, he always nodded encouragingly to whomever he met:

– Yes, we will soon go home again, we'll soon be home...

There was also a song which Ben liked very much about the Prater Park in Vienna:

– UNDER THE TREES IN THE PRATER PARK
THERE IS A PLACE ONLY YOU AND I KNOW
COULD IT BE WE WILL EVER MEET THERE AGAIN?
THEY SEPARATED US, THEY SENT YOU TO THE EAST
AND I AM IN THERESIENSTADT
COULD IT BE THAT WE EVER MEET THERE AGAIN?
BUT FOR DREAMS THERE AREN'T ANY BARRIERS
EVERY SINGLE DAY I KEEP YOU IN MY MIND

The Germans ordered an orchestra to be formed, and when they asked for musicians, Ben offered himself, as he could play the trumpet. He was the only boy in the orchestra, the others were all adult musicians, some of them from a famous orchestra, the Koncertgebouw in Amsterdam. There were no fewer than ten musicians from the Koncertgebouw, and one of them was the first violin, the concert-master himself. Three other Danes were there too, Rebecca's big brother on the violin, and a saxophonist and a conductor from Denmark's radio, so the whole orchestra consisted of more than forty members.

When Uncle Moritz heard Ben had been accepted by the orchestra, he called him "The Wise Trumpeter of Gotham" and laughed mockingly as if he were being very funny. But Mommy was very proud of Ben.

Ben played together with the first trumpeter, Gokkes, while his young wife played the clarinet. She had dark curly hair and sparkling eyes. She was so beautiful... Ben's cheeks turned red every time he so much as glanced at her.

Once, during the rehearsals, one of the violinists got up. He was the one sitting by the last desk of the second violinists, a quiet and modest man, who used to be very reserved. But now he began to play. He'd never done that before, play solo. He played Dvorak's famous Humoresque...

Everyone looked at him in surprise. He was now playing with such fervour, such passion, abandoning himself totally, singing and crying out his sorrow with the music, and... in the finale, at last, he exposed all his rage, vented all his anger at being imprisoned, humiliated, at the threat to his life. It sent a shiver down Ben's spine.

When he had finished playing and the last note had died away, he remained there, letting his bow fall slowly...

For a long while there was complete silence. At long last the first violinist exclaimed:

– This was magnificent... marvellous!

The violinist glanced around at them all, and at Ben. He had tears in his eyes. With his music he had taken them all with him, far far away, beyond the barbed wire, out into freedom...

In the middle of the large square in front of the church, a bandstand was built, and benches and flowerpots were set up for promenade concerts.

Originally they were to play only Jewish music but this was changed, so that they could play all sorts of music. Especially they were ordered to play operettas and other kinds of merry tunes. They played selections from the Czardas Princess and the Fledermaus, and Ben liked very much the intermezzo from Cavalleria Rusticana and the Light Cavalry Overture, in which the trumpets struck up the melody. They also performyed the Copenhagen March, which Ben knew so well from the Tivoli Boys' Guard. The conductor just changed the title, so that it was called the Theresienstadt March. They all thought that was very funny.

When the concert was to begin, it was Ben's duty to bring the conductor, Peter Deutsch, his baton. Ben walked up to Maestro Deutsch, who was waiting for him at his desk, and laid the baton on his music stand. When Ben returned to his own place, they could start playing.

The musicians devoted themselves to the music heart and soul and while performing they smiled at Ben blowing his trumpet as best he could. They regarded him as their little mascot.

– Cheerful as can be! Theresienstadt is such a nice and jolly place to live in, isn't it!

Obersturmbannführer Rahm himself arrived to encourage the musicians. There he stood with his officers, in cap and shining boots, long-legged, cross-armed, fiddling around with his horsewhip, listening with the air of an expert. The Jewish Elder hinted that the SS commandant was a very musical, highly cultured person.

The Café was opened as well. Here jazz was played by the Ghetto Swingers, American music which was forbidden in Germany! Sometimes Ben joined them too: *WHERE IS THE TIGER* or *BEI MIR BIST DU SCHAIN.*

The Sports building was turned into a concert and opera house. They performed Tales of Hoffmann with fine scenery brought from Prague. In the Doll's Aria, the singer moved just as stiffly as a real doll as she sang. Ben was fascinated. They also performed a ballet, Tschaikowsky's The Waltz of the Flowers, and while Ben was playing in the orchestra, Kalle took care of the lights and John drew the curtains.

Verdi's Requiem was practiced with a choir of more than ninety singers and famous soloists. The latter had sung in the greatest theatres of Europe, and now they were singing here in Theresienstadt! It was very hard work to learn the piece, but finally it was performed at a gala at which Ben and Gokkes played the difficult fanfares. SS Commandant Rahm, even Adolf Eichmann and other Nazi bigwigs who had come to Theresienstadt for the occasion, sat in the front row of the audience.

The boys and girls from Ben's home performed a children's opera in Czech. It was called "Brundibar," and was about children fighting for freedom against oppressors. The children played all the parts themselves and, of course, Ben had the trumpet solo in the orchestra. It was fantastic, staged many times, and at the home the boys and girls talked a lot about the experience.

Once they held a festive folk music evening. All the different nationals performed their dances and music. It was a gigantic succes. The Czechs danced in their native costumes, as did the Germans, the Austrians, the Dutch and the Hungarians. They all sang in their own language, and they even presented Jewish folk dances and ballads in Hebrew! A famous singer rendered My Yiddishe Mama in Yiddish. All of it with the permission of the SS Obersturmhanufführer. You could hardly believe it!

The Danish children performed, too. Led by Lea and Rebecca they sang:

– YOU GET SO HAPPY WHEN THE SUN IS SHINING
THAT YOU FORGET ALL YOUR WANT AND WORRY!

And the girls brought down the house!

For such a night, it was difficult to get tickets. Some people gave up to two full bread rations or four cigarettes for a ticket.

* * *

It was not very long before Uncle Moritz began to storm and rage again. One day, when Ben arrives at the hut with his food, Mommy is sitting on her bed crying. There had been an enormous quarrel and everyone in the room had been against Mommy, especially Lea's mother! They no longer wanted to see how Ben was treated, they were living so close to one another that they couldn't help noticing it...

– Circumstances are difficult enough as they are!

And then Lea's mother had called Mommy an unnatural mother!

Ben hugs and comforts Mommy. He doesn't know what to do to make Mommy stop being sad. And Mommy kisses Ben and keps on crying, asking again and again:

– I am not an unnatural mother, am I?

Ben shakes his head, clinging to Mommy, and cried:

– No, you aren't!

Then Mommy claspes Ben, shouting at the others in the room:

– There you are! My Bennyboy is on my side! You can see for yourselves how much he loves me!

And Mommy holds Ben even tighter. But nobody in the room says a word.

When Uncle Moritz arrives, Mommy tells him all about it, and it is a long time before she calms down enough so she could eat again.

Afterwards Mommy said to Ben that he mustn't ever talk to Lea's mother, never again, nor to Lea! Because they had been so wicked towards her, to call her an unnatural mother!

And yet, when Ben was sitting behind the last hut in the evening, Lea came and sat down next to him. The fact was that Lea's mother had also told her not to talk to Ben, so they hardly said anything to each other. But now and then she slipped her hand into Ben's hand, and he acted as if nothing had happened and kept it there.

✳ ✳ ✳

That summer Ben moved out of the villa into a rented room. Sometimes Mommy comes to see him. She always brings him something and sits down to talk, as if nothing had happened between them. When she comes home to Moritz, she tells him that she had been visiting the Jewish old people's home. Ben keeps asking himself why Mother doesn't just tell his stepfather the truth! Moritz couldn't be so stupid, that he does not know where she is going, when Mother sneaks away with a full bag.

One day Mommy even brings her rich sister from America. That has to take place secretly, too. Moritz was certainly not to know anything about it. His aunt presents him with a pencil and notebook. Mother is enthusiastic:

– Ben likes that! He certainly needs it very much, now that he is going to be a learned scholar!

The aunt also brought some cast-off clothes from her millionaire husband, all the way from America, top-quality, almost new! But unfortunately, they do not fit Ben, nor does it pay to have them altered.

Ben enjoys working hard. He attends lectures and studies till the small hours of the night. Scholarships you cannot get until you have passed the first part of your exam, so Ben earns money by teaching German, English and French at the evening school. And Italian, too, although he is only a few lessons ahead of his own pupils. He also collects old newspapers for the paper collection, tries his hand unsuccessfully as a seller of sun ray lamps, gets up in the morning at 6 o'clock to deliver milk and bread, and sells Christmas trees in December, and that was certainly a cold job!

On Christmas Eve he even becomes a popular Santa Claus, riding on his bike from one home to another, handing out presents to little children, and singing Christmas carols with them. He meets sparkling children's eyes when giving them their presents, wrapped in multi-coloured gift paper with bows around them. In this way, even Ben experiences the joy of a Christmas feast!

In every home he is offered a glass of port wine or liqueur, so Ben is pretty well plastered when, finally, late at night, he arrives home.

The three musketeers still stick together. They meet in the students' canteen to have lunch together, but as Ben is studying at the Faculty of Arts, he gradually makes new acquaintances, with others apart from Grete and Kristian, who in turn, find themselves other friends from among the medical students.

Once in a while, Ben also comes to the villa. Birgit and Knud are really pleased each time. Then he goes to the piano and plays, while Grete and Kristian read anatomy.

But Ben can't help feeling the social difference between himself and the sons and daughters of the well-to-do citizens in that respectable suburb of Copenhagen. He doesn't feel comfortable in his shabby clothes in parties in the company of Kristian and Grete's elegant friends.

By himself, Ben also reads Stanislavsky's books about acting and learns the great young male parts in "Ghosts" by Henrik Ibsen, "Winter Solstice" by Maxwell Anderson and even "Hamlet" itself! But it was prohibitively expensive to pay for lessons with one of the great actors in Copenhagen; so, in the course of the winter, Ben gives them up.

* * *

There was great excitement in the ghetto. They not only expected a visit from the Red Cross and a commission from the Danish Foreign Office, but on top of it, a film was to be made about life in Theresienstadt. Therefore the whole town was to be made to look nice: BEAUTIFICATION was the command!

The Jews had to build a playground with swings and sandpits for the small children. Flowers and grass were sown in the square, and the grass seed came from Denmark! The streets were to be washed with soapy water. The pavements must be so clean, that you can lick them! The women were on their knees in the streets, scrubbing with all their might the roadways made of earth. Woe to the person who left a dirty spot...

A new wooden building furnished with tables and benches was built, supposedly a dining hall! The cemetery with the new urns was nicely decorated with Jewish stars, and all the facades of the houses were washed and painted in beautiful colours.

Some of the most distinguished Danes, the chief rabbi and other so-called prominent people, were now to live together as families. Each family got a whole room to itself, with furniture, tables and chairs. Flower pots were placed in window sills and curtains on the windows. The Jew Elder got a big carpet and a grand piano in his reception room, and every person was told exactly what he was supposed to answer to the questions from the Danish visitors. It was extremely important for everybody to look happy and satisfied. Anyone saying anything negative about the living conditions, they would be sent to the Little Fortress. To free more space in the ghetto, 7,000 old people were sent on transport.

Then the Danish delegates arrived. They had a personal greeting to the chief rabbi from King Christian X himself. The rabbi was proud, indeed: Now we could all see that he was a personal friend of the king! The Nazis were all smiles and politeness, but the Danish Nazi from Horserød was there, so that it was impossible to say anything in Danish to the commission about the reality of their situation.

It was prohibited for old and underfed people to show themselves in the streets. Everything looked clean and bright and comfortable. The distinguished guests visited some of the nice Danish family homes, the weather was splendid, and Ben played in the orchestra at the promenade concert in the square. They played melodies from the Merry Widow, and chosen townsfolk in nice clean clothes sat on benches in the sunshine among flower pots, enjoying the music. In the Café, others were having a good time drinking coffee at small tables, listening to cheerful swing music, and in the evening there were concerts, opera and ballet as well!

For the children in the playground, the SS leader had delicious sardine sandwiches. He was smiling, patting them on their sweet little heads, while the children had practiced reciting: "Dear Uncle Rahm, we really don't feel like eating more sardines!"

When the Danish commission on its walk through the town asked the rabbi if the children went to school, he could show them a building with a sign on the front door saying: *VACATION!* But when the holidays are over, the children will be taught again, of course.

Furthermore, the Danish delegates saw how the pea soup was dished up in large quantities, and everybody got lots of potatoes and a delicious meat sauce in the fine new dining hall where a small number of Jews were eating that day. Ben was lucky to be chosen to eat there. He stuffed himself full with the food, and on top of it he got yet another portion, so that he couldn't eat even a bit more.

Well, the commission went home to Denmark again with a greeting from the rabbi, just as personal as the one he had received from the king. They had, indeed, got a positive impression, that everyone actually led a fairly good way of life in the Jewish model town of Theresienstadt.

✳ ✳ ✳

Later on that summer of 1944, the making of the film was directed by an actor among the prisoners, Kurt Gerron. The cameramen and technicians were all professional people living in the ghetto as well. But, of course, everything was done under the control of Obersturmbannführer Rahm. He devoted himself – artist that he was – to putting all his heart into the enterprise.

From the film you could see clearly how well off the Jews were... much better off than the poor German population, who had to suffer from cruel bombardment by the Allies.

In the course of the filming, Ben was made to strike up a dance tune at the Café, where the most well-fed young Jews were called in. They were chosen from among those who looked typically Jewish, preferably with big noses. They were supposed to look happy and to appear to enjoy themselves very much. The scene was retaken several times, until it was to the full satisfaction of the director and the camp commandant.

All of a sudden the professor from the pottery was there again. Ben could hardly recognize him, so emaciated and bruised was he. He had a deep wound on one side of his head. He was modelling a big figure, a mermaid riding a fish, and he was made up so that you couldn't see his wounds while he was filmed. Afterwards, the professor vanished again.

There were scenes of Jews working happily and eagerly in the tailor's and the joiner's workshops. Kalle was filmed working in a shoemaker's shop, and some women appeared producing fashionable dresses and handbags, which in fact were sent to Germany.

Some men, who weren't yet too emaciated, were filmed while they were having a nice hot shower, and Jewish scientists were shown delivering lectures and borrowing books from the library well stocked with volumes from Jewish homes in Prague.

In the film you could see the Jews going to concerts. The audience was handed some clothes from the store, so that people looked well-dressed while they applauded their own Jewish composers and artists.

At the children's opera all the spectators were children. Little Jacob and Lea, with a fine headscarf, were there too, applauding. A film was made of how the children were playing in the kindergarten, dancing and eating delicious margarine sandwiches, and how they were amusing themselves with the Danish clown Hambo.

Ben was also present as a spectator, when they were ordered to watch a football match in the yard of the Hamburger barracks, and he was cheering and yelling when there was a score, as they had been told to do.

Lea participated in a school lesson, where the teacher taught the children Hebrew, and the girls were ordered to do gymnastics in the field, and this was filmed.

The Germans' allotments with the delicious vegetables were filmed too, pretending they belonged to Jewish families, and on a lovely sunny day some of the most beautiful young girls were chosen to splash about in the river, dressed in bathing suits. Commandant Rahm himself participated in selecting them. The filming lasted from early in the morning to late in the evening, so the girls were chilled to the bone when it was finally over. You could actually see from the film how the Jews were enjoying the seaside– and holiday life, while the Germans had to toil and moil in the war industry.

* * *

What they feared most of all were the transports. They knew that they went to Auschwitz, even though it was never said openly, and then they hoped each time that it wasn't... Because in Auschwitz, it was known, there were gas chambers. But that was never uttered in so many words either, as if they could exorcise death, deny its presence, by not pronouncing it aloud. One just never had any news at all from those who went on the transports.

There had been a few labour transports for young men willing to toil in return for being promised enough to eat. Ben had been watching a young Czech packing his things to go on a labour transport. What strong muscles and arms he had... But he never returned either.

When the camp commandant gave a transport order, the Jewish leaders were made to see to it themselves that it was carried out. The register of the ghetto was examined. The Jew Elder Paul Eppstein was very nervous, because if there were any mistakes, he would end up in the Little Fortress like his predecessor.

The transport orders always came as a complete surprise, even though Ben could almost figure it out, as it happened every time just after Commandant Rahm had soothed the council of elders by saying that now all transports were finished.

One could never tell who was to go. Sometimes all sick people, sometimes all healthy people, then only old people, at other times only youths, or only men, or solely females...

One day the order came for all handicapped and mentally ill people. At the youth centre where Ben was living, there were two Mongoloid children in the next room. They were suddenly picked up and disappeared.

Then the Germans promised that henceforth there would be no more transports, and again everybody breathed a sigh of relief.

But when the film was completed, in the autumn, a transport order was given all the same: 3000 men over sixty years old. And then one more: This time 3000 women!

Then everybody despaired. Married couples were separated, children taken from their parents... but one could give oneself up voluntarily to go together with one's partner. Many people ran to the registration office to try to have the order changed, or they tried to buy themselves out... There was a traffic, a bargain with life and fate. People were willing to give anything, bread or jewelry smuggled into the camp, just to remain in dear Terezin, where you were living so well, so securely, as it was said in the song. But there was nothing to be done. Orders are orders.

Those who were chosen for a transport had to report the night before. They could bring a rucksack, and dragged about with them all the best things they had brought or had obtained by trading. They were hardly going to

Auschwitz if they were allowed to bring luggage on the transport, were they...?

The prisoners from Denmark were never selected for transports, and after some time it was confirmed that the Danes were exempted. But could you rely on that? In any case, the Danes in particular were ordered to be transport helpers.

It always left early in the morning. Then they had to help the people who had been waiting all night into the cattle trucks. The German officers counted them again and again, because the number had to be exactly right.

And then a new transport order: 3000 women over 60 years old... and then another 2000!

The departure of the transports could last for weeks. Sometimes the cabaret singers or the jazz muscians from the Café were ordered to come and play, because the SS soldiers wished to have a little entertainment while they were supervising the human beings being loaded into the railway carriages.

That's when the Germans, together with the Jewish entertainers, sang *THERESIENSTADT, YOU ARE MY OWN, THE WORLD'S MOST BEAUTIFUL TOWN*, and it seemed as if the Germans in their enthusiasm actually meant it, that it was so nice to be here...

Now and then they would hit people if they were not moving fast enough: 100 into each wagon! That was twice as many in one car as there had been when Ben was travelling to Theresienstadt. The prisoners had to be helped up and to stand, packed into the carriages like sardines.

When they received the feared call-up notice, it said that they could bring thirty kilos of luggage with them, but of course there wasn't room for it in the train. All their belongings, which they had scraped together, were to be left behind.

All of it was to be collected, and Mommy and Lea's mother were commanded to unscrew the artificial legs and arms of those men who had lost their limbs fighting for Germany in the First World War, before the poor devils were helped into the wagons. Mommy and Lea's mother became very grave and didn't quarrel at all.

– They won't need them where they are going! SS-Haindl guffawed, and it was clear to everybody that the voyage was to Auschwitz anyway. Some cried and whimpered, but most of them didn't say anything, they just let themselves be pushed into the cattle trucks.

People also had to hand in their glasses. An elderly married couple gave Kalle and Ben their gold rings for four cigarettes, which Kalle had obtained. The man and his wife had been married for more than thirty-five years, and now they knew that they would not need their wedding rings, which they had smuggled into Theresienstadt. They might as well profit from the rings for the last time and enjoy the cigarettes together. Kalle and Ben got one ring each, and Ben gave it to Mommy who exchanged it for two bread rations.

The luggage, the glasses and the artificial limbs were loaded into another box wagon. All of it was to be sent to Germany and SS-Haindl took really good care that every bit of it was there. He grinned and guffawed his malicious laugh:

– You see what trickery Jews get up to, to get things, and then they claim that they don't possess anything! They must be able to conjure, these Jewish swine!

One day, when they were to help a transport of old women up into the cattle wagons, one person was missing. SS-Haindl roared that she had to be found or he would send one of the helpers with them instead. They must find her within five minutes! So they looked for her under all the carriages. At last John found her and dragged her out.

She was small and skinny, her hair was white, and she was trembling all over with fright. Haindl went over to her and said kindly:

– So you were trying to hide, little Mummy!

Then the Nazi officer took a knotted stick, lifted it above his head and with a single blow split her skull, so that the blood spurted out while he bellowed:

– Los! Get her up! Up with the others!

John and Kalle tossed her up, while the people in the carriage were crying, terrified. Ben was standing there, paralysed, with blood on his cheek and on his coat. He might have been hit with the stick too, but Haindl just went past him up to the train, pushed the sliding door shut himself and bolted the door with a slam.

Once the carriages were locked, they were not to be opened again. Sometimes the train would stay an entire day or even more before it was finally driven off.

Again it was thought that the tranports had come to an end, and they could count on staying in Theresienstadt. Obersturmbannführer Rahm himself wouldn't say anything which wasn't true, would he? Would anyone dare to assert that the Obercommandant was a liar?

* * *

But in October all hell broke loose. After the performance of Verdi's great

Requiem, the order came that everybody who had taken part in the concert was to go on transport, the orchestra, the soloists and the whole choir, as if they had been performing their own mass for the dead...except the Danes.

Of all that fine symphony orchestra, all at once, only Ben, Rebecca's brother, the saxophonist and the conductor were left. Ben had come to be very fond of the Dutch trumpeter and his beautiful wife. They had almost become his musical father and mother.

Ben took leave of them, with their rucksacks, Gokkes with his trumpet, and she with her clarinet in her hand. Ben knew well enough that they were not allowed to take their instruments with them anyway. Later on he wrote the poem:

> PARTING
> To my friend Gokkes.
>
> YOU WENT TOWARD DEATH
> CONFIDENT – AND SAD
> AND YET – YOU DID NOT KNOW IT!
>
> YOU PACKED THE BEST THINGS YOU HAD
> YOU PACKED THE BEST THINGS WE HAD
>
> AT THE PARTING – AMAZED
> YOU ASKED: WHY ARE YOU CRYING?
>
> I COULD NOT ANSWER YOU

Soon after, everybody who had participated in making the film was ordered on a transport, too. It was expressly ordered! Technicians, the young girls and men who had been bathing in the river and dancing at the Café, all the football players, the young women from the ceramic workshop and the allotment garden, and the little children who had been filmed in the sandpit – however, their mothers could, as a special favour, volunteer to join the transport...

This is how events followed each other in quick succession, one transport after the other. But the Danish Jews continued to be exempted. After each transport it was said that this had been the last tranport, now there would be no more of them!

But then, just as surprisingly, another transport was ordered all the same! 2000 men between 30 and 40 years of age, 3000 women between 18 and 30, 2000 men between 18 and 30, 3000 women over 40, 1000 men and

2000 women over 65, 2000 of one kind and 3000 of another. Even 4000 children from the other children's home had to go off, and then once more 3000 children under 12 years...

There were transports every day for months! They could never feel safe. What was one to do to avoid being selected? Nobody escaped, whatever good reason they could give. An old German Jew presented Ben with his Iron Cross. He had to go, even though he had been a German officer.

There were some Catholics in Theresiensatdt as well. They did not evade the transports either. They had no idea whatsoever that they had more than one third Jewish blood in their veins before they were picked up in their homes by the Gestapo.

The Danes couldn't go on being exempted. But Uncle Moritz trusted the king:

– King Christian X will protect us, he will! Everything else is UNTHINKABLE!

But there were also voices saying that those who weren't really true Danes, the emigrants, the stateless – and Ben was one of them – they shouldn't feel too safe. Because if somebody from Denmark was to go on transport, they would be the first!

One cold morning the Obersturmbannführer ordered Kalle to light the fire in the stove of the railway carriage for the German guard.

It was dark in the wagon when Kalle entered it, so he couldn't see that he had thrown the firewood on the head of somebody who was sleeping there before he heard a roar: It was SS Haindl taking a nap. The German drew his pistol to shoot Kalle, who cut and ran in terror and reached the commandant. The commandant stopped Haindl, scolding him that he had been sleeping. In this way Gestapo Führer Rahm saved Kalle's life.

The famous film director Gerron had probably believed that he would be spared the transport as he had been so co-operative and done his best to comply with everything the Germans wanted. But he wasn't let off either. Just as Gerron was to enter the cattle wagon, he ran out of the row he was in and up to Gestapo Führer Rahm, begging him to let him off, but Rahm looked right through him as if he didn't know him and just shouted:

– Weitergehen, get off!

Finally the people who had been forced to select those who were to go on transport had to go themselves. And they had been so sure they'd be allowed to stay... but no! There was again a special order from the Gestapo that they were to be off! Even the Jew elder, Paul Eppstein, disappeared in a mysterious way. They said he had been shot... Rahm just appointed a new mayor, Benjamin Murmelstein, and he could hardly refuse the honour.

There were now only about 13,000 prisoners left in Theresienstadt where there had been more than 55,000 Jews before. For some weeks it was quiet in the camp, and little by little one began to believe, really, that the transports were over.

Then the order was given: All the rest of the children and young people – except the Danes – were to go off.

* * *

At the youth centre where Ben was living, there were 350 boys and 450 girls between 10 and 16 years of age.

Ben is sitting in the boys' room watching how the other boys are packing. The only one who isn't packing, besides himself, is Fritz. He is sitting in his upper bunk, swinging his legs.

Fritz is quite sure that he, at any rate, is not going on transport. He is light blond, has blue eyes, just like his mother! His own father has told him that he would stay in Theresienstadt until the Germans had won the final victory.

At that very moment his mother rushes into the room. She will take Fritz to camp commandant Rahm himself! This must be a mistake! It cannot be true that Fritz is going on transport! She herself has a 100% Aryan grandmother, so her own mother was 50% Aryan and she herself was, consequently, 25% Aryan. She can prove that Fritz's father is 100% complete pure and genuine Aryan and what's more is a member of the Nazi Party and a high-ranking officer. Anybody can see that Fritz doesn't look the least bit Jewish at all! Fritz is 125% divided by 2 that is 62.5% Aryan, and it is only 6 months since the boy's father divorced her, and he had assured her that Theresienstadt was a very safe place...

Nobody has time to listen to her. They are all busy packing. Ben approaches handsome Pavel. He is standing by the window with a dark curly-headed girl with sad eyes. Her name is Eva Pikova and she too has written a poem:

> – WE WANT TO LIVE
> THE WORLD IS OURS
> WE WILL MAKE THE WORLD
> A BETTER PLACE...

They are holding each other's hand without saying anything. They are just standing there, carrying their rucksacks on their back, waiting. Ben wants to say goodbye, but his throat constricts so that he just shakes Pavel's hand. He doesn't dare look at Eva. Then he turns away and walks back to his bed.

Mr. Klein arrives with the list of names. He calls the boys one by one, ticking their names off the list:

– Jiri, Bentler, Frantisek Brozan, Gideon, Josele, Ruben, Heinrich, Markus, Isak, Ulrich, Frantisek Bass, Pavel...

Handsome Pavel!

– Klausi.

The youngest boy in the room with his mouth organ. He is playing I *DON'T KNOW WHAT IT MEANS THAT I AM SO SAD* while he walks up to the line placing himself behind the others. The teacher goes on calling the names, as if it were a quite normal journey they were going to make:

– Wolfi, Arje, Menny, Stankov, Bachner, Hanus Hachenberg...

His birthday is July 12th, just like Ben's!

– Franzl, Vladimir Flusser.

Flusser broke his leg during a football match last Sunday.

– Leo, Bubi, Poldi.

That's the small curly head with glasses.

– Schlomo, Gyorgi, Gabriel... And Teddy!

Teddy, who cannot keep his bed dry at night.

– Benjamin, Janus, Misha, Petr Fischl, Pavel Bondy, Hanus Löwy, Miroslav Kosek, Juri, Hänschen, Abraham, Heinzl, Dasha, Hellmuth... And Fritz!

All 42 boys, including Fritz! He is also on the list...

His mother has to help him pack, while she keeps on wailing that this must be a mistake. Fritz must go off anyway, in spite of the fact that he has blue eyes and his father is a Nazi, despite having 62.5% Aryan blood in his veins. But he lacks another 4.2%, to arrive at the 66.7% requirement for exemption.

At the end, Ben is sitting there all alone among the empty beds.

How could God allow all this to happen?

✳ ✳ ✳

Ben has been ordered to appear the next morning at 5 o'clock at the transport departure and told by the entertainment section to bring his trumpet. A piano is placed on the platform, and the Ghetto Swingers and the Danish clown Hambo are also present.

All the children are lined up in groups of 100, ten children in each row, boys and girls separately. They have been waiting all night...
At 6 o'clock the German officers arrive. They are supposed to be entertained and it must be really cheerful. The Germans want to hear *THE SONG OF MUSIC* and Ben starts to play, together with the Ghetto Swingers:

> *– EVERY DAY THERESIENSTADT HAS ITS MUSIC*
> *WE PLAY ADAGIO ANDANTE AND ALLEGRO*
> *CYMBAL AND DRUM SAY BUM BUM CHING BUM CHING*
> *ENTHUSIASTIC, THE AUDIENCE IS APPLAUDING,*
> *BUT CAN'T YOU HEAR THERE IS A CHILD CRYING*
> *WHILE THE MUSIC IS SO CHEERFULLY PLAYING?*

> *THERESIENSTADT HAS ITS OWN COURT CHAPEL*
> *THE MAESTRO CONDUCTS THE FAMOUS ORCHESTRA*
> *AT EVERY FESTIVAL AT EVERY DEPARTURE*
> *ENTHUSIASTIC, THE AUDIENCE IS APPLAUDING,*
> *BUT CAN'T YOU HEAR THERE IS A CHILD CRYING*
> *WHILE THE MUSIC IS SO CHEERFULLY PLAYING?*

> *MUSIC GIVES US DELIGHT AND DREAMS*
> *FLOWING AFAR, OUTSIDE THE BARBED WIRE,*
> *CYMBAL AND DRUM SAY BUM BUM CHING BUM CHING*
> *ENTHUSIASTIC, THE AUDIENCE IS APPLAUDING*
> *BUT CAN'T YOU HEAR THERE IS A CHILD CRYING*
> *WHILE THE MUSIC IS SO CHEERFULLY PLAYING?*

> *AND THE VOYAGERS GO OFF... WHERE, YOU MAY GUESS*
> *AND WHEN YOU ARRIVE AT THE DESTINED PLACE*
> *THE ONLY THING YOU CAN BRING WITH YOU*
> *IS THE MUSIC, IS THE MUSIC, IS THE MUSIC...*

Then Hambo is to sing his songs, and the Germans are so amused when he is singing in falsetto, doing his parody of the operatic prima donna who is going to die. Obercommandant Rahm is screaming with laughter when Hambo is wriggling his behind like a lady sobbing:
– I'm dying! I'm dyyying! I'm DYYYYING!!
SS Haindl walks over to Hambo and starts beating him with his whip so that Hambo, yelling loudly, jumps around to avoid the lashes. Goodness gracious, what fun the Germans have! The soldier keeps on hitting harder and harder, beating him with all his might, because it is so funny, when

Hambo wails in his high-pitched voice so that it sounds like a woman crying. There is hardly an end to the fun.

When the children are to get on the train, Ben has to play again. He must pay very strict attention. Imagine if he played out of tune... it is a matter of life and death to hit the right notes. Especially at the moment when Pavel and his other room-mates are to climb into the carriage, his head is swimming, so that he can hardly read the music.

In this way they take turns at entertaining the Germans, until all the children are inside the cattle trucks and the doors are spiked. By that time almost the whole morning has passed away.

* * *

Mommy cannot bring herself to leave when Ben is so angry with her. Furthermore she MUST talk with him. She has not been sleeping nights since the Chief Rabbi spoke to her last Sabbath.

– You have resigned from the community!

Ben stops playing. That's exactly why he did it, to be free from all the gossip and bickering!

– Can't you leave me alone?

To Mommy the community is her extended family, where she has found a secure place. Last summer she had been in Israel and she was enthusiastic. Finally, the Jews had their own country, now they could show what they were worth and defend themselves. Of course she had visited YAD VASHEM, the great memorial hall for the six million dead:

– But you cannot desert your people just like that... and your faith!

– Deserting? What has my people given me then? And my faith! Does it mean anything at all?

– But we are Jews, we must stick together...

– Stick together... that's the very thing people blame us for!

– You who love music and art, will you disclaim our culture and our traditions? The world's most famous musicians and artists are Jews... we have our Jewish heritage!

Ben can't help thinking of Pavel, of Klausi and Teddy, and of Gokkes:

– In Theresienstadt I lived in a room just somewhat bigger than this one, we were 43 boys. Where are they now? Do you think that they were happy belonging to your people, your faith? They have been cheated of their lives, cheated of experiencing love, cheated of having children and being happy with them! I'm the only one of them left alive today!

– Because you were a Dane!

– I was stateless! An emigrant!

– But we did belong to the Danes! We did come home!

– And the other boys? Didn't they have a right to live? It was mere chance that we were spared!

– Then be glad that you belonged to the Danes!

–Mother, you are talking as if it were all right that only the other people were sent to Auschwitz. I had to go to the Aliens' police unit twice a year to have my residence permit prolonged: FOREIGN PASSPORT was written in capital letters on my passport. When I went with the Tivoli Boys' Guard to Sweden I had to have a visa and pass a special passport control while all the other boys had to wait for me. I got my school leaving certificate as a stateless person and the police questioned my teacher Børge about me! It was fifteen years before we became Danish subjects...

– But then you've one more reason to stay in the community!

– You and your community! When I was a boy you forced me to go to the synagogue every Saturday. That was also to please your dear Moritzl! And I was to bow properly, greeting the rabbi, and I had to walk on foot, as you can't drive on a Sabbath, that's forbidden! And in the synagogue you were sitting high up in the balcony, where only the women were to be. You were so high up, so unattainable, just like when I was sitting in the sandbox as a child... I was forced to stand close to Moritz and follow the prayerbook, while the men murmured the Hebrew prayers. The worst thing was Moritz's odour. I breathed his smell in at every breath. I detested his smell and I was scared of him. And then all the strange glances from people when I, a little boy, ran through the streets of Copenhagen with a grown-up's trilby on my head... I must have looked funny! I rushed along as fast as I could to get home and get that hat off: I HATED going to synagogue!

To Mommy the synagogue is the place where you have a good time with the other ladies, show your newest coat to the others, and Mommy can be just as proud of her nice, well-mannered son as the other mamas.

– I wanted so much to bring you up to be a good Jew!

– And what is that? A good man, that I could understand...

– But the community is our fellowship!

– Fellowship? When we came to Denmark we were really far down on the social ladder, we emigrants! They certainly let us feel the difference between us and them, the fine Danish Jews. And you are flattering those people today!

– But, Ben, we do have a common destiny, common roots...

– IN DENMARK I WAS BORN THERE ARE MY ROOTS... Do I have roots anywhere at all? Where do I belong?
– Why are you so negative, Benny? We have settled in well. You are a Dane now! You are having a good time here with your friends, you are well-liked and respected, what else do you want? We belong here in Denmark! You have every reason to be satisfied!
– You are what you are taken for. No matter how much effort I make, I shall be sized up anyway, with my strange name. I am considered an alien, an alien bird...
– Alien bird?
Mommy thinks about it for some time:
– No, Benny! That's something you are imagining. It is not at all like that in reality! You are what you feel you are... And if you feel like that, why do you let us down then?
And Mommy can't help letting a small hope flare up, which she cherishes in spite of all:
– Won't you come home and visit us again?
– Home? With you I have always been an alien too.

✳ ✳ ✳

Now there was room enough to live more comfortably. All Danes, not only the "prominent" people, were now allowed to live as families. Ben moved together with Mommy and Uncle Moritz into a little room with a stove. There were beds standing on the floor, which you could use as sofas, and a table and a window looking out on the street with the beautiful name Town Hall Street.

There were only one or two families in each room. That was naturally far better than before, even though they had to go through one another's rooms. Lea and Rebecca lived with their mothers next to Ben. But Ben was not allowed to say anything when he crossed their room, not even "Good morning." But outside, the children did talk to each other, when their mothers couldn't see them.

It was good to live with Mommy again, but Ben had to look out not to get in Uncle Moritz's way. Ben was now playing in a small six-piece band in the Café. They were four Danes and two Dutchmen who had arrived in Terezin after the great transport. That and the Ghetto Swingers were all the musicians they could muster.

The Danish Ministry had sent a small library of books and reading was now permitted. All in all, with the monthly food parcel, living in the ghetto wasn't so bad as it used to be. There was still a shortage of fuel, so that you had to sleep with your coat on top of the blanket... and it was beastly cold getting up in the morning, when it was 10 or 15 degrees below zero. It could even happen that the Germans stopped the distribution of coal for two or three weeks as a collective punishment for some reason.

Mommy had found a teacher, Mrs. Räuber, a German, who gave Ben English lessons. She got half a piece of bread, sometimes with a slice of sausage, as payment.

It still happened that Ben had to eat his meal in the street, because Uncle Moritz was annoyed with him. Then Rebecca, Lea, or Kalle and little Jacob came to keep him company.

One day John arrived white-faced with fear. He had been sent to the Little Fortress, where he was to fetch some clothes which belonged to a young Danish agricultural trainee. The young man had been sent to the penitentiary, because he had smuggled cigarettes, and now he was dead. John had seen that the prisoners were strung up by their feet in long rows, hanging for hours and hours.

One night, when Mommy and Uncle Moritz must have thought that Ben had fallen asleep, Ben perceived his stepfather's big shadow rising from his bed and walking to Mommy's bed. His parents were whispering a little together and then the dark shadow began to move up and down on top of Mommy while they gasped and panted. Ben was scared to death. It sounded terrifying. Ben remained completely immobile, as if he were frozen in ice. As a matter of fact, he had heard about such a thing, and once when he was ten, a small fox terrier had clung tight to one of his legs with its forepaws and then the dog had behaved strangely. It had jumped up and down, panting, with its tongue hanging out of its mouth. One of the big boys had roared with laughter, saying:

– Now the dog thinks you are his wife!

Ben had kicked it away, pretending that he was well familiar with it all...

But his own mother! She who never talked about such things! For that was, indeed, so awfully disgusting, something so filthy! Ugh, ugh... that his Mommy agreed to such a thing, and with his stepfather, who was so loathsome, his own good sweet Mommy!

Ben couldn't help listening intently. It sounded as if Mommy was moaning. And his stepfather was grunting like a wild animal doing Mommy harm. Then, suddenly, it became totally quiet, and his stepfather sneaked back to his bed. After a little while he began to snore. And so did Mommy...

It was as if Ben, all alone, had been placed in a dark forest with a lot of wild animals around him, and he could see their shining eyes staring at him. He doubled up, and fell asleep.

* * *

Ben is awarded the major scholarship and is admitted to the residence hall, Regensen. Here he finds new friends and enjoys undergraduate life with its old traditions.

Life at the Red Yard was led by a chosen group of students, the head being called the "Sexton." They arranged the balls and parties and led a rebellious struggle against the Warden of the hall who was installed by the university.

At Regensen there were nine clubs, and Ben becomes a member of SHARP, named after the legendary King Vermund's sword. That's why the ten young students have a big sword and a huge bottle as symbols of their club.

One of the traditions was to "water" the novices on one of the first nights, that is, they were "interrogated" about the escapades of olden times, and then led to the bathroom where they undressed, to be sprayed with water from the cold hosepipe. It was performed as an amusing procession, with the Sexton disguised as a judge and the heads of the clubs carrying their symbols. It was to be taken in good spirit and the novices, at the end, would get a glass of schnapps to warm themselves.

Ben was unpleasantly affected by the thought of having to stand naked in front of the others, so he asked the Sexton to be excused from the watering. The Sexton promised Ben he'd be exempted when Ben had explained the reason for his shyness. Ben could just lock his door, then nothing would happen to him.

The following night, when Ben heard noises and loud voices in the corridor, he pushed the cupboard in front of his door. However, the students left him in peace.

Ben is having a good time with his friends. They have long debates and Ben draws attention by contributing witty remarks. He feels really secure and comfortable. When you are tired of studying until three or four o'clock in the morning, you can visit some of the others, still sweating over their books, have a cup of strong tea together, smoke a pipe, discuss matters, or you could read your own poems to each other, play chess or settle Regensen politics to your heart's content.

Then it happens that you sleep so long into the next day, that you do not get out of bed until the charladies have already gone home.

As Ben is earning enough to pay the instalments, he buys himself a piano. The instrument is newly restored, with a strong dark sound, and a pleasure to play.

Ben composes the music for a cantata and conducts the performance himself, with a choir of students, at a great punch blowout where King Frederik IX himself is present. Ben would have wished it had been the King's father, Christian X, who probably was the person to whom Ben owed his own presence today. But King Christian, who fortunately did live to see the end of the war, had died some years ago.

The feast is a veritable war of singers! The clubs get up in groups, singing their battle songs, and Ben sings with his friends with might and main:

- *HERE WE ARE, THE STUDENTS OF SHARP*
HERE IS OUR SWORD, OUR BATTLE SPIRIT...

The other clubs break in with their own songs – the great thing was to shout the others down – so that at the end, all hundred students are bawling simultaneously as loudly as they can!

King Frederik himself makes a witty speech about the students' night life. If the students were not wakened by the king's guard marching through the street at noon with drums beating, past his own old illustrious residential hall, they were unlikely to turn out of their bunks at all! It really was something to be on equal terms with the King of Denmark!

✳ ✳ ✳

One beautiful autumn day, when Ben is coming out of the Royal Library, he runs into Lily in the rose garden. Ben is surprised and curious. Lily is looking marvellous.

– Hello, Lily, nice to see you! What are you doing?

Lily is pleased. She smiles at Ben. It is not quite a coincidence that she is here precisely at this moment. She has been thinking a lot about Ben all this time, and has been here several times to try to meet him. But then Ben had been with somebody else, and she wished to talk to him alone:

– I have a job as a fashion model, but I intend to become an actress. I'm taking private lessons with one of the actors from the Royal Theatre to try to be admitted to the drama school next spring.

Ben is choked. Lily is doing exactly what he would so much like to do himself. He suppresses a little pang of envy:

– Are you really!

It was Ben who had opened Lily's eyes to the theatre world. She is quite convinced it is Ben's greatest wish, too. She comes very close to him to read his face:

– There is nothing so fascinating as the theatre and films, don't you think?

But as Ben's dark eyes are drawing back she changes the subject:

– I heard that Grete and Kristian have been to America. How was it over there?

– It was fantastic! Four of them hired a car and drove across the continent from east to west for six weeks...

Suddenly Lily has become a completely different person, a new personality. She radiates a resolution he never noticed before. He can't get over the fact that she wishes to put into practice exactly that which he is still only dreaming about. Lily had opened, as a matter of course, the gateway to the Promised Land which he, just like Moses, was only allowed to see, but not to enter!

Lily takes Ben's arm while they walk among the roses in their beautiful glowing colours with all shades, from the most delicate rose-pink to the deepest dark blood-red. The air is filled with bitter-sweet intoxicating scents to make your nostrils prickle:

– Wouldn't you like to come and visit me? I've told my mother so much about you!

Ben gives a little laugh. It never occurred to him that Lily would have talked to her mother about him.

– About me? Hopefully something nice!

– Mommy would like to get to know you very much!

Now Ben gets a bright idea:

– We are having a party at Regensen next Saturday, with ladies. Would you like to come?

There was nothing Lily would like better.

✳ ✳ ✳

Now the days are one long boring wait. Uncle Moritz knew from the gendarmes in the postal service that the Americans had liberated most of Italy and France. The Allies had crossed the Rhine and were now standing on German soil, while the Russians had conquered Warsaw and advanced to Vienna. They were on their way to Prague and then it wouldn't be long before they were here. His stepfather had got himself a map on which he used little pins to plot the positions of the frontlines. According to his estimation, the war should have been over a long time ago, before winter ended. But, anyway, it never did seem to end.

Weeks and months passed. Spring was in the air. It was getting warmer and the days were brightening. What would happen when the Russians arrived? And what couldn't be happening in the meantime?

Mommy was working together with the other Danish women splitting mica, Glimmer, as it was called. It was used for German aeroplanes. It was a wearisome job. They were supposed to finish a certain quantity each day, and it was very hard, in the bad lighting, to distinguish the cracks in the material, where you were to slit it into thin sheets with your knife. They started at five o'clock in the morning and worked fourteen or fifteen hours to get it done. The women had to sing all the time they were working... it was an order! They were to be content and happy when SS-Führer Rahm came to check the production. But as long as they were working for the German war industry, they weren't likely to be sent on a transport, were they?

One day a group of Jews arrived from Hungary. They had been walking all the way from the front and looked appalling: Several thousand men in old rags with hollow eyes and emaciated as skeletons, their skin stretched over their bones like tent canvas over poles. They could hardly speak, fatigued as they were. They had no strength left to move any farther and were just lying in the streets and the square in front of the bandstand, groaning and dying, before they were dragged away.

To try to save some of the Hungarians from death, the others collected food from among the Danish prisoners who had their packages from the Red Cross every month. That was the first time Ben saw anybody give any food away.

Sometimes you could see, high up in the light arch of the spring sky, a lot of tiny spots. They seemed to stand still in the air, so high up were they. It was the British bombers. But when Ben looked up a little later, he could see that the spots had moved after all. Simultaneously, the air was buzzing low, but massively and persistently, from the rumbling of the aircraft engines.

Actually, an alert should have sounded, so that people could take shelter in the basements, but then SS-Führer Rahm would have to admit that the aeroplanes were British and that the German anti-aircraft guns were powerless! Besides, the Allies would certainly never think of bombing Theresienstadt. They knew of every single concentration camp and they were sure to leave them alone, Uncle Moritz exulted.

Most of all Ben felt like throwing his cap in the air, shouting hurray and waving his hand at the sky, but of course you must not do that. If one of the

German guards saw it, you would be shot... So Ben acted as if he didn't see or hear the aeroplanes. It was deadly dangerous just to hint that you did not believe in Hitler's ultimate victory.

But when they were alone in their room, even Uncle Moritz would be pleased and smiling. Now the Allied warplanes arrived daily, almost punctually. He would nod and look as if he had ordered them out himself.

On the grounds between the ramparts, where they used to play football, new huts were being built. There were going to be fine new bathrooms, the Obersturmbannführer said. But they were rather worried, as the building of the huts was proceeding at such a pace. There was something mysterious about it, because showers and taps were installed, but no sewers or drains were dug. How could they be used for baths, then?

Nevertheless, nobody would think of the worst of all! They preferred to trust "Uncle Rahm's" assurances, on his honour, about the harmless purpose of the huts. For it couldn't, really be the Gestapo commandant's intention, seriously... It was unthinkable, wasn't it? But was it...? And they did not dare to finish the thought.

Then, of course, you hoped that the Russian and American advances would be fast enough. It was also rumoured that they would let the river flow into the moat and then they were all going to be drowned, but nobody would ever believe that! That was, indeed, *UNTHINKABLE*! Only a sick mind could ever imagine that!

Now the grass in the market-place was fully grown again and the trees had little new green leaves. The sun was really warm, high in the sky every day.

One day a lot of smoke was noticed on the ramparts. John said that the SS-Obersturmbannführer had ordered him to empty all cupboards and cabinets in the offices of the Gestapo headquarters, to collect all the briefcases and take them on his oxcart to the ramparts, where Karl Rahm in person set fire to all the documents. The smoke from the burning paper piles could be seen for three days.

March had passed. It was mid-April already and you kept on waiting and waiting...

* * *

One day during the lunch break, Moritz suddenly comes running like a madman from the Gestapo barracks, where he delivered some mail. He is panting and can hardly breathe. He has seen an automobile with a Red Cross and the Danish flag in front of the entrance of the headquarters. A couple of Danish officers has been talking to the Obersturmbannführer, and then one of the Danes had also spoken to him. Moritz can hardly utter a word from excitement:

– We are going to be liberated! The Red Cross has come to free us! That's what he said: We have come to rescue the Danish prisoners!

Everybody goes completely mad with joy. They run in and out of each others' rooms to pass on the happy news. Mommy goes to Lea's mother and they both sob, embrace each other. All grudges are forgotten, Lea throws herself into Ben's arms, and he hugs her and gives her a kiss on her cheek. It is unbelievable but it IS true! This time it is true, really!

Mommy kisses Ben, and his face is wet with her tears. And imagine, it is her own Moritzl who had seen the Red Cross car first! Isn't it fantastic?

Now they are waiting anxiously. Neither men nor women go to work, and in the evening a row of white buses with Red Crosses drive up in front of the Germans' barracks. It is not the usual rumours or wishful imagination, it is hardly credible...

Ben runs to examine the buses more closely, hiding himself behind trees. The Germans had lied and fooled the Jews so many times before, but there could be no doubt this time, Red Crosses are painted on the white buses... Where might they be going? Were they really going to Sweden or maybe to Switzerland, as some people said? And would they be going too, even though they are stateless?

The next day an order in writing comes to every Dane, and also to the immigrants, to turn up for transport the same evening at nine o'clock.

The whole ghetto is buzzing with excitement. They pack the whole day, and then off to the exit barracks.

The other people in Theresienstadt came and had to be told about it a hundred times before they believed it. They gave those others some food, which Mommy and the other Danes could spare.

Then all were checked and their names taken down, and after negotiations with Commandant Rahm the chief rabbi got permission to marry five of the young men to Czech women, so they could be set free as well.

After a night full of restlessness and uncertainty, a Swedish Red Cross officer came. For the first time, somebody spoke to the prisoners in a friendly and polite manner, and in Swedish, as one human being to another, without yelling and ordering! They could now rest assured. They would try to drive up through Germany to Denmark, and if this was not possible because of the frontlines, they would turn back and drive into Switzerland. The Red Cross had already brought many Danish and Norwegian prisoners back home from the other German KZ-camps, and the Jews were the last ones to be released!

Another whole day went by, and another night. It was a long time to be waiting. But they were short of buses. The food was brought by the kitchen staff and they had to sleep on the ground with their clothes on.

The next morning they were to leave at long last – all the Jews from Denmark, except the fifty-two no longer alive. Gestapo Führer Rahm came to take leave of the Danish prisoners with a smile, almost as if they were parting from a friendly innkeeper with whom they had been on vacation.

Before they all enter the buses the Obersturmbannführer asks Hambo to sing his opera parody once more, and now Hambo changes the words as he is singing in Danish: "Now you are dying! Now you are dyyying! Now YOU ARE DYYYING!"

Everybody applauds with enthusiasm, including the German himself, who doesn't grasp that Hambo is making a fool of him.

The Ghetto Swingers are playing at the gate, as the buses were leaving Theresienstadt. Those left behind are waving and crying. In a way they had been feeling a certain security as long as the Danes were there. What was going to happen to them, now the Danes were gone?

* * *

Lily was at the great banquet at Regensen. There was lots of wine and Ben made one of the evening's witty speeches, while Lily was sitting next to him gazing at him with bright eyes.

After the meal they danced, and while Lily was clinging to him, Ben had the joy of feeling her warm body close to his. He wasn't alone any more, and the emptiness in his chest was filled.

* * *

Ben is sitting with Lily on the silk-covered Louis XIV sofa in the drawing-room of the beautifully furnished villa. There is a view of the well-kept garden, with the trim bushes and pretty herbaceous borders. They certainly had a skilful gardener.

Lily's mother is wearing a smart, slightly provocative black dress, fitting tightly around her svelte figure, and forming an attractive contrast to her wavy blonde hair and pale face with her greyish-blue eyes. She is pouring from the decanter while holding a gold cigarette-holder between her well-cared-for fingers with the pink varnished nails.

First Lily's mother showed Ben over the rooms with the antique furniture, selected with care – they stood for what they were, without being ostentatious – and *en passant* she mentioned that several museums were interested in the Danish paintings she had on the walls. Of course she would never part with them although, by so doing, she prevented the public from admiring them, which in fact, she must admit, could be considered a little egotistic.

Lily had been walking around with them as if she were a guest in her own home. They had also cast a glance into Lily's room in all its disorder, which her mother apologized for with a disarming smile. It was Lily's own area which she ruled over herself! The mother wouldn't meddle in the way Lily dressed for anything in the world, either! Mother and daughter each had her own taste!

– Another sherry?

Ben would like another drop, and another cigarette is lit for him as well, while he is wondering why there is no mention of the father at all. It was not like Lily to be so quiet either. Her mother leads the conversation:

– I hear that you are a good piano player... We also love classical music in this home, don't we, Lily? We often go to concerts when the orchestra of the Royal Theatre is playing.

While they are drinking out of the beautiful crystal glasses, the low music from the radio has stopped and is replaced by the news. In the silence you can't help hearing:

– ...This morning Israeli fighters have been bombing villages in the South of Lebanon in return for alleged guerilla attacks. More than twenty civilians have been killed, mainly women and children...

Lily's mother pours a third glass for Ben and with a smile she turns her eyes towards the big Venetian cut-glass chandelier.

– Bach, Beethoven and Brahms, the three great B's, don't you think?

And her mother sighs as if she were listening to the most wonderful music at this very moment. Then she looks significantly at Ben:

– My daughter would so very much like to be on the screen. And you are soon going to become a Master of Arts, I hear?

Ben is sipping his sherry. He is a little ill at ease with Lily being so silent next to him. He looks at her and she is smiling at him. Ben answers politely:

– I have just passed the first part, so it will take another four years.

Now the radio announcer can be heard quite clearly:

– ...The United Nations Security Council has condemned Israel's aggression. Israeli troops have closed the border...

Lily's mother gets up with irritation and switches off the radio:

– Those Jews... There is always trouble with them!

Ben gives a start:

– Trouble with them? They must be allowed some place in this world to live.

The lady has sat down with the young people again and has apparently already forgotten what it was all about:

– What do you mean?

Even though he actually doesn't feel like it, Ben goes on:

– Those Jews, as you were just saying...

– Oh, them!

Lily's mother shrugs her shoulders. There is nothing which she could care less about. Ben won't let go:

– The Jews have been persecuted for centuries, expelled from everywhere, from all countries, treated unjustly...

Ben is just about to tell her what he has experienced himself. The lady quite unexpectedly becomes aggressive:

– Persecuted? Unjustly? Then there must be a reason for it, mustn't there!

Lily's mother is under the impression that this sympathetic young man hardly knows anything about Jews:

– Otherwise they wouldn't be persecuted, would they? You just have to see how they stick together, all of them, always, exploiting the rest of us. My husband... the things he had to put up with! And it did cost him a lot of money! Because he wouldn't think badly of other people, although he had been warned and did business with the Jews anyway! It is not without any reason at all that people don't like the Jews, Hitler was, indeed, right...

Ben can't believe his ears:

– Was Hitler right? You can't seriously say that!

Lily is sitting there quite silently, while her mother nods affirmatively:

– I am certainly not joking, young man. Look how they press themselves forward everywhere, sponging on the rest of us! All they want is to dominate the whole world, they do... Wall Street, high finance! They own all the newspapers and decide what we are to read, poking their noses into everything. There is no place where you can be free from them, no... you can recognize that race everywhere!

Ben is quite indignant:

– But it is not true! Hitler's racial theories are a forgery. Jews are in no way different from other people! If you go south to Italy, Spain or Austria, most people have brown eyes and dark hair. It is only here in the northern countries that people are blond and have blue eyes. Besides, all human races are equally good! So if the Jews did belong to a different race, as for example, the negroes... Why, it is nature which gave them the dark skin, so they can better withstand the strong sun...

Lily's mother is categorical:

– You are so young. You have such a sterling character, and it is only praiseworthy that young people want to improve the world, but no matter what you say... It is a fact: Jews are different!

Ben has to take a deep breath to calm down. He glances at Lily, who remains silent. Then, quite patiently, he tries to formulate very clearly what he will say:

– Jews are human beings who have a common religion, or a common culture if they are not religious. They can belong to all sorts of races, a Chinese who is converted to Judaism certainly remains a Chinese! There are also Jews who are red-haired or fair, although most are dark-haired, because they come from Mediterranean countries. You cannot see if a Spaniard or a Greek or a Tunisian is Jewish...

Lily's mother cannot help liking Ben's eagerness; the trouble is that this young man certainly doesn't know any better.

– You bet I can! You can sense it at once! The way they behave! My husband always said so, too!

It now strikes Ben like lightning.

– Your husband is, perhaps, a Nazi?

– Oscar is an idealist! During the war he wasn't afraid of standing forward, acknowledging his attitude with head erect, fighting for a cleaner world, for a worthy Denmark we don't have to be ashamed of! My husband was true to our country, ready to defend it against the Communists and the Jews.

Ben doesn't know if he should laugh or cry:

– It's almost ridiculous! It's to turn everything upside down! Jews can't be Communists and dominate high finance at the same time! The Nazis stole the Jews' property, their money, and killed them on top of it! It was Hitler who aimed at getting world supremacy! That is exactly what is so vile, that's the grievous injustice!

Now the lady gets angry. She has had to swallow a lot of things, indeed, in the years after the war.

– Injustice! My husband was convicted! And all of us do have a right to have our political opinions, don't we! One party is just as right as the other, that's why we have a democracy! And Oscar never hurt a fly, but THEY had him convicted! Because THEY again have been taking over judicial appointments, that's the way they are! They are cheating us all, greedy as they are! Always money, money, money! My husband used to say: "It's a pity that Hitler didn't get them all..."

Until this moment Ben had simply believed that Lily's mother didn't know better. Now he realizes that she is serious. He thinks of his comrades from the room, of handsome Pavel, of Fritz and Klausi with his mouth organ. Lily, whom he had completely forgotten, is looking at him with her big eyes. He isn't angry any longer now, only sad:

– Have you ever known any Jews... personally?

The lady has certainly seen them for herself:

– You can believe me! A tailor's family was living in our street...it was before we got this villa and, of course, we would have liked to support them. They didn't have too much, and then all these children. We aren't at all that bad you see! My husband had a suit sewn and then the Jew cheated him over the material!

Should Ben tell her now that he was Jewish himself?

– And then, in your opinion, all Jews are to be exterminated, because he cheated your husband over the material?

The lady is lighting up another cigarette with a graceful gesture:

– How naive you are nowadays, you young people. It's nothing but propaganda, all of it. Hitler wanted only to teach the Jews to work, to do something instead of exploiting the rest of us. And the tailor was one of those who was always currying favour. His obsequious way of smiling! And he couldn't even speak Danish properly. What are they doing here in our country, those people, if they don't even care to learn our language? And they twang through their big noses, and they are flat-footed...

To Ben it seems as if he were attending a satirical play:

– It is indeed incredible... grotesque! After what you know now about the concentration camps where six million Jews were eradicated, more than Denmark's entire population!

– That's also the usual propaganda lies, so many Jews didn't even exist in all of Europe. There were three million at the most...

– Do you mean that murdering three million people is only half as bad?

Lily's mother gets aggressive again:

– What about all the poor German soldiers who died frozen to death at Stalingrad? Nobody talks about them!

Ben is thinking of his father:

– WHO STARTED THE WAR? Was it the little tailor family? And where are they all, the Jews who lived in Germany, Holland, Russia, Hungary, Austria? And Norway, where not even fifty of more than a thousand survived! Or Paris... Did they never exist, never live?

Lily's mother doesn't like to be on the defensive:

– That's something they have invented to make us have compassion on them, so they could steal Palestine from the Arabs without any decent people protesting. You can see for yourself: the radio and all newspapers are on the side of the Jews! They have made the Germans incur everybody's wrath, so cowardly are they! They are not a bit better than the Nazis themselves! Nobody talks about the poor Palestinians, whom they have murdered and kicked out of their country! They are making themselves conspicuous everywhere. Slum landlords, swindlers the whole lot of them... you can smell them at a great distance!

– You can smell them...?

The lady gives vent to her pent-up hatred:

– You just have to learn to pick them out, you can't avoid recognizing them at once with their Jew noses! They never look straight in your eyes... It's their bad conscience!

Ben feels as if he is being strangled:

– What about me? I never defraud other people, I am not especially interested in money. But I know good Christians who are so avaricious, that they even grudge themselves anything.

– What do you mean?

Ben leaps to his feet:

– What about my Jew nose, as you put it so beautifully? I'm not at all flat-footed and I'm looking straight in your eyes!

Lily's mother is taken aback:

– But you are not... are you...?

– Both my mother and my father are Jews... so I am a Jew too!

For a long time they are silent. The mother is furious that she had given herself away:

– It was mean of you not to say anything, it was mean, indeed, to make me talk...

– When I introduce myself I don't say: "How do you do, I am a Jew"! You don't say either: "Hello, I am a Nazi"... "Heil Hitler" is not in for the time being, or is it?

The lady's face is stone-hard:

– It was really shifty of you, that's all that one would expect from such a... There you can see that I'm right!

There was no reason to say any more. Ben looks at Lily:

– I'm leaving now... are you coming?

Wordlessly, Lily gets up and leaves with Ben.

✷ ✷ ✷

There were twenty-two buses crammed with people and luggage. They were sitting close, but it didn't matter. Ben was sitting by the driver and could watch them passing through the countryside and the towns. He hardly dared talk to the driver, but Kalle constantly talked about seeing his fatehr and his big brother again in Sweden.

Beside the Swedish driver, a German soldier sat with his rifle, so you had to be careful not to show too much joy. Imagine if the Germans changed their minds at the last moment! You also had to keep wearing your Jew Star.

Mommy was sitting behind Ben with his stepfather. All the time she murmured: "Thank you, dear God, because you have saved us, thank you, dear God..."

Lea and her mother were sitting farthest back in the bus, and when Ben turned around, each time he looked right into her big eyes.

When they went through Dresden, they drove for hours, and all they saw was bombed-out smoke-blackened houses, smouldering heaps of ruins. Once in a while the drivers had to get out and remove burning beams from the road, so that they could continue, or else they were forced to turn back, trying to drive along alternative streets, before they got through the town.

They had been driving all day when, late in the night, they arrived in Berlin. Now the important thing was to manage to get through before the Eastern Front and the Western Front met.

That's when the air raid began. They all had to get out of the buses and lie down in the roadside ditch. The bombs crashed around them, the whole sky was lit up with flames from the burning buildings, while the long cones of the anti-aircraft searchlights slid to and fro in circular movements high up in the sky above them.

When the bombers had finished dropping their bombs – it was still dark night – they got on their buses again and drove off, away from the burning city. After another whole day's ride – several times getting off the buses to hide in the ditches when aeroplanes flew overhead – they arrived in Hamburg, Ben's native city, which looked like an immense desert of ruins. Only a few people here and there were seen trying to find their things among the destroyed houses. The streets were filled with rubble or were full of holes. They had to sleep most of the night in their buses until they got off again. In the morning they arrived at the Danish border.

KRUSÅ it said on the sign. What a relief! Now the German soldier's power was broken. He did, as a matter of fact, remain in the bus, but now nobody cared about him any longer. Jubilant with joy, everybody tore off their Jew Stars. John had a knife. Wherever had he got it from? He had taken off his own star long ago, and now he helped Mommy and Uncle Moritz get their stars off. The Swedish driver had a pair of scissors, which he lent to Ben.

It was a strange feeling to liberate yourself from that curse which you had sticking to you. At first Ben threw away his star. Off! Out of the window! But then he picked somebody else's off the floor of the bus. He was going to preserve it and show it to his children one day!

They got real rye bread with butter and cheese, and real fresh cow's milk! They had completely forgotten what it tasted like! Ben drank one glass of milk after another till his stomach felt utterly stuffed!

The Danes at the border were smiling, waving flags and shouting: "Welcome home!" and throwing cigarettes, chocolates and biscuits through the windows of the buses, and there was much smoking and much munching!

But the Germans were still occupying Denmark. While the convoy of white buses with the Red Crosses continued through Jutland, Ben saw young German soldiers trudging along the highway, exhausted and dusty in their ragged uniforms. They were so young, many of them couldn't possibly be more than one or two years older than Ben. They could hardly lug their heavy guns, which they were carrying on their backs or over their shoulders in all sorts of irregular ways to ease the weight. They certainly did not look very cheerful.

In the town of Odense they stayed for the night in the school gymnasium. All the people were so kind and helpful. You could hardly believe it. A delicious hot meal was served, meat and sauce and potatoes, just as much as you could eat!

When they drove on the next morning, the bus Ben was in crashed against a lamp post. The driver had been inattentive for a moment, tired as he was after the long ride.

Fortunately nobody was hurt, but it was a nasty shock. They had to be distributed amongst the other buses. Ben and John got into the bus for the sick, where they had to stand between the stretchers all the rest of the way to Copenhagen.

One of the sick old people was Grandma. She had become tiny and thin and was blind. Ben didn't speak to her, pretending he didn't know her at all, in spite of the fact that it was his own Grandma.

They were to continue by ferry to Sweden. While they were waiting in the harbour, some of them were greeted by friends who had arrived to bid them welcome. If Kristian and Birgit and Knud had only known that Ben was here, surely they would have come too...

They went on board the ferry sailing across the Sound to Malmø. Now they could take leave of the German soldiers, who had been guarding them. It was quite incredible!

Ben stood all the time in the prow of the ship, watching the Swedish coast coming nearer while the houses over there got bigger.

But when they set foot on Swedish soil, Ben was disappointed: now they were guarded by Swedish soldiers, who also had rifles with fixed bayonets and who looked just as unapproachable as the German soldiers. Nobody was allowed to move a single step, they had to remain standing on the same spot. It was certainly not a welcome like the one in Kruså!

Then – still under surveillance – they went by train, in a railway carriage for human beings, to a camp, where they were examined by a doctor, who only touched them wearing gloves on his hands. Here they were going to be in quarantine for three weeks.

It was a camp of huts in the middle of the country. There was a fence around it also. But there was no barbed wire, and the Swedish soldiers weren't quite so dangerous after all.

After their arrival, Ben found Kalle with his mother and little Jacob mourning and weeping... Kalle's father and big brother had both been drowned in the Sound when, a year and a half ago, they tried to get to Sweden in a rowing boat

They lived only three or four to a room and they had many visitors. Even Uncle Moritz's sister and her husband came to talk to Mommy and his stepfather. They brought a bag of apples. Ben could have two or three apples and he munched them with great pleasure.

John, Rebecca and Lea had been sent to another quarantine camp.

They all got plenty of food as they had to recover. Ben weighed only 20 kilos. He had hardly grown, even though he was going to be fifteen in another three months.

If only it didn't all take so long! All were impatient to be set at liberty.

They had been rescued and were luckily out of danger. Yet it was hard to put up with still being confined.

* * *

It was a magnificent spring day in Sweden. The sun was warm, so you could really feel it. Ben had found a hole in the fence and every day he crawled through it and walked out into the surrounding forest. Here, there were no people, here he was all alone. And he enjoyed it! Nobody stood over him. He enjoyed walking about in a world which belonged to him entirely, without anybody to control him, to make decisions for him and over him, to be on at him... To be all alone, in the midst of nature... to breathe in the free, fresh air!

Ben looked around. The sky was a gleaming azure. The birches had not come into leaf yet. But the scent of the spruces and pines was so strong, that Ben was almost narcotized.

He lay down on the thick soft mat of green moss and let the sun bake him thoroughly, so that he was warmed through to his very bones... And as he lay there in his new-found freedom, he had a rushing and growing feeling in his body, he felt a power inside him which was new, which he had never known before. He opened his trousers and felt the joy of petting himself, so that it was thrilling and trickling all through his body, and he experienced, for the first time in his life, how at the climax of pleasure, vigorous drops came out of him which fell steaming upon the warm ground and were absorbed by the earth.

Ben was surprised, even though he actually had had a certain feeling that this would happen to him, but at the same time it was as if Mommy was standing behind him saying: "Ugh, ugh, ugh!" And he was ashamed...

Nevertheless, Ben could not refrain from running into the forest secretly every day to be alone to do it.

* * *

Every evening they listened with excitement to the news on the radio and at last the message came, which they had been longing for so much.

In the middle of the news, the BBC announcer from London interrupted the broadcast and, after a short break, he said, all excited, that he had just received a message saying that the Germans had surrendered!

What hilarity and joy! Everybody was cheering, shouting hurray, dancing about with tears in their eyes. Mommy first kissed Ben and then Moritz.

Ben even expected that his stepfather might congratulate him, too. But Moritz, as usual, ignored Ben as if he weren't there at all.

Denmark was free again! It was the 4th of May 1945! On the radio they played the national anthem *Our Beautiful Land*. Everybody stood up singing:

> *– AND OLD DENMARK SHALL REMAIN*
> *AS LONG AS THE BEECH REFLECTS*
> *ITS LEAVES IN THE BLUE WAVES*
> *REFLECTING IN THE BLUE WAVES.*

Now the war was over. Now Ben actually was to have his watch back. But his stepfather acted as if he had forgotten all about it. As he looked at the watch many times daily, surely he couldn't avoid thinking of it. Anyway, he kept the watch without mentioning a word.

The week after, they were allowed to travel to Stockholm on their own. They each received 250 crowns from the Swedish state. Ben's money was paid to him personally, too, as Mommy was not to sign for him. Mommy then allowed him to decide all by himself what he would use it for. Ben wished to buy a brand-new bicycle. He had never owned one. This was a very sensible idea! Mommy went with him into a shop in the main street of Stockholm, where Ben chose a smart beige-yellow bicycle with special elegantly curved handlebars such as they used in Sweden, and with a powerful bell which could easily be heard at a distance!

Ben could hardly believe that it really was his own, that he really owned a completely new bicycle... but it was so!

While Mommy and Uncle Moritz stayed at a hotel for about a week, Ben was with his stepfather's sister and her husband in one of Stockholm's suburbs.

The aunt was very kind to him, even though she was his stepfather's sister. It was quite incredible! She fed him stewed rhubarb with thick cream. Ben liked it very much.

✶ ✶ ✶

Ben is lying in his bed, looking toward the window. Lily rests her head on his arm, hiding her face against his neck. They had cycled all the way home to Regensen without exchanging a word, while thoughts rumbled in Ben's head after the confrontation with Lily's mother.

Lily had followed Ben because she had no alternative. It was as simple as that. It was as if her mother didn't really concern her. All she wanted was to be with Ben. She had been thinking of him ever since he came to her class after the war.

Ben can catch a glimpse of the lit-up Round Tower outside the window. It was there, keeping an eye on him in such a friendly and confident manner, like a loving round father from on high. Then his eyes run over the piano. In the glow from the window the keys glisten in the dusk like white teeth in an open mouth. He liked to have the feeling of the cold-warm, hard-soft ivory surface of the keys against his fingertips, when he touched them cautiously and affectionately or when, with the full weight of his arms and body, he hit them with his fingers stretched like hammers of resilient steel.

Ben turns Lily's head towards himself. Her blue-black eyes are shining brightly, looking inquiringly at him. He feels the warmth of her body, his fingers stroke her arms. He puts his hands round her firm white breasts, breathing like two downy young birds.

Lily, too, is exploring Ben's smooth fragrant skin with her hands, touching his shoulders and neck, gliding further down to his chest and around his back, drawing him tight to her. Her lips search his mouth. Ben kisses her, tasting her warm bitter-sweet breath.

Impulsively, they cannot get their clothes off fast enough. Their young bodies are like magnets. They feel each others' burning skin, touching each other everywhere simultaneously. In Ben a strength is breaking out which amazes him, and Lily follows him. They clutch at one another like two abandoned children alone on a distant planet, and Lily is open for him. He is so welcome with her! She is carried away by his strength, floating with him dizzily between the earth and all the stars. All their accumulated longing for love is redeemed. Ben utters a cry of triumphant delight that almost makes him lose consciousness.

Slowly he loosens himself from her, while a sweet pain flushes through him. Lily nestles against him again, breathing in his hot steaming body with all her senses and pores open, with the animal desire of a she-cat.

Ben has never known himself in this way:

– Unbelievable! It's reality, it's true! It is simply incredible! It has happened. Now... the two of us together!

Lily leans her cheek against his chest:

– I love you, Ben... Although I almost was afraid of you before. You sounded like a warrior, like a savage, like Tarzan himself!

Ben, rather flattered and also amused:

– Tarzan, of course... me Tarzan, you Lily!

Ben imitates Tarzan, howling:

– Uuuuh, Tarzan has brought down the dangerous lioness, uuuuh!

Both of them laugh and kiss each other again.

For a long time they lie still. Ben feels light, as if he were floating in weightless space, losing himself in Lily's arms, enjoying his sensation of being victorious:

– Here we are lying then, you the daughter of a Nazi, with me, a son of a *YIDDISHE MAMME!*

Lily rises up on one elbow and looks Ben in the eyes. She has something important to say:

– I have always wanted you!

– But I thought that... it was Kristian?

Lily is all frankness now:

– It was because I felt that you, you and Grete, belonged to each other, and then I thought that Kristian... I was taken aback, so mad, when I found out that Grete and Kristian were to be engaged!

Ben kisses Lily's breasts very softly. All the tensions of the day have completely disappeared.

– Are you serious about becoming an actress?

– I have been thinking about that for a long time, too.

Ben has no doubt that Lily is speaking her mind. Maybe she could give him the courage he didn't possess to try seriously himself... But now Ben won't think of anything at all, right now he just wants to enjoy the present, to be with Lily. He embraces her again and they become one living being... to fall asleep in each other's arms.

* * *

The tower clock of Regensen strikes five brittle strokes as Ben wakes up, feeling Lily's quiet breath against his cheek. Her face, with its high forehead, straight nose and curved mouth, surrounded by thick blonde hair in a broad garland over the pillow, radiates nothing but peace. Her eyes stir a little under their closed eyelids. Then she opens her eyes. In her sleep she could sense that Ben was watching her. She smiles contentedly, running her fingers through Ben's dark curls. He gives a little laugh:

– What won't your mother think of us now?

– It's a matter of total indifference! Mama only repeats what she has heard from Dad. And I can't help it, can I?

– That's true...

Nevertheless Ben is shocked:

– I've never heard anyone say it so openly!

Of course Lily had spoken to her father about it when she learned of the tragedies of the war:

– To me my Dad said that he did not have the slightest idea about the concentration camps.

– Do you think it is true, what he said?

– Yes, I do...

After a while Lily is spontaneous:

– Ben, I would so much like to be someone special for you!

Ben gets a sensation of a pain, as if it were too to good to be true, as if he couldn't, weren't allowed to accept it. He gets up:

– It is dawning now. Come, I will walk you home.

* * *

Lily and Ben place their bicycles by the garden gate and steal up the path. By the front door of the mansion he kisses her goodbye before she will slip up into her room without being noticed. Just then the door is torn open from inside the house. It is her mother. For a moment they stand there, all three of them, in a stone-like trance. Then the lady grasps Lily's arm firmly, pulling her out of Ben's embrace, dragging her inside the door. She is white-hot with rage:

– Up you go, up! I have been waiting for you all night without shutting my eyes! You ought to be ashamed of yourself!

Then she turns towards Ben, full of hate:

– What have you done to my daughter? Such a... Such a...

And she slams the door in his face.

* * *

The first thing Mommy and Ben do when they get to Copenhagen is to visit Kristian. They are all waiting by the front door, with Mrs. Vestergaard. Ben throws himself into Birgit's arms, and then father Knud lifts him up in his strong arms:

– You don't weigh anything, my boy! But we will see to that!

When he sets Ben down on the ground again, Ben heads straight for

Kristian and presses him tightly. And then once more he goes to Birgit and she holds him tight as if she will never let him go again.

Kristian observes his mother: She is crying at last! When Ben was caught, Birgit had become completely silent. All she said was: "Has he been caught...?" But she didn't cry, Kristian noticed that. Nor when the postcard arrived from Ben, who was out there when he wrote that he was all right. Kristian thought of Ben every time he saw the German soldiers in the street... Maybe Ben would never come back, while he himself just went to school and had to do his homework every day. All this time his mother did not laugh either, that is really heartily. But now she is crying again! Now she also would be able to be really happy again. He had been missing his mother being really content.

Ben feels Birgit's body trembling as she holds him tight. He would like to cry too, but he cannot. He didn't cry either when he was captured in the church loft, or in Theresienstadt. Not even on Liberation night on the 4th of May, when everyone else had wept and Uncle Moritz had tears in his eyes...

The big dog easily recognizes Ben, too, jumps gleefully up at him, laying his forepaws on Ben's shoulders, barking and licking his face.

Now they are going to have lunch on the terrace, where they can look at the garden with the big lawn and the trees, and the bushes where the boys have their secret cave.

Birgit asks Ben what he would like to eat most of all. A fried egg on a piece of rye bread! He had not tasted that yet, not even in Sweden, so Mrs. Vestergaard goes into the kitchen to fry a fresh egg for him, and Birgit spreads a really thick layer of butter on the bread, so that it melts as the hot egg is placed over it. Ben has not eaten an egg for over eighteen months.

During lunch, Mommy asks if Ben can stay with Kristian for some time. Other people had taken over their old flat and they were not likely to move out, so first of all Mommy has to find a place to live...

Knud and Birgit not only want Ben to stay with them for a while, but they insist that he should live with them always. Ben could have the room next to Kristian. The two boys glance at each other. That's exactly what they had always wanted!

It suits Mommy fine, too. The boys are so beside themselves with joy that they run out on the lawn jumping on top of each other while the dog leaps around them, giving tongue to its joy, wanting to play with them. Now, down to the cave. There is exactly enough space for the dog to fit in.

* * *

The next day Ben brings his new bicycle. How smart it is! Kristian is really impressed.

– Shall we go for a ride at once?

– Of course!

And the two boys jump on their bicycles. Off they go through the residential neighbourhood of Hellerup.

Suddenly Ben cuts and runs, racing round the corners, so that Kristian can hardly keep up with him, rushing at a terrific speed, pushing down like mad on the pedals, using all his muscles, pumping with his legs, clutching the handlebars with all his might, while he gasps for breath, spurting faster and faster, until he brakes with a shriek from the tyres in front of the school gate.

Then he waits, until shortly after Kristian with a groan catches up with him. Both boys have to wait some time till they recover their breath.

– Are you off your nut, old chap, to clear out like that?

Ben bubbles with joy:

– But it's so fantastic, man! Can't you grasp that? That I can just ride to the right... or to the left... or straight ahead... just as I please! Nobody is there to prevent me from going where I wish! I can ride along with nobody forbidding me to do so, with no one to stand guard over me with a gun, who will shoot me or imprison me! The streets are mine! It's not only other people who can walk the streets. I am free, I can ride where I want to, freely... It's fantastic!

And Ben bellows so that the whole world can hear him:

– I am free. I am FREEEE!

Kristian is mute for a while. He has missed Ben a lot... Then he nods towards the school:

– She isn't there any longer, you know... Mrs. Arnold-Hansen. She and her husband, both of them, have been dismissed.

Ben is glad, but not completely satisfied. There was something he would have liked to ask her about.

* * *

Mommy and Ben went to see their old flat. To begin with, the people who were living there wouldn't allow them to come in at all.

– None of Mommy's things are left!

But then, finally, they reluctantly let Mommy glance inside.

– Look, there are our curtains!

Ben pulled Mommy's arm when they were walking through the rooms. But these people claimed that they were their own curtains, and Mommy shushed Ben to be quiet and ignore it.

In Ben's room the bookcase with the rounded corners which he had made himself was hanging on the wall, with the big book about animals which he had got for his Bar Mitzvah standing on it. But the two books from his birthday about Indians weren't there...

– That's my book!

But the boy who lived there now said it belonged to him. Then Ben took the book and opened it so they could see that he had written his name in it. So the boy had to give it back to him, but when Ben asked for his two Indian books, which he certainly had bought himself, the boy answered that they had never been there and hastily looked the other way. Ben was convinced that he had hidden the books somewhere else...

Ben, of course, also wanted to get his bookcase back, but both the boy and his parents asserted that it most certainly was theirs! Ben was completely dumbfounded that they could tell such a lie! If only he could get hold of the teacher, he would surely remember that Ben had made the bookcase himself. Then he remembered the time when Mr. Ermelin had hit him, so Ben didn't feel like looking him up.

Mommy thought that now that Ben had his book back, it was useless for him to kick up a fuss about nothing.

* * *

When they were down in the street again Ben was deeply ditraught:

– It was certainly mine, I made the bookcase myself... Why didn't you help me to get it back?

Mommy explains:

– We must be pleased that we got out alive, you must understand that, Bennyboy!

Miss Berg, the woman to whom Moritz gave power of attorney when they had to run away, had sold all their furniture. The armchairs had been sold for five crowns each, the sofa for twenty crowns, and the whole dining-room suite with the large carpet for one hundred crowns.

Ben is amazed:

– But it was an Oriental carpet!

That's how it was! Miss Berg had given them all the receipts and the amount of money was correct. Miss Berg had allowed Mommy and Uncle

Moritz to sleep in her dining-room till they managed to find another flat. Mommy couldn't, in all decency, complain after that.

Luckily Miss Berg had kept Mommy's fine silver box with cutlery for twenty-four places, which Mommy had inherited from Grandpapa. Mommy had at least got that back. Mommy also went to the second-hand dealer who had bought her beloved piano for fifty crowns. She was offered it back again... for 500 crowns. When Mommy thought that it was very expensive, the dealer said that she was under no compulsion to buy it.

Ben can't comprehend any of this:

– Why was it all sold so cheap?

– That's because nobody really reckoned we would ever return.

✶ ✶ ✶

Ben now wanted to know what had become of his own father. They tried to track him through The International Red Cross, but all they could get for an answer was a statement from the hotelier in Paris where Ben's father had been living: Aron was arrested by the Gestapo in the summer of 1943 and deported to Poland. They had no further information to offer about his fate.

✶ ✶ ✶

The salt wind on the port side makes the sail swell and the boat glides swiftly through the water.

Every now and then the sun hides roguishly behind a cloud, as it commonly happens in the Danish summer, only to emerge again, and just as you think it is there, it disappears again. The sun teases the Danes in this way year after year.

The two brothers are lying in the bow following with their eyes the white foaming waves breasted by the pitching prow of the boat. They are enjoying diving with the boat into the dark green trough of the sea and then, with a sucking motion, being lifted up again by the enormous power of the water, swinging with the varying rhythm of the waves, while the warm breeze blows through their locks and the sunlight caresses their tanned muscular bodies. From time to time they let their arms hang over the rails, feeling the cold water rush its way through their fingers.

Kristian thinks of the time when they were boys. Ben had so often been sad, and when Kristian had asked his parents why, they had answered that they couldn't do anything about it.

– Do you remember, the only time I was ever at your place, Ben? We were having dinner with your stepfather, we didn't even dare to exchange a look or say a single word! The painful atmosphere, the fright he inspired in us, the horror he radiated! It sends a shiver down my spine to think of it! I never will forget that... And you have been living with that man all those years! And every time I think of that gym cupboard at school...

Father Knud is sitting in his sunhat with his indispensable pipe, holding the tiller with a firm hand.

He is in a magnificent mood. Our little Denmark is, indeed, a wonderful country to spend a holiday in. The consultant is content. He has left a long working year behind him. If you just take a real vacation, relaxing completely, then it doesn't matter that you work hard every day. But you must let go of every thought to do with your working day, and then please yourself with a drink. That's the whole secret: Smoke and drink, but take a holiday!

Birgit has heard it so often. She always brings them something refreshing. However, not only that: she is also the one who knows how to listen, to be silent and to comprehend. She smiles and waves at her boys in the bow. Ben waves back. Suddenly she seems to him to look different. Hasn't she lost rather a lot of weight...?

Now Knud is waving his cap signalling Kristian to take over the tiller.

Ben remains lying on his back, glancing up at the sky. A couple of white seagulls, wings outstretched, sail in wide circles above them. Then a familiar hand is stroking his forehead, quietly and for a long time. It is Birgit who has sat down next to him:

– Your mother phoned me just before we left...

Can't Mother ever leave him alone? Does she also have to be down on him far out at sea?

– Will she involve you in it too? It's my private affair, to resign from the community, isn't it?

– But she is so terribly sorry. She does care so much about you, Ben!

– Does she?

How can Ben ever be in doubt? Birgit feels so sorry for Tanya too...

– But don't you think it's true?

– I have done everything to comply with mother, instead of doing what I wished to do myself! I have renounced... And all the same she is always anxious. It's sickening. She is always thinking that I'll fail. She claims that I am causing her distress, that she suffers so much for my sake...

– Is it really necessary that you resign from the Jewish community? Your mother says that you are ashamed of being yourself.

Ben glances over the glittering crests of the waves. He can feel the reproach: Desertion! He cannot reject it entirely either:
– I'd like to be anonymous, like the rest of you, not always be pointed out! By the way, it is dangerous, too. It was the card index of the community which the Germans went by at that time.
Birgit gets upset:
– But that was during the war... That won't ever happen again!
Ben had also been convinced that now the whole world MUST have realized how much the Jews had suffered... And the enthusiasm when the United Nations recognized Israel! But just what hadn't happened since then, all the things he had experienced in discussions! And not even ten years had passed since the war...
– Won't it ever happen again? Will you guarantee that?
Now Birgit really must protest:
– But it is impossible, now after Hitler! And certainly not in this country, where there is no anti-Semitism at all! It is not like the Danish mentality to be like that!
– Are you convinced of it? What do you know about what people are hiding behind the nice faces they show to others? Things won't disappear just because you deny their existence.
Birgit has to laugh:
– Aren't you a little silly, my dear boy? People have become more sensible, fortunately, haven't they?
– Do you really think so? When they haven't learned anything for two thousand years?
– Ben, it hurts so much to hear you saying things like that! I have never noticed anything of that kind, not the slightest!
– YOU haven't, I believe that! It depends on which people you keep company with, and if they know you... But I have! Not with many people, as it isn't so popular to be an anti-Semite at the moment, and fortunately most people are decent people, but...
– It isn't true, it can't be! It simply mustn't be true, I won't believe it!
– When people don't know that I am Jewish, they will tell me things: Short condescending comments, shrugs of the shoulder, ambiguous hints betraying their prejudices. It may even take place openly, although that is an exception...
Birgit feels her bosom press together, so much so that she gasps for breath:
– It's not possible Ben, unthinkable...
– UNTHINKABLE? Would I say such things to you if they weren't true?

Birgit is mute with grief. Tears trickle slowly down her cheeks. She looks at Ben: wouldn't he withdraw what he had been saying?

Ben takes Birgit's hand and holds it tight, without speaking any more.

On the Danish coast Kronborg Castle rises proudly, surrounded by its wooded bastions, while they sweep past Elsinore on the green rolling waves gurgling quietly against the boat's side.

* * *

At the Tivoli Garden's first season after the liberation, Ben joined the Tivoli Boys' Guard again. His comrades hadn't the slightest notion where Ben had been, thinking he had been in Sweden all the time.

In the meantime, two boys younger than Ben had advanced to playing first cornet, so Ben was set to play the second cornet. They didn't take into account that he had been playing in the orchestra in Theresienstadt. The bandmaster was so strict, that all the boys trembled in fear of him. He even demanded that Ben should write out the sheets of music for the time he had been away, and he scolded Ben as if it were Ben's own fault. Despite this, Ben was glad to be with his friends in Tivoli again.

For the first part of the summer holidays, Ben remained in town to play in the Boys' Guard. He lived all alone in the big villa, while Kristian and his parents went up to the Cabin by the seaside.

When the Tivoli Boys Guard had its summer holidays, Ben immediately rode down to the seaside on his new bicycle and managed the sixty kilometres so swiftly, that he reached the Cabin by lunchtime.

And so they were together again, Ben and Kristian. They swam in the fresh waters of the Sound and rode, as they used to do, to the Trolls' Forest, where the trees with their gnarled branches looked like living witches. Birgit brought lunch on her bicycle, as she always did, and Knud saw to it, that they would most certainly not forget the schnapps bottle, as he always did. A good dram was about the healthiest thing you could get, the consultant declared, while the boys were racing along on their bicycles ahead of the parents.

Ben did tell them about how he had been caught in the loft of the Gilleleje church. In any case, he did not feel like talking about what he had experienced in Theresienstadt, and neither Kristian nor his parents questioned him about it.

At the Cabin the boys had their fun catching flies with their hands, becoming so good at it that they never missed.

Both boys loved to draw. Kristian was best at drawing the dashingly smart flashy American cars. He could draw them exactly as they were in reality, whereas Ben was best at drawing horses: Beautiful slim saddle horses or big thickset dray horses.

He told about the horse he had modelled, when he was at the pottery workshop in Theresienstadt. The next day Birgit brought him a big lump of clay and asked Ben to make a horse for her. In the days that followed, he modelled a clay horse, with legs rearing, flying mane and a long flowing tail. But when everybody had admired it, he got up early the following morning and broke it into a thousand pieces. Birgit was alarmed that Ben destroyed his own work in this way, but why he did so he truly didn't know himself...

They sailed around Zealand again. Kristian and Ben had a marvellous time! They sang modern American melodies from the radio, moving their heads and their entire bodies to the jazz rhythm: "Open the door, Richard... da dum da dum da dum... Get up those stairs, mademoiselle... da da, da dum, da dum dum..."

At night the boys slept in a small cabin all by themselves. That's when they told each other pirate stories for a long time, until they fell asleep. In the last school year of the occupation, Kristian had been in a secret alliance with teacher Børge: Twice a week, when they had Danish for the first lesson, the schoolmaster had placed a pile of pamphlets from the underground press, covered by old newspapers, behind the bicycle shed in the schoolyard. Kristian had put the papers into his school bag and, bicycling in the district, tossed the pamphlets into people's mail slots, while Børge had ticked him off in the school attendance register as being present. Neither Knud nor Birgit had had the least idea about it, and the alliance and its aim was so secret that his parents were not to know anything about it even now, after the war was over. Ben had to swear not to tell anything to anybody.

∗   ∗   ∗

After the summer vacation, it was agreed that Ben was to go to school in Kristian's class, although he had missed over two years. Kristian was going to help him with mathematics.

During the first months of school, Ben had extra lessons in the afternoon, which Børge gave him privately and voluntarily, and it wasn't long before Ben was able to keep up with the rest of the class.

Mommy saw to it that Ben had piano lessons again, and he liked to practice for hours on the grand piano in the living-room of the villa. When he visited

Mommy and played on her piano, she was so pleased to hear him play Chopin's Polonaise.

∗ ∗ ∗

Every May 11th, the lime tree with its new light green leaves stands in the middle of the rough paving-stones in the yard at Regensen. The least the lime tree can do is to smarten itself up to look its best, on its very own birthday! The day is celebrated in style, according to all the traditions! A white gloved hand is tied to the trunk of the lime tree and all the students walk up to the tree to shake hands with it, congratulating it one by one.

That is followed by a great party at the tables around the tree, with lots of sandwiches, beer and schnapps, speeches and songs in honour of Virgin Lime, the only virgin in the Red Yard! The big bottle belonging to the SHARP club also comes into good use. It circulates under the tables, so that those who need to relieve themselves don't have to take the trouble to leave the banquet during the pleasures of the feast. At the end, all the students walk in single file out of Regensen's gate, crossing Merchant Street and up on top of Christian No. 4's own Round Tower, from where they throw toilet rolls down at the gaping passersby.

Ben enjoys participating in Regensen life, writes parodies and satires and takes part in the annual revue performance, which the Warden's wife has a far too touchy temperament to watch.

But in spite of the cheerful undergraduate life, for long periods Ben suffers from stomach pains. Actually he had them since he came home from Theresienstadt. The doctor at the Hall diagnoses a duodenal ulcer. Often, Ben must get up at night to boil himself a plate of gruel. It doesn't taste good, but it soothes.

∗ ∗ ∗

During summer vacations Ben travels in Europe as a guide. It is exciting to see the countries, experience the freedom of passing through borders he never dreamt of, guiding his tourists to Paris, Vienna, the Riviera, the beautiful mountains of the Tyrol, sailing on the Rhine. War was far away in the past, nobody mentioned it, when Ben jovially touched glasses with a jolly German wine grower, even though the question sometimes flashed through Ben's mind, what had this man been doing years ago as a German soldier...?

Several times Ben served as a guide in Rome, sharing his enthusiasm for the Eternal City with his tourists, the intense Roman way of enjoying life, the food, the wine and the charming Roman women who walked the streets as if they were dancing.

Here he was comfortable amidst the beautiful palaces. There was a kind of solidarity between the historical ruins and the modern improvised traffic which, in spite of apparently total chaos, unsnarled anyway in the city of miracles. Here he felt accepted. Nobody pointed him out because of his strange surname or scoffed at him when he said he wanted to be an actor.

With special enthusiasm Ben placed himself at the Forum Romanum – upon the very same spot where Antony had stood two thousand years ago with Julius Caesar's murdered body in his arms – he would recite Antony's dramatic speech from Shakespeare's play, to the loud applause of the appreciative party he conducted.

What a wonderful sensation, to be admired when he displayed his talent, in the sun, in the limelight, on the renowned historical stage under the triumphal imperial arches!

In such moments of success he forgot he had spotted a small newspaper paragraph. Lily had been accepted by the Drama School of the Royal Theatre, together with five other hopeful aspirants.

* * *

One day Ben got a parcel by post from Prague. He opened the package: My fountain pen! I had never expected to see it again. It will come in useful for writing school exercises. But Moritz had still not returned the watch to Ben. His stepfather certainly ought to give it back to him voluntarily, but patience was of no avail; so Ben finally had to ask him for it. Moritz gave it to Ben without thanking him by so much as a word.

The watch had been worn, scratched, and it kept bad time. Ben took it to a watch repairer who said it was not worth repairing. Anyhow, Ben wasn't fond of the watch any more, either.

Now came the first Hanukkah at liberty. During the Christmas vacation, the former prisoners from Theresienstadt were offered a free trip to a holiday resort at Lidingö near Stockholm. Mommy and Ben left without Uncle Moritz, who had important business to attend to.

It was such fun to meet John, Kalle, little Jacob and Rebecca again. In Sweden there were miles of white snow! What fun to be sledging down the hills, and what tremendous snowball fights they had!

Lea and her mother hadn't come along. She thinks that she is too distinguished to be together with the rest of us, was Mommy's opinion. Actually, Ben had been very keen to meet Lea.

The last evening they had a party. Everybody was to dress up. Mommy got the idea that Ben, who was still small and thin and could still fit into Mommy's size 36 shoes, should put on Mommy's clothes, her blouse and skirt and her bra padded with a pair of stockings. Mommy made Ben up herself and combed his full curls which could easily have been a girl's, and then Ben went down to the party.

John and Kalle had dressed themselves as pirates. They couldn't recognize Ben and thought he was a fine lady. What a lark when everybody thought that Ben was a girl! He walked about smiling, swinging his hips, and when somebody at the party asked why that lady hadn't dressed up, they couldn't believe it when he answered that he was a boy.

The following summer Knud, Birgit, Kristian and Ben were to sail to the Swedish Skerries. At the last moment it emerged that Ben, because he was stateless, needed to have a visa. It would take six weeks to get it. Doctor Knud tried to persuade the Swedish Ambassador to speed up the issue of the visa, but it was not possible to make an exeption. So Ben, regrettably, couldn't go with them.

* * *

Confused, Ben wakes up as somebody is knocking at the door. It's only eleven o'clock in the morning. Mommy clasps her hands:

– Aren't you up yet, dearest Bennyboy! Well, you students certainly enjoy life! You sleep half the day away and have a good time all night... Now come and have a look what your Mommy has brought you: Two fine shirts. I found them at a sale. Just imagine, they were so cheap, only half price! First I was going to give them to Moritzl, but he didn't want them, and then I immediately thought of my own Benny! You could certainly use a couple of new shirts. You students look a perfect fright, living in your own world, and not caring in the least how you dress.

Ben is cross. Yesterday he had met a girl at a concert at Broadcasting House and she came home with him. Ben had played for her and it had gone late. Imagine if she had stayed. What would mother have been able to get out of that then? And those idiotic shirts which not even Moritz wanted!

– You can keep your shirts!

Mommy is thunderstruck:

– But... don't you want them? Believe me, they were, indeed, so cheap, there was only a tiny defect which you can hardly see.

And Mommy holds one of the shirts in front of Ben's chest with enthusiasm:

– Look for yourself, how it suits you...

– I don't want your cheap shirts!

– Sweet Bennyboy, think of all the poor people who would be delighted...

– Then give them to the poor in Africa or wherever, God damn...

When Mommy is confronted with anger, she always reacts by ignoring it. Benny doesn't mean it, he isn't serious, he has inherited his temperament from his father! Mommy just wants to enjoy her son:

– That's all right, Bennyboy, I'll soon find somebody who would like to have the shirts, if you insist that you don't... How about your examinations, did you pass?

Ben goes to the sink and begins to brush his teeth:

– It was...

– And what did they ask you about? Were they nice to you? What are you reading at present, is it Schiller or Goethe or Stefan Zweig? I just read his great book on Maria Stuart.

– Does it matter?

Ben's refusal hurts. Mommy finds something else to talk about. She had been to the theatre the other night:

– Imagine, Moritzl and I saw I WANT TO BE SOMEBODY ELSE, yes, exactly the same play in which you had the principal part when you were at grammar school... I was thinking of you all the time. But Moritzl didn't want to see it then, so now he saw the play anyway, and I told him that you had played the lead at school and that they had all applauded you and been impressed by you! At school we shook hands with Kristian's parents after the play!

– Yes, Mother, you were talking about the play and you praised Kristian, enlarging upon how well he had played, upon how sweet Grete had looked, you talked about all the actors, one by one, you were so enthusiastic: But about me... not a single word! As if I had not been on the stage.

– But I couldn't boast about how talented you were when Kristian only had that small part compared to you! Besides, both Doctor Knud and Mrs. Birgit praised you, so that I was very proud!

– I was waiting for you to say something, mother. You only had to say: "Well done, Ben!" Since then you actually never mentioned that I played in

I WANT TO BE SOMEBODY ELSE. I remember that very clearly. You weren't fond of it at all...

Mommy had been sitting in the dark among the spectators, weeping:

– It's because I was so miserable... You had played in such a way that I really thought that you wanted to be somebody else that, indeed, you were in earnest!

– Does that surprise you? It was really the role of my life! I didn't need to play it, I was just myself!

– Ben, I know very well that you would rather become an actor. I remember it as if it was yesterday, when you read Slovenly Peter aloud, and with all the right intonations. You were a real little actor even then, at three years of age... You were so lovable, you always did what Mommy told you, you were such a good boy...

– Yes, because if I wasn't a good boy... there was only death!

Mommy becomes totally confused:

– Isn't that a strange thing to say?

– Don't all the children in Slovenly Peter die if they are disobedient? They do get punished and mutilated, if they don't do as Mother tells them to!

– Are you becoming insane, Benny? That is not in the least true! You were so fond of that book, knew it by heart! All children love that book, and the lady at the dentist's really thought that you could read...

– I still know it by heart: Poor Kaspar died because he couldn't swallow the disgusting soup and Paulinchen burned to ashes. Her mother didn't even mourn for her, only two cats wept over her death!

– Sweet Benny, they are only innocent, amusing stories! Dear me, how you do take it much too seriously...

– Don't you think I took it seriously when Konrad the Thumb-sucker had his thumbs cut off?

– But it was only to break children of a bad habit. It wasn't meant so severely at all!

– How should I, a three-year-old, know it was not meant seriously?

– But you were never a bad boy like the others, Benny!

– You bet I was not! With all the horrifying frightening stories! I was your obedient little soldier, in Horserød I certainly chose to go with you! Soldiers go out to kill or to be slain themselves... And then you weep salt tears, you poor, poor mothers!

– I really think that you are ill, Ben... an innocent children's book! Thousands and thousands of children have been delighted by it. And you no longer suck your finger, now that you are a grown-up, do you?

Ben smashes the mouse-rinsing glass in the sink with a loud crash:
– It was Konrad's only comfort! Because his mother leaves him all alone!
He has only his thumb to suck! But he is not even allowed to do that, as his
mother threatens him with the tailor with the big pair of scissors! And then
he does it all the same. And the punishment is merciless! The executioner
mutilates him, first one thumb: CUT! And then the other thumb: CUT! There
they are, lying on the floor, two bleeding bits with the blood gushing out of
the two big holes where his thumbs had been!
Ben shakes his hands in front of Mommy:
– Look, I am bleeding, I am still bleeding, look mother!
Mommy screams and hides her face in her hands.
It takes a while until Ben calms down again:
– And the righteous mother didn't give him his figs either, which she
actually had bought for him. That's what happens if you are disobedient, no
punishment is harsh enough!
Mommy looks frightened at Ben:
– Ben... I'm so afraid for you that you'll never be able to fend for yourself,
either as an actor or...
– I am studying for a sensible profession now, God damn it!
Immediately Mommy tries to calm herself:
– Well, then everything is all right! You take so many worries away from
your little Mommy, now that you have become sensible at last, Bennyboy.
That's certainly the very best thing for you, my dear! If only you would
complete your studies...
Now Mommy has said the wrong thing again!
– But WILL you not understand me, Mother: I want to do what I myself
think is best for me! I myself am able to think! Why don't you support me
in what I will do myself?
– But I do! I did say that if you really wanted to become an actor, then you
should always try for it all the same. And then, of course, I hoped that when
all is said and done, you would realize...
Ben's stomach hurts so that he can hardly breathe:
– You see that I have given it up!
Mommy becomes sad:
– But I did say that you could always try later, when you had passed your
examinations...
– It's not what you are saying which is decisive, but what you are hoping
for me...
– You have given up the stage yourself, it was your own choice!

True. He had made his own choice. But had he had the freedom to choose? When he first had confided to Mommy that he would like to go on the stage, Moritz was certainly by no means to be told! Ben can recall that feeling of doing something forbidden! When later the stepfather learned about it, he even made Ben look ridiculous! Ben again gets that sucking feeling, as if he had been knifed in the stomach:

– It is true, I gave it up myself... But for whose sake?

– Why didn't you try anyway, then?

– Because you condemned me in advance! I'd starve like the children in the book!

– But it's because I love you... I'm sure you would certainly break your neck, and you cannot bear to suffer defeat!

– You have always been so damned afraid for my sake. As if I couldn't stand on my own feet. If I wished to take a swim you would, instead of letting me learn the strokes, out of sheer fear that I would drown, rather cut off my arms and legs to prevent me from going bathing! There I would sit on the beach amputated, watching how all the others are splashing, in the sea. That's the way you always wanted to save me!

To Mommy it always was a matter of survival:

– If you had been talented enough, you would have accomplished it in spite of my resistance!

– Your RESISTANCE?

For an instant everything turns black for Ben. Then a thousand colours whirl inside his head. Only little by little he comprehends what his mother has been saying...

– Resistance! Not only did you not support me but... my God! It's only dawning on me right now: You have opposed me purposely! You have been against me! Behind my back! While you have been lulling me with your feeble-minded worries...

Ben looks at his mother who suddenly becomes a stranger to him. At this moment, something ceases to exist, something which goes to pieces just like the machine he once dreamt about:

– You have deceived me... deluded me!

Mommy is frightened. She senses that something irrevocable has occurred:

– For your own good, Ben! I've always fought for you like a lioness, for what's best for you! I have done it all because I love you, Ben, because I am your mother!

Ben is petrified:

– You aren't my mother any more.

Now Mommy's heart stops beating:

– Ben, how can you say such a thing... What can I do? You cannot abandon me just like that, Benny, it's unnatural! Let's talk about it, for God's sake!

– There is nothing more to talk about. It is too late.

– No Ben, it is never too late!

Ben has always relied, totally, unshakably, on one thing: That when it really came to the point, Mommy would side with him. That's what he had been trusting in blindly:

– It's too late.

Mommy feels as if she is on the bottomless sea and cannot keep afloat:

– Ben, you mustn't toss me over. You have always been my only consolation when I was in despair, then I had you...

Ben feels hatred growing inside him. Mommy has been choking him with her love all the time, sucking him out, drying him out like a flower which was never given water... He tumbles on his bed hiding his face in the pillow:

– I will never see you again! My mother is dead...

Now Mommy is weeping:

– Ben, I love you... I do love you, I do!

Ben won't hear it, stops his ears.

Mommy is looking uncertainly at him. She would so much like to take him in her arms, give him of her tenderness... But there are bounds which she can't overstep. She does not allow herself to do that. She takes her coat and bag. Moritz is waiting for her at home and he will ask where has she been so long. Silently, she shuts the door behind her.

⁎ ⁎ ⁎

Ben dreams that he is an Egyptian mummy lying in a coffin, wrapped in taut bandages so that he cannot move. He fights to free himself, calls for help, cries out that he is not dead, that they laid him in there by mistake, but he cannot utter a word. A woman with a cloth over her head sits by him, strokes his cheeks gently and feeds him an eggnog beaten up with sugar. Then she rocks him, humming a song until he is completely quiet and has given up resistance.

⁎ ⁎ ⁎

Kristian and Grete have come to lunch in Ben's locum. They must spoil themselves a little. Ben has bought a delicious home-made liver pâté and sausage in the delicatessen next to the synagogue. He opens some bottles of beer:

– One for all and all for one!

He is in an excellent mood and doesn't notice that Kristian and Grete are unusually quiet:

– When I guide my tourist party to Frascati, we go down to a wine cellar where I have made reservations in advance. Now it's like this... The Frascati wine doesn't taste especially strong, but it happens to be stronger than you think, and although I do warn the guests, they quickly get noisy and flushed after only two glasses. Sometimes I have to support some of them when they are reeling back to the tourist bus, but they are enjoying themselves...

The lack of attention seems so striking, that Ben starts wondering:

– I don't think you are very cheerful today?

Kristian hesitates a little:

– We are thinking of getting married soon...

Ben is taken a little by surprise, a slight pang... even though he has become used to the thought that this is going to happen:

– I must say! But weren't you going to wait until you had finished studying? After all, there is not so much longer to go...

Ben watches them carefully:

– You don't seem to be delighted either?

Grete is very solemn:

– It's because Birgit is ill...!

Ben's heart stops for a moment:

– Really ill?

Kristian has never before realized his true feelings about what he is saying now. He recalls when they were boys... the day when his mother received the postcard from Ben from down there.

– Actually, mother changed entirely, Ben, when you were captured... And she never actually got over it, even after you came back. She wasn't ever the same again. Something went to pieces inside her.

Ben's heart is beating so loudly that he imagines the others can hear it. Kristian is clutching Grete's hand:

– I assume that you will be our best man, Ben. It's next Saturday.

Ben is stunned. His head is in a whirl:

– Next Saturday... So soon?

They continue to eat in silence.

* * *

That winter, playing Mozart's Fantasia and Sonata in C Minor, Ben becomes fascinated by Mozart's letters, radiant with his brilliance and dramatic musical genius.

Add to this Mozart's father's affectionately admonitory attitude to his young hothead of a son, who wants to conquer the world. It is exciting to read about the Wunderkind's travels to Paris, London, Vienna and Rome, where Wolfgang, together with his sister, were admired by emperors and princesses.

What fascinates Ben so much is the warmth and solidarity of the Mozart family: Father, mother, brother and sister! Ben takes an active interest in their difficulties and successes, in Mozart's amorous and bubbling naughty letters to his cousin, letters which scandalized the serious German musicologists, who knitted their brows in indignation. Ben feels empathy with Mozart's courage and joy towards the stage, almost as if he were related to him.

Mozart's father not only recognized his son's talents, but even gave up his own employment as a composer to devote himself entirely to his son's musical educaion. The father demanded a lot from the boy, but he supported him with all his heart, enabling him to develop freely as a musician and as an artist.

Mozart's letters from Paris, where his mother had fallen ill and died, are moving and exceptional in their affectionate tactfulness, when he tells his father the tragic news.

To Ben's regret, in the last few years of the father's life, it came to a quarrel between father and son. As an adult, Mozart found his own way, made himself independent, both as a man and as an artist...

* * *

In the large bedroom, Birgit is lying in bed with her eyes closed. The curtains are drawn in the darkened room. Only a bedside lamp casts a dim gleam over her face. She is a shadow of her former self. Pain has ravaged her in recent months, but now a new peace has transfigured her features, as if she already felt the great peace of mind which human beings only seldom experience in their lives.

A vase with yellow flowers fills the room with scent. Knud, Kristian and Grete are silent. They are listening to Birgit's breathing, which from time to time seems to cease completely. Knud is talking very softly:

– Have you told Ben?

Grete nods. Now Birgit opens her eyes. She wants to say something! They

bend down to her. Kristian sits down nearest to his mother's pillow. She grasps his hand, caressing it, clutching it to her breast, and is now looking quite clearly into his eyes. Her voice is distinct:
– Ben!
Kristian, taken aback, looks at his father and at Grete. Then he leans his cheek against Birgit's:
– But mother, it's me...
Birgit looks at Kristian. Her eyes are transparent, stars shine from inside them:
– Ben...
She lays her other hand upon Kristian's hand and stops breathing.

For a long minute Kristian sits very still, with his hand in his mother's hand. Knud closes Birgit's eyes with cautious fingers, helping Kristian draw his hand out of Birgit's hold.

Just then Ben arrives, springing up the broad stairs. He had been at a lecture and hadn't received the telephone message till just now. He had ridden his bicycle all the way like a madman.

At the threshold of the bedroom he stops, looking inquiringly at the others. He can read the answer in their faces. Only with extreme difficulty is he able to approach the bed.

There she is, lying peacefully. She looks as if she is asleep.

* * *

The sunbeams shine dazzling out of a sun low in an otherwise pale sky. Breath from the many people dressed in dark clothes steams like miniature white clouds in the ice-cold air. They talk, but very softly, falling silent when entering the church. The arched light space with the richly coloured tessellated window was decorated with flowers.

The vicar talked briefly about Birgit's warm humanity and the void she left behind her. It was simple and moving.

Ben tries to comprehend that it actually is Birgit lying there in the white coffin covered with yellow and ochre chrysanthemums. So that is the reality of death... that a life you have known always, all of a sudden, ceases forever and can never be called back!

Ben can't get used to the thought. To him it had always been a matter of course that Birgit was there, just as he himself was there. She was a part of his life. She had been there as a confident firm support, for him to take refuge in any time: And then, from one moment to the next, an instant which couldn't be measured, this life has come to an end.

And here he is now, looking at the white coffin, with Kristian, Knud and Grete... and with all the others whom she has also left behind alive...

In accordance with Birgit's wish they sing:

– ALWAYS FREE AND EASY WHEN YOU ARE WALKING
THE ROADS THAT GOD MAY KNOW
EVEN THOUGH YOU SHALL REACH YOUR DESTINATION
ONLY AT THE END OF THE WORLD

How much wisdom in this simple sentence: To walk free and easy! To own the freedom of being yourself, to have reached serenity, where you do not exert yourself unceasingly any more, where you do not aspire to a goal you will never reach... To be cheerful, at peace with yourself, not nagged any longer by an empty sucking longing, but walk the roads God may know... No more hastening from one place to the next, without attaining satisfaction from your own existence, but being free and serene! Not any longer, like Cain, wandering restlessly through life with a mark on your forehead: To live in harmony with your inner and outer world.

This calmness of mind some people – but far from all – attain only after a long life of struggle, after some decades of reckoning with themselves and the whole world, just as Siddharta only found his own heart of hearts as a ferryman by the remote river, having no ambitions, no desires, but just following the waves of the waters flow muttering past and knowing – comprehending – that one wave is followed by the next and the next again, without termination. To trust that the source of life never will be exhausted, that it, like the river, will keep flowing on and on, and at last will be engulfed, entering into a blissful unity with the boundless sea.

Birgit had had this knowledge. She was born with this sense of ease, as a gift from God. She knew the road and had walked on it with security and confidence simply by letting God in her own soul guide her, blessed like Abel who never had the least doubt where to set his foot upon the firm ground which carried and supported his weight at every step, so that he was living with the earth underneath him and the timeless vault of heaven and the universe above him.

At Birgit's funeral Ben realized for the first time, in spite of the fact that he had known so many people who weren't alive any more, that he could die himself too, that his own life was limited to a relatively short span of years and could cease to be in an instant, without his being aware of it himself.

Together with Knud and Kristian, Ben carries the coffin out of the church. Then the coffin is lowered into the earth.

* * *

Doctor Knud is eating slowly, doing justice to the food. There is harmony in his wrinkled face, surrounded by thick silver hair, the distinguished nose in a pronounced profile.

He is sitting in the high-backed armchair at the end of the massive oak table. That is his chair. He has always sat there, just as the furniture stands firmly on the floor with broad legs, exactly where it has always belonged.

Ben's glance travels from the painting of the blue jug in a black frame to the painting of the red flowers. These pictures have hung in their place since he came here from a foreign country as a boy of six. Everything is as if it had never been different and as if it could never change. And yet... Birgit was missing, although the curtains, the furniture and the plants still smelled of her.

The consultant lays his knife and fork down, smiling at Grete:

– Really delicious meal, my girl, really delicious.

Grete receives the compliment, although it actually was Kristian who had brought the roast home and Mrs. Vestergaard who had made it up. But Grete has supervised it all carefully and dished up, so that everything is as perfect as if Birgit had done it herself:

– Truly, it is Kristian who deserves the credit for the roast.

Kristian is smiling:

– I would like to pass the credit on to the butcher, or rather to his wife. If only you flirt a little with her, her husband will give you a good piece of meat. You never know if it is to keep his wife for himself... she is a delicacy too, absolutely not to be sneezed at!

They all laugh with satisfaction and relief. Ben inserts politely:

– At any rate the credit is due to the lady of the house.

Knud is a little moved:

– I know very well that we are all thinking of how good it was when she was among us. If only she had been here tonight! Well, in our family we don't believe in being down in the mouth. It wouldn't bring her back. Let us enjoy all the good memories, all the rich years we have had together, common events... the summer holidays, and not forgetting the weekdays. It would have pleased her if she saw us here, and who knows, maybe she does! She passed away, assured that we would stay together and be all right together. She felt very strongly about it.

Ben is looking at the three faces, so confident in him:

– Yes, that's right. It is good, safe and at ease to be here.

For Knud it's a pleasure to have his two boys around him, and then Grete, of course. She is now replacing Birgit:

– Yes, Ben, feeling secure is the most important thing in life.

Ben impresses the words in his mind to make himself completely aware of what he is saying:

– A place where you really are protected, where you don't have to alter yourself or adapt yourself to be accepted, a place where you are welcome...

Grete has to intervene, because it hurts her so much that Ben is incessantly arguing in a circle with his doubts and restlessness!

– And you have always had that right here!

Ben smiles a little apologetically at her:

– Yes, Grete, of course, it is true!

Knud gets up:

– Thanks for the meal, it was delicious!

They can have their coffee in comfort in the library. Tonight he is going to smoke his good old meerschaum pipe, which he acquired on a journey to the Far East when he was young. He always chooses that pipe when he really wants to indulge.

Grete goes out into the kitchen to make coffee.

– Ben, you aren't leaving without clearing the table, are you!

Kristian is calling Ben, so he too has to join in collecting the plates and the glasses and take them into the kitchen, in brotherly harmony with Kristian.

Grete is already in full swing, boiling the water. All three of them help one another to put away the washing-up. That can wait for Mrs. Vestergaard tomorrow. But now, as it is Kristian's task to serve the brandy, he must join his father in the study again.

Ben has been thinking and examining his soul during the passing years. Was something wrong with him or...? Now he is determined to know the reason, whatever it may be:

– Grete?

Grete is sure to have a presentiment of what Ben is going to ask her. Ben puts his arms around her:

– I have been interrogating myself again and again... Now tell me, Grete, why, WHY precisely?

She puts her hands upon Ben's cheek. Her eyes are shining:

– You have so many dreams, Ben, so many high-flying schemes... *FLY BIRD FLY!* The bird flew so high, too close to the sky for little me... And where was I? There was no place for me in your dreams.

Grete relaxes her touch and again becomes the little attentive woman with both feet on the ground:

– Come now, we must join the others. You take the cups and I take the pot.

* * *

Comfortably recumbent, Knud is sitting in the winged armchair puffing vigorously at his pipe, so that the aromatic blue-white smoke rises in waves, disappearing in the darkness among the leather-bound books on the top shelves of the library.

Kristian fills the glasses with the round paunches: Just so much that you will not spill one drop if you tip them even slightly. Only in this way can you enjoy the original brandy properly: You inhale its bitter-sweet aroma through your nose and mouth before you let the priceless drops moisten first your lips, then your tongue, and then, at the end, you let the precious liquor seep slowly, all by itself, through your pharynx and your throat, to arrange itself in your stomach and from there radiate a pleasant warmth that spreads through your entire body. Doctor Knud knows how to appreciate the small, but important trifles of life.

Grete is pouring the coffee. It too has the fragrance of quality. It's not like wartime, when the only thing you could be quite sure of was that it was made of anything except coffee beans.

– One for all and all for one!

Kristian raises his glass, looking at Ben who has thrown himself down on the deep sofa.

Ben has a fancy for reviving the devil-may-care atmosphere of the old days. He touches his arm and bursts out theatrically:

– Ouch my arm, alacka-day! Help poor me! A doctor! Call hither a doctor before I expire!

Grete and Kristian are game at once. They are playing physicians-in-ordinary who, with solemn gestures, examine and feel the prince's bad arm while Ben groans and moans. Kristian shakes his head with a worried face, reciting:

– This patient is suffering from morbus biceps braccialibus. It is due to the fact that you bend your elbow a little too often!

Kristian looks inquiringly at his father:

– What do you think, professor?

Knud nods and laughs:

– Or it is due to the fact that you bend your elbow a little too little!

Grete lifts her glass, speaking with the drawling voice of the consultant:

– We must immediately retrain his arms, dear colleagues, with physiotherapeutic treatments, putting his peristalsis into motion and simultaneously flexing his extremities, that is bending the elbows, gentlemen doctors!

They all drink and Ben moves his arm up and down, looking very surprised:

– Upon my word! The medicine has had an immediate effect: Look my arm is completely recovered, pliant and compliant!

What rejoicing at the speedy recovery! Ben makes a royal gesture chanting:

– Alas, what a sad change, as the old poet said!

Kristian pretends to be deeply moved:

– What a touching melody our pathetic knight Ben strikes on the strings of his harp. What a noble melancholy he intones in his trembling voice! Listen how it sounds of bygone days!

It was as true as true could be! Grete recalls their Danish lesson:

– Do you remember Børge's enthusiasm for Earl Haakon?

Kristian glances at Ben, and there is an unmistakable glint of recognition in the eyes of both.

Grete walks over to the window and looks out into the dark night:

– It's snowing again. It's freezing; at least 8 to 10 degrees.

For a long time silence hums in the half-lighted room. Their minds set out on long journeys, thinking about what once happened and flying on to something which might happen one day...

– Do you remember the parties we had, Kristian? Your birthdays! The two of us fighting on the stairs against the rest of our class!

Kristian cheers up:

– We still have our musketeer costumes and swords. The other day I was in the loft looking for them in the cupboard. They were there, including our plumed hats. I should like us to go up, get them and have a real duel!

The consultant now remembers something:

– Ben, didn't you take a large piece of layered cake with whipped cream once, stuffing it inside your shirt?

Ben laughs, a little moved:
– I wanted to bring a piece of it home to Mommy. I thought that she should taste a piece of it as well. God, how I looked when I got my shirt off. Mother was awfully upset and I meant so well!

Now something else comes to Kristian's mind:
– Daddy, do you remember when Tarzan taught us to swim? You forced us to go swimming, no matter how cold it was. We had to swim, didn't we, Ben?

– And the water full of jellyfish! And Tarzan made us duck our heads under the water when we did the crawl. You certainly didn't like that, Kristian, you always stuck your head up into the air when you were swimming, while I was swallowing water, coughing and spluttering!

Knud doesn't think it was so terrible after all:
– I did go swimming in the fresh waves every day myself too, to set a good example! Even in stormy weather during the summer when the waves were several metres high... You liked it too, you boys! But you weren't very keen on it when the water was only 14 or 15 degrees...

Kristian's father gets up to go to bed:
– I think I'll leave you young people alone now. Good night to all three of you!

For a while the trio sit silently together. Grete has a feeling of oppression, almost like a presentiment of an imminent parting, a fear that their fellowship might end one day:
– We will always stick together, the three of us, won't we?

Ben is thoughtful too:
– Who knows... maybe our roads really will part?

Kristian can feel this vague pain too, but he will not allow himself to suffer, he must rebel against it:
– Stop it, you two! Or we will actually end up being sentimental and the noble knight Ben will start blubbering. Shall I call the fire brigade and ask them to bring a towel?

It is, in fact, easy enough to be tempted to abandon oneself to depression, but then Ben pulls himself together:
– You are right Kristian, forgive and forget the past. It's the future that matters. What did old Adam Oehlen Beerswiller and his faithful disciple Børge say? To the future!

Kristian answers promptly:
– To the future is all right, but it is the present that matters: To the present!

* * *

They had felt like getting some fresh air in their lungs, although it was already late at night. Without intending to, as they had said to Grete that they were only going for a short walk, they had come farther away from the villa than they planned. Past Triangle's round building with the tortoiseshell roof, they were walking on the rampart of the Citadel. For years they had more or less subconsciously avoided this place, but on this clear night it was as if their feet had taken them there by themselves.

It had stopped snowing. The trees stood there white-powdered like fairies, reaching their outstretched arms with crooked fingers up towards the blue-black sky. From on high, the points of stars shone immovably in the clear frost. Beneath their feet it crackled each time they set their feet in the snow, as if they were walking on dry white clouds.

Ben breaks the silence:

– Look at the stars, Kristian. They are so far away and yet it is as if you could catch them with your hand, put them in your pocket and take them home.

Kristian takes a deep breath and puffs it out so that his breath projects out of his mouth like white steam. He breathes in the ice-cold air again and tastes it, chewing the crystal molecules of air. He couldn't imagine living anywhere else. He belonged here, that's exactly what Ben had been saying at dinner:

– Yes, we are safe and at ease here in our little Denmark.

Ben feels that little sucking in his midriff which comes like a small pang in the pit of his stomach, whenever he hears the matter-of-fact way in which others say: "Our little Denmark..."

When he said it himself, there was always a shadow of a doubt in his mind. It was as if he were standing outside a window, looking into the well-lit living room where everybody was dancing and amusing himself, without missing him at all. Well, he might be invited to come in, but they would continue to dance and he would just stand there watching them. It did not matter if he was there or not, and even if they asked him to join in the dance, he always felt like a guest, while the others belonged there. Because they were born there...

– Yes, you feel fine in your little Denmark WHERE YOUR ROOTS ARE, WHERE YOU BELONG...

Kristian gets annoyed. Now why this tone of reproach in Ben's voice again?

– Stop it, Ben, you are unbearable!

– What do you mean?

Must Kristian perpetually watch out not to hurt Ben? That is really beyond endurance too!

– Stop complaining all the time, as if you weren't... You are doing fine! We are both doing well! In a couple of months you are a Master of Arts and I am a doctor! God damn it, man!

– It wasn't what I wanted to be...

Kristian understands Ben better than Ben suspects:

– You haven't found your right place, have you?

– Exactly!

Ben feels again the solidarity between them:

– That's what matters, Kristian. That life has a meaning and the day has a sense when you get up in the morning. What else are we living for? Anyway, why do we have to be shelved or labelled so that you can't get anywhere? Locked up! My right place is where I have my freedom, where I can have pleasure in what I am doing!

Surely enough, Ben is right! But he keeps talking and talking... As if Kristian had no problems! He just didn't talk so much. Were there any people at all living in total freedom?

– You yourself chose to study linguistics, chose your niche yourself. You have got an education...

– Yes, but is it enough to have an education? It's a choice that determines the rest of your life.

Ben thinks of the confrontation he had with his mother and his stepfather:

– Must we choose an education just because it is proper to do so? For the sake of your family or to be acknowledged by society? Must we always just adapt ourselves to others, disregarding our own original wishes?

– Original wishes?

Did anybody ask Kristian about his wishes when he was a boy? Was Kristian ever allowed to make his own choice?

– You once said something when we were studying in our garden. It made me look into myself, but then I pushed it aside all the same. You said: "It has always been decided that you were to become a doctor!" And now I am becoming one! It was determined before I could make a decision for myself!

– You have always been satisfied, haven't you! It was the right thing for you! At least you have never expressed yourself differently.

– Yes, that's correct, I haven't.

Kristian must admit that. He has never allowed the slightest doubt to cross his mind. He never imagined anything but becoming a doctor and writing the thesis. For his father's sake... And he was surely going to do it, he had promised that to his father, to avenge the offence. But did he himself really wish, in his innermost self, to become a doctor?

– You have a chance to change your mind, Ben, if you will...

– I don't know what I will... If I have a will. Unlike you, I have always been dissatisfied with what and who I am. I have always desired to be somebody else! The two of us have known each other our whole life, Kristian, but there is still one thing we avoid mentioning... something we never had out.

Ben glances around. Not a breath of wind stirs. They are standing on the top rampart just like then, years ago, but now it is icy cold and the black earth is covered with white snow, gleaming dimly in the silent night.

– It was here!

Kristian knows but tries to delay the inevitable all the same:

– What was here?

Ben is quite sure of what he is saying:

– You never forgot it, no more than I have. It was here you said JEW to me!

Kristian had often thought of this matter in the course of the years. Why did he say it, why? But he had been so full of hatred, at that moment he had really wanted to touch Ben in the raw. Only afterwards you reason... But he had given Ben to understand clearly that he regretted it. Kristian won't defend himself:

– Ben! I have a right, too, to be angry with you, don't I! I'm sorry, indeed, that I said it, but it is not only you who has a reason to be angry!

Ben is looking over the frozen water:

– I'll never forget it as long as I live.

Kristian would like to clear the air between them, but he won't pay Ben anything he doesn't feel he owes him. There had been things that he never told Ben, because he wanted to show consideration... Now he grasps Ben's arm, shaking him:

– A Jew or not a Jew... Ben you are my brother! Think of our cave! Of our oath! You are not different from other people. But you make yourself different! You point out all the time that you are something special, placing yourself on the outside. People get annoyed. The things you have experienced... Don't you think that I sympathized with you? But I couldn't help it, could I? And it is as if you are shifting the blame on to the rest of us!

Ben thinks of his father, whom he never got the chance to know:

– Six million people died in the gas chambers.

– Will you stop it, Ben! You are talking about the same things all the time! It is tragic... dreadful. Well, that's how it was... But it is disagreeable to be reminded of it perpetually. You end up thinking: Spare us! It's so long ago now, we heard about it so often! It is over now! Can't you conceive that? It's over! A thing of the past! And you are not different...

– I have been spat on because I am Jewish!

Ben has that undigested lump in his stomach, because things haven't been settled. What had become of justice? Few Nazi war criminals had been brought to justice and convicted, most of them had been set free again already. Everyone would prefer to forget it! As if what had happened was of no importance at all!

– Everybody is what he is regarded to be! And, consequently, I am considered to be a Jew, baptized in spittle and contempt!

And the thought makes Ben sicken to such a degree that he begins to yell, with all the power of his lungs, into the black night:

– Jew! JEW! JEEEEW!

Ben's wallowing in his debasement makes Kristian furious. Can't he stop scratching at his own sore?

– Isn't that a pity! Poor, poor Benny! It is enough to make you cry snot, it really is! Can't you bloody well realize that you are troubling people with your claim for compassion? They get resentful! You want their sympathy, you want them to suffer with you, sure, you can do that for a while, but in the long run they don't like to do it. You make yourself pitiable, and then people despise you! Is that what you want to be? Pitiable? You estrange people with your commiseration for yourself. You achieve exactly the opposite of what you desire, when you are always making great play of your sufferings. You are demanding too much of people and then they don't like you and turn away from you.

Kristian makes a decision and picks up a handful of snow:

– That's just what you need! Serves you right!

Kristian mashes the cold snow in Ben's face, wiping it all over his head:

Ben is literally cooled down. Then rage gushes forth from him. Quick as lightning, he fills both hands with snow, throwing it at Kristian:

– And this is for you! And this! And this! And this! Because you have always had everything, and I had nothing! Because you always had everything! Everything! Yes... everything!

Now Kristian also flings snow at Ben. They are shovelling snow at each other, heedless of the cold, out of sheer excitement, telling each other all the truths they have kept to themselves for so long!

– The moment of truth, Ben! But you can't even bear to hear the truth when I am telling it to you for once... I, who have always shared everything with you!

They are gasping for breath as they throw the snow, so that their muscles are shrieking:

– But it was your toys Kristian, not mine! And I will tell you a truth, that you won't have any doubt about: I always wanted your toys, your soldiers and ships and tanks! My own mother once brought you a car, which I did not even dare to wish for! And then you got it, from MY OWN mother...! And I will tell you one more thing: I wanted to be you, I did! Be you, you! I wanted to be you!

The two young men are equally strong. So they also used to be when they were boys, but in their fights then, it was generally Ben who won, because he was more infuriated. Now Kristian takes hold of Ben, knocking him down and pressing him into the snow with the weight of his body. Their faces are close up as they glare into each other's eyes:

– I never cared a damn about that lousy car your mother brought me! I never liked to play with it! But you did! And it was my toys, my soldiers, my ships! You... you should always be allowed, my mother said! You were always in charge of my toys, you held on to my toys, you did!

While they fight and snort they are rolling, embracing each other, down the slope, so that the snow swirls up around them. At this very moment Ben hates Kristian, because it was true, it was, what he was saying!

– And I was supposed to be grateful for it! Do you want me to pay for it? Your toys! Go to hell!

Ben tries to wrest himself free, but Kristian holds him in a vise-like grip:

– And mother always said that my toys also belonged to you... and I had to submit to that!

At last Ben manages to get loose, forming more snow in firm lumps, throwing them at Kristian:

– This is your payment! That's it! And one more! And one more! And I had a bad conscience out of sheer gratitude, because I couldn't pay you... I, poor devil! Now I'll pay you back! To hell with gratitude! To hell with the damned gratitude!

Kristian attacks Ben again and pushes him into the snow:

– A bad conscience! I had that, damn it! Because I could see from your miserable mug how you envied me!

– Yes, I envied you!

Ben is almost crying with relief at getting it out, yelling with joy and groaning at the same time:

– I envied you! The hell, I did! I envy you! I envy you! I do envy you!

Ben liberates himself by rolling out of his coat and flies at Kristian again, so they both tumble over, sliding down the last slope:

– And your father gave you 10 crowns to buy all that Meccano! And you owned all the Tarzan books! All 19 Tarzan books!

Ben gets hold of Kristian's neck, gripping it so hard that Kristian is just about to be choked, so he can hardly bring out the words:

– Because they were my books, my Meccano! They were mine! They were mine! Mine!

Ben has a pain permeating through his whole body:

– Yes, by God! They were yours, indeed! They were yours! Yours! YOURS!

While they are wrestling they roll out on the moat ice. Finally Kristian manages to relax Ben's hold:

– I could feel, all the time, that you wanted it all... you spoiled my pleasure in owning anything at all! You wanted everything I owned!

And now Kristian screams out his innermost truth:

– Even my mother! Even my mother you wanted to take away from me! My own mother!

Ben shouts and weeps at the same time:

– What about Grete, then? What about Grete?

Kristian is fighting to recover his breath:

– I have... I also have a right to get what I want to have! I also have a right to fight to have the one I love... And my mother died for your sake! It was for your sake! Mother died for your sake! And she was my mother! My mother... my mother!

They are both pitching blindly into each other. Ben is screaming like a baby facing death:

– She was also... MY MOTHER!

Just then they both stop fighting and remain lying there. They are both sobbing, embracing each other, clutching at each other, seeking comfort from each other. They have come out with everything that they had kept inside themselves. They have found each other again.

The ice cracks under them and Kristian slides into the icy water.

Like lightning, Ben crawls a little backwards and lies down reaching for Kristian, who is holding onto the edge of the ice, struggling to pull himself out:

– Help me, Ben! Help me, help...

Ben stretches out his arm and gets hold of Kristian's hand, trying to pull

him up, while a sense of mortal fear squeals in his head: Oh my God, don't
let it happen, don't let him drown!
– Be careful Kristian, pull now, pull! Not too hard! Watch out!
But as Kristian is about to pull himself out of the water, the ice floe on
which Ben is lying breaks, turns half about, so that Ben's torso goes under
water and he has to let go of Kristian.
Ben holds his breath under the icy water. With one hand he grasps the
bottom edge of the ice floe, sinking his fingers and his nails like a wild beast
into the hard ice to turn it over again.
He will not die! Just as in Theresienstadt, where he had been convinced
that even if he had been locked up in a gas chamber together with a hundred
other people, there would have been a small hole in the wall just for him,
through which he would have been able to get a breath of air, so that he could
hide under the heap of dead bodies and survive when they opened the door
of the gas chamber... As the only one of them all, he would escape death,
because he was born to survive.
With all his strength Ben manages, with a jerk, to pull the floe on an even
keel again, and gets his head above water. He is gasping for breath. He
tightens his whole body like a steel spring. Then throwing himself backwards,
pushing the floe into the water with his hands, he takes off, and rolls over
on the solid ice, before everything goes black and his head is down with his
face upon the frozen surface of the ice.

✶ ✶ ✶

Ben wakes up with a start. Had he been gone for a second or for a whole
lifetime? He raises his head anxiously and looks down into the hole in the
ice.
Kristian is not there any more.
Ben can't comprehend it. He looks down again into the darkness of the
water, reflecting the stars, scintillating and swaying in the ripples. His hands
are still hanging in the icy water... Are they really his own fingers? He cannot
feel them at all, but now he is aware of the cold beneath him, slowly coming
up, spreading through his body, crippling him.
He can't stay here... Gathering his strength, he manages to sit up. His eyes
search the sky. The stars are so infinitely far away. You cannot expect any help
from THEM.
Turning around he discovers the figure lying motionless behind him.
– Kristian!

He slides up to him swiftly, lifts his head, shaking him cautiously:
– Kristian!
Kristian's face is lifeless, he does not breathe. Ben weeps desperately, tears Kristian's mouth open with his fingers, presses his lips against Kristian's and blows with all his might, fills his lungs and blows, again and again, puts all his strength into blowing harder and harder... Rising up on his knees, he grabs Kristian's feet and drags him to the bank. He presses his head under his brother's body, lifting him upon his shoulders, climbs the slope from where he had just glided – ages ago.

Now he runs along, keeping Kristian tight with his arms round his neck. He stumbles forward like a madman, while his clothes, his hair and his eyebrows are beginning to ice over, stumbles across the ground slippery with snow and doesn't notice at all how beautifully the trees stretch their snow-covered white branches up into the blue-black night.

At long last he is by the phone booth. Carefully he lays Kristian down, and with a great effort he manages to push the door open with his back and to slip into the small, square box.

Ben's fingers are frozen stiff but finally he succeeds in dialing 9-9-9.

He can't utter a word when he hears the impersonal voice of the operator:
– This is the police... Hello... hello...
At last he finds his tongue:
– An ambulance... Port East station... emergency, hurry up, quick!

He runs back to Kristian, kneels down, hugging Kristian's head, and, putting all his vigour into it, he blows again into his mouth and keeps on blowing... until, at last Kristian, feebly, begins to breathe.

In the distance the air resounds with the howl of the ambulance siren approaching.

* * *